Dying in the Wool

Also by Frances Brody

A Medal for Murder

Dying in the Wool

Frances Brody

MINOTAUR BOOKS

A THOMAS DUNNE BOOK

NEW YORK

This is a work of fiction. All of the characters, organizations, and events portrayed in this novel are either products of the author's imagination or are used fictitiously.

A THOMAS DUNNE BOOK FOR MINOTAUR BOOKS.
An imprint of St. Martin's Publishing Group.

DYING IN THE WOOL. Copyright © 2009 by Frances McNeil. All rights reserved. Printed in the United States of America. For information, address St. Martin's Press, 175 Fifth Avenue, New York, N.Y. 10010.

www.thomasdunnebooks.com
www.minotaurbooks.com

Library of Congress Cataloging-in-Publication Data

Brody, Frances.
    Dying in the wool / Frances Brody.—1st U.S. ed.
        p. cm.
    "A Thomas Dunne Book."
    "Originally published [2009] in Great Britain as a paperback original by Piatkus, an imprint of Little, Brown Book Group"—T.p. verso.
    ISBN 978-0-312-62239-8 (hardcover)
    1. Women private investigators—England. 2. Missing persons—Fiction. 3. Fathers and daughters—Fiction. I. Title.
    PR6113.C577D95 2012
    823'.92—dc22

2011038154

Originally published in Great Britain as a paperback original by Piatkus, an imprint of Little, Brown Book Group, an Hachette UK Company

First U.S. Edition: February 2012

10 9 8 7 6 5 4 3 2 1

In memory of Peter

Note

Bradford once had its mill millionaires who owned more Rolls Royces per silk top hat than London. The mills are silent now. Those that did not mysteriously catch fire years ago have been converted to other uses.

Bridgestead will not be found on any maps nor Braithwaites Mill in the trade directories.

Dying in the Wool

1

Spinning the Yarn

My name's Kate Shackleton. I'm thirty-one years old, and hanging onto freedom by the skin of my teeth. Because I'm a widow my mother wants me back by her side. But I've tasted independence. I'm not about to drown in polite society all over again.

Seven o'clock on a fine April morning, cosy under my blankets and red silk eiderdown. Through the open curtains I looked at the blue sky with its single small white cloud. In Batswing Wood, a blackbird sang. A crow alighted on my window ledge, head tilted, beady eye peering as I swung myself out of bed, planted my feet on the lambs-wool rug, stretching and curling my toes. Crow visitor turned tail, plopping a parting souvenir on the window sill.

Time to start the day. From downstairs came the sound of the letter box, first a rattle then a series of gentle thuds as post hit the mat.

As I brushed my teeth, a horse clip-clopped along the road towards Headingley Lane.

The back door opened. Mrs Sugden would be at her self-appointed task. She would clank round with bucket and shovel, stepping along the little path to the road, and scoop up horse muck. Manure. Good for the roses, she says. Waste not, want not. But how much fertiliser does one garden need?

A small mountain of horse dung grows between the coal shed and the fence that separates the back garden from the wood. Resident armies of flies and bluebottles delight in its stench.

Knowing that some people, particularly my mother, hold my way of life and pastimes odd, I don't like to interfere with Mrs Sugden's manure habit. For a reason I dread to fathom, my housekeeper has appointed herself horse muck monitor for the neighbourhood.

I live a short cycle ride from the centre of Leeds, not far from the university, and from the General Infirmary where Gerald once worked as a surgeon. Ours is the lodge house, sold off by the owners of the mansion up the road when the new occupants cut down on staff. A neat extension provides Mrs Sugden with her own quarters, a situation which suits us both.

Because of the university and the infirmary, we have our fair share of soaring intellects in this part of the world, though I don't count myself among them. My nose for solving mysteries comes from having a police officer father, a poke-your-beak-in persistence and an eye for detail.

Dressing gown round my shoulders, I sat on the bed and pulled on my stockings. Knees are a very strange part of the anatomy. Mine are too bony for my liking. As I contemplated my knees, I thought of the mystery I have not yet solved. My husband Gerald went missing, presumed dead, four years ago.

Like a sleepwalker, I allowed his and my family to persuade me into claiming insurance, transferring the house into my name, and drawing down his legacy. Financially, I am secure. I do the things we humans have devised to find some meaning in life. The sleepwalking is at an end, yet my world stays out of joint.

Try as I might, I have not yet been able to find an eyewitness to Gerald's last moments, or to discover the circumstances of his death.

The only news of him, if you could call it that, can be summed up in a few words. Captain Gerald Shackleton of the Royal Medical Corps was last seen in the second week of April, 1918 on a road near Villiers-Bretonneux, following heavy bombardment. There had been gas in the valley and many casualties. Gerald had taken up position in a quarry, his stretchers and supplies stored in a large cave. He had written to me that there was so little he could do in a first aid post – just make the men feel better for having him there. A shell hit the quarry. His stretcher-bearers were killed and supplies destroyed. The few men that were left set off to walk to Amiens. I tracked down a lieutenant who spoke to Gerald on the road. The lieutenant said that there was barrage after barrage. Somebody must have seen Gerald again, just once. Somebody must know what happened.

Four years on, one side of my brain knows he is dead. The other side goes on throwing up questions.

It was after Gerald went missing that I began to undertake investigations for other women. I have uncovered some clinching detail about a husband or son, some eye-witness account from a friend or comrade. As late as 1920, I tracked down a soldier who had lost his memory, and reunited him with his family. One officer I traced last December remembered only too well who he was and from where he hailed. He had simply decided to turn his back on family and friends and begin a new life in Crays Foot, cycling to work each day at the Kent District Bank.

I wake in the night sometimes, startled, with the sudden thought that Gerald may still be somewhere on this earth – not dead but damaged and abandoned.

Searching for people and information, sifting through the ashes of war's aftermath, drew me deeper into sleuthing. Where I failed for myself, I succeeded for others. It's something useful I can do.

The enticing aroma of fried bacon drifted up the stairs, snuffing out my reverie and propelling me towards the wardrobe.

Opening the wardrobe door makes me groan. I can pounce on something wonderful, like the pleated silk Delphos robe, my elegant black dress, stylish Coco Chanel suit and the belted dress with matching cape that you can't get a coat over. These outfits are squashed by pre-war skirts, shortened to calf-length, divided cycling skirt, and the shabby coat I wore when setting off with the other Voluntary Aid Detachment women and girls from Leeds railway station back in the mists of time. Fortunately I have several afternoon dresses. Mrs Sugden and I peruse the 'Dress of the Day' in the *Leeds Herald*. She can make a fair copy of almost anything and I am an excellent assistant.

I pulled on my favourite skirt and took a pale-green blouse from the drawer, vowing to shop this very week and become highly stylish. I topped off my outfit with a short military-style belted jacket. To go downstairs in anything less substantial would draw Mrs Sugden's warning to 'Never cast a clout till May goes out'.

Glancing in the mirror, I brushed at my hair. Before the war, I wore it long. In some ways long tresses made life easier, except on bath night, but I shan't grow it again. If hair could speak, I suspect it would express a preference for length. It takes against me and has to be forced with water and brush into lying down.

After breakfast at the kitchen table, I poured a second cup of tea and reached for the post.

Mrs Sugden busied herself at the kitchen sink. She has a look of Edith Sitwell, with the high forehead and long nose people associate with intelligence and haughtiness. She turned her head and primed me in her usual fashion. 'You've only two proper letters. One from your mam.'

It would not amuse my mother to be called 'your mam'.

I slit open my mother's letter first because it would be bound to contain instructions of some kind.

4

Mother reminded me that she had booked our railway tickets to London for 11 April, a week on Tuesday. I like Aunt Berta and wouldn't want to miss her birthday shindig. She and Uncle Albert live in Chelsea, in a house that expands as you enter.

'Don't bring that same black dress,' Mother wrote. 'You have worn it for the last three years. And before you say you will wear the Delphos robe, don't forget who passed it on to you and that it is practically an antique. We will shop in London but before that I will catch the train to Leeds this coming Monday. You and I will visit Marshalls for an evening gown. It is time for a burst of colour.'

I'm sure there must have been a time when I liked shopping for clothes. Hmm, Monday. Today was Saturday. It might not be so bad. I could do that. Would have to do it. Yet ... I might as well admit now that my aversion to buying a new evening gown is compounded by the totally illogical feeling that if Gerald does by some miracle come back, and we go out to celebrate, I ought to be wearing something he will recognise. I know that makes me irrational and a suitable case for treatment but there it is.

The brown envelope held my application form for the 1922 All British Photographic Competition, closing date 30 June. I have been a keen photographer since Aunt Berta and Uncle Albert bought me a Brownie Outfit for my twentieth birthday. I still remember the delight in cutting the string, folding back the brown paper, opening the cardboard box and discovering item after item of magical equipment. There was the sturdy box camera, 'capable of taking six $3^1/_4$ x $2^1/_4$ inch pictures without re-loading', the Daylight Developing Box, papers, chemicals, glass measuring jug and the encouraging statement that here was 'everything necessary for a complete beginner to produce pictures of a high degree of excellence'. I subscribe to the *Amateur Photographer* magazine and occa-

5

sionally attend the slide shows and discussions of the local club here in Headingley but have never yet entered a competition.

'I think I shall enter this photographic contest, Mrs Sugden.'

She peered over my shoulder as she picked up the teapot. 'Why shouldn't you? You're at it often enough. Just don't ask me to pose.'

She made a dash for the kitchen door, as though I might whip out a camera there and then and tie her to a chair.

With almost three months to the closing date, I would have plenty of time to choose a really good print of one of my old photographs, or to find a new subject. Most of all I like taking photographs of people, people absorbed in doing something, or just being themselves.

Through the window I watched Mrs Sugden empty the teapot. She does not tip tea leaves on her dung heap; that must remain pure. What a challenge it would be to photograph a pile of manure danced on by flies and bluebottles and to do it so vividly and with such art that viewers of that picture would pinch their nostrils. Perhaps not.

I left the fattest letter until last.

Tabitha Braithwaite has a neat, sloping hand like a schoolgirl's. She gives letter Ls a generous loop. An amateur analyser of handwriting might say she was a generous person, and that would be true.

Her missive covered several sheets, the handwriting becoming larger with each page. As I read it, I forgot to breathe. Our paths had crossed twice during the war, when we were with the Voluntary Aid Detachment. Since then we had met at the opening of the Cavendish Club in Queen Anne House. We were both huge supporters of a club for VAD women in London. Since then we had exchanged letters at Christmas. It must have been in one of my letters that I told her about my sleuthing and the success I have had in finding missing persons.

I had no idea Tabitha had carried such a burden all this time. Not once had she breathed a word about her own personal anxieties and her loss. The gist of her letter was this: her father went missing in August, 1916, a month after her brother was killed on the Somme. Now she is about to marry, and has this great desire that is sending her half-mad. She has a picture in her mind of her father, walking her down the aisle. The wedding will be on Saturday, 6 May at a church in Bingley.

I read the letter again, searching for an explanation as to why she had waited over six and a half years before deciding to instigate a search for her absent parent. Of course, that word came up, that little three-letter word that speared us all. War. But Mr Joshua Braithwaite was a civilian, master of a mill.

The war slowed down normal life. In peacetime if a man went missing, boulders would be rolled back to find him. In wartime, men without uniform seemed less important. Mr Joshua Braithwaite should have been an exception. Between the lines of her letter, I sensed a feeling of shame attaching to the situation. This would explain her reluctance to talk about it.

Mrs Sugden came back into the kitchen and rinsed the teapot under the tap. 'Anything interesting, madam?'

She calls me madam when she is being nosy. I swear she senses when I have a new case about to begin. She can be a great help and is the soul of discretion.

I heard myself sigh. The letter troubled me. 'It's a request for help,' I said quietly. 'Sounds like an impossible situation.'

Mrs Sugden pulled out the chair and sat down opposite me. She leaned forward, folding her hands.

'It's from a Miss Braithwaite. We first met at a hospital in Leeds during the war, then again in France.'

I couldn't call Tabitha Braithwaite a great chum as we didn't know each other all that well, but what we'd been

7

through gave us a special bond. 'It's about her father, a mill owner who disappeared in 1916.'

For once, Mrs Sugden didn't try to read the letter upside down but gazed at me with that look of piercing sympathy that makes me wonder who she lost as a young woman. I have never asked.

Mrs Sugden's eyebrows lifted the high forehead into a thoughtful crease. 'And after all this time she wants you to find him?'

I looked again at the last page of Tabitha's letter. 'Yes. But that's not all. She wants to engage me in a professional capacity. To reimburse me for expenses incurred she says, and to pay above my usual rate because of the short notice.'

For a moment, Mrs Sugden and I sat in stunned silence. I have helped relatives search out missing persons as a kindness, not a paid service. I could not decide whether to be thrilled, terrified or insulted by the offer of money.

To save Mrs Sugden the strain of upside-down reading, I turned the letter towards her. Frowning, spectacles perched low on her nose, she read. Her thin work-worn fingers, nails ridged with age, turned the pages slowly. She is a fast reader as a rule, devouring novels and exchanging sensational paperbacks with a vast network of female book lovers across Headingley and Woodhouse.

When she had turned over the last sheet, she bit her lower lip as if to aid thought. 'Well then, at last someone's doing the right thing.'

'Searching for her father?'

She pushed the letter back to me across the table. 'That an' all. But it's her offering to pay you for your trouble that impresses me. You're recognised. You're making a name for yourself.'

'It's only because she knows me.'

'And knows how you come up trumps.'

What bad timing. I would love to help Tabitha

8

Braithwaite, but with Mother's shopping expedition, and the following week off to London, it just couldn't be done.

'I read something of this case at the time.' Mrs Sugden's memory never fails to impress. She mops up newspaper stories like a blotter dabs ink. 'Wasn't he one of them Bradford millionaires?'

'Not exactly Bradford is it? The Braithwaite mill is in Bridgestead, between Bingley and Keighley.'

She made a dismissive gesture. 'Same difference. It's all out in that direction.'

'What do you remember about the case, Mrs Sugden?'

'It's a long time back. A lot's happened in the last six years.' She took off her spectacles and polished the lenses on her apron. 'I do recall my surprise that a man such as Mr Braithwaite should get hisself in bother.'

'What kind of bother?'

'You couldn't get a proper tale out of it. Just the feeling that there was more to it than met the eye. I do recall it was around the time of the tragic explosion at Low Moor. A cousin of mine was one of the firemen who lost his life.'

She picked up the morning paper and slapped it down in annoyance. 'Look at that. Just look at that.'

Her bony finger accused an item headed "The Varsity Boat Race Name the Crews". 'Typical,' she said. 'They can name a bunch of young rowers, but did they name my cousin and the other firemen who lost their lives? They did not. Didn't even say where the explosion happened.'

'We had censorship. You couldn't read a weather report, in case it helped the enemy.'

'Dozens of working people lose their lives, no names no pack drill. One toff goes off the rails and we hear about that all right.'

If Mrs Sugden could edit *The Times*, she would make it very clear what was news and what was not.

She opened the kitchen drawer. 'But if the lass wants

9

you to find her dad . . .' Rooting among the bottle openers, string, tape, sealing wax and tape measures, she found a jotter and a stub of pencil. 'I better scratch out details of where you're going. Just to be on't safe side. No doubt your mam'll be turning that telephone red hot.'

'I don't see how I can help Tabitha, at least not before her wedding. She's getting married in . . .' I consulted the letter. 'Five weeks.' I watched Mrs Sugden copy down Tabitha Braithwaite's address and telephone number. 'Obviously I'd like to help her. But people must have looked for him at the time. The trail will be stone cold.'

What I didn't add was that it terrified me to be thought of as a professional sleuth, accepting payment and expenses. Now I half regretted boasting to Tabitha that I traced the errant officer to the Kent bank when a professional investigator had failed.

It would be fraudulent to take money from Tabitha. I'm not a proper investigator, just stubborn, and sometimes lucky. My usual contacts for tracing missing soldiers were through the regiments. Officers and men were always willing to help. This was different. Yet the challenge of Tabitha's request pleased me. If I could find out what happened to Joshua Braithwaite, a civilian with no regimental links to exploit, a trail gone cold, it would be a real achievement. It might change me in some way. I'd have an entitlement, would earn respect. As it is, I'm a sort of lady bountiful of the dead end. The person a wife or mother turns to when she does not know how to find something out for herself, or when all lines of enquiry turn cold.

So why shouldn't I take on a difficult task and accept money?

It might at least excuse me from short-notice dress-shopping trips.

Mrs Sugden raised her high forehead, creating a perfect set of horizontal lines. 'You've said yes already.'

'No I haven't.'

'I can see it in your eyes. You can't resist.'

I tucked Tabitha's letter into the inside pocket of my jacket. 'It won't hurt to look into it. Since you remember reading about Joshua Braithwaite in the newspaper, I'll go to the *Herald* and see whether I can unearth that article you mentioned.'

And any others that there may have been, I thought to myself. I would grab a notebook, and cycle to the newspaper offices. Touch of swift pedalling and I could be there in twenty minutes.

Mrs Sugden brightened. She likes me to be out of the way for an hour or two. It leaves her free to lavish attention on the dung heap, which receives the contents of her chamber pot.

'What do I say if your mam rings?' she asked.

2

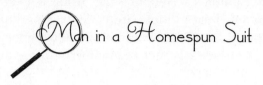

Man in a Homespun Suit

I cycled onto Headingley Lane. No one had told the month of March to skedaddle and give way to April. A chilly gust blew against the back of my neck, so cold it tickled. Sails on a bicycle would be a good idea, to be hoisted in a favourable breeze, providing extra power.

On Woodhouse Lane, by the edge of the moor, a telegram boy took it into his bonce to race me. For a while we were neck and neck, earning a curse from the rag and bone man we overtook. That curse slowed me down, but not the boy. He streaked ahead before pulling in front of me, daring me to brake or swerve. He turned his head, raising his too-small cap and grinning at me like a gargoyle. I waved defeat.

Go on, spotty lad. Something has to cheer your day before you end up under a tram.

I slowed down at the top of Albion Street. Sandwich boards on the kerb, and posters in the window proclaimed the day's headline news. "Irish Bill Becomes Law – Mr Churchill and the New Agreement."

All of a sudden, I had misgivings. The folly of my mission seeped through me, like when you have sat too long on a damp stone during the break in a walk and not realised until you arise that your skirt is wet. I would need to be discreet about my enquiries. Tabitha would not thank me if some reporter guessed my task and her father's story found its way back into print.

The doorman suggested that I park my bicycle round the

back of the building. I wheeled the bike through an alley to a flagged yard where men in shirtsleeves and waistcoats were heaving tied bundles of the second edition onto a bogie to be pushed through the alley, ready for loading and delivery to the sellers and newsagents throughout the city.

I leaned my bike against the railings and made my way to the front office. A florid-faced porter chewed his pencil over a diamond-shaped crossword puzzle. He didn't look up, having that air of regarding the general public as too much trouble altogether.

If I were a bona fide investigator, I would have a card and some justification for poking my snitch in.

'Hello. I'd like to see copies of the newspaper from the summer of 1916 please.'

'Public library, madam.' He did not look up.

'I want to buy some back copies.'

He chewed on the pencil, as he raised his eyes and gave me a cool glance. 'If you want to buy a back copy, you have to know the date.'

'I'll know the date when I've looked for what I want.'

'Public library. Our library here, it's the company's archive, for access by the reporters.'

I knew very well that I could consult papers in the public library, but hoped that somewhere during the course of my visit I might be able to dig out that extra revealing titbit of information about Joshua Braithwaite.

I did a Mrs Sugden and read one of the porter's crossword clues upside down. 'Are you stuck on 4 across?'

His eyes met mine, with a hostile glare.

What was the matter with him? Perhaps he'd got out of the wrong side of bed, or didn't like women. I pressed on regardless, saying somewhat apologetically, 'I'm a bit of a crossword fan myself.'

We had to solve four clues together before he melted a little. I took advantage of the crack in the ice to push him a little further.

13

'I'm researching for a friend who's writing a play set in the summer of 1916. I need to get some local flavour of what was going on, just for background, and to take him some newspapers to have handy.'

The lie sounded reasonable enough to me, and also to the porter. He put down his pencil.

Pushing my advantage, I smiled sweetly. 'My playwright friend says how the press is our country's fifth estate, neglected at our peril.'

'True enough,' granted the porter. He lost his slouch and sat upright.

'I expect you're regarded by your friends and family as something of an expert on current affairs?'

'There's summat in what you say,' he said in a wistful voice that made me think there was no truth whatever in what I said. 'No one but the editor and the printers see the headlines afore I do.'

'And you're the gatekeeper for this great newspaper. In medieval times, you'd have worked the portcullis.'

I'm sorry to say that resorting to smarmy flattery is not a new skill. A detective's card might eliminate such a requirement.

A light went on in his eyes. 'I know who might be able to help you.'

'I thought you might.'

'Our Mr Duffield.'

Five minutes later, the porter returned with a courtly gentleman, aged about sixty, wearing a well-boiled white shirt, a dark-green silk bow tie that would not look out of place on a stage magician, a worn tweed jacket and baggy flannel trousers. Corpse-white of skin, he had a mane of suspiciously black hair that swept his forehead like the rush of an incoming tide.

He extended a hand in greeting. 'Eric Duffield, newspaper librarian.'

'How do you do, Mr Duffield. Kate Shackleton.'

14

'I remember you from a benefit do at the Infirmary. Dr Shackleton's widow. Superintendent Hood's daughter.'

I felt myself blush, with both pleasure and annoyance. For once, couldn't I simply be Mrs Kate Shackleton?

Mr Duffield smiled, showing a tombstone row of yellow fangs. 'Well then, Mrs Shackleton, if you'll come this way we shall see whether the *Herald* may be of service to the daughter of the West Riding Constabulary. You're researching for a playwright I understand?'

Did I detect disbelief? Possibly. I muttered something that sounded like agreement.

Mr Duffield escorted me without further words along a corridor with offices to our left, and on to a still narrower corridor leading to a lift. On the second floor, the lift creaked to a stop. We stepped onto the landing.

'Have you worked here long, Mr Duffield?' I asked as he led the way to a pair of heavy double doors.

'Thirty-five years, starting out as office boy.'

'You were not attracted to reporting?'

'Far too frenetic an activity for me, Mrs Shackleton. I prefer to dwell with the ghosts of yesterday's stories.'

The large room was full of shelves stacked with binders, along the walls and across the centre of the room. Under the high windows were a couple of old oak tables and straight-backed chairs. The librarian took pride in explaining his index system, then turned to me with a penetrating glance. 'What precisely interests you?'

I wanted to ask him did he remember the case of Mr Joshua Braithwaite of Bridgestead. It would save me time but I did not want to risk bringing the Braithwaite case to public attention.

'Really, it's more background than specifics. I'd like to see copies of the paper for July and August, 1916, please.'

I chose a spot at the woodworm-eaten table under the high window. After a couple of moments, Mr Duffield returned, bearing a heavy binder, and placed it with a thud on the oak surface.

I opened the binder and began to look at the newspapers, reading of Bradford City Council's debate on the government's appeal to postpone the August Bank Holiday, which did not meet with approval from the people of Bradford. I read of war honours, air raids, the Wesleyan conference, wages in the dyeing trade and the death toll in the Canadian forest fires.

The story appeared on Monday, 21 August. It bore no relation to the information in Tabitha's letter.

Under the heading "Mill Owner Saved by Boy Scouts", the article read:

Mr Joshua Braithwaite, 50, respected mill owner of Bridgestead, was saved from drowning on the evening of Saturday, 19 August by intrepid boy scouts. A first-rate troop under the leadership of Mr Wardle was camping out in Calverton Woods.

At about five p.m., three bold lads strode to Bridgestead Beck to fill their billy-cans. They were surprised to see Mr Braithwaite, a teetotaller and stalwart of Bridgestead Chapel, lying unconscious in the water. It is thought that Mr Braithwaite suffered a dizzy turn while out walking.

The younger of the scouts ran to raise the alarm. Two older boys showed great presence of mind in pulling Mr Braithwaite to dry land. Thanks to the speedy intervention of the resourceful young chaps, Mr Braithwaite was brought to himself. In a weakened state, he was carried on a makeshift stretcher to the home of the local doctor who insisted that he remain there overnight, under close observation. Mrs Braithwaite was sent for and hastened to be at her husband's side where she remained through a night-long vigil.

I made notes, not wanting to ask for a copy of the paper and reveal my true interest. There was nothing in the following day's paper. My hands were now black with printer's ink. I turned to 23 August. There was the piece about the explosion "at a munitions factory in Yorkshire" that had so annoyed Mrs Sugden because of its lack of detail and failure to mention her cousin. It was issued by the Press Bureau, authorised by the Ministry of Munitions, and seemed to me a fair account. 24 August. Still nothing more about Braithwaite. To keep up my pretence of being generally interested in the whole of summer 1916, I made random notes about the King's surprise visit to soldiers in France, the extension of government control over the wool and textile trade, and why there is no substitute for Horlick's malted milk.

Immersed in his index cards, Mr Duffield looked up as a young messenger boy brought in more papers, placed them on the counter and beat a hasty retreat. I wondered whether the librarian ever felt overwhelmed by the sheer weight of cataloguing everything that ever happened.

'Find what you wanted, Mrs Shackleton?'

'May I see September please?'

For the whole month of September, there was no reference to Mr Joshua Braithwaite. I closed the binder.

'You look puzzled,' Mr Duffield said as I stood up to go.

'Strange what counts as news,' I said, 'and how some stories don't appear at all and others peter out. I suppose editors were so very preoccupied with the progress of the war, and sensitive about what not to say.'

'You're thinking of the munitions explosion,' he said gravely.

I was not, but chose to agree with him. 'Yes, a big explosion like that in which so many people lost their lives.' Mrs Sugden would be glad to hear herself quoted as if she were scripture. 'All those firemen dead in the

17

course of their duty, and not a pip of acknowledgement.'

'We did have one reporter who picked up on the Low Moor story. He wrote a good account as I remember, but it was spiked. The editor could only use official sources. The reporter gave me a copy. If you leave me your address I'll look it out and send it on to you.' Mr Duffield looked entirely satisfied with himself having, as he thought, sniffed out the true subject of my interest.

It suited me to let him think that he was right. 'The reporter won't mind?'

'He'd be delighted. Poor chap died in 1917 – apoplexy if you ask me, fury at wartime censorship and not being allowed to do his job as he saw fit. He covered that area around Bradford and Keighley.'

'Thank you. I'd like that.' I took a deep breath and put on my most throwaway voice, with only a touch of interest. 'I expect he wrote up that strange story about the mill owner, dragged from Bridgestead beck by boy scouts.'

He frowned, as though trying to remember. 'Ah yes. That was a rum do. That was August too – and usually such a quiet month on the domestic front.'

We stood by the table. He turned to the article about Joshua Braithwaite and scanned the piece, running fingers through his black hair. If the dye came off, it would blend with printing ink. He struck me as a complex man. The dramatic green silk bow tie indicated a devil-may-care chap who did not mind what others thought of him. The dyed hair suggested something contrary, vanity or a desire to fit, not to be thought too old for the job.

He looked up from the article. 'Will this stay within these four walls, Mrs Shackleton?'

'Of course.'

'We didn't hear any more about Mr Joshua Braithwaite because it wouldn't have been very good for morale to report that someone of his standing hadn't the spunk to face up to losing his son.'

18

'Are you saying he was trying to drown himself? That it was an attempted suicide?'

'Same reporter, rest his soul, Harold Buckley. Used to complain that if a story wasn't spiked it was in danger of being "smoothed out" by the editor. Bit of an old die-hard radical, anything political, anything to challenge the bosses and Harold was there. He covered the founding of the Independent Labour Party, that's how far back he went. It was just up his street to spill the beans on a Bradford millionaire, a bloated capitalist.'

'How was his story "smoothed out" as you put it?' I asked, as Mr Duffield escorted me back to the lift.

He looked round quickly to ensure we were not over-heard. 'Apparently, and this was according to old Harold, our millionaire mill owner wanted to be left to die. There was talk of a prosecution for attempted suicide. Then Braithwaite disappeared into thin air. The man must have had enemies or Harold wouldn't have heard about him.'

The lift clanked me down to the ground floor. Why hadn't Tabitha mentioned the beck, the boy scouts and the stories of suicide? She must be saving that treat.

I cycled home from the newspaper library, leaving the smog of the city behind. April sunshine streamed through the trees on Woodhouse Moor, creating a pattern of branching shadows. I wondered who, back in August 1916, had gone to the newspapers with the Braithwaite story.

A familiar car sat outside my gate – one of the sleek black Alvis saloons favoured by West Riding Constabulary HQ. It could mean only one thing. Dad had decided to pay me a visit. Either he had psychic powers, which would not in the least surprise me, or Mother had telephoned and winkled my fledgling plans from Mrs Sugden.

I wheeled my bike into the garden with a sudden dread that something might be wrong. Dad didn't usually visit me during the day, not when on duty.

'Dad!' I called as I opened the front door.

He emerged from my tiny drawing room, lowering his head so as not to bump it on the door frame. He smiled. 'Hello, love.' He was wearing his smart superintendent's uniform with gleaming buttons. His easy manner quelled my anxieties. 'My sergeant's in the kitchen, having a cup of tea with Mrs Sugden. We've been at the Town Hall for a meeting. Just did a bit of a detour to speak to a chap at the cricket ground regarding an inter-force match.'

As a young chap, Dad played rugby and cricket and still picked up a bat now and again.

We looked at each other. He raised an eyebrow in answer to my unspoken question. The cricket ground detour had provided his excuse to call and see me. I knew that Mother had spoken to Mrs Sugden, and then managed to get word to Dad.

'How's Mother?' I tried to keep the suspicion from my voice.

'She's very well. Would be even better if you'd agree to go shopping with her on Monday, but I understand you may have other plans.'

The annoyance started somewhere around my toes and eased its way up. Mrs Sugden may be the soul of discretion, but not where my mother is concerned.

'Dad! I'm a big girl now.'

'I know, I know, love. And I suppose I'm to blame for the sleuthing.'

'Yes. I suppose you are.'

'Inherited, eh?' He winked at me.

I laughed. 'Almost certainly.'

The truth is, I am adopted and so any aptitude I have for investigation is not an inheritance of the blood. Perhaps it arose from a fascination with polishing Dad's silver buttons, or having a failed police bloodhound as a pet.

I was adopted as a baby, when Mother thought she

20

would not have children. When I was almost seven, she had my twin brothers. By then I must have passed the trial period because I was not returned to sender as surplus to requirements.

I call the little wood at the back of my house Batswing Wood because a glossy dark green ivy grows there whose leaf forms the shape of a bat's wing. There are maples, sycamores, elms, beech trees, a bracken fern and toadstools. A pregnant-looking oak, massive growth protruding from the middle of its trunk, takes centrestage in a flat raised area of the wood where local children sometimes perform their magical plays on summer afternoons.

In a clearing, Dad and I sat on a bench hewn from a fallen beech tree by some long-ago gardener. I told him about Tabitha's letter and my visit to the newspaper library.

Dad entered into the spirit of the case straight away. 'How have Mrs and Miss Braithwaite coped in the past six years? Until it's established to a court's satisfaction that a man has died, the financial assets are frozen. And who's been running the mill?'

'I don't know.'

He stretched his legs. The bench is too low for a tall man. 'Sounds as if there could be a lot of practical difficulties. I'm surprised the widow hasn't applied for presumption of death before now.'

'From Tabitha's letter she's obviously hoping he'll be found alive. Missing doesn't mean dead.'

I had said the wrong thing. Dad went quiet. I knew what he was thinking. *Why doesn't Kate accept that Gerald won't be coming back? Missing only means: No one saw him die and lived to tell the tale. Presumed dead means blown to smithereens.*

'I expect I'll find out more when I speak to her,' I added quickly. 'From her letter, I don't think it's about money.'

He shook his head. 'People never do say what it's really

21

about. The court will expect to hear that all attempts to locate Braithwaite have been exhausted.' He watched a squirrel run up the oak tree and dart across the branches, heading towards the big house. 'From what you say, Kate, this won't be like the cases you've taken on before, not like finding information for some bereaved soldier's relative. You'll be stepping into a different sphere. Bradford – Worstedopolis, wool capital of the world. Hard brass at stake.'

'It's different in another way too, Dad. Tabitha must think I do this work professionally. She's offered to pay me, and I'm inclined to say yes.'

To my surprise he gave me a broad smile. 'Couldn't be better. Fits perfectly. After all in the last couple of years you've probably tracked down more recalcitrant husbands and sons than a small police force.'

He swayed slightly, with that gleeful involuntary movement that means he expects he is about to get his own way. My suspicions were roused.

'What do you mean "Fits perfectly"? What fits?'

'I have a suggestion to make. There's a chap lives not a mile from here, in Woodhouse. He's ex-force, face didn't fit, so he left. Since then he took on short-term security work for a shoe company who had rather too many boots walking away. Now that's at an end, I'd like you to meet him.'

I turned to him, protesting. 'Dad! I can't promise a man permanent employment.'

'Take him on for this case. See how you get on. Don't forget you'll be off to London for Berta's party. And we're there over Easter. You're not going to let your mother down over that are you?'

'No.'

He was winning me round to the idea. But I still felt a tug of reluctance. Yes, it could be useful to have someone to help. After all, Sherlock Holmes had Dr Watson. On the other hand, I'm my own woman. An ex-policeman sounded a daunting prospect. Bound to be a know-it-all.

Dad made a steeple of his fingers. 'Your mother worries. She tracked me down to the Town Hall and bent my ear this morning. If I can tell her you have a chap utterly fearless, straight down the line who'll . . .'

'I don't need protection.'

'. . . who'll be your assistant and take on some aspects of the work. If you do that, then I think I can persuade your mother to leave you alone to . . . to get on with your life.'

There was a gulp in his voice. He wanted me back as much as she did. They don't see that if you're thirty-one years old, it's too late to be a little girl again. I was in the big bad wide world and had to do something, or I would go mad.

'Need to stretch my legs.' Dad stood up. I took his arm as we walked along the path to circle our way round Batswing Wood. 'I know how you feel about wanting to make your own way in the world, Kate, but there are limits, even for someone as independent as you. You've searched out military men before – with a lot of goodwill from their comrades and officers. This will be a different world. From what you say about the missing Mr Braithwaite, it'll be useful to ask a few questions in the Bradford Wool Exchange. You won't hear the swish of a skirt there, unless it's an early morning cleaner.'

'Hang on a minute . . .'

'You need someone who'll do a bit of leg work.'

A branch of mistletoe caught my skirt. I stopped to untangle myself. 'I like to see who I'm talking to, Dad, weigh them up, try and understand what they're *not* saying.'

'You need to know what your own strengths are and not be afraid to accept help. If this young woman is due to be married in how long . . .?'

'In just over a month's time, on the first Saturday of May.'

23

He let out a soft whistle and shook his head. 'Even I would think twice about taking on that kind of job. You'll be hard pressed to get any kind of conclusion without help.'

We had circled the wood and reached my back fence. Through the kitchen window I could see Dad's driver, leaning across the table, lighting Mrs Sugden's cigarette.

I thought over Dad's words. Perhaps it wouldn't hurt to have help, just this once, given the urgency of Tabitha's request. 'What's the name of this ex-policeman, security man, pursuer of missing boots?'

'Sykes.'

'As in Bill Sikes? Notorious villain, slayer of Nancy?'

'Not Bill, Jim. Jim Sykes. He's 35 years old, a married man with three children. You'll need to pay him at least two pounds a week, so cost that into whatever you charge for the job.'

'I haven't said yes. Either to the job or Sykes.'

'Meet him. See how you hit it off.'

I did not want Mr Sykes to come to the house, or for me to go to his, in case we did not get on and I had to decline his services. We were to meet on Woodhouse Moor, a little after six that evening. I would rendezvous with Sykes on the second bench, as arranged through Dad.

I wore my belted dress with matching cape, and Cuban heels with the strap. This seemed to me a businesslike look. The damp evening air felt fresh and sweet. A light rain started as I reached the moor. I unfurled my umbrella. Suddenly, the situation struck me as comic and absurd. A little voice in my head mocked the whole business and said that I should be wearing a red rose between my teeth, to fling at him and say, 'You are Jim Sykes, son of Bill the slayer of Nancy. I claim my prize.'

Since telephoning Tabitha and arranging to meet her on Monday, I had tried to recall all I knew about mills, worsteds and woollens. From my thimbleful of knowledge, I remembered that Harris tweed, Irish tweed, Scottish tweed and for all I know Yorkshire tweed are sometimes lumped together under the name "homespun". Then I spotted him.

It seemed appropriate that here was a man, sitting in the centre of a bench, wearing a homespun suit, a pulled-down trilby and highly polished brown boots. Perhaps the brown boots were his bonus from the shoe company for whom he had acted as security man. They looked new.

He tilted his head towards the sky as if asking the drizzle how long it might last. His umbrella remained furled. At first glance, he appeared totally unconcerned with all around him. At second glance, I saw that he missed nothing. Likely he had a pinhole in the back of his trilby for the convenience of the eye in the back of his head.

Wiry and wary, he sat bang in the centre of the park bench, as if daring any other person to claim a seat.

Although he had not appeared to notice my approach, he leaped to his feet and raised his hat in a pleasant manner.

We shook hands and he moved along the bench, making room for me, on the dry spot where he had previously perched. Fortunately the brief spit of rain stopped so we did not need to negotiate umbrellas.

A good four inches shorter than Dad's six foot, Sykes was six inches taller than me, with the kind of pronounced cheek bones, ears and nose that make me think of the skull beneath the skin, and of poor Yorick. That leads me on to imagine that here's a man who will look at himself in the mirror while shaving and know that he must make the most of his short time on earth. Not very logical, but I can't always help the trains my thought catches. He was clean shaven, though I had for some reason expected a handlebar moustache. He had bright intelligent eyes, with the sort of bags under them that I associate with mothers

25

whose children keep them awake in the night.

Dad had told me that Sykes' face didn't fit. That his boss got the wrong man for a robbery and told Sykes to let it go, but Sykes wouldn't. 'That's being a good copper in my book,' Dad had said. But in Sykes' nick it was seen as insubordination. He would never rise above pounding the beat, and with the worst shifts his sergeant could throw at him. When I asked Dad could he not have intervened, he said that it did not work like that. Sykes resigned.

For a few moments we exchanged words about how long Mr Sykes and his family had lived in Woodhouse, which was five years, and how long I had lived in Headingley, which was eight – since Gerald and I married in 1913 after our whirlwind romance. Of course if I took off my time away in the VAD, I had hardly lived in my little house at all until the end of the war.

Behind us some lads began to kick a ball about. A woman wrapped tightly in a musquash fur coat walked along the path, talking kindly to two Pomeranians who trotted alongside her.

'How well do you know Bridgestead and the mill business, Mr Sykes?'

He turned to me with a solemn glance, as formally as if I were an entire board of directors interviewing him for the post of bank manager. 'I don't know Bridgestead at all, madam. But I have family who work in the mills.' He told me about his aunts who worked in Listers Mill, and of the spinners and weavers who were his ancestors. 'My knowledge should help me to blend in and not arouse too much suspicion while making enquiries.'

'Where would you begin? My father mentioned the Wool Exchange.'

'That would be on the list certainly, Mrs Shackleton, especially on the meeting days, Monday and Thursday. But I might begin by finding out which public house

Braithwaites' workforce frequent. There's gossip to be picked up over a pint and some of it proves useful.' He paused, giving me a chance to question him.

'I shall visit the Bridgestead village bobby, Mr Sykes. Is there anyone you could draw on for information?'

He looked thoughtful. 'There's one or two officers in Keighley who'd be willing to talk to me about what they remember of Joshua Braithwaite. If you agree, I'd like to find out what I can without revealing my connection to you.'

'Why would that be, Mr Sykes?'

'Call it a copper's instinct to play his cards close to the chest. But I believe there are two kinds of people in the world – them that cough out information and them that gather it up.'

He made the work sound as though we would be walking about offering a spittoon to passers-by.

'And how would you keep your connection to me secret, and yet find out all you wanted to know?'

'I'd have some good story – as I expect you may have.'

I had not thought of that. 'Until I see Miss Braithwaite, I'm not sure how I'll proceed.'

I told him what I had read in the newspaper library and about the librarian's story from the reporter on the scene that Mr Braithwaite had tried to commit suicide.

Sykes shook his head sadly. 'Attempted suicide's a nasty business. And it muddies the beck, if you'll pardon a pun.' Sykes let out a sigh. 'The Keighley lads will tell me whether they had the bloodhounds out searching for a body.'

Without our having formally agreed to a working arrangement, I realised with surprise that we were already jointly on the case and were discussing who would do what.

I would speak to the family and the village constable, and try to find out whether there had been family or financial difficulties. Sykes would quiz the workers, Keighley CID and connections at the Wool Exchange.

'My father says two pounds a week would be an appropriate remuneration,' I said, thinking it best to get this out of the way.

'He said that to me too. And there'd be any expenses I might incur, travelling, standing a drink, and so on.'

'So perhaps you would like something on account?' I took a folded five pound note from my pocket and handed it to him.

He grinned for the first time. The smile lit his face and I saw the relief. He would go home to his wife and children and say that he had a job.

He extended his hand and this time the handshake was stronger and held longer. 'Thank you. You won't be sorry.'

'I'm going to Bridgestead on Monday. I suggest we meet, say Tuesday evening and compare notes.'

He nodded. 'I'll take the train to Bingley, that's nearest.' He took out a notebook and wrote the name and telephone number of a hostelry. 'I know the landlord at the Ramshead Arms. He owes me a favour and will give me a room if necessary.'

'Six o'clock. And if I can't make that time for any reason I will telephone Mrs Sugden and she'll send word to you.'

And that was how I came to work professionally for the first time, and to employ Jim Sykes, the man in the home-spun suit.

3

 The Silesian Merino Shawl

Early on Monday morning, the sun shone brightly in a crisp blue sky. It was the kind of day when you look through the window and expect that it will be warm, only to get a chilly surprise when you put your nose outdoors. I loaded the boot of my Jowett convertible with portmanteau, camera bag and walking-stick tripod. I had packed my Thornton-Pickard Reflex, useful with or without a stand. The tiny Vest Pocket Autographic Kodak slid into the notebook section of my satchel. *The VPK is to other cameras what a watch is to a clock*, as the slogan goes. In other words, easy to lose at the bottom of your handbag. Mrs Sugden shook the travelling rug and folded it carefully.

Setting off can be a trial.

Mrs Sugden will say, 'Have you got the map?'

'Yes.'

Two minutes later: 'Have you got your driving goggles?'

'Yes.'

A minute later: 'Is there petrol in that there can?'

At which point I pretend not to hear, and have totally forgotten what it was I meant to remember.

In spite of the sunshine, it would be a chilly ride. My motoring coat is a great fleecy swaddler with detachable lining. It saw me through the war and is way out of fashion, but it makes me feel safe, secure and immune to traffic accidents.

I pulled on my tasselled motoring hat and gauntlets.

'Have you got . . .' Mrs Sugden began.

I turned on the petrol tap.

'If I haven't got, it doesn't matter.' I switched on the ignition. 'I'm going to Bingley, not the North Pole.'

I turned the choke to rich and pressed the starter button. You will gather from this that my motor is modified for easy use, and I don't apologise for that so there.

Mrs Sugden waved. 'Go careful!'

'I will.'

Rain during the night had dampened the roads so they were not so very dusty. Once out of Leeds, I made good progress, through villages, past farms and mills, keeping an eye on the signposts and milestones.

I thought about the time Tabitha and I last met. It was almost two years ago, June, 1920, at the opening of the Cavendish Club. All through the war, we VAD girls had nowhere in the capital to call our own. Afterwards, that was put right and Tabitha and I were among the supporters of the campaign for a club that women could afford. Since then, the two of us had promised in our Christmas letters and summer postcards to meet up, never doing so until now.

We had arranged to meet in a café on Bingley High Street. Once parked by the side of the road, I shed my antique coat, swapped the tasselled hat for a cloche, and set off to find the café.

Looking over the red and white check curtain that hung across the lower half of the plate glass window, I saw her. With one hand she held a cigarette, with the other she twirled at a strand of her blonde curly hair. She has the quality of a Dresden doll, with neat features, a snub nose and bow lips.

The bell rang as I opened the door. The waitress, taking away Tabitha's full ashtray and placing a clean one on the table, blocked me from view. Then Tabitha was pushing back her chair, and coming towards me. I was about to hold out my hand when she gave a beaming smile, grabbed me and pulled us into a clinch. We kissed each other on the cheek.

'Kate, thank you so much for coming! I'll order another pot of tea.'

After the preliminaries about my journey and whether I found my way easily, she said, 'You're so kind to come at such short notice. I hope you don't mind my turning to you for help. You were always so capable. Do you remember I couldn't think straight when that poor chap in St Mary's died under my care?'

I nodded. 'You'd become attached to him.'

She sighed. Her fingers played a silent requiem on the tablecloth. She looked much younger than her thirty years, almost like a schoolgirl.

'You get to the bottom of things, Kate. You tracked down the brother of that Cavendish waitress.'

'Even though he wished I hadn't.' I smiled. 'But I think people have a right to know the truth — no matter how hard it is.'

You can never tell whether someone will immediately blurt out every single detail of their story, or sidle up to the matter in hand so slowly as to trip over it. Tabitha is a sidler-up and tripper.

Finally, she said, 'I look for Dad all the time. Just before I came in here, an old chap went shuffling by the ironmonger's and I thought, is that him? It wasn't. It never is. But I don't stop looking you see. Sometimes, if there's a knock on the door, I think it's him.'

'Would he knock on his own door?'

She lit another cigarette. 'No. But none of it has to make sense. I even dreamed he came back, walking through the fields from the mill, with some other men, saying he'd not been lost at all and we'd only thought him lost. Mind you, it'll be Easter a week on Sunday. Resurrections and all that.'

31

'So you think he's lost, and not dead?'

'He's not dead. I'm sure of that.'

'How can you be so sure?'

'I just am. I know in my heart and soul. You know when someone is dead.'

There was logic to that. But just because you knew when a person was dead, that did not mean you could be certain that someone was alive. There seemed to me to be a shade of difference between her declaring him 'not dead' and asserting that he was alive. Perhaps he was not dead because she could not bear that.

When someone has gone missing, there is always that edginess, that looking out of the corner of the eye. Even when your head knows that he will never come back, that part of you that hopes beyond all reason just won't give up. When trying to find out what happened to Gerald, I had spoken to his colonel, pushing him for names, survivors who might have some scrap of information for me. He grew impatient. In the end, he said, 'My dear madam, please understand that the words "Missing in Action" frequently mean "blown to smithereens. Nothing left to identify".'

If she saw the shadow cross my eyes, Tabitha thought it was for her.

'It's come between me and Hector, my fiancé,' she confided in a low voice as if the waitress would be listening, ready to spread gossip, which perhaps she would to make up for having to watch everyone else eat egg custards. 'He practically holds his breath and turns purple if he suspects I'm going to harp on about Dad again. At first he was patient but now . . .' She blew a perfect smoke ring. 'If you can't find an answer for me, Kate, I've got a horrible feeling this wedding will never happen.'

'Tabitha. I can stay with you until Saturday. The following week I must go to London for my aunt's birthday dinner. It would be more than my life's worth to back out. Then we have the Easter weekend. Let's see whether I can be of any help. Perhaps by this Friday we shall have a better idea.'

We left the café and strolled around the market town. I told Tabitha I wanted to stretch my legs, which was true. But I also kept an eye open for the Ramshead Arms where I would meet Sykes on Tuesday evening. I suddenly felt absurdly competitive with him. I wanted to find out as much as I could – just to prove that it wasn't necessary to swagger around male preserves like the Wool Exchange and the local pubs to get to the bottom of a mystery.

Women with shopping baskets hurried by. A furniture van unloaded a desk outside the solicitor's office. Tabitha steered me on a compulsory visit to the stone church with its fine tower where she and Hector would marry.

'There's a lovely set of bells. I do hope you'll come to the wedding, Kate. I posted a formal invitation this morning. Sorry it's a bit late.'

She seemed reluctant to walk back to the car. We stood on the packhorse bridge and listened to the water. 'What arrangement do we come to, Kate? About fees and so on?'

I should have sought advice on this, but I hadn't. Mental arithmetic is not my strongest point, but if I were to pay Sykes' wages and expenses, for at least a month, that had to be taken into account.

I played for time. 'You can pay me on completion. I shall give you a report – verbal or written, as you please, whether I'm successful or not, and send an invoice.' This waffle allowed me to put off saying an amount. 'It's difficult to be precise about costs without knowing how much investigation may be involved but . . .' I pulled a figure from the air and said it quickly so that it would not sound made up. '. . . let's say thirty guineas.'

She sighed and turned her back to the wooden parapet. 'It would be worth three hundred guineas to me, three thousand – no, it would be worth all I have to see my dad again.'

The enormity of the task made my knees go weak. Perhaps there had been dust on the road after all. My mouth and throat felt suddenly dry.

'Tabitha, some people would have applied for presumption of death long ago, to enable a life insurance claim to be made, and access to bank accounts and assets. How have you and your mother managed all these years?'

She took my arm as we walked back past the church and along the main street to the car. 'We are all on the board of Braithwaites Mill, Mother, Uncle Neville and me. Any two of us can deal with the finances, sign cheques and so on. The company provides our living. Mother and I have our own financial resources. I would give up everything to find Dad.' She pressed my arm tightly, like a plea.

'I can't make any promises, Tabitha. I'll try, that's all.' I folded down the car's top and opened the door.

Tabitha has a mercurial quality of switching moods in an instant. She pulled off her hat as she slid onto the passenger seat. 'There's nothing like the wind in your hair to make you feel free as a bird.'

As I chugged the car forwards, an old lady made a dash for the other side of the road, pretending not to see me. Perhaps she was after compensation. If I ran her down, no doubt I could add it to Tabitha's bill, along with my legal defence fees.

Tabitha ignored our near miss. 'Drive straight along, past the corn merchant's. It'll be a right turn by the Co-operative Store.'

We left the town behind. I felt alarmingly satisfied so far, having found out a little from Tabitha about the Braithwaites' financial background, and, just as importantly, having located the Ramshead Arms where I would rendezvous with Sykes.

Hawthorn bushes edged a country lane. Daffodils still

held tall. This was far from the dark satanic mills I had pictured.

As the road made a bend, I caught a glimpse of horse-drawn barges on the canal.

She was twisting her hair again, making a ringlet around her index finger. 'We've a way to go yet. The road runs between the canal and woods. No one ever comes to Bridgestead. We're a bit remote from modern life really. Seems strange, after all of you-know-what.'

I did know what. The what that came to seem 'normal' during our time as VADs had probably sent us slightly mad.

She punched my arm, a little too hard. 'Do you remember the time when there were too many of us trying to get a billet in London for just one night . . .?'

'Yes. And we ended up piling into my aunt's house and Betty Turnbull sneaked down in the night and made a midnight feast of our breakfast.'

'Betty Turnbull! Then she came back upstairs and snored fit to shake the roof . . .'

We started to laugh. A rabbit dashed from the hedge and dared me to run it down. Another second and I would have had the makings of a fur muff but I swerved, barely avoiding the ditch.

I restarted the car and chugged along sedately, enjoying the fresh air until we passed a farm where the workers were busy muck-spreading.

'It makes such a difference when the sun shines! You live in a lovely area, Tabitha. I'd imagined it much more cobbles, chimneys and clogs.'

'Oh we do that too. But we've some pretty spots nearby. Do you ride?'

'Rarely. It wouldn't be fair of me to keep a horse.'

'We all ride. Mother's a keen horsewoman.'

Something in her voice hinted at a possible obstacle to our investigations.

'Does your mother know I'm coming to stay, Tabitha?'

'Y-e-s. Only, to be truthful, she doesn't know why. I thought once she got to know you, I'd sort of raise the matter of finding Father in a day or so, when I mention what you do.'

'I can't work like that, Tabitha. I must have straight dealings. And if I'm to investigate properly, I'd need to talk to people. Naturally I'll be discreet.'

She reached out and touched the windscreen with her fingertips as if to deflect a shock. Her voice rose. 'Other people?'

'Yes. The local constable, and whoever else was involved. I'll need a list.'

The tips of her gloved fingers left tiny imprints on the now dusty windscreen. Her arms fell helplessly to her sides. 'I suppose so. I hadn't thought of that.'

It struck me that she hadn't thought of very much.

'Time is of the essence. If you really want me to try and help, I must start straight away. I'll need you to give me a photograph and a description of what your father was wearing, where he was last seen and by whom. What was his state of mind when he went missing, whether he had transport, what his possible destinations may have been. The more you can tell me about his interests, friends, acquaintances, business associates, the better.'

'Yes I suppose so,' she said flatly. 'Mother won't like it. Uncle Neville won't like it. We can't involve the business. He'd hate that. You don't know what mill people are like, Kate. They play everything so close to the chest, never wash dirty woollies in public.'

I thought perhaps I did have a notion of what they may be like given that it had taken Tabitha this long to confide in me and that she seemed daunted by the thought of how much information I would need.

'Look, you don't have to go on with this. I'll come in, say hello to your mother, we can talk over old times and I'll drive home in the morning.'

36

She sighed deeply. 'Can I talk now? Can you listen and drive?'

'Yes.'

'That little lane over there takes us on a byway and off the beaten track so that we come to Bridgestead the long way round. You drive. I'll talk.'

I was not entirely sure my supply of petrol would run to a detour. I pulled in by a five-barred gate. In the field beyond, a horse and foal grazed, the foal looking up at us.

'I'm listening.'

She fidgeted with her engagement ring. For a moment, it distracted both of us. I stared at a sizeable rose-cut diamond flanked by rows of glowing single-cut diamonds and with shoulder-mounted square-cut rubies, glinting in the afternoon sunlight. 'I have to try to find Father before the wedding. It's the right thing to do, whatever anyone else says.'

'What does everyone else say?'

'That everything was done at the time. The police searched. Mother offered a reward for information. She assured me that everything would be done to find him. I wasn't able to do much, going wherever the VAD sent me. Oddly enough, it was on the day we met that he went missing. Do you remember? On that ward full of poor men with shell shock.'

We were silent for a few moments. The foal lost interest in us and tottered after its mare. In the far corner of the field, a crow swooped.

'I read a newspaper account. It said that your father was found by boy scouts, and saved from drowning. Do you believe there was any reason why he may have wanted to take his own life?'

She shuddered. 'That's not it. That's not it at all. He didn't try to take his life.'

'How can you be sure?'

'I just know it.'

'We have to look at every possibility. I believe your brother was killed just weeks before your father was found by the beck.'

'Yes.' She clasped her hands, twirling her thumbs.

It felt cruel, making her talk about her brother.

'Poor Edmund. There were just the two of us. Edmund volunteered, but then everyone did, didn't they?'

'What happened?'

'He was killed on the first day of the Battle of the Somme. But Dad was stoical, as we all were. He wouldn't have attempted to take his life. He wasn't a despairing kind of man.'

'Can you tell me about the last time you saw him?'

For a moment, she looked as if she would cry. 'I'm afraid my mind's gone a bit of a blank.'

'Try.'

A blackbird trilled in the hedge, as if nothing in the world could ever be out of kilter.

'It would have been a Sunday dinner, sometime that month. August. There were just the two of us. Mother claimed a headache. Truth to tell she could hardly bear to be in the same room with Dad, not since Edmund was killed.'

'Why was that do you think?'

She shrugged and shook her head. 'I don't know all the ins and outs. She thought Edmund shouldn't have joined up, at least not so soon, and that he only did it to get away from Dad, and from having to stay in the mill. We were busy producing khaki, so Edmund could have avoided the army.'

For the moment she seemed to have run out of words.

I restarted the car.

Following Tabitha's directions I drove up a steep cobbled street of densely packed two-storey cottages, past a school with high windows.

'If you look over to your left, you can see the mill chimney. We'll continue up the main street. You'll soon find your bearings.'

The row of houses gave way to a solid stone building with sturdy pillars and portico. 'That's the Mechanics' Institute. The lecturer comes from Keighley. Just up ahead you'll see the chapel. Dad was on the committee. Uncle Neville takes an active interest.'

'Is your family very religious?'

'Not in an out of the ordinary way. Mother and I are Church of England thank goodness. Gives you a much better class wedding. A chapel do would be so ordinary and plain. But all mill masters have to make a show in some chapel direction, and encourage their hands. It's what keeps the mills in motion, Dad always says.'

'Is Uncle Neville your mother's or your father's brother?'

'Dad's cousin, so I suppose not a fully-fledged uncle, but the nearest we've got. Head towards the mill and keep going.'

I caught sight of a humpback bridge and heard the sound of running water. 'Is that the beck?'

'Yes. Dad was found by the stepping stones, where we used to play.'

We stopped to take a look.

Standing on the solid old sandstone bridge, we watched water play over rocks, murmuring and rushing as if to keep an important appointment.

'He was a smashing dad, Kate. I love him. I want him back. See just there, by the stones, that's where Edmund and I used to play, trying to make a dam, fishing, that sort of thing. Dad painted a picture of us once.'

'So he didn't entirely lock himself away in his work, if he found time to paint?'

'Mills can be monsters – eating up lives – but he did sometimes paint.'

39

In as neutral a tone as possible so as not to seem critical, I asked Tabitha why she had left it so long before deciding to search for her father.

'Mother said everything that could be done at the time was done. But you see, I didn't do anything, being off in the VAD. And I must do something, otherwise it'll haunt me forever that I didn't try.'

'Have you made any enquiries?'

'People are so close-mouthed, or they say what they think I want to hear. I'm hoping you'll be better at getting the truth than I've been. Someone must know what happened to him.' She turned to me. 'Here I am rabbiting on and I haven't even asked how you are yourself. You had a telegram too, just as we had for Edmund.'

'Not quite the same.' I kept my voice steady, feeling foolish to let hope betray me. 'Mine was a missing telegram. I tried to find someone who saw Gerald on that last day. The nearest I got was a sighting in the late morning, before the big bombardment, a sighting of Gerald walking along a road.'

I didn't say all those mad things about waking in the night and imagining that he walked to safety; that he lost his memory; that he works as a peasant in a remote spot, not knowing who he is and that one day . . .

The Braithwaites' elegant stone villa was of an unusual design. The centre comprised four storeys. Adjoining either side were extensions of two storeys, giving an impression for all the world like a person resting on her elbows. Shutters, the same dark green as the front door, framed latticed windows.

'Grandma had it built around 1900,' Tabitha said. 'It was terribly modern at the time.'

To the right and left of the house stood outbuildings, stables and garages. Neatly planted flowerbeds and a bare-looking rose garden flanked the drive. A fountain in the Italian style played in the centre of the beds.

'We've a tennis court round the back, if you're brave

40

enough to bear the April breezes.'

'Where shall I park?'

'Oh just any old where. Briggs will see to your car.'

I brought the car to a stop and stepped out. Tabitha followed, pausing on the running board.

'I wasn't entirely truthful when I told you Mother knew you were coming.'

'I'm not expected?'

'I didn't know if you'd come.'

'But I said I would.'

'I know. I'm so ... I'm such a big baby about some things. I can't explain it.'

'Do you think she won't want me here?'

'It's not her. It's me. I thought you might change your mind, or have an accident, or find something better to do and then I'd look a fool and she'd say, "Oh that's Tabitha all over, makes a plan and nothing happens."'

'I wouldn't just not turn up.'

Tabitha suddenly looked like what my mother would call a bag of nerves.

'I know, I know. I want my head examining. I always expect something terrible to happen. I so much wanted you to come, but was afraid to count my chickens. This is going to sound mad, and like wedding nerves, but I don't believe anything good will ever happen if I don't find Dad. My life will just unravel.'

I'd seen this sort of response before. In 1919 I was maid of honour for a girl I was at school with, and it was touch and go in the end. She and her childhood sweetheart had come through the most terrible times with great strength. Then, when life promised happiness – a wedding for heaven's sake – she went to pieces, saying that she knew for certain that nothing in life would ever go right again and to pretend otherwise was tempting fate.

I touched Tabitha's arm lightly. 'Better tell your mother about me.'

41

'At least your room is ready. Becky knows you're coming. She's very reliable and will look after you. Leave your bags.'

I picked up my canvas bag. 'I'll keep this with me. It's my photographic equipment.'

'Right.' She hesitated at the steps of the house, turning to me. 'Thank you for coming. I'm sorry I'm such a drip. Hector knows you're coming, but not *why*. Whatever you do, don't mention to him that you're investigating Dad's disappearance. He's so sensitive. Perhaps he thinks Dad might turn up and put the brakes on the marriage.'

'Why would he do that?'

She blushed. 'Because Hector's ten years my junior, and everyone expects that he'll find some useful occupation on the board of the mill. Well, why shouldn't he?'

Was this her way of telling me that Hector was marrying her for money? If that ring was anything to go by, he was no pauper. 'It's a family business and your husband will be family . . . That's how it works, isn't it?'

Privately I wondered whether Hector knew something about Joshua Braithwaite's disappearance that Tabitha didn't.

A soft wool shawl in rich shades of purple and mauve lay folded on the cushioned window seat. The walnut bureau held an inkstand, pen and paper. A vase of daffodils stood on an occasional table. Someone had thought of everything.

The latticed window looked on to open moorland. The sun had moved almost out of view, causing the dry-stone wall to cast a long shadow onto the rockery.

The floor of the dressing room provided a suitable place for my cameras and equipment. Bringing my photographic stuff served a dual purpose. After talking to Sykes, I realised that an investigator needs cunning and reserve. If I drew attention to myself around Bridgestead, it would be as an amateur photographer and thus I would allay suspicions. That was my theory at any rate.

In truth my desire not to be parted from my cameras may have been more to do with attachment to my gentle hobby. It is a pastime that changes a person's outlook. I remembered my excursion to Whitby when I first made really good use of the camera. A school friend was recovering from a bout of fever and the doctor ordered sea air. All these years on, I can remember quite clearly the fishing vessels bobbing on the bay, the austere outline of ruined Whitby Abbey, casting its shadow at dusk, the limping pie and peas seller pushing his cart. Even when my photographs did not do justice to the scene, which was most of the time, simply framing the views developed a photographing habit that changed my way of seeing. A photographer's eye sharpens memory from a vague or hazy recollection to a clear image of an everlasting moment. Owning a camera gave me a new interest in people and landscapes, in markets and busy streets. It is a way of looking outside yourself and at the same time gathering up mental albums of memories.

It was in Whitby I met Gerald. He and a friend were there for a weekend fishing trip, staying in the same hotel as my friend and I. He gave up one of his fishing trips to introduce me to Frank Meadows Sutcliffe, that wonderful photographer of local people and scenes. After seeing his work it was a toss-up whether I would throw away my camera or reach for perfection. He set me on the path of photographing people going about their business, getting on with their work and lives, pausing for the camera, and for eternity, or for as long as photographic chemicals will allow eternity to last.

Mr Sutcliffe took our photograph and when Gerald and I left his studio, even though we had known each other for only hours, something was settled between us without the need for words.

43

As I closed the closet door on my photographic equipment, there was a knock on the door. Becky the maid scooted in a young houseboy who deposited my portmanteau. At the same time, I heard horse hooves on the flagged courtyard below.

Tabitha had said her mother was out riding. I went to the window in time to see Mrs Braithwaite sitting upright on her horse, its head tossed slightly to one side.

She dismounted quickly and gracefully. Before her riding boots touched the flags, a groom appeared to take charge of the chestnut bay mare. She patted the horse's neck and spoke briefly to the groom before turning towards the house. Her dark bobbed hair gleamed in the late afternoon sunlight. She seemed to glide up the steps to the house in such a slow deliberate way that I expected her to leave an impression on the air after she sailed through it.

Slowly, I changed from my motoring outfit into an afternoon dress. It occurred to me that Mrs Braithwaite looked like the kind of woman who could browbeat the entire West Riding police force and hire a small army of private detectives. The task ahead seemed suddenly more daunting. If no one else had traced Joshua Braithwaite, what on earth made me think I would?

Tabitha tapped on the door. 'Are you ready to come and meet Mother? It won't take her long to change out of her riding togs. I've told her you're here.'

Tabitha now wore an exotic Chinese silk smoking suit decorated with bridges, nightingales and bashful lovers. A long ivory cigarette holder peeped from the top pocket.

I sat down on the window seat. 'Just one more thing, Tabitha. You and your mother know everyone. All the questions I'm going to ask, she probably already has. From my brief glimpse of the way your mother dismounts, I'd say she's a very capable woman.'

Tabitha joined me on the window seat. 'You can't tell a

44

person's character from the way she rides a horse.'

'Perhaps not.' I said.

Tabitha picked up the shawl. She shook it out – a swirling intricate pattern in the most exquisite shading, from lightest violet to darkest purple, with a delicate fringe.

'This is Silesian Merino, it's the finest wool in the world. The bulk of German sheep are merino crossed with native breeds, but the Silesian is highly prized. This shawl was a gift from Mr von Hofmann, a chemist who had his own dyeing company. Before the war, he and his family were our regular visitors. We used to go to concerts together. There's an area in Bradford, off Leeds Road, called Little Germany. That's where Germans had their warehouses and offices.' She folded the shawl carefully. 'Some people said Dad was too close to the German merchants, and especially too close to Mr von Hofmann. But they were friends. That's all. When they all had to leave, go back to Germany, there was cruel talk. People said we were German sympathisers. Uncle Neville wasn't included in the lies, but Dad was. I think all that talk, all those feelings might have got in the way of finding out the truth when Dad went missing. People were so fierce at that time. One old lady in Bingley dared not take her dachshund for a walk because it was a German dog. There were nasty scenes in Keighley, German shops burned.'

'Do you believe someone might have harmed your father because of his friendship with von Hofmann?'

She screwed up her face in a look of horror and froze in the act of producing a packet of cigarettes from one of her many pockets. 'That never even crossed my mind.'

'It's unlikely,' I said quickly, 'but I'm trying to look at the possibilities.'

Unlikely because, why would someone with a powerful grudge wait two years to act on that grudge?

She inserted a cigarette into the ivory holder. 'All that

stuff about our being Germany sympathisers had evaporated by then. It was only ever tittle-tattle. The von Hofmanns left. We all plunged headlong into the war effort. Edmund enlisted the minute he was old enough. I'd signed on for the VAD. No one could say we're not patriotic. We were producing army khaki in the mill, weavers working all hours.' She lit her cigarette. 'But this just goes to show that you can ask hard questions. I can't. And even if I could, people wouldn't tell me the truth. They'd talk behind our backs, but not to my face. And it's all too personal to go to some anonymous private detective person who wouldn't understand. That's why I asked you, and why I'm telling you all this. If you hear nasty stories, don't be shocked. I just want the truth, whatever it is. I need to know. I can't move forward otherwise.'

I nodded. 'I understand.'

She looked suddenly about to crumple into tears. 'I'm not sure you do understand, Kate. I'm not sure I do myself. When we came back after the war it took me about two years to recover from a kind of emotional shell shock. Then for two years, Hector and I were dancing a minuet around each other. He's so young. For us to dance to the same tune, I had to make myself different – play at being young again. Act as if there were no dark side to the moon. But I'm thirty years old. My father's missing. I've done nothing to try and find him.'

The drawing room was a vision of cream, black and chrome, all sharp angles and geometric shapes.

Mrs Braithwaite sat on a curved black leather sofa, flicking through a copy of *Tatler*. She wore a calf-length day dress that would easily have doubled as a chess board.

'Mother, this is Mrs Shackleton. Kate, my mother, Mrs *Joshua* Braithwaite.'

There was a barely perceptible change in the air between them. On hearing Joshua's name pronounced so deliberately, Mrs Braithwaite winced.

'How do you do, Mrs Braithwaite.'

'Pleased to meet you. I hope you'll be comfortable with us. You two must have had extraordinary experiences in the VAD. And my daughter tells me you're a keen photographer and will be taking photographs . . .'

Perhaps she noticed my dismay. If Tabitha could not come clean to her mother, we would not make progress. Mrs Braithwaite tailed off, as if expecting me to own up to my vice and say what I intended to snap. Tabitha had obviously made up a story about my visit. 'An old friend from the VAD.' True, I had taken photographs at the opening of the Cavendish Club but hadn't made much of it. As far as I remembered I had never even talked about photography to Tabitha until today when she saw me unload the equipment.

'There's a little more to my visit than that, Mrs Braithwaite. I'm sure Tabitha was about to tell you.'

Tabitha blew a smoke ring. She narrowed her eyes. 'Er, yes. I'll ring for tea first, shall I?'

I could hear her brain whirring as she made for the bell pull.

'Oh never mind that!' Mrs Braithwaite walked across to the black lacquer cocktail cabinet. 'I'm sure we'd all like a cocktail. Name your poison, Mrs Shackleton.'

We gathered ourselves around the low stainless-steel and glass table. I named my poison, and asked that Mrs Braithwaite call me Kate.

'Then you must call me Evelyn.'

We chatted about the photographic opportunities in Bridgestead and surrounds. Not until Tabitha mixed a second lot of cocktails did she finally spit out the reason for my being there.

'The thing is, Mother, the truth is I specially asked . . . well, you might remember my telling you that Kate had some success in finding that officer chap that everyone

47

thought was missing and he'd started a new life in Sidcup, abandoning his wife.'

Mrs Braithwaite raised her eyebrows to show how impressed she was. 'Yes. You did mention that.'

Tabitha continued. 'And when we were in London, staying with Kate's aunt – she's Lady Pocklington of course – this person, Turnbull . . .' Tabitha gave me a meaningful look, intending me to go along with her story, '. . . Turnbull stole a diamond brooch. Kate got to the bottom of it.'

My mouth dropped. Poor Betty Turnbull had eaten two eggs, which since we were all on rations was considerably worse than snaffling diamonds. At least if Tabitha were going to boast about my achievements, I would have liked accuracy.

Evelyn narrowed her eyes and looked at Tabitha across her cocktail glass. 'Have you lost something?'

Tabitha flushed with annoyance. 'I said it last week and you completely ignored me. Don't you think Daddy should be at my wedding?'

'Well, no, Tabitha, I don't, for the simple reason that a dead man would not make much of a positive contribution. I'm sorry to be so blunt.'

A tap on the door interrupted us. The dressmaker had arrived for Miss Braithwaite's fitting. Tabitha shot to her feet, having forgotten all about the appointment.

'I'll ask her to come back another day.'

'Not at all,' I insisted, trying not to appear too relieved. 'You must have your fitting.'

'Yes, do go,' Evelyn said impatiently. 'Perhaps there'll be alterations and so on, or extra lace to order.'

'All right. But only if you'll come up and see me, once I have the dress on.'

When she had gone, Mrs Braithwaite leaned back on the sofa and looked at me steadily. Her hair was almost black. Her eyes were brown and her face chiselled, like the countenance on a china figurine. Fine lines around her eyes, mouth and throat gave away her age. She was the kind of woman who would look young, until seated beside a twenty-year-old. Her beauty would draw some photographers, yet her face seemed strangely empty and lifeless. A slight frown betrayed annoyance.

She set down the cocktail glass with a sigh, as if it had made her a promise and then disappointed.

I felt awkward about being a guest in her house and an investigator into something so painful and personal. Really, Tabitha had placed me in a difficult situation. I owed her an explanation. 'Mrs Braithwaite . . .'

'Evelyn.'

'Evelyn, I've had some success in tracing missing persons since the war. As a result of that, Tabitha asked me if I would look into the mystery surrounding her father's disappearance. But if you'd rather I didn't stay here, or . . .'

'Then Tabitha has taken leave of her senses. What little thought she has was entirely diverted into snaring a chap. Having achieved that, she now thinks all she has to do is want a miracle and it will happen.'

'And you think it would be a miracle if your husband were to be found?' I gave Evelyn an encouraging look. When she did not continue, I forged ahead, overcoming my discomfort at the situation. 'Tabitha believes her father is alive.'

Evelyn rearranged her ankles. 'How much did she tell you about Joshua's disappearance?'

'I know the date, and the barest of circumstances. I should very much like to hear about it from you.'

She rose and walked away from me towards the window. A great sighing breath seemed to let all the air from her body. After a moment she turned back, and opened the door of a black lacquer cabinet from which she produced a silver-framed photograph.

49

'This was the two of us. Joshua and Evelyn – on our wedding day.'

I looked at a slender, elegant young woman with smiling eyes. She sat on a straight-backed chair, wearing a long white dress, her veil tossed back over her head. The man standing beside her looked proud and erect, yet not very tall. He had a wiry frame, a small moustache and smooth fair hair. They were a good-looking pair. People often appear so solemn in a formal photograph. These two looked as though they couldn't wait to laugh.

'You look happy, both of you.'

'Oh we were happy, for a long time, when the children were small.'

She took the photo from me. 'Tabitha looks like neither of us. She takes after Joshua's late mother. She'll turn frumpish in later life. Edmund was like me.' She indicated another photograph, this time not hidden in the cabinet but holding pride of place on a hexagonal cocktail table. A fine-featured young man dressed in regimental uniform looked out at us with the kind of intensity that always unnerves me. Perhaps it is the way I look at a photograph, but when it is a young man, a soldier or a sailor, I can always tell whether he is dead. The eyes tell me.

Evelyn reached out a finger, as if to stroke his face. 'He was taller than his father.' She drew herself up. 'I brought height into the Braithwaite family.'

The maid chose that moment to tap on the door.

Evelyn replaced the photograph on the table with great gentleness. 'What is it, Clara?'

'Miss Braithwaite has her gown on and would like you to come and see.'

'Very well. Tell her we'll be there shortly.'

It crossed my mind that Tabitha may have anxieties about her wedding, and rather than face them had decided to worry about her long-gone father. Perhaps the best thing I could do would be simply to let her talk, to be her

50

friend for a few days. Not much detection would be involved in that, but with so little to go on regarding her father it might prove the better course of action.

I asked was there a photograph of Mr Braithwaite that I could borrow. She took an album from a drawer in the cabinet, and handed me that along with the wedding photograph. 'You're a widow I believe?'

'Yes.'

'Tabitha can be somewhat insensitive at times. You've no need to go up to see her. She ought to be aware of how so many women have had to entirely rethink their lives.'

'It's all right. I can bear to see her in her wedding dress.'

'No it's not all right. Let her wait. I'll tell you all you need to know, and then perhaps you'll see why you'd be wasting your time looking for Joshua Braithwaite. There are a few simple facts.'

I waited. In my experience, simple facts can be baffling and mysterious, leading to more layers of 'simple facts' and complexities and intrigue that make Sherlock Holmes stories seem utterly straightforward.

She arranged herself carefully on the sofa, smoothing her dress. I slipped a couple of photographs from the album then took the opposite chair, and waited.

'My husband attempted suicide. Why? I've given this a lot of thought – I've had plenty of time to do so. Possibly it was because he drove my lovely son into the army. My boy was killed one week after his posting. Joshua knew I would never forgive him.'

'You must both have been distraught.'

'I was distraught. He was full of self-pity. With Edmund gone, there was no one to take over the mill.'

'Are you sure he attempted suicide? Could Mr Braithwaite have found himself in the beck as a result of a blackout, a stroke, something of that sort?'

'His health was perfect.'

51

'But men in perfect health do suffer heart attacks or . . .'

'In the weeks leading up to that night, he had been moody, morose, not his usual aggressive self.'

'Aggressive?'

'He attacked life as though it were his enemy. He had to beat everyone, be top dog. Of course he kept that hidden, under a bluff, brash exterior. But he sized everyone up – business rivals, associates, workers. He manipulated the world to his advantage. I didn't complain. It led to a satisfactory life for me and my children. But as I said, I'll keep to the simple facts. Tabitha doesn't like inconvenient information. She wants to be happy. She was always a child with unreasonable expectations.'

'Did he give any indication that he meant to take his own life? From the way you describe him, he does not sound like a man who would fall into despair.'

'Someone had beaten him. His own son died a heroic death, turning his back on everything that Joshua stood for. He had been bested. He saw the contempt in my eyes and he couldn't bear it.'

'Was there a note?'

'Yes. There was a note.'

'Do you have it?'

The newspaper account had not mentioned a note. Nor had Mr Duffield.

Evelyn shrugged. 'I can't remember what became of it. He was found and arrested. The note was held, by the police I think.'

'What were the circumstances of his disappearance?'

'Constable Mitchell committed him to the local hospital. He walked out the following day.'

'What measures were taken to find him?'

'The police searched. His workforce took part.'

'When?'

'The next day.'

She looked at the door, as if planning an escape to the wedding dress fitting. I needed to know more.

'It would have been hard for him to face people, after what happened.'

She gave a bitter laugh. 'He never cared in the least what other people thought. He was too selfish. Besides, he would have gone on denying that he attempted suicide.'

'In spite of the note? Was it ambiguous then?'

'I can't remember.'

'When was the last time you saw him?'

'On Friday evening – the day before he was found in the beck. We passed on the landing. He insisted I come to his room, that he had something important to say.'

'And what was that?'

She shrugged. 'Don't know. I told him he might well have something to say, but I didn't want to hear it. Now of course I wish I had listened, if only out of curiosity.'

'What do you think it may have been?'

She paused. 'I'd rather not speculate.'

'Did he leave his affairs in order?'

'Oh yes. He did that all right.'

Either the newspaper account was wrong, or Mrs Braithwaite was lying.

'So you didn't see him after he was found?'

'No. Why should I have tried to see him? So that he could gloat – pretend that his grief at Edmund's loss was greater than mine?'

She still seemed angry with Joshua. If he came through the door at that moment, I could imagine cocktail glasses whizzing through the air, aimed at his head.

'Is there any relation or friend he would have gone to?'

'The police did pursue that line of enquiry. If you're asking me was there another woman, almost certainly. One that he would have gone to? I doubt he cared for anyone that much. He cared about the business. He cared about things – his cars, his house. He was selfish and materialistic. He scoffed at higher things, at anything he didn't understand.'

'And yet he was prepared to die and leave all that behind?'

'In his self-pity, yes. Don't waste your time, Kate. I know he's dead.'

'How can you be so sure?'

'If he were alive, he would have found himself some brilliant barrister to contest the charge of suicide and he would have come back to claim what's his.'

'Do you object to my taking on the case, for Tabitha's sake?'

'You'll be wasting your time. Don't do it.'

'Do you withhold permission?'

She looked as if that was exactly what she wanted to do. I remembered what my father had said – that it would be necessary to show all attempts had been made to find the missing person.

She stared at the material of her chess board dress, closed her eyes for a moment as if dazzled, and then stared at me.

'Tabitha seems determined to torment herself, and me.' After a long time, she said, 'You won't find him. It will only prolong her pain, feed her anxieties. I'm sick of telling her to look to the future.'

'Tabitha desperately wants to try, and I'd like to help her.'

She sighed. 'The police house is on the High Street. Tell Constable Mitchell you have my reluctant permission. If you do by some remote chance find Joshua's bones on the moors or his remains at the bottom of a tarn, you might be good enough to tell me first. I should naturally want a Christian burial for him, but would hate to have a funeral delay Tabitha's wedding. At her age, this is probably her last chance to leave the ranks of surplus women.'

I wanted to keep her in the room with me a while longer, having the feeling she may never be so frank again. 'Do you really and truly feel in your heart that he's dead?'

I didn't believe I had asked that question. There was a sudden glint of compassion in her eyes. I felt my cheeks turn pink but kept my eyes locked on hers, willing her to say more than her 'simple facts'.

'I don't feel anything in my heart, as you put it. Not for him.' She hesitated. 'I did my duty. I gave him a son and he squandered that son. My Edmund didn't enlist out of patriotic duty. Oh, that was the clothing on his reason. He enlisted to get away from his overbearing, ambitious, narrow-minded father. The week before Edmund enlisted, he got drunk, with his young friends in the village. Joshua horse-whipped him. If Edmund had waited just a short while longer, the Battle of the Somme would have taken place without him and he may have come through. I begged him to wait, but he wouldn't.

'Look for Joshua Braithwaite, if you must, Kate. But I warn you, he was very good at wasting other people's time. Only Joshua could go on doing that from beyond the grave.'

After that, I chose not to see Tabitha in her wedding finery, but retreated to my room. I took out my notebook and while the recent conversations with the two women closest to Joshua Braithwaite were fresh in my mind, wrote out what each had said. A little voice in my head muttered about the dangers of opening a can of worms.

You can rush at a matter too quickly. It can be valuable to let a question or two simmer while doing something else. A useful something else would be to inspect my temporary dark room.

Becky had clearly been told to look after me. She was about eighteen years of age, with red hair, a wide mouth and a gap between her front teeth, like the Wife of Bath.

She led the way towards the chosen spot, along the back hall that took us into the servants' quarters.

'I've told Robert no end of times over leaving that boot blacking box there.' She bobbed down and moved the offending box to the other side of the hall, giving it a fierce shove with her foot for good measure. I wondered whether the annoyance was for Robert rather than the box. Not for the first time, I felt that ridiculous emotion that I suspect might be envy, which is mad. I wouldn't change my life for hers, nor for anyone's. But girls her age will have men to marry. Robert won't be swept off never to return. What did her generation feel, looking at us, the surplus women? Probably she saw me as a different species altogether.

By the scullery door, she stopped, uncertain I would really and truly want to tuck myself away in a poky corner.

'Here we are, madam. I specially cleared it out for you.' She flung open the door. 'I've done what you said – that there slab's where you can put your photographic stuff and that.' She pulled down the blind, then went into the passage, closing the door, leaving me to see whether the room was sufficiently dark.

In the cool, silent scullery I placed the palms of my hands on the uneven stone slab. It is strange how you need to wait to find out whether what first appears to be a dark room truly is so. Once my eyes grew accustomed to the darkness, I noticed that the merest sliver of light found its way through the side of the blind. Above me, a woman plodded wearily on the stairs – one of those worn-out servants in rich households whose weariness is only too clear if you choose to watch or listen.

As if to assure me that she was still there, following her directions to ensure I had all I needed, Becky called, 'Is it dark enough, madam?'

I opened the door. 'It'll be perfect. Thank you. I'll hang

this towel next to the window blind, and that will do the trick.'

'It's like the black hole of Calcutta, madam.'

It was far better than many spots I'd found myself in. Once, Gerald stood guard outside the lavatory on the L&Y train so that I could develop a print of Clitheroe Castle.

I began to take the dishes from my bag. Becky returned quickly. She had cut out a piece of cardboard. Bold letters proclaimed: PRIVATE. KEEP OUT.

'Thank you very much, Becky. What a good idea.'

She smiled and blushed at her own initiative. 'You don't want some nosy parker opening the door on you and letting the light in to spoil all your hard work do you?'

She pinned the sign to the door with a drawing pin. Shifting her weight from one foot to the other, she bit her bottom lip and said all in a rush, 'You won't be taking photographs of any of the staff I don't suppose?'

I had to pull out my hanky to stop a sneeze. She had swept the floor and the dust would need to settle before I could develop photographs.

'You'd make a very good subject, Becky.'

She blushed and her eyes lit up. 'My mam'd be that pleased to have a photo of me.'

The evening was still light. We stepped out into the back courtyard where washing hung on the line. In the distance, a horse neighed in the stable. Beyond the fence, a couple of lambs bleated for a sheep that was trying to escape her responsibilities.

Becky pushed a few stray strands of hair behind her ears. She wore a black dress, white cap and white apron – the colours of modern photography. To me, black and white symbolised past and present, hope and loss. Yet I couldn't say which colour represented what. The two of them together touched me in some way, saying capture this moment, there might be no other.

Doorways are a favourite of mine, a person framed in their doorway – with that sense of belonging to a place and time. The interior remains just out of view, forever a mystery.

'Becky, I'll take a photograph of you as if you've just come out of the door.'

She was not a girl for staying still. I wanted to capture that sense of restless movement. I had left the Reflex upstairs but the VPK would do. It takes a tiny picture but is sharp enough to enlarge.

'Unpeg that tablecloth from the line. Make as if you're just about to shake it.'

She stood in the doorway, clutching the cloth to her, biting her lip.

'Look this way! Let the cloth loose.'

I clicked the shutter. 'I don't suppose you remember Mr Braithwaite. You were probably too young.'

She began to fold the cloth with deft movements. 'I wasn't working here, that's true, but I do remember him. He sometimes read the lesson at the Chapel Sunday School, and gave out the prizes.'

'Did you ever win a prize yourself?'

'Oh no, thank goodness. I would have been too shy to go up for it.'

'You're not shy with me.'

'You wouldn't make a person feel all confused and out of place. To my childish way of looking at it, Mr Braithwaite seemed very stern. I'm sure if he had given me a prize book, I would have dropped it. I deliberately missed two Sundays, so as not to have full attendance.'

She reached for a clothes basket.

'When you heard what happened to Mr Braithwaite, were you old enough to understand what was going on?'

'Oh aye. My brother, he was one of the boy scouts that found him.'

I closed the camera and slipped it into my pocket.

'Indeed? That must have given him a jolt.'

She put the tablecloth in the basket. 'He was with two other lads, bigger than himself. They stayed and helped Mr Braithwaite out of the water. Our Nathan, being the youngest, he was sent to run for the scoutmaster.'

'Did Nathan help in the search, when Mr Braithwaite went missing from the hospital?'

'Oh no. Mam kept him well away. She didn't want him finding a dead body and having nightmares the rest of his life.'

We stood by the door in the evening sunlight, reluctant to go back into the dark house.

'Was your mam surprised when Mr Braithwaite was never found?'

'She didn't know what to think. There's lots of places round here a body could go missing. Caves, deep tarns, old mine shafts.'

A few light drops of April rain began to fall.

'So you believe he's dead?'

'It's what they say. Lizzie Luck, she told Mam – in confidence like – that we wouldn't see Mr Braithwaite again. Right or wrong, Mam took it to mean he'd passed over.'

'Who's Lizzie Luck?'

'Lizzie can tell the future, and give messages from the other side.'

'She lives in the village?'

'Just beyond. Look over, you see't mill?'

'Yes.'

'Just down from that there's the humpback bridge across beck. She's in the little old cottage.'

'I might just let her tell my fortune, for a bit of fun.'

'She works in't mill, so don't go yet.'

'What time should I go?'

'You'll hear mill hooter go for finishing time. Give her half an hour to have a bite of tea.'

4

Crêpe-de-Chine

Lizzie Luck's tiny cottage, its side wall bowed with age, looked as if it dated from the seventeenth century, making it older than the other village houses. Crossing the hump-back bridge, I noticed a woman in the garden.

She had gone inside by the time I opened a low, rickety gate and stepped onto a crazy-paving path. Neat trenches lay ready for onions or potatoes. In this cool, shady spot a few brave snowdrops still survived by the fence along with purple and yellow crocuses. By the door, a sawn-off upturned barrel provided a pair of garden seats. From its perch on the scoured windowsill, a black cat glowered at me, its marmalade eyes catching the glow of the evening sun. When the door opened, the cat bounded down and strolled inside.

It was hard to judge the age of the woman who answered my knock. I guessed somewhere in her forties. She wore a long black skirt, grey-blue blouse and grey cardigan. Through the open door, I saw that a floral pinafore had been discarded on the chair-back – perhaps not fitting the dress requirements for a teller of fortunes.

I introduced myself, told her I was staying with the Braithwaites, and asked was she Lizzie Luck, and if so would she be willing to tell my fortune.

The smile set her eyes twinkling. 'It's not me calls meself luck. That's other folks' name for me. I'm Lizzie Kellett.' She waved me inside, with a quick glance across to the humpback bridge, to check whether we were observed.

I stepped into a cold room with a flagged floor. A black leaded range gave home to a struggling fire. An enamel bowl stood on a low cupboard by the window. Next to the bowl lay a bunch of cuttings from the garden and a sharp knife. A square deal table, a small rocker and a larger bentwood chair, a couple of buffets and a dresser completed the room's furnishings.

She assessed me as I peeled off my gloves and took a seat by the table. 'Will you take some refreshment?'

'No thank you. Becky at the Braithwaites thought you'd be at the mill until half past six, Mrs Kellett. I'm glad to find you home.'

'Loom's down,' she said glumly. 'There'll be no more weavin' today.' She took the buffet beside me. 'Please speak to my face, so I can see your lips. I'm half-deaf from the weaving.'

In a businesslike fashion, she gave me the price of reading my palm, and the somewhat higher price of a tarot reading.

She brought a dark-red chenille cloth from the dresser, disturbing the dust in the air as she spread it across the table with a flourish. A faint odour of cedar came from a carved box as she opened it, and took out a pack of cards.

She placed her hands flat on the table and closed her eyes for a moment. 'I don't need to look at cards to know thah's lost someone. There is a parting of the ways.'

There is also a mourning brooch and wedding ring, I thought. I swear these people can smell a widow a mile off. Oh here's a sad soul, good for a guinea or two. Psychic robbery.

As if sensing my disbelief, she said, 'It's not just the outward signs. I see loss in the form of an aura.'

And you hear it in the tinkling of coins, I wanted to add.

She examined my palm. As we both leaned forward, I caught the whiff of cheese and onions on her breath.

My life would be long, she told me. I had been well-placed, and lived a leisured life, though it had not always seemed as if I would. She saw some disruption in my earlier life. My childhood road had two forks, and mine was the fortunate path.

Goose bumps shivered along my spine. These people, I swear they pick up on something – though who knows what. I didn't even remember my adoption. But that was her art, I guessed. In spite of my rationality, I was filling in the gaps she left.

The cards revealed that I would be going on a journey. I encouraged her, confirming that this was so, and soon. If I did not catch the train to King's Cross next week, seats reserved by dear Mother, the prediction for my long life might prove mistaken.

What she said next jarred with her previous pronouncements.

'Sometimes to be still is the best course.' She looked at me, waiting for a response.

Perhaps she had some inkling of my mission to find Joshua Braithwaite and was warning me not to waste my time.

Undaunted by my failure to respond, she began to lay out cards, with encouraging remarks about my future.

'At Miss Braithwaite's wedding, catch the bouquet,' she instructed. 'There'll be a stranger, an older man, who'll change the course of the future for thee. Only don't judge off first appearances.'

'I'll be sure not to.'

I found it difficult to believe that I would find true love outside the church in Bingley, in spite of Tabitha's assurance that the C. of E. delivers a high class wedding.

I tentatively voiced my reason for being there, feeling sure that a proper detective would not have gone through this charade. 'The one person Miss Braithwaite hopes will turn up at her wedding – besides the groom – is her father.'

She did not respond to the bait but instead said, 'Have you seen Miss Braithwaite's wedding gown?'

'Not yet. She had a fitting today.'

'It's crêpe-de-chine. Mr Stoddard had a special loom set up. He asked me to weave it. It's as fine a piece as you'll see in England if I do say so meself.'

She went to a drawer and took out a sample piece of shimmering ivory. 'Feel that.'

The silky fabric slid across my fingers. 'It's beautiful.'

'That's the end piece. I asked if I could cut it off for a keepsake.'

'You must be very proud to be the one weaver chosen to do this.'

She smiled, pride in her work transforming her into a glowing subject for a photograph.

What kind of detective will suddenly forget all about the questions she needs to ask and see the potential for an album entry?

Weaver, broad face, tight mouth, eyes deep set under arched brows, sloping shoulders, sinewy hands, perched on the upturned barrel by her door, woven fabric in her hands. Still just sufficient light outside, and with a bit of luck and careful timing I might have my winning picture for the photographic competition.

I forced myself back into detective mode.

'Are you able to say whether a man exists in this world or the next, Mrs Kellett? Will Tabitha get her wish to see her father? She's sure he's still alive.'

With that mixture of guile, mockery and outspokenness familiar in Yorkshire, she said, 'If you'd said sooner, I could have asked the cards.'

'I don't think you need to do that – not after all this time. A woman of your sensitivities must have a view on the matter.'

There was a slight stiffening of her shoulders. 'He will be there in spirit. Miss Braithwaite is by way of being what we call a sensitive herself. Perhaps the feeling she has comes from the spirit world. Her brother Edmund came through to her, you know, in this very room.'

She seemed as proud of her ability to summon spirits as of her weaving.

'The bairns used to play out there, Tabitha and Edmund, paddling and fishing by the bridge. Edmund's spirit found its way home. He come into this very kitchen.'

If I were Edmund's spirit I would have preferred my own room at the villa. But then, I'm a mere know-nothing mortal.

'Did Mr Braithwaite ever find his way here, in body or spirit?'

She watched my face more carefully than lip-reading warranted. Her own lips stayed tight shut for a moment as she gave me a questioning look.

'Tabitha would love to find him,' I said again. 'If anything comes back to you about where he may have ended up, or what may have happened, we might set her mind at rest.' I produced my card and handed it to her. 'In case you have any thoughts. I'd like to help my friend if I can.'

She opened the table drawer. 'I'll keep it safe. If I come up with a communication from the spirit world, I'll send word.'

She replaced her tarot cards in the cedar wood box.

'May I ask you something else?'

'Go on, though I'm not forced to answer.'

'Was Mr Braithwaite something of a ladies' man?'

She looked at me quizzically.

'I'm only guessing,' I said. A sober man found cut and bruised in the beck. A jealous husband might be an explanation.

'Mr Joshua Braithwaite,' she said, giving the name more syllables than it deserved. 'When he was younger – and don't say this to Miss Braithwaite – he'd chase after anything in a skirt, in spite of being a bigwig in chapel.'

'Did Mrs Braithwaite know?'

'She'd be a fool not to. A woman always knows.'

'He must have had enemies.'

'I don't know about that.' She got up and placed a log on the fire, turning her back to me so I had to wait to ask my next question.

'Have you been in touch with him?'

She looked at me sharply. 'How could I be?'

'You said just now that if you come up with a communication from the spirit world, you'll send me a message. So you must believe he's dead.'

'Let's just say I know what I know. He's dead. I haven't told Miss Braithwaite. I didn't have the heart, not after her being so upset over her brother.'

She picked up the money I had paid her and slid it into a Rington's tea caddy on the mantelpiece.

Beside the tea jar was a postal order stub for ten shillings. I wondered who she sent money to. She quickly slipped the stub in the caddy.

Being a fully-fledged investigator was turning out to be a little unnerving. She was wary of me, although I tried to be sympathetic and encouraging. What did she have to hide?

The cat had heard the log go on the fire. It came to sit on the rag hearth rug. The larger bentwood chair was covered in a piece of army blanket with patchy stains in green, blue and black.

'Does your husband work in the mill?'

'Aye. He'll be in presently.'

My signal to go. 'Thank you for the fortune. May I take your photograph holding your woven piece?'

She looked at me in horror. 'Why ever would you want to do that?'

'Because I'm trying to become as good at taking photographs as you are at weaving. I'll let you have a copy to stand on the dresser.'

She agreed, reluctantly, more for the sake of her crêpe-de-chine than for herself, I thought.

While she damped and combed her hair, I paced out the distance from the barrel seat and I set up my camera and tripod on the path. In the pale evening light, I reckoned I would need an exposure of two seconds.

She sat stiffly at first, until I chatted to her about the garden. 'Do you use much horse manure?'

'Aye. Among other stuff,' she added mysteriously, stroking her woven piece as if it were a cat.

I clicked the shutter on a woman who would keep her own counsel as close as the weave in her cloth.

I thanked her for posing, then folded down my tripod. 'What does your husband do in the mill?'

'He's in the dyehouse.'

The beck ran noisily across the stones yards away. I tried to make my words sound casual, like an after-thought. 'Where was Mr Braithwaite found, by the boy scouts?'

'Over there – by't waterfall.'

'You're so close by. Did you see or hear anything that day?'

'My hearing was better then, but I heard nowt. I knew the boy scouts was out and about. I kept my door shut.'

'Did your husband hear anything?'

'It were Saturday night. He were off having a pint and a game of dominoes.'

I thanked her for her time, and cut up the bank, towards the humpback bridge. Not an auspicious start to my enquiries. That old Yorkshire saying seemed appropriate. See all, hear all, say nowt. Eat all, sup all, pay nowt.

Tabitha had told me that the Bridgestead police house accommodated the village constable, his wife, the younger portion of their family, a border collie cross dog and an elderly canary. This hub of law and order for the village

66

and surrounding areas occupied a position close to the post office. It announced itself by the cast iron black and white Yorkshire Constabulary house plate. I rang the bell.

Constable Mitchell was a big man, well into middle age, with intelligent eyes and a quickness and grace that belied his size.

He pulled out a buffet for me. 'If you'll give me just a moment, you'll have my full attention. Only I promised the wife I'd finish this. It's her father's eightieth birthday tomorrow and I've the ship to put in yet.'

An antique whisky bottle about eighteen inches long lay on a piece of linoleum in the centre of the big oak desk. Notebooks, report books, inkstand and pencil holder had been pushed aside to make way for the delicate work of creating a ship in a bottle.

'I've always wanted to know how a ship goes in a bottle.' I perched on the tall buffet and watched.

When you are watching someone work expertly, time stands still. I forgot why I had come. There was an 'ocean' in the bottle already, with an indentation where the ship would lie.

'How do you get the sails in? That's what puzzles me.'

'You have a tiny hinge on the masts. Look.' With his little finger, he indicated the place.

He lowered a sail. At its base, a scrap of silk formed a hinge. 'I'll attach a thread. That allows me to bring the mast back on its hinge, into a vertical position. Once it's in the bottle, I release the thread, and cut it.'

Like every other mystery in the world, I thought, once it's been explained, it's so obvious.

Constable Mitchell probed the 'ocean' gently with a small tool. 'You have to make sure it's thoroughly dry.' He sniffed at the bottle.

Satisfied, he dipped a brush in glue. He stroked glue onto the base of the tiny hull and bowsprit, not more than six inches in length. With a tweezer-like tool and a steady hand, he inserted the base of the ship onto its indentation.

He replaced the lid on the glue and put his tools away.

'Don't stop for me.' I wanted to see what he would do next.

'It has to dry. Putting a ship in a bottle takes patience. Now what can I do for you, madam? I'm sure you didn't come to Bridgestead to learn how to put a ship in a bottle.'

Why did I have the feeling he knew exactly what brought me to Bridgestead? The telephone on the wall seemed to me to smirk. I suspected my father had already put in a call. What Constable Mitchell said next confirmed my suspicions.

Gently setting his precious bottle at the back of the desk, he turned to me. 'That's my tea-time break over. It wouldn't do for me to appear a slacker in your presence, Mrs Shackleton. Who knows what levels that might be reported back to?'

'I guessed as much.' I forced a smile. 'You have no need to worry on that account, Mr Mitchell. My father thinks highly of you.'

'I was surprised he even remembered me.'

'Are there any objections to my looking into Mr Braithwaite's disappearance?'

He shook his head. 'When a person remains missing, the case is still open, but after all this time nothing new has come to light.'

He passed me a scrapbook, opened at cuttings relating to the Braithwaite case. Some of them I had read in the newspaper offices, but not the ones from the local paper. The editor of the weekly *Bingley Bugle* maintained a cautious tone. In the first article the name of the Bridgestead man 'found in the beck' was withheld. It was not until two weeks later that a photograph of Joshua Braithwaite appeared, giving an account of his disappearance.

Constable Mitchell waited until I had finished reading the cuttings.

'It was one of the worst days of my life, having to arrest Joshua Braithwaite for attempted suicide. And the man was in no fit state.'

'Tell me about it.'

'I'll do better than that. I can give you my report from the time.' He opened a desk drawer and lifted out several notebooks, looking at the covers for dates. 'It didn't help that he was found in a spot where a suicide had happened three years earlier.'

The image made me shudder. 'How awful. By the waterfall?' This was what Mrs Kellett had said, although Tabitha had pointed out the shallow area near the stepping stones.

'Yes, by the waterfall. If Braithwaite hadn't been pulled out when he was, he would have drowned, like the weaver and her children.'

'That's terrible. Poor woman.'

He found the notebook he was looking for and returned the others to the drawer. 'It was a sad case. A poor soul at the end of her tether. It was said she wouldn't give up her children to be farmed out from the workhouse.'

I would never look at the idyllic spot again without imagining the despair of that woman. It took an effort to make myself concentrate on Joshua Braithwaite.

'I can imagine that a woman might seek to end her life in that way, if she is truly despairing. Perhaps it's my prejudice, but it seems to me a more female method of dying. Would Mr Braithwaite have chosen that way out?'

'Men are just as likely to drown themselves. Mills are all built by the water. Canals and becks have made a last resting place for many a poor labourer.'

He found the page in his notebook. 'My writing's not very legible. I'll read it to you.'

'Thank you. Do you mind if I jot down one or two points?'

'Feel free.'

I took out my own notebook and listened. Policemen have a flat, unemotional way of talking when reading from their notes. Mr Mitchell was no exception.

'Here goes. "Saturday 20 August 1916, six pm. Summoned to an incident reported as suicide attempt at beck, beyond old bridge. Mr J Braithwaite on the bank, soaked to skin, in recovery position, supervised by Mr Wardle, scoutmaster, who claimed Mr Braithwaite was found drowning, but reluctant to allow self to be dragged from beck. Mr B not coherent. Cut lip, bruising, lost a shoe. Makeshift stretcher ... Mr B fetched to police house. Wardle urging charge of attempted suicide. W says concerned about impressionable lads witnessing event. Sent for Dr Grainger from Milton House. Dr G pronounced no immediate danger. Watch kept in night by self and wife." That's the first entry.'

'So he stayed here the night? One of the papers mentioned he was at the village doctor's house.'

'We'd had no doctor in the village since 1915. Dr Grainger's the army medic, at Milton House.'

He turned a page in his notebook. 'Now we come to the following day. "After satisfactory night, Mr B somewhat recovered. Denied attempted suicide but no explanation as to how he got into beck. Said he remembered running and tripping – that was his explanation for cuts and bruises. A teetotaller, Mr B insisted had not touched a drop of drink. Mr B transferred to the temporary Milton House Hospital, pending further investigations.'

He closed the notebook.

'Couldn't he have been taken home, Mr Mitchell?'

'Good question.' He put the notebook on the desk.

Even after all these years, I could see that the memory of that night still rankled. 'It's a pity Wardle found him and went round shouting suicide. If it had been up to me, he could have been home and in his bed within the hour, no more said.'

'Couldn't you have overruled Wardle? You represent the law here.'

'I was in a difficult position. Wardle had a troop of boy scouts ready to swear to the fact that they'd found a potential suicide. And Wardle's brother's a magistrate in Keighley.'

'What did Mrs Braithwaite have to say?'

Constable Mitchell seemed reluctant to continue. 'You're staying with them?'

'Yes.'

'Perhaps you should ask Mrs Braithwaite yourself.'

'It's Miss Braithwaite who's keen to find her father.'

He seemed to be weighing up how frank he should be. Eventually he said, 'I telephoned Mrs Braithwaite, asking her to come. She said no. If anyone could have ridden roughshod over Wardle, she could. She could have pooh-poohed the whole business. As it was, reporters from Bradford and Leeds were here within the hour. They came on motorbikes.'

'Did you believe the story of how Mr Braithwaite came by the cuts and bruises?'

'His Humpty Dumpty tumble? It's possible. But I did wonder . . . this is a little delicate . . .'

'Mr Mitchell, I was in the WAPC at the start of the war. There was nothing delicate about my work there, or later when I drove an ambulance in France.'

'Yes but this is a little close to home.'

'I have heard he was something of a ladies' man.'

'Then I can say it. I wondered whether some irate husband had just cause to give him a walloping.'

The story began to sound like a Thomas Hardy tragedy. The fall of a local notable whose fault was not in his stars but in himself.

Constable Mitchell sighed and continued. 'I don't need the notebook to tell you what happened next. My wife sat with him for a short while, to give me time to cycle up to the Braithwaites', since Mrs Braithwaite wouldn't come into the village. There was no note in his study, no indication of anything at all out of the ordinary. And she hadn't changed her mind about not wanting him home.'

'What about in his office at the mill? Was there a note there?'

He shook his head.

'Mrs Braithwaite mentioned a note.'

My guess was that she remembered correctly, and had decided not to make it known at the time.

The constable raised his eyebrows. 'Did she now? Well, all I can say is that I went to the mill the next morning. In the country, it's not like the towns where you can despatch another constable. There was just myself. Besides, I was reluctant to disturb Mr Stoddard. His wife was dying. So I went to the mill early the next day – no note, nothing.'

'Mr Stoddard?'

'Mr Neville Stoddard. He's Mr Braithwaite's cousin. I'm afraid all the work of keeping the mill running fell on his shoulders. I daresay you'll meet him shortly.'

'Yes, I expect so. You didn't charge Mr Braithwaite with attempted suicide?'

'No. It might have been better for him if I had. If I'd been less scrupulous about trying to get at the truth, I would have done what the scoutmaster wanted, had him charged and committed to prison. Instead, I came up with the idea of asking Dr Grainger to keep him under observation. I telephoned my sergeant at HQ. He spoke to the inspector and got his agreement. Dr Grainger, he grasped my predicament. The transfer took place on Sunday morning. Mr Braithwaite was supposed to be under observation and isolated.'

'Why wasn't he brought before a magistrate on Monday morning?'

72

'The magistrates were fully scheduled for that day – conscientious objector cases. He'd been timetabled for Tuesday morning, by which time he'd skedaddled.'

'What happened?'

'When I interviewed staff at the hospital, it was like yapping with the three wise monkeys. They'd seen nowt, heard nowt and would say nowt.'

'Do you have a theory?'

He shook his head. 'I was hopping mad with Dr Grainger. Of course, when I got to know him better I could see how he let it happen. His head's in the clouds most of the time. He goes in for talking cures. Well, a talking cure only works if you've kept the feller there to talk to.'

'Mr Mitchell, what do you believe? Is Mr Joshua Braithwaite alive, or dead?'

'I have to keep an open mind.'

'But which side would you come down on, if you had to?'

'Sometimes, I think someone wanted him done in, and they succeeded. Other times, I remember what a wily old bird he was and I wonder whether he's living the life of Riley with a femme fatale in Brighton.'

'If someone did want him dead, who would it be?'

He turned the tables. 'You're very good at asking questions, Mrs Shackleton. It's a pity the force doesn't make better use of females. Who do you think, from your investigations so far?'

'Too early to say. Business rival? Former employee with a grudge? Wronged husband? It's sometimes the spouse, especially if that spouse feels betrayed and aggrieved.'

He raised his eyebrows and gave a cautious, tentative, 'Yes.'

'But there has to be method as well as motive. Mrs Braithwaite couldn't have duffed up her husband and thrown him in the beck.' I didn't say *in spite of her having brought height into the family.*

73

We looked at each other without speaking. Constable Mitchell tugged at his shirt collar. Neither of us said, *She could have paid or persuaded someone else to send him on his way – to death or oblivion.*

Mrs Mitchell came in carrying a tray of tea. She smiled at me, but quickly looked at the ship in the bottle, checking on its progress for her father's eightieth birthday.

Constable Mitchell introduced us.

'Mrs Shackleton and I were talking about Mr Braithwaite,' he said.

'Poor man.' She set the tray down carefully. 'If he did go off, then good luck to him and leave him be, but I don't think he's to be found this side of the grave.'

'Kate Shackleton!' a fair-haired, red-cheeked young man with pale-blue eyes bounced across the Braithwaite drawing room, smiling a greeting. 'Tabby told me to look out for you. She's upstairs with my mother going over some important matter to do with a veil. I'm Hector Gawthorpe, the fiancé.'

We shook hands and agreed how pleased we were to meet.

Hector cocked his head to one side, listening. When no noise came from the stairs, he said, 'They'll be ages yet. I'm glad we've caught each other. I hope you'll be coming to dine with us in a couple of days' time – it's a meeting of the families . . . pre-nuptials and all that.'

'I think perhaps I'd better not, if it's family.'

'Tabby insists, and mother will be pressing an invitation on you the moment she comes down. I'm afraid there'll be no getting out of it, if you'll still be here.'

I smiled. 'In that case, I give in.'

'Tabby told me you two know each other from ages ago.'

'Yes.'

'From the war?'

'We were both in the VAD.'

He sighed and seemed to deflate. 'All of you who came through that, it's as if you're a different species somehow. You saw so much. You have a way of being with each other that's . . . I don't know. Those of us who weren't there . . .'

'Really, I try not to think about it too much. And I'm sure Tabitha is glad to have it all behind her. We've hardly talked about it at all.'

I didn't say that that was because we hadn't yet had the time. I'd no doubt that candles would burn late into the night, and we would go over those days.

He rubbed at a spot on his cuff. 'I know why you're really here. She hasn't told me, but I'm not entirely dense.'

I waited to see what else he would say.

'I'm right aren't I?' he said, looking at me sadly, like a little boy who can't join in a game.

'I don't know. Why do you think I'm here?'

'To look for her father, of course. Well? Am I right?'

'Yes.'

'And?'

I shrugged. 'It's been a long time. I'm not sure that I'll succeed where others have failed.'

He leaned forward, sighing. Dropping his head towards his knees like a damsel recovering from a faint. When he straightened up, there was a hardness in his face, so that he looked much older. 'We'll hit the rocks before we begin. I don't understand why she has to go on looking. It gets worse instead of better. I honestly think she won't marry me if she doesn't find him. It obsesses her, night and day. Yet all through our courtship, she pretended enough for me to think I was the one who mattered. Now it's Dad this, Dad that. If only she'd been here for him and so on and so forth. I feel so helpless, as if it's somehow my fault.'

'It's traditional I suppose, for a bride to be walked to the altar by her father. It's only natural . . . that she should be thinking of him, wanting him to be there.'

'Is it? She has her Uncle Neville, and she has me.'

'It's not a reflection on you, Hector.'

'Oh but it is. And she won't find him, and it will always be there, between us, as if it was somehow my fault.'

'How could it be your fault?'

'The nearest person always takes the flak. We all know that.'

'She simply wants to know, one way or the other, and I shall do my best to try and help her. People do sometimes turn up after years and years. It has been known.'

He ran his hands through his hair. Something about his gesture seemed so young. I realised he must still have been at school when Joshua Braithwaite went missing. And if he were still at school . . .

'Do you remember much about that time, Hector?'

He shifted uneasily on the sofa. 'I hate leather sofas. We shan't have one.'

It was tactless, but I had to say it. 'You must have been what? Fourteen, fifteen at the time?'

'Yes.' He stood up and went to the window, then suddenly turned. 'I don't talk about that time. It only serves to remind us both that Tabby was already grown up and off doing important things and I was . . . I loved her even then. I used to read those stories about knights and ladies, and I was the knight, and she was the lady who might give me a favour to carry into battle. But of course she was the one who went off to war, and I . . . '

'And you were what, Hector? In the boy scouts?'

He nodded.

Footsteps on the stairs. Tabitha's voice. A woman laughing.

I said, quickly, 'Sometime, will you talk to me about that? Your time in the scouts, and when Mr Braithwaite went missing?'

'Only if you promise not to tell Tabitha.'

'I can't promise that.'

'Then I can't talk to you about it.' He avoided meeting my eyes. 'Anyway, there's nothing to tell.'

Tabitha and her future mother-in-law swept into the room, looking so happy. Tabitha introduced me to Hector's mother, Mrs Gawthorpe, a stout cheerful woman with a round open face.

She shook my hand warmly. 'Tabitha was just telling me about how you and she met at a hospital in Leeds.'

'St Mary's,' Tabitha said.

5

Hospital Linens

Monday, 21 August 1916

TABITHA

Nurse Tabitha Braithwaite had been working since five
a.m. They were short of staff in St Mary's. One of the
domestics had not turned up for work. Tabitha collected
the urine bottles. She assisted men who could not manage
alone. There were drinks of water to distribute, floors to
be mopped, surfaces scrubbed down, teas handed round,
then breakfast. On the shell shock ward, some bad cases
needed help with everything. Their shaking got in the way
of the most basic tasks.

The man in bed ten lay beyond speech now. Yesterday,
when he arrived, she had begun to write a letter for him.
He grew tired and they agreed to finish it today. The letter
crackled in her pocket as she walked. Under the sheet and
counterpane, his knees jerked. For two or three seconds,
his legs would be still and then a foot would raise the
covers as though it thought itself in a match, ready to take
a goal kick.

With one hand cradling his head, holding him still, she
helped him drink, putting the hospital cup to his lips. His
baby bird mouth gaped. A low groan came from somewhere deep inside as water trickled onto his chin. His
twitching jaw made a clicking sound. Not having his notes
yesterday, she had left the 'T' on his forehead, alerting

Sister, uncertain whether the tetanus injection had been given to him.

Now she walked round with the doctor and ward sister, pad in hand, making notes, feeling fraudulent. Nurse they called her. But her training had been rushed and felt haphazard.

At bed number ten, while the doctor and sister conferred, Tabitha gently wiped the T from the man's forehead. The tetanus injection had come too late to prevent lockjaw. The patient had a name: Stanley Spence. Stan to friends and family. Tabitha knew this because yesterday evening, when he was still clinging to hopes of staying in this world, they began the letter. She recognised his accent. He was from Keighley, a millwright. When she told him she was the daughter of Braithwaites Mill, he chuckled. It tickled him to have her look after him. A boss's daughter.

By quarter to three she felt frayed at the edges and leaned against the wall in the sluice room. There was a shudder, as if someone in the adjacent room had hammered on the wall. The vibration rattled a shelf, causing a urine bottle to fall and break. That was all she needed. More work. At least it was empty. Tabitha went to find a dust pan and brush.

'Is someone hammering?' she asked.

'It felt like a tremor, a quake,' Sister said. 'It's upset the men on the shell shock ward.'

Tabitha had seen men die before. But this seemed so unfair, to have come all this way, to be so near home and yet to be beyond hope. She should be off duty now but would not go. Stan Spence's hands shook. Wool-gathering fingers folding and unfolding grasped the air.

She took his hand. He sighed. Something inside him seemed quieter now, reassured by her touch. She had placed screens around the bed and pulled her chair close.

A stranger's voice startled her. 'I've come to relieve you.'

Tabitha turned. A young woman appeared by the side of the screen. She slid into view and stood by the bed. Tabitha did not want to be relieved. She felt knotted to the chair. This was where she would stay, for eternity, or at least for Stan Spence's eternity.

'Sister sent me.' The woman went round to the other side of the bed. She was about Tabitha's age, with an open friendly face, smooth healthy skin and lively eyes – too alive to belong in this corner of last resorts.

She perched on the edge of the bed. You weren't allowed to sit on the beds. Sister was a stickler over that.

'Sister says report to the office,' the woman said gently. 'You're off duty.'

Tabitha did not trouble herself to shake her head. The man in the bed did enough shaking for both of them.

His other hand flailed on the counterpane. The intruder took his hand and held it. Each of them stroked a hand, Tabitha on his right, the intruder on his left. Stan Spence seemed calmer, and to sigh, but only for a moment.

It was as if invisible bolts of lightning jolted Stan's frame. Some sound came from deep inside him, a terrible rasping noise, like a machine that needed more than oiling.

Tabitha leaned forward and encircled him in her arms to hold him still. He rolled towards her, and back, and towards her. Some powerful leaping motion seemed to propel him forward, as though to catch the thin-spun thread of his own life.

And then he was still, and grey as undyed fleece. That change in his skin seemed too sudden, too dramatic, too unnecessary. As if Death was laughing, and impatient. *I've got him now. He's mine.*

Tabitha stroked his still hand, and thought of him strolling among the looms of a mill. The man who could fix things and get the weaver working again. She knew he had children. He mentioned them in his unfinished letter.

She thought of Edmund, her brother. Killed in action, the telegram had said. She thought of how he had held a cricket bat, and how he always said she held it wrong.

Stan Spence must have held a cricket bat, and laughed, and hit a ball for six. She hoped so. *Howzat?!* Edmund had called. *Out! Out!*

Tabitha watched the intruder close Stan's eyes and cover his face.

They walked side by side back to the nurses' room. Tabitha went to tell Sister that Stan Spence had died. She felt for his letter in her pocket, and wondered what to do. She was too tired to think, worn out and useless. Her brain had turned to lint.

Sister told her to get herself off duty now, and rest.

The woman who had tried to relieve her made them cups of tea, using the old tea leaves in the pot because that's all there was till tomorrow. The woman didn't speak, but everything about her quiet confident movements spoke sympathy and understanding. It soothed Tabitha to have someone else there, making the tea, saying nothing. The woman had chestnut hair, caught with combs at the nape of her neck. She wore an ambulance driver's uniform. She looked as alert and intelligent as Tabitha felt insipid and undone. Even something as simple as letting her legs walk her off duty posed an insurmountable task.

The woman set down the tea and took out cigarettes, lighting Tabitha's for her.

The action, and the deep inhalation, brought Tabitha back to life. She remembered that she had been on the go for twelve hours without time to stop, until now.

'Sister called you Braithwaite,' the woman said. 'What's your Christian name?'

'Tabitha.'

'I'm Kate. Kate Shackleton.'

Tabitha took Stanley Spence's letter from her pocket. If

81

she did not do this now, her courage would fail. She would finish Stan Spence's letter. Setting her cup on the desk she reached for the scratchy communal pen and dipped it into what was left of the scrunchy disgusting ink. Not looking at what had gone before, she wrote, *Must say ta ta for now, Your loving husband, Stan. Kissses to the children.*

Earlier that day she had checked his address from the records and written an envelope. She folded the letter carefully and reached for the envelope.

Kate looked over her shoulder. 'Is that for the man who just died?'

'Yes. But what do I do? Mrs Spence will receive this letter and think her husband is alive. Then a telegram will come. I can't put PS I am dying. PPS I have died.'

'Where does Mrs Spence live?' Kate asked.

'She lives in Keighley,' Tabitha answered. 'Not far from the railway station. Stanley was a millwright. He thought it was a hoot to be cared for by me. We have a mill, you see.'

Sister looked in on them. Tabitha and Kate exchanged a swift glance as Tabitha slid the letter into her pocket. Sister would insist on doing things by the book, posting the letter, arranging for notification in the usual way.

'I told you to take some rest, Braithwaite,' Sister said. 'And haven't you a home to go to, driver?' She had forgotten Kate's name.

Sister clomped out. She put the whole of her foot on the floor at once, not heel first in the usual way. They listened to her plod along the corridor.

'She makes more noise than a woman clattering to the mill in clogs,' Tabitha said.

Kate started to laugh. 'Take some rest, Braithwaite!' Kate giggled.

'Haven't you a home to go to, driver?' Tabitha demanded, shaking with laughter.

'Isn't it terrible to laugh?' Kate said.

82

'I know.'

'I have petrol enough to take you to the station. Would you get a train to Keighley at this time, and if you did, could you get back?'

Tabitha felt some energy returning. 'Yes. I can do that.'

She felt she owed it to Stanley Spence. What fury would Mrs Spence feel when she found out how close Stan was to coming home. How near, and yet gone forever.

And that was how Tabitha came to call home, unexpectedly, for a brief visit.

It was mad to have done it, to have gone to see Mrs Spence and break such news. At nearly midnight, she had no chance of getting back to St Mary's. She found a cab driver willing to urge his tired horse to take them to Bridgestead. She left him on the drive while she went indoors to find the fare, expecting to have to bray on the door to wake the house.

The door was open. The housekeeper emerged in her dressing gown. Dad wasn't there. Mother wasn't there. Tabitha had to scrabble about in her room until she found some cash.

When she had paid the cab driver, she asked where her parents were. On hearing that her mother was with Aunt Catherine, she hurried towards the mill house, forgetting her exhaustion, running across the two fields. Aunt Catherine must have taken a turn for the worse. Tabitha could not bear another death. Please God, don't let her die too. Not today.

Aunt Catherine was sleeping. Tabitha and her mother went into the big dining room. Under the gaze of the stuffed birds, Tabitha felt a pang of fear in her guts.

'Where's Dad? Where's Uncle Neville? What's wrong?'

'I didn't want to worry you,' her mother said wearily. 'Something's happened. We had a bit of bother over the weekend with your father. Now he's disappeared.'

'What do you mean "bother", what kind of bother? What's happened? Where's Dad gone?'

There was a frantic edge to her mother's voice when she said, 'Neville's out looking for him.'

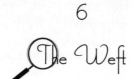

6

The Weft

When meeting someone for the first time, it's good to have a little information about them. All I knew about Tabitha's Uncle Neville Stoddard was that unless Tabitha's miracle happened and Joshua Braithwaite was found alive and well, Tabitha would walk down the aisle on Uncle Neville's arm. I also guessed that without Uncle Neville's steady hand on the tiller, Braithwaites Mill would have sunk.

Neville Stoddard's office held a table containing books illustrating what the well-dressed gent would be wearing next season, a large desk, at which he sat, on the telephone, and shelves stacked with rolls of fabrics, grey blanket material with a red stripe, plaid rug and uniform-style navy. I examined the fabrics while waiting for his call to end. When it did, he put down the receiver and offered me his hand with a disarmingly friendly smile.

He pulled out a chair for me. 'Tabitha's told me why you're here. How are you getting on with your investigations?'

'Not very well, so far.'

'Thanks for bringing your photographic stuff. And a tripod too.' He picked up a bobbin, rolling it on the desk, like a child might play with a toy car. 'I used to dabble in photography a little myself. The camera will be useful.'

'Oh?' I was curious as to why he had asked me to bring a camera.

'Thing is, I'd rather not stir up a hornet's nest of speculation over Joshua. The workers will look at you and see a lady photographer, interested in mills and weavers.'

I smiled at this. 'As it happens I intend to enter the All British Photographic Competition. I hope to find an unusual subject.'

He slapped his hands on the desk. 'That's settled then.'

'Does that mean you don't want me to talk to your employees?' I added hastily. He wasn't to know that Sykes would do that for me. But Sykes would only be able to talk to men in pubs. There must be female employees who might have something useful to say.

He shook his head emphatically. 'Nothing to be gained from upsetting the workers. Rule out that line of enquiry, save yourself some time.'

He leaned back in his chair, rather precariously, looking at me with what seemed like admiration. For a moment I feared for the back of his head against the window sill. At school when I had broken my arm, I leaned back on my chair and couldn't manage to lever myself up again. Ever since that day, seeing someone tilt a chair gives me the collywobbles.

'Tabitha tells me you'd like a tour of the mill?'

'Yes. I've never visited a mill.'

'Then you've missed a great deal of muck, a lot of stink and enough noise to blow down Buckingham Palace. Let's start here.' He pushed back his chair and stood up. 'This is Joshua Braithwaite's office, and I make no apologies for purloining it. I'm holding the fort until he returns.'

He said it as if the words were meant to ward off further questions. I stayed put.

He sat down opposite me, in the second of the visitors' chairs. 'Whatever anyone else says, Mrs Shackleton, I choose to believe that Joshua has gone to warmer climes, for his health, and will return. I say it at the Wool Exchange. I say it to customers, and I say it in the Mechanics' Institute. I needn't say it at the chapel, because folk there have the courtesy not to ask.'

'And do you believe what you say?'

'My job's not belief, except when it comes to The Almighty. My job's to run a mill to the best of my ability.' He reached for the bobbin from his desk and spun it between his palms. 'We were all flummoxed by his disappearance, didn't know what to make of it. You can't pluck an explanation out of thin air when there isn't one. I decided to shut up the questions with my warmer climes remark. If you say something loud enough and often enough, folk stop asking.'

'It must have been hard for you when he left.'

A fleeting look of hurt altered his expression, making him look suddenly younger than his fifty-something years. 'It was hard. To be frank, it was terrible. We did everything together, from about the age of fifteen when I came to live here. Technical college – sitting exams together, learning the trade together. Having fun too. We used to run, when we were younger, take part in the fell races. I miss him, very much.'

I'm not here to pity him, I told myself, though in that moment I did.

'I understand the official explanation you give. I'd probably do the same. But I can't really work out what happened. What was Mr Braithwaite's state of mind?'

'He was feeling low-spirited, heartbroken over Edmund's death.' He sighed. 'And Tabitha was away from home, of course, doing her bit in the VAD. I believe that's where you met?'

'Yes.'

'I'm glad she's got a friend to stay. To tell you the truth, I think that's what she needs more than anything, a female friend. Joshua isn't going to turn up for her.'

'Were there any business worries?'

'Come on, let me show you round. You can get a feeling of how good business is – and believe me, it was even

87

better in 1916. That was our best year in decades. Bring your camera and choose a view. There's plenty of light in the weaving room. If you can bear the racket, you might get a good photograph. Make an extra copy for the office, and the village hall, and you'll have friends in Bridgestead for life.'

In each office, he told me what work took place there: Purchasing, Sales, Invoicing.

On the corridor, I asked, 'What do you purchase?'

'Yarn, from the worsted spinners. We're weavers and dyers. Joshua was a good businessman. He left the firm in great shape and I've ensured it stays that way.'

One office was Quality Control, another Wages. 'I'm very popular on Fridays. I take the wages around myself. Keeps 'em on their toes.'

I noticed that although he had the local accent, similar to Evelyn Braithwaite's, now and then his vowels would lengthen, as if he had spent his early life somewhere else.

On the stairs, he said, 'We were exceptionally busy during the war.'

I listened carefully. Would this be his roundabout way of talking about Joshua, *during the war*?

'Be careful, Mrs Shackleton. It's slippery just here. Someone's come up in muddy boots.'

'You were exceptionally busy during the war,' I prompted.

'We had to increase wages to keep our staff. Some of the men had answered the call to enlist. We needed to find overlookers – the machines have to be kept running. That was when it paid off that we had a loyal workforce. Look after them and they'll look after you. We took work from firms in Leeds, where men had more choice of employment. A lot of owners were still lagging behind in their outlook. Prepare your ears for a shock.'

I could already hear deafening noises, slamming and banging and the roar of machinery.

He raised his voice, 'Don't expect to hear a thing on this floor. It's full of looms all going flat out. We were down for a few hours yesterday, waiting for yarn. We're making up for it today.'

Before he opened the door, the choking stench of engine oil filled my nose and throat. I made a deliberate attempt not to stagger back when he opened the door as the smell, although it hardly seemed possible, grew even more over-powering.

The noise was literally deafening. No wonder Mrs Kellett asked me to face her for my fortune-telling, so that she could read my lips. I had all on not to put my hands over my ears. Small wonder she had become 'half-deaf' as she put it. At the far end of the room a thundering roller moved the woven cloth to a workshop on the floor above. I caught sight of Mrs Kellett. With a barely perceptible movement, she nodded to me.

Stoddard hadn't noticed Mrs Kellett's greeting, which I guessed was what she intended.

At that moment, Stoddard was speaking to the manager. Neither could possibly hear a word the other said. The conversation was conducted entirely by each watching the other's lips.

The women, faces alive and expressive, were mouthing conversations across the frames. Sometimes they would laugh, but not a human sound could be heard, only the clatter, crash and clang of the looms with their monstrous metal teeth, shuddering wheels and moving belts.

Everything about this mill felt dangerous. If a man wanted to commit suicide, he could do it here. And if that man were rightfully entitled to enter walkways, climb steep open stairs, cross floors where rattling machinery might crush the unwary, a death could look like an accident. Though it would be a horrible way to die.

Stoddard nodded encouragingly, expecting me to photograph one of the looms. The noise shuddered its way into my being, setting every part of me on edge as I found a good spot to stand. Light flooding in from the windows behind, I focused the picture – a single loom and its operator.

Stoddard waited until I had taken a photograph.

He spoke to me on the stairs, on the way to the floor above, but the noise still rang in my ears and I could not make out what he said.

I told him that I would like to take a photograph when the machines were still. It would be like catching a lion as it snoozed.

On the top floor there were more looms. He pointed to a loading door in the wall. The crane had been hoisted up from the floor below. A worker leaned out of the door to draw in a cart that swayed in the air outside, a dizzying height above the ground. As the man held the cart, Stoddard stooped and leaned in to help, unhooking the cart from the crane. Carts of folded cloth stood by the wall. High rods just below the ceiling level ran the width of the room. On two of the rods tents of cloth were drawn down by eagle-eyed women who caressed the cloth into folds.

'They're inspecting and marking it,' Stoddard said. 'From here it goes to the burlers and menders.' He nodded to workers in the centre of the room. 'They pick up the flaws and put them right.' Stoddard spoke briefly to one of the women who wielded her needle at a piece of cloth.

He watched my lips as I said, 'It seems to me you're a bit of a burler and mender yourself, Mr Stoddard.'

He laughed and on the landing said, 'You're a smart lass. I don't know why you're wasting your time trying to do the police out of a job.'

On another floor was the packing and despatch department. Parcels of cloth were fastened with string, loaded onto carts and wheeled across to the door in the outside wall where once again the crane came into operation.

'Well?' he asked as we walked back to the main doors on the ground floor. 'What do you think to the place?'

'Impressive.'

In the yard, I stepped carefully round puddles of coloured rain. A small, wiry man with huge arms manoeuvred a large bogie, loaded with yarn. Stoddard beckoned me to look. 'This yarn we're just taking delivery of, it's dyed in the wool – pre-dyed. What you'll see next is our own dyehouse. This is where we do piece dyeing, after the cloth's been woven.'

In the doorway of the dyehouse, he said, 'Now you best just put your head round and take a peep. It's filthy, foggy, it stinks and the dye flies everywhere – onto your skin, into your hair and clothes.'

'And you don't have women working in here?'

'It'd be a rare woman that'd have the muscles for it. Looks messy and haphazard, but there's a high level of skill involved in achieving consistent colour. These workers have served a long apprenticeship.' He nodded towards a man wearing a flat cap and another with a shock of red hair. 'They're father and son.'

The man whipped off his cap, then scuttled away so as not to have to speak to me.

Stoddard called another man who seemed less shy. 'Kellett!' He introduced me. 'Tell Mrs Shackleton what we do here.'

Kellett stepped to the doorway, whipping off his cap. So this was Lizzie Luck's husband. He was stocky, pugnacious and had a claw of a hand. Industrial injury, or war wound?

'Good afternoon.' He fixed me with a bold stare, as if asserting his authority over this, his world.

'Good afternoon, Mr Kellett.'

He waved his arms to the great shed of a room where Stoddard went to seek out one of the workers. 'This is the dyehouse. In some places they call it a shed. We all know

91

it as well as we know our own house, so dyehouse is a good term for it. Every man jack here has served his apprenticeship and knows his work – or he wouldn't last two minutes. Our first job is to make the stuff stable like. That's why it's hotter than hell in there, begging your pardon. We scour the cloth to shift muck and grease, any other whatnot picked up as it's gone along. Then we dye and dry the fabric – tentering that's called. Looms was down yesterday and so we're behind-hand. Someone'll be working late tomorrer night to finish off – and that some-one'll be me because I'm foreman.'

Beyond him inside the dyehouse were wooden struc-tures, with rails above them. Some looked as if they could double as bathing huts. There were deep oblong vessels with cloth suspended from a contraption above.

'I expected great half barrels.' I didn't add that I'd also thought to see giant wooden spoons.

'You been looking at school picture books. They stopped using the Thiess barrels around 1900.'

Suddenly steam rolled towards us, coming in waves from the far end of the building. The place was full of steam. Wafted with it came a smell like rotten fish and decaying flesh.

'Dyehouse fog, we call it.' Kellett replaced the cap on his head. 'Hear that high boiling noise?'

'Yes.'

'There's a vortex as the steam hits cold. Listen for the low rumble. When it stops – goes quiet like – you have to turn the steam off quick or it boils over.'

'What happens if it boils over?'

'You run.' He laughed. 'And you better not stand too close to that barrel, missis.'

I hadn't realised I was leaning against the barrel. I moved away. 'Why's that?'

'It's full of piss, begging your pardon. We use it to soften't wool.'

'Thanks for telling me.'

Only when he took his leave and turned back to face the fog did I realise what it was about his speech that marked him out. He didn't thee and thou as his wife did, as if deliberately bringing his talk into an idiom that would suit mine.

Stoddard came to the doorway, followed by the red-haired youth and two other men.

'I've twisted their arms into having a photograph taken,' he said, winking at me, determined to keep up the fiction that I was here solely because of my interest in photography. 'Where would you like them to stand?'

This time I used the tripod, lodging it in the cracks between the cobbles. As I focused the Reflex, Stoddard called for Kellett to come back and take his place for the group photograph. The men joshed each other and awkwardly pretended to jostle over pride of place in the line. In the end, they formed themselves around Kellett who was not the tallest but managed to make himself look the most important.

Usually I enjoy taking a photograph, but suddenly the light felt wrong. Aware that I was keeping them from their work, and that they had been coerced, I nevertheless decided to make the most of the opportunity and asked them to move further into the yard, away from the shadow cast by the dyehouse.

Picture taken, I thanked them and walked back across the yard where Stoddard waited for me. From the vantage point of crossing the yard, I could see the usefulness of the hoist that transported materials from one floor to another up and down the four storeys of the building. There was a sense of danger about the door openings. An unwary person could easily step to their death. The thought made me shudder. The heavy chain with its huge hook clanked as it lowered a swaying cart from the fourth floor to the ground.

If Joshua Braithwaite had wanted to commit suicide, he

could have done it here, when the mill was closed. Or way off on the moors somewhere out of sight. It did not make sense to me that he would have tried to drown himself in a shallow beck within a few feet of a cottage and where boy scouts camped in nearby woods.

Stoddard was talking to me again, about the deliveries of yarn. I'm here to find out about Joshua Braithwaite, I reminded myself, not to become an expert on mills or even to find the perfect subject for the All British Photographic Competition.

'How do things work administratively, Mr Stoddard? Do you have meetings and so on?'

'Evelyn and Tabitha are on the board. We meet once a month. I have meetings with my managers, from each department, once a week.'

'I'd like to see the board minutes, please.'

'Why?'

'Perhaps I'll pick up something that's been missed. I still don't feel I know enough about Mr Braithwaite's state of mind.'

'I've already told you his state of mind. Saddened by the loss of his son. And I'm sure you've spoken to Evelyn. There's nothing to be gained by reading our commercially confidential information.'

'But . . .'

'Really, it would go against the grain for me to do that. We mill owners are very secretive. And don't forget, as far as our employees are concerned, you're here because of your interest in the mill, and photography.'

There was no more to be said as we walked back to his office.

The impressions jumbled together in my mind. I could hold on to only a vague notion of what I had seen, the noise and the smells overriding any sense of what process followed what. A bent old woman creaked into the office, her arthritic hands shakily clutching a tray of tea and biscuits.

94

He pulled a face. 'You haven't stirred my tea!' he called.

She grumbled a reply. I had a feeling this was a regular exchange between them. It made me warm towards Stoddard.

When the tea lady had gone, I said, 'I know you don't want to talk about it but . . .'

'Digestive?' he offered me the plate.

I took a biscuit.

'I have a routine, and a good workforce. Mrs Braithwaite has a shrewd business head. Between us we have steered through some difficult times. It's fortunate that Joshua wasn't a man to hold power tight to his chest or we wouldn't have had the authority to carry on.'

Under his attempt at modesty, I sensed a pride in his own achievements.

'Tabitha did tell me that she and her mother are on the board and that the three of you continue the business. It does puzzle me that Mrs Braithwaite has not sought to have her husband declared dead.'

'I believe she'll wait the full seven years.'

That magic word seven, seven leagues, seven seas, seventh heaven and seven sins.

'And are Mrs Braithwaite and Tabitha . . . I mean do they know the business well enough to be of help?'

He paused, and smiled. 'Ask me another question.'

'Do you think Mr Braithwaite tried to commit suicide?'

He picked up his fidget bobbin, holding it in both hands, turning it, sighing.

'Did you do sports at school, Mrs Shackleton, or were you one of these young ladies educated at home?'

'I play tennis. I ride.'

'As I mentioned, when we were boys, Joshua and I were both keen runners. Lots of people round here take it up. You test yourself, against the elements. You run, and when you feel you can run no more, you keep on running.'

'Are you saying he was not a man to give up?'

'I think that day, when he was found, he'd been out running and taken a tumble. That's my guess. When he said he wasn't trying to top himself, he meant it. It's just that he was unfortunate enough to be found by people who wanted to believe differently and he didn't have enough strength – or perhaps the will – to persuade them otherwise.'

'Your theory about a new life – in a good climate – where do you think he may have gone? And what would he have used for money?'

'Joshua provided for Evelyn and Tabitha. He left the company in good heart, and the workforce secure.'

'But he had other money?'

'Is it likely Joshua Braithwaite stashed away money?! Does the sun rise in the morning? If he is dead, there's probably money in accounts that will go unclaimed forever, money that should rightly go to Evelyn.'

'What do you believe? Is he dead, or alive?'

'Tabitha's clutching at straws, but what young woman wouldn't on the eve of her wedding?'

'There is just one other thing, Mr Stoddard. It seems such a coincidence that he disappeared on the day of the Low Moor explosion, when so many people were killed. Is there any possibility that he would have gone in that direction?'

He lay his fidget bobbin down and rolled it back and forth on the desk. The fidgeting had begun to disconcert me. I wondered whether he had one of those slight stammers where movement acts as a distraction.

He seemed not to want to begin. 'I've wondered that too. There's nothing I haven't imagined, nothing I haven't thought about. But I can think of no reason he would have gone there.'

'Did Mr Braithwaite leave a note?'

'What kind of note?'

'An explanation? A suicide note?'

'Good heavens no. Joshua sometimes left notes about this or that to be done, or something to be added to the minutes for the next meeting, but there was no note of the sort you have in mind.'

I decided not to mention that Evelyn Braithwaite had said that there was.

'Perhaps his stumbling into the beck was a cry for help.'

Mr Stoddard gave up on his bobbin. He placed the backs of his hands on the desk in a gesture of surrender. 'That's a bit deep for me. If you said that he came over queer, took a dizzy turn, that might make sense.'

'Why did no one send for you when Mr Braithwaite was found in the beck?'

'Out of consideration I expect. My wife was dying.'

'I'm sorry.'

'No. You're right. They should have come for me. I would have seen to it that Joshua was taken home. The local scout troop had been camping out in the woods. There was a lot of that sort of activity then, perhaps you'll remember something of it yourself – self-sufficiency, training lads up to take their place in the front line. They went to their scoutmaster. He's dead now, poor man, but he was the brother of a rival of ours. That's how the whole thing became public so quickly, and such a scandal. That's why I started to say what I did, about warmer climes.'

'But surely even a rival would baulk at accusing a man of suicide. He would have understood the necessity to keep up morale in wartime.'

'The scoutmaster understood we'd almost put his brother out of business.'

The telephone rang. Mr Stoddard called through to his secretary in the next office, 'Not now, Dorothy!'

'Not many more questions, Mr Stoddard. But what do you believe happened after Mr Braithwaite was taken to the hospital at Milton House?'

97

'I'm really and truly not sure. I've come up with all sorts of ideas during the intervening years, and none of them seem satisfactory. Some say – I don't listen but I know what they say – he was overcome with shame at being accused of attempting suicide, and went somewhere to finish what he started. If so, why didn't we find a body? Did he somehow find his way to a new life? I can't see it. He would have been in touch. He would be here for Tabitha's wedding. Now is there anything else that I can do for you?'

'Yes. I'd like a souvenir of my visit – a bobbin like yours.'

'Easy!' He handed his bobbin across the desk. 'They're ten a penny.'

He insisted on escorting me from the building, through the yard, past the house within the grounds where he lived, and out as far as the gate.

The mill hooter sounded the dinner hour. My stomach rumbled, but I had to develop my photographs, and keep my appointment with Sykes. I hoped he would have been more successful than I had been so far. One advantage of working alone is that you are not measuring yourself against anyone else. Now that Sykes had come to work for me, that changed. Which of us would find out that useful little fact that would act as a key to the Braithwaite mystery? And who would get to it first?

7

Twisting-in: joining the threads of an old warp to a new warp.

The Ramshead Arms is a market tavern some hundred or so years old, built to replace a much older coaching house. I parked a little way off in case any inhabitant of Bridgestead might be conducting business in the town and spot my car outside.

Sykes must have been looking out. He came to meet me. We exchanged a brief greeting then entered the Ramshead Arms by a side door and turned into a small function room.

There was something almost awkward and boyish in the way he had thoughtfully arranged for plates of sandwiches and glasses of cider to be set out on a large oak table at one end of the room.

At the other end of the table was an open valise containing bathing suits.

'My cover story,' he said. 'As far as the staff and customers here are concerned, I'm a traveller in bathing attire.'

Having missed lunch while developing and printing my photographs, I tucked into a ham and mustard sandwich. He took a striped plain navy and a two-tone bathing suit and placed each one carefully on the table, betraying great enjoyment in his play-acting. 'Just in case we're interrupted.'

It struck me that my five pounds payment to him on

account had gone a very long way. As if he read my thoughts, he said, 'I have the bathing suits on sale or return.'

It was time to pool our information.

I brought out my gallery of characters, suggesting that I go first. Sykes studied the Braithwaites' wedding photograph, alongside a photograph of Joshua Braithwaite at a Wool Exchange function, and by the sea with Tabitha and Edmund, shading his eyes.

We looked at the photographs intently, as though the man himself might speak.

'Joshua Braithwaite is or was about five feet five inches tall,' I said. 'Spare, energetic. He and his cousin Neville Stoddard were great fell runners in their youth. He's teetotal, pillar of the chapel, a womaniser, and a good businessman. His son was killed in July 1916, on the Somme. According to the cousin, who runs the mill, Braithwaite was brought exceedingly low by Edmund's death, as you might expect.'

Sykes swallowed a mouthful of his best Yorkshire ham sandwich. 'Low enough to try and top himself?'

'His wife thinks yes. Tabitha says no. Stoddard won't admit to Braithwaite's having attempted suicide. He says he was not a man to give up easily. Stoddard won't say outright that Braithwaite is dead, though I'm sure he believes that.'

Sykes stabbed at Evelyn on the wedding photograph. 'Why hasn't she had Braithwaite declared dead?'

'She believes he's dead but as far as I can gather wants to wait the full seven years. Perhaps it's for Tabitha's sake. Evelyn's main concern just now is to see the wedding go smoothly. Hector, Tabitha's fiancé, is ten years her junior. He resents the investigation. I'm hoping to get more out of him but he's reluctant to talk in case I tell Tabitha and it reminds her of how young he is – as if she didn't know.'

'Can't you give him assurance that what he says won't go any further?'

There was a hint of criticism in his voice which made my reply sharper than I'd intended. 'It's her investigation. She'll be coughing up. My obligation is to Tabitha Braithwaite, and the truth.'

He shrugged and wiped his mouth with the serviette as if attempting to button his lip.

'I play it straight. That's why Tabitha asked me and not some tuppence ha'penny private detective, or an ex-policeman.' I polished off the cider, wondering had I made a big mistake taking on this clever Dick.

'Touché!' He smiled. 'But my point is, it's the result she's after, not every bit of tittle-tattle on the way to it.'

For a moment we were silent, picking up each of the other photographs from the table, like playing snap without hope of a match. I told him about each person in turn. Evelyn, not sorry to see the back of her husband, claiming there was a note but not remembering its contents; Tabitha, who blamed herself for not being there; Edmund, much mourned young soldier whose death may have prompted Joshua Braithwaite's suicide attempt; Hector, the former boy scout who knew more than he admitted; Stoddard, cousin and friend of Braithwaite's youth who had held the fort at the mill; Mrs Kellett, on the upturned barrel outside her door. I explained her special insights into who had reached where and who did what in the afterlife and her certainty that Braithwaite had shuffled off this mortal coil. Lastly I showed him the photograph of the dyeworkers, including Kellett, whom I had not yet spoken to except concerning the workings of the dyehouse.

'Kellett interests me.' Sykes picked up the photograph. 'That's him?'

'How do you know?'

'By his description. The dyeworkers go for a pint after work. I stood them a round last night in the Gaping Goose. Only Kellett's the one who jumps in to get the

101

overtime, so he wasn't there. Just as well because they may not have been as forthcoming about him if he had been. Must be a bit of a comedown for him, to be back in the dyeworks. He had his moment of glory.'

'Do you mean the injury? He's missing his left hand. He has a sort of claw. It's tucked up his sleeve in this photograph.'

'He joined up in 1914, after a row with the missus and an argument over a pay increase that wasn't forthcoming. He came out in 1915, due to his Blighty wound.'

'Are you saying it was a self-inflicted injury?'

Sykes shrugged. 'Don't know. But I do know that some men made their own wounds worse, to keep from going back to the front. And a hand or foot injury – that's always the easy one to self-inflict. It's his left hand, and he's right handed.'

I knew well enough about war injuries. I'd once been asked by a doctor in France to bandage the arms and legs of men to stop them from scratching their wounds worse so that they would not be sent back to the front. We all knew what they were up to but said nothing. It would have been a court martial offence. If Kellett had shot his own hand off, he must have been desperate.

'The moment of glory I was thinking about was when he came back.' Sykes selected the photograph of Braithwaite with his business colleagues and set it alongside the photograph of Kellett and the dye workers. 'Did anyone mention a German connection?'

'Tabitha said there was talk about a friendship between their family and the von Hofmanns and that because of it there was some local suspicion of Braithwaite.'

'Did she say why?'

'Just that they were thought to be too close. She mentioned Little Germany, an area of Bradford where the merchants worked.'

'There was a bit more to it than friendship and fine

buildings. I picked up on a little gossip at the Wool Exchange that confirmed what the dyeworkers said. Before von Hofmann left the country, he and Joshua Braithwaite came to an arrangement. See, our textile industry was hugely dependent on German chemistry, and German dyes. With that source cut off after the outbreak of war, there was real difficulty. Anyone who could get their hands on the German dyes that were in storage here stood to make a fortune.'

'And Joshua Braithwaite was that man?'

'Indeed. Of course he did it at arm's length. Kellett came out of military hospital in 1915, with his honourable discharge and his demob suit . . .'

'And he knew all about dyes.'

'Exactly. Oh Braithwaite made the right gestures, for appearances' sake. He sold the picric acid to the Bradford Dyers' Association at a proper price. They had a subsidiary – the Low Moor Munitions Company, formerly Low Moor Chemical Company. The picric acid was used to manufacture high explosives. Low Moor Works got the picric acid, but there were a lot of other dyewares Braithwaite had come by. The shortage was so drastic that the Braithwaites of this world could name their price.'

'Braithwaites would have needed the dye for themselves surely?'

'Some of it. But if you compare Braithwaites with mills the size of Salts and Listers, they're small fry. They'd get away with far less. They were weaving khaki, you said?'

'Yes, according to Stoddard.'

'Khaki was produced from two olives, white, light-blue and purple. But some dyers threw in all sorts of stuff. It wasn't unknown for the khaki to turn pink or blue once it'd had a day's outing in fair or foul weather.'

'So Braithwaite was making a lot of money out of these dyes. I wonder how much.'

'According to my informants, Kellett was on the road

103

selling dyes between 1915 and 1916.' Sykes pulled out his notebook. 'I made a few notes as soon as I was out of the Goose and out of sight of my dyer friends.' He flicked the page. 'To give you an example – Chicago Blue 6B, eleven pence a pound, was sold in Bradford for ninety shillings a pound – diluted. And Braithwaite had access to the von Hofmann warehouse. He got in before war was declared. Don't know where he shifted the stuff but shift it he did.'

It made me feel indignant. 'That's just greedy. He was already a millionaire.' Footsteps trod the corridor. I returned the photographs to my satchel.

Sykes fingered a bathing suit. 'Profiteering. A lot of it went on.'

The footsteps passed. 'No wonder Stoddard goes about saying Braithwaite's decamped to warmer climes. He could afford to.'

Sykes gave me a quizzical look. 'It would have to be warmer climes like Cornwall or Devon. I can't see Braithwaite making his way to the South of France at the height of the Great War.'

'So do you think Kellett may have had a grudge? If he did the selling and Braithwaite picked up the profits?'

'Not as simple as that. They say Kellett has a fair whack stashed away, and that he'll surprise them all one day and go off to Bradford-on-Sea – to some grand bungalow on the cliff tops.'

'Bradford-on-Sea?'

'It's their nickname for Morecambe. They say Kellett keeps on working because he's adding to his pile.'

'He's turned into a miser?'

'Don't know. I hope I'll get the chance to talk to him. What did Mrs Kellett have to say?'

'I got the impression she's happy to rake in as much money as she can herself. Nice little sideline in fortune telling. She did have a postal order stub on the mantelpiece. Perhaps that was a payment towards the dream bungalow.'

'Could be.' Sykes consulted his notebook. 'Have you come across one Arthur Wilson yet?'

'No.'

'He's related by marriage to Miss Braithwaite's fiancé, Mr Gawthorpe. So he'll be more closely connected with the Braithwaite family soon. Wilson works in the mill as weaving manager.'

'Stoddard did have a conversation with a man in the weaving room as he showed me round, but I didn't get a name.'

Sykes leaned back from the table, relaxing his shoulders. 'Apparently this Wilson chap invented a new type of loom picker and Braithwaites patented it. These loom pickers are being manufactured in Sowerby Bridge and sold across the world. Wilson received an outright payment of twenty-five guineas, according to my informant at the Wool Exchange.'

Not for the first time, I began to feel a little out of my depth. 'What is a loom picker when it's at home?'

'It's part of the mechanism that drives the shuttle across the loom. A picker needs to be strong enough to do its job but not so tough that it snags the weave.'

Sykes picked up his pencil and turned to a fresh page in his notebook. He sketched out a slim vertical column that he labelled "picking arm", with a horizontal extension from the top. 'So you have the long picking arm, and across the top you have the picking stick, with a strap wound around. The strap drops and to that strap you attach the picker.' He sketched a small shape on the end of a strap. 'All sorts of materials have been tried, buffalo hide, rawhide, asbestos coated with rubber, canvas. Leather pickers last longer but cost more than canvas. If the leather's too thick it won't cling round the picking stick. So through the years, you get lots of experiments, and it's not until they're put into action that you know whether you've got a winner or a dud.'

'And is Wilson's loom picker a winner?'

'It's selling. So having accepted an outright payment in 1915, Wilson has simmered ever since. And it was with Mr Braithwaite that he settled on the outright payment.'

'A motive then?'

Sykes looked thoughtful. 'Yes if it was in anger. But it wouldn't be logical to murder the man you might still negotiate with.'

There was a tap on the door and the handle turned. In an instant, Sykes pulled an order pad towards him. 'You've made a good choice, madam. The striped attire is on track to be our best seller this year . . .'

The waiter approached us. 'Everything all right, sir?'

Sykes confirmed that everything was satisfactory. I handled the bathing suit as the waiter cleared the table and Sykes filled out the order form. 'And the two-tone? The two-tone is popular with the stouter-figured lady.'

'I shall take a dozen of each.'

When the waiter had gone, Sykes gave a sigh of relief. 'There's only so much you can say about bathing suits.'

He produced an Ordnance Survey map and unfolded it on the table. He had marked the beck, the mill and the Braithwaites' house.

'I like to have a map to see where I'm going, and more importantly where the villains might come and go.'

'We don't know that there are villains, Mr Sykes. Just the missing man and the people who miss him.'

'Or say they do. And there's sure to be villains. If it's all the same to you, Mrs Shackleton, I'd like to be the one that puts the handcuffs on the villain. I miss that part of the job. Now where's that hospital, Milton House? Is this it?'

I scanned the map. 'See just there – Laithstone Hill. Somewhere there.'

Sykes held his magnifying glass over the map. He leaned forward with the air of a general planning a military campaign. 'So he went from home, to the beck, to the police house, to the hospital and then we know not where.'

'And we don't know how he came to be in such a state at the beck. I'm hoping Hector can help, though there's a possibility some angry husband got to him.'

'No one at the Wool Exchange hinted at business problems, and apparently 1916 was a good year,' Sykes said.

'Yes. All the same, I'd like to take a look at the minute books in the mill office, so I'll need to get in after hours. I suppose you have skeleton keys and all that sort of thing.'

Sykes' face lit up as though I'd suggested a thrilling safari. 'I'm sure we'll manage it. What makes you think there'll be something useful in the minute books?'

'I don't know that there will be. But when someone says I can't take a look . . .'

'Someone like Stoddard?'

'Exactly. Then I know the one thing I have to do is take a look.'

Sykes nodded. 'The no-stone-unturned approach. Sometimes you can turn over an awful lot of stones and find only a few woodlice and beetles, but if you don't turn the stones you'll never know.'

As he began to pack up the bathing suits, I thought of summer and sand under my toes. I reached out for the striped suit. 'I'll take that one.'

'Done!' He wrapped the bathing suit in tissue paper.

'How much?'

'Not a penny. I wouldn't dream of profiteering at the expense of my boss. I sold five of these in the hour before you came and I'm quids in.'

Perhaps there was a good reason why Sykes' face didn't fit in the police force. I had a sudden picture of him in Leeds market on a Friday evening, flogging truncheons and handcuffs to passers-by.

I smiled to myself as I walked back to my car. It was one

107

of those lovely sunny evenings when the light is so sharp, the best part of a dull day. I breathed in the aroma of the shops along the street, fresh bread at the bakery, the earthy smell of potatoes outside the greengrocers, the sweet and powerful confusion of tobacco scents as someone opened the door to the tobacconist's.

'Hector!'

We practically collided. He pulled off his hat and beamed at me.

'Just the person I wanted to see. Do you have moment, Hector? Could we find a spot to have a chat?'

He looked alarmed. 'What about?'

'About the time Mr Braithwaite went missing?'

He spotted a young man on the other side of the street and waved. 'So sorry. I'd love to but I'm here to meet my best man and there he is. There's not much I can say about that time anyway, nothing Tabby can't tell you. She got home from the VAD whenever time allowed. She'd come home to visit her parents and was ever so concerned about her Aunt Catherine. Sorry to be rude, must fly.'

He replaced his hat, saw a gap in the traffic and made to cross the street.

'Why was she concerned about her aunt?'

He called back to me as he stepped off the pavement. 'Poor Catherine was so very ill.'

8

ndlewick

Thursday, 17 August 1916

STODDARD

Catherine lay back, propped on her pillows. He had noticed that for other people his wife willed herself into attention. Afterwards she would slump, exhausted.

Evelyn Braithwaite, wearing a blue linen dress, her hair wound into a loose knot, sat by the bed. She held a heavy cluster of tomatoes in her hands, nine growing from a single stem.

Catherine looked at them. 'You've brought me the vine.'

Evelyn placed the tomatoes on the white candlewick counterpane. 'Smell that,' she said to Catherine. 'They're the first to ripen.'

Stoddard hated the rank tomcat smell of new tomatoes. He watched as Catherine touched the red fruit with great tenderness, her thin fingers testing the hard green stem.

'You've brought me summer.' The tomato vine slid from Catherine's hand. She looked across to the window at a square of sky.

It was almost seven o'clock in the evening. The sun would be over Laithstone Hill. Stoddard wanted to go running on the fells, feeling the wind behind him, the earth solid under his feet. He wanted to run back in time to a simpler world – before war, profiteering, before this cruel illness gripped his wife. There was time to run. Run in the light, run in the dark, no difference to Stoddard. He knew the lie of the land as well as the lines on Catherine's ravaged face.

He had almost not entered the sick room, thinking to leave the women alone. Now he stepped up to the bed and picked up the vine. He placed it on the washstand.

'I'm all right,' Catherine said. 'You go for your run.'

'Yes, leave us to praise junket,' Evelyn said. 'I've brought a dish, made half an hour ago. Will you taste some, Catherine? It might give you strength.'

'I'll try.'

Catherine would always try, Stoddard thought. She would try, and try and try.

He could barely move from the spot. Sometimes he would look at Catherine and forget to breathe. Strength. We placed such store on strength, Stoddard thought. Build yourself up. Take a cup of tea. Pull yourself together. Face the world. Get a bit of backbone. But what if you did all of those things, and none of it availed?

The spoon travelled to Catherine's mouth. The junket should have slithered down her throat but seemed not to know that.

'That's it,' Evelyn said. 'Do you remember the day I bought this dress material?' She held the spoon again.

Catherine turned her head away, very slightly and Stoddard thought she was refusing, that she had decided to eat no more. But she said, in that flat way her words came out now, 'I spotted that material. The day we went to Brown Muffs.'

'You did. You said it would suit me.'

'I'll leave you alone to chat,' Stoddard said.

Now was his time to go running.

But he couldn't bring himself to leave the house. That morning's paper lay on the dining table. He began to read news of the war, but the words did not connect with that part of his brain that made sense of things.

The music holder on the piano held Catherine's sheet music – the last tune she had played – some nonsense about a little girl in blue. He slapped the music into the piano stool and folded the holder back into the top of the piano.

Sitting down at the dining table, he picked up the morning paper, glancing at headings. The King meets President Poincaré, pays a surprise visit to soldiers, Russians make Great Move Forward.

Well, good for them, someone needed to move.

Evelyn came downstairs. She sat opposite him at the table. 'The nurse is with her now.'

'I'm glad you've come, Eve.' He folded the newspaper and set it aside. 'Catherine perks up for you.'

'I knew she'd remember this dress.' She leaned forward, elbows on the table, hands lightly clasped. 'We're turning out to be an unfortunate family, Neville.'

'Like many others.'

'I suppose.'

'Will you have tea?'

'I'd prefer something stronger.'

Evelyn was the only woman he knew who drank Scotch. He poured from the decanter – two stiff ones. 'Water?'

'No.'

She sipped at her whisky. 'Has Joshua said anything to you?'

'What about?'

Not the damn dyestuffs again. Every time Stoddard went to the Wool Exchange, he felt the envy and anger. Joshua pooh-poohed his scruples, saying everyone was at it.

'None of that money went into the firm did it?' Evelyn asked.

'What money?'

'Oh stop it Neville! From the German dyewares. You know what I'm talking about.'

111

'No. He kept that separate.'

'When are we due a board meeting?'

'I'd have to look at the diary.'

'Talk to him would you, Neville? Tell him you're drawing up the agenda and so on. Try and find out what he's up to.'

'We usually do the agenda the week before.'

'Arthur Wilson's on the grumble about not being properly compensated for his invention.'

Stoddard folded the newspaper carefully. 'First I've heard. He and Joshua sorted it out between them.'

'We can't afford to lose Wilson.'

'Wilson won't go anywhere. Where did you hear this anyway?'

'Lizzie Kellett if you must know.'

'Eve! Half the congregation is consulting that meddling woman, crossing her palm with silver. People accuse mill owners of war profiteering. What about her?'

'Yes well this wasn't a message from beyond. Marjorie Wilson told Lizzie that Arthur Wilson feels aggrieved. Apparently Joshua gave him an outright payment for his invention and he wants royalties on any future sales. He's saying that Kellett made a small fortune from peddling German dyewares.'

'One has got nothing to do with the other.'

'He says an honest man should be fairly treated. He wants his name on the invention.'

'Well then, let Wilson put up the cash to develop it. We've all on keeping pace with producing khaki.'

Evelyn slid her glass across the table for a top-up.

'You don't know what it's like living with a teetotaller. You were very fortunate to arrive in Bridgestead when you were past the age of being harangued into signing the pledge.'

He refilled their glasses, and gave up on the idea of running on the fells tonight. 'Don't worry. Joshua's distracted. Each of you is trying to cope as best you can in your own way. And don't let Lizzie Kellett get you in her clutches. It's cruel of her to make out she can get messages from the other side.'

Evelyn shook her head dismissively. She gazed into her glass. 'Don't fuss about me falling for Lizzie Luck's nonsense. I went to keep Tabitha company the last time she was home.'

'Tabby should know better.'

'All girls want to know the future – especially now. Will any of them have a future, that's the question. She's expecting that chap of hers to be back home shortly with God only knows what sort of wounds.'

Stoddard frowned. Now she had stepped on his lay preacher's toes. He didn't like God to be evoked in connection with the war.

She waved the glass under her nose, savouring its aroma.

'Joshua's been so secretive. He went off somewhere last weekend. He took the motorbike and sidecar.'

'Let him. It will be all right.'

She didn't believe him, he could see that.

She drained her glass and stood up to leave.

In the doorway, he put a hand on her shoulder.

'Everything will be all right for you, and for Joshua and for Tabitha. I'll see to that. You have my word, Eve.'

When he saw her out, she unexpectedly kissed his cheek.

'I nearly said something so stupid, Neville.'

He could smell her hair. 'What was that?' he asked softly.

'That Catherine was lucky – to have you, I meant.'

'It's not luck, Eve. The lord takes the ones he loves best and he's chosen Catherine. Perhaps she's to find Edmund and bring him to peace.'

'Now who's sounding like Lizzie Luck?'

If anyone else said that to him, Stoddard would have exploded into a sermon. But for Evelyn, he had immense patience, immense forbearing.

9

 Fashion plates

I sat at Tabitha's dressing table, looking at myself and at Tabitha behind me. Wearing a loose gymnasium suit, she moved through a series of postures. A sharp scent of vinegar wafted from her. Climbing onto a footstool, wand in her hands, she stepped from foot to foot, raising the wand above her head.

'Do I stink of vinegar?' She had laced her tepid bath with aromatic vinegar prior to exercising, as advised in the magazine article.

'Only slightly,' I said kindly.

'Try that cream,' she ordered. 'A wrinkle on the face is like a crinkle in a piece of tissue paper. You'll easily smooth it out.'

Cautiously, I dipped my finger into the home-made face cream. It had a pleasant, flowery aroma. 'What is it?'

'Becky makes it. What is it, Becky?'

Becky left off laying dresses on Tabitha's bed and with a solemn manner came to stand beside me. 'You take an eggshell of mutton tallow, warm over water in a double boiler, half as much of sweet almond oil, and scent with five drops of rose geranium. Best put on at night, but I'm sure it'll work. You don't have a lot of wrinkles, Mrs Shackleton, just a few from laughing. Unfair that. You have to laugh.'

When she said that, I did laugh. There was something absurd about the intensity of these preparations for an evening at the Gawthorpes. But Tabitha felt uneasy about meeting Hector's relations. She had begged me to set aside any thoughts of detection today, so as to give her moral support.

'What will you wear tonight?' Tabitha asked when Becky disappeared on an errand.

I had brought in my Delphos robe and picked it up to show her. It's a simple tunic of pleated silk, in gorgeous colours that you wouldn't think to mix: turquoise, purple and orange.

'Kate, it's stunning! I have a shawl that will go with that perfectly.'

'Aunt Berta bought this in Paris in 1908.' I always mean not to tell people the history of my peculiar wardrobe, and then I blurt it out.

'That's amazing.' She stroked the gown. 'Paris seeps through my fingertips.'

'Really I could have done with buying something new for her birthday party next week. My other evening gown is black and I've strict instructions from my mother not to wear it.'

Tabitha held the dress against her and looked at herself in the cheval mirror. 'I'd love to wear your Delphos. Why don't we do a swap for tonight? And if there's something of mine you like, you can take it to London.'

'What a good idea!' I had been wondering how I would fit in a shopping trip and now I wouldn't need to. We looked at Tabitha's selection of evening gowns. Eventually, I chose a satin ankle-length barrel-shaped dress in two shades of blue, narrow at the bottom but with a centre vent to the knee so that with a bit of luck I wouldn't trip and break my neck.

That settled, Tabitha sat down to watch me apply the wrinkle-vanishing cream, a thoughtful look on her face as she scrutinised me. 'You look about twenty-six. How old do I look, Kate? Tell me the truth. They're all going to be looking at me tonight, totting up the age difference between me and Hector.'

115

It wasn't so much that Tabitha looked old, just that Hector was such a very young twenty-one.

'You look younger than me, Tabby.' I had no idea whether she did or not. It is difficult to say how old someone looks when you know very well they are your contemporary.

Her face lit up with pleasure. 'Really? Thank you, Kate. It must be Becky's cream that does it. Avoid your eyes.'

She watched me smooth in the cream. I replaced the lid carefully, wondering whether to speak my thoughts or stay silent. I took the plunge.

'Are you sure about your feelings for Hector? Because if you are, a few years age difference doesn't matter does it? Is he the one for you?'

She sighed. 'I'm not sure of anything. When he's not here, I love him no end. When we're together, I still love him, but he is very sensitive. If he thinks he doesn't have my one hundred per cent love and affection, he turns moody. Was your husband like that?'

'No. But he was often so very busy. We didn't have as much time together as we would have liked, because of his work at the infirmary, and then the war.' Not wanting this to turn into a discussion of widowhood, I said, 'What does Hector actually do when you're not together?'

'He goes into raptures over motor cars, adores the whole business. Of course it's expected that he'll find his way into the mill, but the thought of that clouds the poor boy's brow.' She came to sit beside me at the dressing table. 'He keeps an eye on the land and that sort of thing,' she said vaguely. 'His family own half the houses in the village, where our workers live. Mother and Uncle Neville think it's a good match from that point of view, but Hector and I don't think along those lines at all. We both want children.'

'I'm sure he'll be a loving father.' And I meant it, Hector being such a child himself.

116

'I know he'll never give me cause for doubt. Hector says he's always loved me, all his life long. I'll make it work, Kate. It'll be up to me to do that.'

'Because you're the older party?' I couldn't resist that and smiled at her through the mirror.

She slapped at my arm and we both laughed.

'I can laugh, you can't!' she ordered. 'Wrinkles! Let the cream do its work.'

The Braithwaite Rolls-Royce glided up a dirt track festooned with lanterns towards the Gawthorpes' large square manor house in which lights blazed in every room.

Evelyn has an internal combustion engine in her solar plexus. She presses her belly button and it switches on. That is my only explanation for how she can burst into life as she crosses a threshold, switching on a smile that wipes out history. Perhaps I do the same myself, though I fear not so successfully.

Stoddard, handsome in his dress suit, took my arm. 'Glad you're here to swell our numbers, my dear,' he whispered. 'There are more of them than us.'

Hector looked as though he would burst with joy at the sight of Tabitha. He rushed forward to kiss her before leaping to introduce me to his father. He seemed genuinely concerned to make me feel at home.

It was not as large a gathering as I had expected from Tabitha's trepidation. Mr and Mrs Gawthorpe were about sixty years old, Hector being their late and only child. Mr Gawthorpe gave off a military air. Big game souvenirs decorated the walls: horns, a buffalo head, a tiger skin.

Trays of drinks were walked about the room, with dandelion and burdock laid on for abstainers. One stout fellow, wearing a pledge badge, seemed suspicious even of the dandelion and burdock, sniffing loudly before he took a sip. This man had cornered poor Hector. I caught the words 'my invention', 'part of the family', and 'right-

117

ful dues', so this must be Wilson, weaving manager and inventor of the loom picker.

I approached Wilson cautiously but was intercepted by the vicar, a round, jolly man who misheard my name and relationship to Tabitha and thought I was Hector's cousin, Cecily Stevens. Once we had got over the mistake, he was able to tell me the history of Bingley. I listened with polite interest. He had not met Mr Braithwaite, so I drew a blank there.

Hector was by my side as the vicar fell into conversation with the real cousin Cecily, a tired-looking woman in her mid-thirties.

'The stout fellow talking to Mother is Arthur Wilson,' Hector said, confirming my guess.

'He looks familiar.'

'I'll introduce you. You probably saw him at the mill. He's manager of the weaving shed and a relation of my mother's by marriage. That's his wife, Aunt Marjorie, sitting in the corner. They say he beats her.'

'Charming relations, Hector.'

He took my arm. 'Come and say hello to my Aunt Marjorie.'

'Just a sec, Hector.' We were momentarily in an oasis of quiet. At last I had Hector alone. I tried to manoeuvre him onto the terrace where we would not be overheard. 'If we go outside, you can perhaps help me with a bit of a puzzle.'

A look of alarm crossed his face.

I lowered my voice. 'About the time Mr Braithwaite was found, I believe you were camping nearby.'

As if he hadn't heard me, Hector signalled to Marjorie and I had no option but to walk across with him as he said, 'Poor Marjorie all on her own as usual. She's dying to meet you. Asked me about your car. I told her, the Jowett's a grand motor. Didn't I say that, Aunt Marjorie?'

Marjorie Wilson was as far away from her husband as

possible. A tiny figure, she perched on a gold-leaf painted chair. She smiled sweetly, pushing back a wispy grey hair that had escaped from the small wobbly bun on the crown of her head.

Hector introduced us and then slid away.

'Ah yes. I heard you looked round the mill.' Marjorie took rather a large drink, emptying her glass quickly as a maid approached to top up the sherry. 'And you have a motor car.'

'I do.'

'Excellent,' she said. 'I like you already.' She made elaborate motions for me to draw up a chair beside her and be confidential. Breathing into my ear, slurring her words hardly at all, she said, 'You're looking into Joshua Braithwaite's disappearance.'

Before I had the opportunity to pursue Marjorie's remark, Stoddard was by my side, introducing me to Roberta Stevens, mother of cousin Cecily.

A tall thin woman with a disapproving glare, she shook my hand cautiously as if she expected me to ask for a loan. For a moment I wondered did she realise I was wearing Tabitha's dress. But Aunt Roberta was someone whom Tabitha had not yet met, so the disapproval was either part of her personality or to do with some other aspect of me.

'Will you be going to hear the Hallé Orchestra when they come to St George's Hall?' Stoddard asked her. 'Your husband tells me you're a music lover.'

The disapproval fled from Roberta's face. 'My daughter is a music lover. Have you met Cecily yet?'

It fell to Cecily's father to walk me in to supper. Mr Stevens is what is generally called a man's man, but he made a valiant effort to talk to me about his connections with the railway company. I responded by talking about the Leeds to King's Cross train which I would be boarding next week.

119

Under cover of the murmur of chatter while we were taking our seats, I asked Mr Stevens whether he had met Mr Braithwaite. Unfortunately he had not. Stevens sat to my right and the vicar, who had a voluble amount of praise for the soup, sat to my left.

'What do you think of this unholy alliance between Bolsheviks and the German Empire?' Stevens asked Stoddard.

I did not hear Stoddard's opinion as the vicar had a good deal of praise for the game pie. 'I'm a bachelor,' he confided, somewhat hungrily. 'My cook is adequate, but this is a treat for me, a real treat.'

From across the table, Aunt Roberta, as though we were bosom pals, bellowed, 'I'm not sure in what capacity my nephew Hector will involve himself in the mill. That's yet to be decided.'

Stoddard shot me a quick, amused glance, to tell me that Aunt Roberta's remark was aimed at him rather than me.

From Stoddard's left, Cecily blushed at her mother's clumsiness and began to tell us about a new novel she was reading. 'This clever young couple set themselves up as detectives. A mystery man is about to offer the woman a job . . .'

It was a relief when the time came for us ladies to leave the table for the drawing room where, while we were at supper, dozens of candles had been lit. Cecily resumed her telling of the novel involving a secret treaty and a Russian conspiracy.

Tabitha and I slipped away onto the terrace, on the pretext of not wanting to hear the end of the story because it would spoil the reading of the book. The sky had darkened and was filled with a million stars.

'I don't know why I was so nervous,' Tabitha said. 'They're all right, really. I just thought there might be more of them. The vicar's a sweetie.'

'Yes he is.'

'And in no time at all I shall become Mrs Hector Gawthorpe. Tabby Gawthorpe. I like it, Kate. I'm happy!'

'Good. Then I'm happy for you.'

The men returned bringing the smell of cigars and murmur of talk about railways, Lloyd George and Bonar Law, and the John Bull Victory Bond Club.

I stayed on the terrace when Tabitha went back inside. My only exchange with Wilson the weaving manager and inventor had been hostile, on his part not mine. He did not approve of women driving motor cars, he had said. When I tried to initiate some neutral conversation he gave a non-committal grunt and turned away.

Sweet Hector. Boy scout to his marrow, he spotted me and brought me a brandy. 'Are you all right, Kate?'

'Just grand. Wanted some air that's all.'

'It's good of you to come. And thanks for being Tabby's friend.'

'Hector, about that time when you were camping out with the boy scout troop, and Mr Braithwaite . . .'

'Not here,' he said. 'Not now, Kate.'

Then when and where? He edged away.

On the first Saturday in May, these people would be reassembling, with me among them having failed miserably to turn up the bride's father, dead or alive.

I sipped at my brandy, thinking of the hopelessness of the task. The rich scent of jonquils wafted from the garden below. I wondered what flowers Tabitha would carry in her bouquet. That's when I overheard Evelyn.

'What? What is it, Neville? What are you doing?'

'Just looking. You're lovely tonight, both you and Tabby.'

'You're quite the bee's knees yourself.'

'Eve, there's something I must ask you.'

A pause. An uneasy, 'Oh?'

121

I put down the brandy glass and sank down onto a stone bench against the balustrade.

Stoddard's voice was low. 'I hoped this matter might just arise naturally somehow, but I did promise myself that I would speak.'

Evelyn sighed. 'Is it about Wilson? Was he blathering on again? I expect now Hector's coming into the business Wilson will be wanting a change of name for his precious invention, and a share of whatever preposterous sum he thinks we made on it.'

'Forget Wilson. Eve, you know I've done my utmost for you and Tabby.'

'Yes you have. And with Tabitha's marriage, we both know that Hector is going to be pushed by his family to get his feet under a desk. He's not cut out for it.'

'This isn't about the business. It's about us. You must know of my high regard for you.'

Pressing my palms against the cold limestone of the bench made them cool. I touched fingers to my temples to stop the sudden throb.

'Yes, Neville, and I . . .'

'Evelyn, let me speak. Do you remember just before Catherine died? You thought she was rambling . . .'

'It was the morphia. That happens.'

'There was sense in her ramblings. She'd told me . . . to marry again.'

'I know.'

Indoors, the string quartet began to play. I missed Evelyn's words. I should have moved away.

Stoddard spoke softly. 'When the seven years is up, when we can say Joshua is dead, I want us to marry. I swear I'll make you happy.'

'Neville, that's mad. We're cousins.'

'No we're not. Josh and I were the cousins. You and I . . .'

'Don't do this, Neville. Don't say these things.'

In silence, Evelyn and Neville moved from the shadow

of the wall, along the path towards the fountain.

A maid came out, carrying a tray with liqueurs. I refused.

'I'll take a glass if you don't mind,' a shrill anxious voice called. 'And one for my friend!' Before I had time to object, Marjorie sat beside me, placing the two glasses on her side of the stone bench. As an afterthought, she offered one to me.

'You're welcome,' I said. 'I've had enough.'

She took a sip of liqueur. 'What a wonderful phrase that is. *I've had enough.* Yes. I like that phrase. Not many people know when they've had enough.'

I turned to look at her, so thin and angular. When she raised her glass, the sleeve of her gown dropped back to reveal a purple and yellow bruise on her forearm. 'I expect you're right.'

'Kind of you to say so.' She polished off the first liqueur and set down the glass. 'Refuse nothing but blows my dear, that's my advice.'

'I'll remember that.'

'So you have a car.' She had that drunk's habit of seizing on a snippet of information and making much of it in a sombre voice, to appear sober.

'I do indeed.' She was more than half-cut. I did not know whether there was any significance in her lowered voice when she had mentioned Braithwaite earlier, but I would try and find out. I encouraged her to keep talking, asking about her connection to the Gawthorpes.

'I'm Hector's sort of aunt – a second cousin sort of aunt.'

'I see.'

'It's the one thing I do right, as far as Arthur's concerned. Being related merits an invitation to where it matters. And with young Hector, we'll have a relative on the board.' She started to laugh.

'What's funny?'

'Oh don't mind me. I get cabin fever. When I'm let out

123

into society I go a little mad. You were looking round the mill, photographing looms. You'll have met my husband. Weaving manager.'

She was tippling on the second liqueur. It sparkled in the light from the drawing room and the garden lanterns. 'We don't have drink in the house, you see, or not officially. My husband signed the pledge on the same day as Joshua Braithwaite – just boys they were.'

Why did people do it? Why do teetotallers marry inebriates? Why does a halfway decent man like Stoddard fall for a cold, brittle woman like Evelyn Braithwaite?

'You're looking into things aren't you?' Marjorie Wilson swayed unsteadily, as if trying to bring me into focus.

'Yes. I'm hoping to find out what happened to Joshua Braithwaite.'

'You think he was murdered, don't you?' she whispered, leaning close to me.

As coolly as I could, I said, 'It had crossed my mind.'

'He was thick as thieves with Paul Kellett.'

'Really?' It occurred to me that we were a little public for too many confidences. I was about to suggest a walk in the garden when she leaned so close to my ear she shoved me into the wall.

'You think my husband killed him because of being diddled out of his dues over the lightweight loom picker don't you?' When I didn't answer straightaway, she said, 'So you don't know about that? Well never let it be said I put his head in a noose. Only he did say, A poor man doesn't get his inventions taken up that easy, that they either come to nowt or get robbed by folk who've got the brass to turn a plan into reality.' Mrs Wilson gripped my arm so hard that it hurt. She said, 'Is he a killer? I look at him sometimes across the table and I think, Is he? Did he do it?'

We looked through into the room. I could not see the

124

portly Mr Wilson, enemy of women drivers.

'What makes you think that, Mrs Wilson?'

'I can't make up my mind. It's all a mix-up. He's violent. He'll kill me one of these days. He'll never change. I won't stay. I won't let him. You wouldn't, would you? You wouldn't stay with a violent man?'

'No I wouldn't.'

She swayed unsteadily. 'I'm going home to pack a bag. If I had a car I would get in it. As it is, I shall go to the railway station.'

I took her arm. The two of us walked with great precision and fairy strides down the stone steps of the terrace into the garden. My borrowed barrel dress did not aid movement.

A massive shape lurched from the shadows towards us, bumping against her and knocking both of us off balance. A great hound of a dog, it then lolloped ahead of us, threatening to trip me, wagging its tail, licking Mrs Wilson's hand.

She rested a hand on its broad back. 'Good dog, Charlie. Good dog.' We swayed towards the line of motor cars. 'He always follows me. He's uncanny for knowing my whereabouts.' She waved at one of the cars. 'Come on, Kate, you are a modern young woman. You can assist me in this.'

I held my evening bag between the dog's slobbering jaws and Tabitha's satin dress, hoping to keep it safe from slaver.

'Where will you go?'

'If I go to my daughter, he would come after me. I shall find lodgings. Lizzie said to do it. She had a lodger once, the bonniest lass in the mill.'

A car rolled towards us.

The chauffeur stepped out and opened the door. Marjorie pushed me in. The dog followed. She clambered in herself, helped by the chauffeur.

'Home, Anthony! And don't spare the horses.'

'Very well, Mrs Wilson.' He gave a long-suffering sigh. In the mirror, I saw him eyeing the dog.

'Of course,' she whispered, 'it would help to know who got to the safe deposit box.'

'What safe deposit box?'

'Joshua Braithwaite's of course. If he got to that, then the bird could have flown. If he didn't, then that would clip his wings.'

'Where was this safe deposit box, Marjorie?'

Her eyes had closed. She let out a gentle snore.

We drove along dark narrow lanes to a house where a single light shone in the window.

'Wait here please, Kate. Wait with Charlie.'

The dog licked my ear.

I waited.

She went inside.

It was terribly restful to sit in the dark in the back of a car, just waiting.

'She won't come out again,' Anthony said cheerfully.

Charlie growled as Anthony spoke.

'The dog doesn't like me. But it's nothing personal. He doesn't like any men.'

He opened the door and the dog bounded out, whining at the front door.

It all seemed too much, as if I had fetched up in a madhouse. Rather than helping Tabitha, if I told her everything I'd probably destroy her. Overhearing Stoddard and Evelyn and now learning about mad Wilson and his invention, there were more motives than I could keep steady in my aching head.

I only shut my eyes for a moment.

When I woke, Anthony the chauffeur was opening the car door. There was no sign of Mrs Wilson or her dog. We were in the wrong place – back at the Braithwaites.

'I brought you home, Mrs Shackleton, since you'd fallen asleep. But if you wish to return to the Gawthorpes . . .'

'No. Please just give my thanks and apologies. Perhaps you could say I had a headache and didn't want to spoil the party.'

In the morning, Becky brought me tea. 'You've slept very late, madam.'

'I was with someone . . . a lady and her dog. Is she all right?'

'Ah yes, you was seeing Mrs Wilson home,' Becky said tactfully. I felt a little queasy. Too many of Evelyn Braithwaite's cocktails before we set off probably.

Tabitha came to see me, bringing Andrews Liver Salts, a glass of water and a pot of tea.

She looked pale and drawn.

'What's the matter, Tabitha?'

She shook her head, biting her lip, reluctant to speak.

I felt suddenly guilty for having left her in the lurch. Perhaps something terrible happened after I deserted. 'Was it the party?'

'Not the party. That went all right. There's been a most dreadful accident. It's Paul Kellett. He's dead.'

10

Dyehouse fog

Paul Kellett rubbed the back of his hand across his forehead to shift the sweat. Since half six this morning he'd
been hard at it. Standing in the doorway of the dyehouse,
he drank in the evening air and took a swig of warm beer.

Overtime to finish the job, and he was the one to claim
it.

Uniform material, always uniforms. Dyeing black for
the police, navy for the conductors, grey for the commis-
sionaires. That's how they keep us in our place, Kellett
knew. Wear this, wear that, tip your cap, show respect.
Oh he could do that all right, as long as there was summat
in it for number one.

Where was his Oxo tin and his snap? He took out his
sandwich.

It wasn't only toffs could take themselves off to
Morecambe Bay to live out their days in a cottage by the
sea. The working man could do it an' all, if he set his mind
hard enough at the task. If he took care of number one.

Kellett would surprise them all. There'd be a day when
he was washed white. He'd have clean hands, and hair free
of the dye, like the time when he wore his suit and went
on the road. His chest would clear up too. On that day,
he'd breathe free.

He had picked the spot where his house would be built,
in Heysham overlooking the bay, where you had the finest
sunsets in the wide world.

He wouldn't be a mean bastard neither – he'd invite his

dyeing mates over to stop the night. Lizzie would bake a pie. They'd be the proper host and hostess. Mein host. That made him smile. Mein host. Thank you Herr von Hofmann, especially for the crate of permanganate of potash that Mr Bigshot Braithwaite never spotted. That was his entirely, that little lot. Kellett's only regret, that he could have driven an even harder bargain.

Not long now for the new start. And it would all be down to cleverness. All down to the fact he knew his job inside out and upside down. He'd experimented with the dyes. He could reduce the process time, but only he knew that. So tonight there'd be one time on his clocking out card, and it wouldn't include his going over home to wash hisself down and have a bite of supper and a pipe by the fire.

The trick about pulling in brass was not to be too fussy whether it was a big amount or a little. Oh it was big money in the days he was relabelling and selling the German dyes. Twenty sales for Joshua Braithwaite, one sale for Kellett's back pocket. He'd liked that life — wearing a suit, having summat to sell that folk would give their eye teeth for.

Reluctantly, he put down his emptied beer mug and turned back into the dyehouse fog. The boiler was at it full blast. Metal grinding on metal, whistle and squeal, the high bubbling noise, and the low rumble.

He yawned. Not getting any younger. Bloody tired, weariness seeping through him in waves. Ten yards at thirty-six inches to dye. He'd have it done in no time, no time at all, and out to dry.

He didn't notice the silence. It seemed to be inside his head, a sudden stillness that came over him sometimes when he thought of how it would be to live by the sea, looking out over that vast swathe of ridged sands at low tide, imagining the worlds beyond the roaring ocean, and the peace, the sweet peace of never having to set foot in a dyehouse again.

129

And then it happened, and he knew it was happening, but somehow his body had gone all slow, like when he had been marched to the front line in a state of exhaustion and putting one foot before the other took such great effort.

Even as his hand and claw grabbed the valve and he started to turn, and turn, he knew it was too late. Only one hand to turn with, the claw useless for this job. It took ten or fifteen good turns before the valve would shut off the boiler. And . . .

He started to sweat. His body told him to run but as he turned his back on the boiler, the dye burst out with an angry rush, hot and black, knocking him to the floor, to the hard setts on the floor of the dyehouse and then it was covering him in black waves and he thought of the sea and how he would take off his shoes and roll up his trousers.

Somehow he struggled to his feet, hearing human screams as the roof exploded, hearing screams that were his own and his tiredness had gone now but he didn't know how he moved, fast or slow, only that he moved and one thought pounded through his scalded burning body.

Water.

He ran across the mill yard, ran to the low wall, catching sight of his own dye-blackened hand, the sleeve that hung loose, the skin falling from his arm. Screaming, he jumped into the icy water of the canal.

Someone had heard the explosion. Lizzie ran across the beck, up the bank, past the big bridge, into the mill yard.

The dyehouse was swamped. Parts of the roof had fallen in, with tiles and bricks on the ground near the wall. A broken beer jug lay among the collapsed bricks in what had been the doorway. Across the yard was a trail of black dye.

She knew her heart would burst, but kept running, shouting, calling his name, so that when she saw him, she had no breath left to speak, only looked at him there in the water, blackened, flailing, staring at her with terror in his eyes. She began to climb down to him. He shook his head. She saw the redness of his tongue against the black as he tried to speak. Then the canal took him. She ran along the bank towards the weir.

A fallen branch stopped him. She waded down, to her thighs, to her waist. Paul screamed as she touched him, and then was silent.

Lizzie's own scream tore through the air.

11

Cropping: Shearing loose fibres or yarns from the surface of the cloth to give it a smooth texture.

LIZZIE

Lizzie Luck never saw any need to leave the village. The old people were dead now, parents and gran. Lizzie had inherited her gran's tarot cards, and her knack for the fortune game.

Lizzie's younger sister left to work in the clothing trade in Leeds. Only she was never satisfied. Money, money, money, that was her tune on the harp. Later, she'd gone to work in munitions. Lizzie took the train to Leeds one Bank Holiday Monday to visit. The sun never shone there, never penetrated the smoky air. If that was the big city, you could keep it.

Another time, Lizzie took a train to Bradford to see her brother and his wife. What a smoky hole that was! Oh the shops were big and fine, the arcades grand, and the market teemed with everyone and everything, but it was all too much. She only ever went there one other time – to the Spiritualist Church.

Long before the noisy weaving shed turned her deaf, Lizzie liked the peace and quiet and her bit of a garden to grow potatoes, herbs and whatever else she could coax from the ground when the beck and the canal allowed. She liked the way her house turned its back on the mill and its

132

bowed wall gave the village a cold shoulder. She gazed onto fields where sheep and cattle grazed.

Living alone suited Lizzie, after growing up with seven and eight in the two-room house. But Paul Kellett blew in from Keighley in 1913, looking for work. He helped her up one icy day when she slipped and came a cropper on the cobbles. He looked down, she looked up. It was as simple as that. She hadn't expected to find love at the grand old age of thirty. But he was tender, kind and funny. He could imitate bird calls, tell jokes, play the harmonica. They married within the month.

He took over the entire house with his inventions and experiments. She wondered they weren't poisoned after he used her pots and pans for God knows what type of dyeing mix. He'd stir the dye stuff in with water, using her wooden spoon, boiling it up to dissolve it, more than once causing an explosion. He claimed the fastest green dye in England. He dyed her grey cape forest green and insisted she wash it. It was her fault when the tub turned emerald.

Then it was a new type of gas-fired machine for close-cropping the cloth, only the gas bottle wouldn't supply the right amount. It would come out a useless trickle or a destructive blast. Next came the printing roller, where the fabric rolled over it instead of it rolling over the fabric. Only Braithwaites weren't doing patterns. He'd taken his model to the mill office, but to no avail.

'Damn Braithwaite! He let me explain every angle before he said no!'

That was when Lizzie found out about Paul's nasty side. She gave as good as she got. Took the broom to him.

'Paul, Paul, calm yourself, man. We'll never have a bairn if we're like fire and oil.'

Being married to a genius, especially an unrecognised genius, was no easy matter.

She took him to bed. After they had made love she read

his palm and saw that the future would bring him better fortune. That was the night she conceived, but the baby did not come to term.

He never knew about the baby.

He joined up in 1914, angry that nowt had materialised from all his grand ideas.

Lizzie took in a lodger, Agnes, a bonnie weaver who kept her company. Agnes kept her counsel over Lizzie losing the bairn.

Paul was back from the front within the year, missing part of his left arm, and with a claw sticking out of his cuff where his hand should be. She thought that would be an end of the inventions but it was only the beginning. He set his heart on making his fortune, so as to retire to Morecambe. It would take just one grand idea.

So Lizzie lost her lodger. Agnes cried when she left, took herself off to Bradford, to be somewhere no one knew her.

Paul went to enquire about his old job.

When he came back, he bubbled up inside – not with his usual indignation. Lizzie thought at first he'd had the nod about one of his inventions.

He took a bar of Sunlight soap with him to the public baths.

On Monday, he dressed in his suit.

'I'm going on the road.'

'Doing what?' She imagined him with a pick and shovel, digging ditches. Then tramping, knocking on doors, begging for bread. That's what on the road meant to her.

'Selling. I'm going on the road selling.'

'Selling what?'

'You see it did pay to come up with all them inventions. Because you have to learn to silver tongue in order to explain them. Me and my silver tongue are going on the road.'

'Selling what?' she asked again.

He tapped the side of his nose. 'Best you don't know. That's between me and my employer . . .'

'Who?'

'Don't ask. It's all above board. But if anyone at the mill enquires, you know nowt.'

He'd come home from his selling, spread notes and sovereigns on the table. When he went down to the cellar to stash his loot, she warned him, 'That cellar floods.'

After that he kept the money in a locked chest under the bed.

'We'll buy a place in Morecambe. Neither of us will ever work again.'

They took the train and explored. It was Heysham they fell in love with. Dreams of a life of ease sent them into raptures. A house on the cliff top – nothing less would do.

But the money was never enough. Always he wanted just a few quid more.

When the selling stopped, he didn't want to go back to the dyehouse. He took a job as an orderly in the hospital.

'Just a few quid more. Besides, there's clever men will be coming to that hospital. Officers. One of them might have the imagination to develop a gas-fired cropping machine.'

When the war ended, she thought they would go to Heysham then, though it would be a wrench to leave the place she had lived all her life for the wilds of the coast. It would be bleak in winter. Perhaps he felt the same, not ready to leave this village and everyone he knew. Not ready to reach for the dream in case it dissolved and left only a green stain in his imagination.

Just a few quid more.

Back to the dyehouse.

Just a few quid more.

12

Roving: The combed tops from thick slivers of wool, from which yarn is spun.

I kicked myself that neither I nor Sykes had spoken to Kellett about his time 'on the road' with the dyewares, making money for Braithwaite. If any of the Braithwaites Mill workforce would have an out of the ordinary connection with Braithwaite, it would be Kellett. And now he had met his death in a most shocking way.

Better get Sykes back over here. Taking paper and an envelope from my writing case, I wrote him a note. It was still early enough for him to receive the letter by second post. I would take it to the box myself, and hope that he would not be too perturbed by where and when I asked him to meet me.

I put on my navy pea jacket, beret and gloves, slipping the letter into my pocket. The sky looked fine enough when I stepped outside, but there was a chill in the air.

Tabitha waited for me on the humpback bridge. We would pay our condolences to Lizzie together. From the bridge, we saw one of Lizzie's workmates entering her cottage.

'When you told me that your father was found by the stepping stones, how did you know?'

I was curious as to whether, in spite of Hector's secrecy, she had realised that he was one of the 'rescuers'.

'I can't remember how I know.' She sounded miserable, as if she had failed a test.

136

'Constable Mitchell said it was by the waterfall.'

'Then I don't know why I thought of the stepping stones.'

'Is there any reason he would have come to the beck? Is it on the way to or from somewhere? A short cut?'

She thought for a moment. 'It's a special spot, where Edmund and I used to play.'

We walked down the bank and sat on a flat rock.

'I think I told you that Dad once did a painting of the two of us, playing just there by the bridge. He dashed it off in no time. You see he didn't have much opportunity for that sort of palaver, as he called it, once he took over the mill. He was a younger son and hadn't expected to have the responsibility, but his older brother wanted none of it and went off to South Africa, so father had no choice.'

I didn't want to hear about an older brother in South Africa. My immediate, suspicious response was to imagine the chap returning secretly, slaughtering his kith and kin and waiting in the wings to leap on his rightful inheritance.

'This uncle, is he still alive and well in South Africa?'

'Oh no. The poor man died in a typhoid epidemic.'

I sent up a silent prayer of thanks at not having a complicating factor in the investigation.

Tabitha plucked a blade of grass and slid it from its stem.

I did what I usually do when at a loss for words – set up my field camera to take a photograph of the scene. It would be good to have an image of the location where Joshua Braithwaite went missing.

'I wonder you don't tire of carrying all that camera stuff around with you,' Tabitha said, pushing her hands deeper in her pockets.

'Let me take your picture, Tabitha. By the bridge, here, then further along.' I did not say, By the waterfall.

137

'I don't feel like having my picture taken. Mrs Kellett might look out and see us. It would look heartless.'

'You're right.' All the same, I looked down into the reflector finder. She frowned as I photographed the stepping stones. Next, the waterfall became my focus.

There was a mystery here and I hoped the beck would surrender its secret.

When I concentrate hard, the world turns silent. Blinkers shut out what I do not need to see. When the concentration stops, the world roars back, taking me by surprise. As I looked again at the beck, it had streaked with brown, from the discharge of effluent upstream. Had Braithwaite objected to being rescued? Perhaps he had just slipped and the boy scouts were over-zealous. One hears jokes about boy scouts assisting old ladies across a road, whether they want to be on the other side or not.

As we left the spot, I noticed the tracery effect on the water's surface – sunlight filtering through the leaves. There was so much in the world to photograph, so much to experience.

Mrs Kellett's visitors left the cottage. Tabitha and I walked along the path to the Kelletts' gate. I was determined that after we had paid our visit, Tabitha would walk me round all the places that meant something to her and her father. If the secret of his disappearance lay in the landscape, I would find it.

Lizzie Kellett was sitting in her bentwood chair, her shawl pulled round her, the black cat on her lap. It arched its back as we went in, not at us but at Mrs Wilson's gigantic dog that meandered from under the table to greet us.

I patted its head ingratiatingly. 'Good dog, Charlie.'

Marjorie Wilson sat in the smaller chair. She had a pinched and tired look. I wanted to ask was she feeling better after last night but she made no sign of remembering that I had escorted her home so I said nothing.

Cat and dog locked eyes.

'Corner, Charlie!' Mrs Wilson ordered.

Charlie ducked under the table and lay down. The cat relaxed, but kept a watchful pose.

Tabitha said. 'We just wanted to say how very sorry we are for your loss, Mrs Kellett.'

Mrs Kellett looked as if she would never get up again. She was slumped like an old woman, her mouth turned down, her hands on the cat as if it would breathe for her.

We perched ourselves on buffets. The dog sniffed at my ankles.

'I didn't know your husband, but I did take a photograph of him outside the dyehouse, with his workmates.'

I would make a print for her. It would be easy to cut the other workers off.

She stroked the cat's head. 'He shouldn't've died. He was too good at his job for that to happen. Summat went amiss.'

Tabitha took a sharp gulp of breath. If machinery or equipment had failed, then it would be the Braithwaites' responsibility.

'He never made mistakes.' Mrs Kellett looked directly at Tabitha. 'Summat went wrong.'

'What might have gone wrong, do you think?' I asked.

'Don't know. Summat, that's for sure. It shouldn't've happened.'

Tabitha gulped. 'It'll be looked into, Mrs Kellett,' she said in a worried voice. 'The coroner will investigate. I expect the factory inspectors will be going over everything.'

Lizzie snorted. 'Factory inspectors! What will they know?'

'Uncle Neville says the dyehouse will be out of action now, and we'll ...' Tabitha's voice trailed off as if she wished she had not begun this line of thought '. . . contract the work out.'

139

Mrs Kellett began to weep silently. She pulled a handkerchief from her sleeve and pummelled it in her hand. For a moment, the four of us sat in silence. The room had shrunk.

Mrs Wilson gave a keen look at Tabitha, and then at Mrs Kellett. Then she took her leave, saying she would come back later. The dog ambled after her sniffing at my camera bag. I felt suddenly embarrassed at having brought it. Force of habit.

There was a loaf and seed cake on the table, and a pot of stew on the hob by the fire. Mrs Kellett's previous visitors had proved more practical than Tabitha and me. I was about to break the awkward silence by asking whether there was anything I could do.

Mrs Kellett got there first.

'Paul only had a jug of beer and a sandwich. Someone must've slipped summat in it. He wasn't one to let an accident happen. Accidents don't happen, they're caused – that's what he always said.'

'Why would someone do that?' Tabitha asked, her eyes wide with surprise. The colour drained from her face. Out of pity, or because of the implications for the mill?

'Why? Jealousy, that's why. Jealous of what he'd made of hisself. Jealous of what he'd got. Jealous of what we planned.'

'What did you plan, Mrs Kellett?' I asked. I remembered Sykes telling me of the money put aside from war-time profiteering in dyewares, the dream of a cottage by the sea.

She sniffed and wiped her nose. 'A new life, that's what. And now there's no life at all. They knew he'd summat put by. Only he never got to enjoy it.'

'Who knew?' I asked gently.

'They all knew,' she said vaguely, spreading her hands with such a violent motion that the cat abandoned her. It leaped on the table and sniffed disdainfully at the bread and cake. 'Everyone in the dyeworks knew. He'd invited 'em all to come and visit. In his imagination he were already walking on the beach, watching the sunset over Morecambe Bay.'

Tabitha began to cry.

I felt utterly helpless, and somehow at fault. I did not see how there could be a connection between Kellett's death and Braithwaite's disappearance, or my investigation of it, but now it was too late. Would one of the dyeworkers have had a motive for wanting to see Kellett dead, I wondered. But perhaps Mrs Kellett simply could not accept that her husband could be taken from her in such an arbitrary way, a way that reflected badly on his workmanship, his expertise in his job. 'Did you mention these suspicions to the constable?'

Her mouth set in a grim line. 'He wants it down as a workplace accident. That'll suit his books.'

'Could you bear to tell me about how you found him, and whether he gave any indication as to what might have happened?' I asked.

She sat up straight. 'Aye. Every unbearable detail. Why should I be the only one plagued with nightmares?'

She stared at her hands, folded in her lap, as though to look into the room or at us would come between her and the images in her mind. She told us how she heard a blast, and knew straightaway what it was. How she ran, and found him in the canal, scalded and burned.

She looked across at me, and at Tabitha, with a defiant stare. 'He give me a look that was love, a look that was love and sorrow. And I caught his breath and summat on it that shouldn't have been there, summat sweet and bitter. He were poisoned.'

She said this calmly and with such conviction that it rang true to me.

'Poisoned,' Tabitha repeated, mouth open in horror, eyes wide.

The weakness in my limbs fixed me to the spot. I made

myself take a few deep breaths.

'I'll talk to the constable. Tabitha, will you stay here with Mrs Kellett a while longer?'

I walked slowly up the bank, towards the bridge, carrying my camera bag which I shouldn't have brought and which had grown heavier. The smell of burnt wood, ashes and the harsher tang of chemicals caught my throat. The mill yard seemed ominously quiet. No bogies clattered across the cobbles. No bales of yarn were hauled up on the crane. The destroyed dyehouse was taped off. A glum Constable Mitchell stood guard.

'Fire brigade chief's on his way from Keighley, supposedly with a factory inspector if one can be spared. They want to look at the scene, decide whether it was avoidable, any culpability to apportion.'

'Mrs Kellett thinks it wasn't an accident.'

'I know. She believes someone poisoned him or doped his drink. But she was the one brought him a sandwich and a jug of beer.'

'If it wasn't an accident . . .'

From not far off came the sound of an approaching car.

Mr Mitchell raised an eyebrow for me to make myself scarce. 'Best let the experts do their job. If they tell me owt, I'll pass it on.'

I took the hint.

'Where can I leave my bag? Tabitha and I are going walking and I don't want to drag it with me.'

We left Lizzie's house with slow steps. I asked Tabitha to take me to the places she and Edmund had walked with their father as children. It was not just that I hoped to glean knowledge of the landscape, but Tabitha seemed to talk more freely out of doors.

The day was fine and dry, with a blue sky, gentle breeze and ever-changing clouds. We walked briskly, higher and further, savouring the air and the view. In this timeless landscape, questions of life and death seemed somehow part of a larger pattern, and not new and sharp and unique to us.

'Are there any hiding places your father could have taken shelter, when he left the hospital, just to keep out of the way until the hoo-ha died down?'

'There are caves, and old mineshafts. Last September, I paid a caver to do a search for me. It was scary, because it can be dangerous. All the while I wondered, what if the man dies? He has a wife and children, and what if he dies on my errand?'

As she spoke, I understood why Hector might resent her search for her father. Anxieties, regrets, a permanent state of guilt and mourning were not exactly the qualities a groom would hope for in his bride.

'What did the caver report?'

She flung out her arms, as though taking in the whole of the moors. 'He said that it wasn't possible to search every cave to every depth. But he gave me a map, dotting the places he and others had explored, since August 1916. I hoped there might be traces that Dad had camped out. But the chap seemed to think I was expecting the worst. He said that all the men round here know about father, and if ever a body is found . . .'

'Come on, Tabitha, let's get out of this wind.' I felt a sudden need to be on lower ground.

'He did mention there'd been a fire in one of the caves. That could have been lit by Dad or . . .' She trailed off sadly without finishing her thought, pointing to what she regarded as a path, though I couldn't see it. 'This is the quickest way.' She looked at me doubtfully. 'If you don't mind running.'

Once you begin to run down a fell, you cannot stop. I leaped over loose scree and tiny rocks, slid down a grassy slope, jumped over a great hole in the ground.

'Keep going!' Tabitha urged, running just ahead of me.

143

I didn't dare take my eyes off the ground, but a question was forming in between the leaps and jumps. I called to her as the wind blew up and whipped my cheeks. 'Last September, did something prompt you to ask the caver to search?'

'Don't think so.'

'Was it in any way a special month?'

'I got engaged.'

You got engaged to an ex-boy scout who could tell us both what he knows, but doesn't choose to.

She came to a halt in front of me so that I almost ran into her. The path levelled out a little, so we could stop running.

We paused for a rest where a stream gurgled down the hill. Tabitha produced two apples. I peeled off my gloves and cupped my hands in the flowing water for a drink.

Tabitha frowned. 'I know what you're thinking. Dad was found by boy scouts. Hector was a boy scout.' She bit into her apple and munched slowly.

A young rabbit peered fearlessly from among a patch of bracken. We watched as it first nibbled at a blade of grass, then bit into the bracken, as though on its first solo outing, testing what would be good fodder.

'And have you asked Hector about it?'

She swallowed. 'It got us into a bit of a row. Hector doesn't like being reminded that he was a boy scout when I was in the VAD. Frankly, neither do I. He said Dad was found by a boy called Humphrey Longfellow, who emigrated to Australia with his family, and by a young lad whose name he can't remember, and that the young lad fetched the scoutmaster.'

That fitted with what Becky had told me, although in Becky's story two older scouts had found Joshua Braithwaite, and her brother was the younger lad who had been sent to tell the scoutmaster.

A look of desolation came over Tabitha's face. 'If Hector truly loved me, wouldn't he help me? Wouldn't

144

he want to know what happened?'

I wasn't sure how to answer, except to say that it seemed to me he did love her, and perhaps wanted her to look forward and not back.

I ate my apple to the core. Tabitha left hers half-eaten, a treat for the baby rabbit, wherever it lurked.

From where we stood we had a good view of a snaking road, and beyond that hills and fields. She pointed to a building nestled into the fell.

'That's Milton House Hospital. You can see it from here but not from the road.'

Dr Gregory Grainger of Milton House had reached the top of my list of people to talk to.

'What's Dr Grainger like?'

'He's a very clever man, widower, about forty years old, quite good-looking.'

'Really?' I raised an eyebrow, hoping to lighten her mood. From her description he seemed a far better match than young Hector.

She laughed. 'He's a bit full of himself. If you take a shine to him, you'll need to look sharp. Everything's being packed up at the hospital. It's closed now. He'll soon be gone.'

It was mid-afternoon when Tabitha and I returned to her home, still early enough for me to change and set off to see Dr Grainger. She came to the gate with me, to set me on the right road for Milton House Hospital. It was a drive of a couple of miles, and then a choice of taking the car up a dirt track, or parking by the side of the road and walking.

Rather than risk the Jowett's tyres, I left the vehicle and walked. From the fell where we walked earlier, Milton House had appeared a stone's throw off the road. After ten minutes' hike up a steep hill, without sight of the house, I began to suspect I had lost my bearings. Keep climbing, or strike out to the left? Tabitha had not mentioned a cattle grid or barn. There must be farms nearby. Could one of the farms have provided a bolt hole for Joshua Braithwaite, I wondered. As far as I could see, fields were bounded by dry-stone walls. Meagre trees, ready to come into leaf under sufferance, dotted the land-scape at a distance from each other, as if uncertain of their welcome.

As I was about to retrace my steps, the hospital came into view. Like other buildings in the area, the house was of stone. That its high surrounding wall was of neat Elizabethan bricks, weathered by wind and rain, surprised me. It seemed a contrary choice in a landscape dominated by dry-stone walls.

The big front gates were shut but not locked. I decided not to enter at the front but to circle the house for any obscured exits Braithwaite may have found. The path round to the left of the house took me by a clump of gorse bushes and a side gate, locked and overgrown. At the rear of the property stood a small gate in the centre of the back wall. It was secured by a bolt which I had no trouble in reaching and releasing.

The path led to an unsteady-looking porch. Next to that, French windows stood open, a pale curtain blowing gently from one of them. Framed there, unmistakeably, was Evelyn Braithwaite. She wore her riding garb. She would surely come in my direction. I stayed by the gate and watched. She and the man with her were unaware of me, eyes only for each other. She raised her face, as if for a kiss. He lowered his head. Their lips touched.

Had there been all the time in the world for my inves-tigation, I might have disappeared back to my car and not confronted Evelyn. For a moment it occurred to me to do just that, but most likely she would see me on the path.

Quickly, I retraced my footsteps, so that when she

146

emerged from the back gate she would think I had just arrived.

'Evelyn!' I called.

We were a few yards apart. I could not make out the look on her face, but her body froze. She stood, hand on the gate, until I came near.

'Kate, what are you doing here?'

'I wanted to see the last place your husband stayed before his disappearance, and to talk to Dr Grainger.'

'Have you . . . have you been here long?'

'Just this moment arrived.'

She seemed relieved, and yet unsure what to say next.

'Have you an appointment with him?'

'One of the advantages of being an investigator is that you can occasionally pay a surprise visit, even to a gentleman.'

She forced a smile. 'If Tabitha had thought of that she may have been tempted to follow your hobby herself. How is your investigation going, may I ask?'

'Not very well.'

'I won't say I told you so.' She flicked her riding whip. 'Well, excuse me. I left my mare tethered by the stream.'

I admired her coolness in not attempting to explain her presence, or to say anything that Dr Grainger might contradict.

I approached the French windows just as Dr Grainger was closing them.

'Pardon me arriving unannounced. Mrs Braithwaite did offer to introduce us. Kate Shackleton, friend of Miss Braithwaite.'

He took my hand, yet looked beyond me, as if to see whether Evelyn was still about. 'How do you do, Mrs Shackleton. Grainger. Dr Gregory Grainger.'

He offered me a chair. His desk was placed so that he sat with his back to the window. Perhaps the view onto the garden and the moors beyond distracted him. His patients, sitting in the chair he offered me, would have a wider perspective, onto the moors.

It doesn't hurt to lie sometimes. I apologised for the intrusion and looked him in the eye. 'I tried to telephone to you, but there was a problem on the line.'

He gave a small, amused smile that said he knew I was lying.

We were appraising each other. A lean man, alert and athletic-looking as though he burned off energy through every pore, he gave the impression of having a mind that was never still.

'I'm sorry to say you've caught me at an inconvenient moment. But how can I help you?'

I saw no point in a photographing-the-scenery cover story, so came straight to the point.

'Miss Braithwaite has asked me to look into her father's disappearance. It's her last-ditch attempt before she marries – still hoping to get news of him before the wedding.'

He raised his eyebrows and shook his head sympathetically. 'Sad business. Poor girl.'

If I read the language of his body correctly, he seemed relieved. He relaxed back in his chair. Why? Perhaps he expected me to mention Evelyn's departure, and, not knowing what she may have said to me, feared contradicting her. On the other hand, maybe he really was anxious to get on.

A chaise longue stood too close to the wall, its dark-red velvet cover leaving a mark on the lighter wallpaper. Did his talking cure involve his patients lying down and closing their eyes? Officers back from the horrors of the front must have lain there, dreading the spectres that would materialise. Just for a moment, the living dead seemed to shuffle across the room.

'Since I've called at an inconvenient time, I'll come straight to the point, Dr Grainger. Mr Braithwaite was brought here by Constable Mitchell on Sunday morning, 20 August 1916. By the end of the following afternoon, he was gone. Do you have any ideas or thoughts about him, or about that time, that might give me a clue as to what happened to him?'

He gave me a reproachful look as though believing I had called unannounced in order to catch him out. 'Constable Mitchell took my statement at the time. He interviewed staff and patients. I did not keep the gates locked. Why should I? I had opened this hospital only seven days previously – a hospital, not a prison.'

'I don't understand how a man of Joshua Braithwaite's standing could disappear into thin air. It's a puzzle, Dr Grainger.'

He sighed, and nodded agreement, making a steeple of his fingers. 'I didn't know the man. I spoke to him for about ten minutes when he was first admitted. Since the family have asked you to look into this . . .'

I corrected him. 'Tabitha Braithwaite asked me.'

The slightest flush of embarrassment darkened his features at my unspoken hint that Evelyn didn't give a tinker's damn about her husband's fate. He shuffled papers on his desk, glancing none too surreptitiously at his watch.

'Miss Braithwaite may be reassured that during my brief consultation with him, her father denied attempting suicide. She may be less comforted to know that the human mind is far more complex than we credit. I have known cases of unacknowledged death wish, sometimes coupled with mounting paranoia.'

'Are you suggesting that was the case with Mr Braithwaite?'

'I can't offer a prognosis on so superficial an acquaintance with the man. It was to oblige Constable Mitchell that I agreed to admit him. I left him in the charge of an orderly, but I take full responsibility. It had been a diffi-

149

cult time for me – having been in France, and my move here to open a new facility. That day I needed some air. I went for a ride on the moors. It was hours after my return that I discovered Mr Braithwaite had gone. To tell you the truth, my first thought was that he had taken himself home. I telephoned PC Mitchell. The rest, you know.'

'That's the trouble – the rest I don't know, and neither does anyone else.'

He tapped a pile of papers into a neat pile.

'Normally, I'd be more than glad to talk to you, but I'm literally on my way out. I've a talk to give at the Mechanics' Institute. I've to finish writing it and really haven't another second to spare.' He reached for his diary. 'Would next Monday be any use?'

'Afraid not. Family commitments will take me away for a few days.'

He looked back at his diary. 'If you could be here at eleven on the dot tomorrow, I could spare you half an hour, Mrs Shackleton, though I'm not sure I've anything useful to tell you.'

'Thank you. I'll be here tomorrow. I'm sorry to be such a frightful nuisance but I did promise Tabitha I'd do my best, and leave no stone unturned.'

By eleven o'clock in the morning, he would have had time to speak to Evelyn. The puzzle was that they had not already decided what he should say.

I stood up. 'What is the subject of your talk?'

He opened the door. We stepped into a dark hall.

'The symbolism of dreams. I have made something of a case study of the dreams of the men who have been in my charge over the past years.'

We had reached the front door. 'Will you mind very much if I look around the grounds? It's such a lovely setting for a hospital.'

He looked at me steadily as though about to question my interest in horticulture. He shrugged. 'Be my guest.'

150

His response was less than gracious, but I thanked him and stepped out into the late afternoon sun. It was that time of evening when a stillness pencils through the light, as if the world holds its breath.

The gardener was hoeing between rows of onions. As best I could, I tried to engage him in conversation, making inane remarks about root vegetables. Men who are attached to the soil become unused to speaking. After ten minutes of monosyllabic replies, I gave up. To this gardener, I was just another well-meaning, well-to-do female, sticking in her nose where it wasn't wanted.

I walked round the grounds, as if the walls of the house might give me some message from the past. Surely some orderly or kitchen maid would venture out to offer me a cup of tea and a vital piece of information. None did. After twenty minutes, I gave up and walked back to the car.

Driving back into the village, I stopped by the Mechanics' Institute and read the notice on the board.

Tonight – 7 p.m.
Dr Grainger
Lecture – the meaning and therapeutic value of dreams

I prevailed upon Tabitha to have an early tea and come to the lecture. We slipped into the back of the hall at 7 o'clock and found a couple of seats on the end of a row.

I realised he had lied about needing to finish writing his talk. His notes consisted of a set of cards that he did not refer to once. This was a speech he had given many times. He spoke with confidence, and a tone that seemed just right for his audience, not talking down to them. As I watched and listened, I forgot that I was there as part of my investigations and was caught up in his fascinating account of men's dreams and nightmares.

*

151

The next morning, promptly at eleven, Dr Grainger and I sat opposite each other in easy chairs, glasses of sherry in hand. He seemed more relaxed than the day before, sitting with legs crossed, leaning forward slightly as if to show a great interest in whatever I might have to say, looking at me as though no other person in the world existed or ever had existed.

'I'm sorry if I was less than hospitable yesterday, Mrs Shackleton. Any other day I would have shown you round the grounds myself.'

'Did yesterday's talk go well, Doctor?' I decided not to flatter him by admitting that I was there.

He smiled with pleasure at my apparent interest. 'Very well, thank you. I have a great deal of material to draw on. The interpretation of dreams can be a useful aid in helping soothe the troubled mind.' As he spoke, he became enlivened with enthusiasm. 'I feel I owe it to the men I've worked with to write a book, so that something good may come out of this – a new approach to dealing with mental anguish.'

His passion for such a deep and disturbing subject intrigued me.

'I should think that will be a hard book to write.'

His glance shot to a mound of papers on the desk. 'It's finding the time that's difficult, what with the hospital closing and all the paperwork that goes along with that.'

'And you? Where will you go, when the hospital closes?'

He cleared his throat and took a sip of sherry. His legs twisted around each other in a way a contortionist might envy. I wondered whether the shiftiness in his manner was not because he cared whether I knew his plans but that he cared that Evelyn should not.

'That's still up for discussion. I've had offers.'

That didn't surprise me in the least. One offer no doubt came from Evelyn. It astonished me that he had chosen

Evelyn over Tabitha. But I supposed Evelyn was available, and Tabitha was not. When did his relationship with Evelyn begin, I wondered? It must have been convenient for the two of them that Braithwaite disappeared. I looked into my sherry glass, in case he guessed my suspicions.

'Would these offers you've had take you away from this area?'

'Possibly. An old professor of mine has the job of setting up the Maudsley Hospital. It should have opened before the war but everything was put on hold. It's scheduled for next year.'

'Would that be Professor Podmore?'

In his surprise, he uncurled his legs. 'You know him? How extraordinary.'

I felt my hackles rise. He saw me as some country hick who never set foot off the beaten track. 'He's a regular visitor at my aunt's house. I don't know him very well myself, but shall be seeing him next week, at her birthday dinner.'

'What a small world.' He stood up. 'Will you have another sherry?' He filled my glass. 'Just within these four walls, I have already said yes to Professor Podmore's suggestion. It's too big a challenge to turn down. And he's very sympathetic towards my plan for the book. Positively encouraging in fact.'

My half hour stole on. Somehow I felt it would be extendable.

'One misses society,' he sighed, 'tucked away in the country for years.'

'But the value of your work,' I flattered. 'It must have been greatly appreciated by so many of your patients.'

'Some of whom I cured sufficiently for them to return to the front.'

'That must have been hard.'

'Harder for them. Poor chaps.'

It was time to come in for the kill. 'I can see that Mr

153

Braithwaite may not have been such a great priority.'

'Perhaps not.' He twisted the sherry glass in his hand. 'Of course with hindsight, he should have been. I have had the chance to go over his file, if you have any particular questions. You understand that I wouldn't be divulging information as a rule, but under the circumstances . . .'

'What was his state of mind?'

Grainger walked back to his desk and stood, hand on the chair-back, looking at a set of notes. 'I barely spent ten minutes with him. My notes say I would have explored possible paranoia. He believed the person who came to his aid – the scoutmaster I mean, after the boy scouts found him – had a grudge against him.'

After he had consulted his notes, Grainger stood straight and alert, as though ready for the new life ahead of him. I suddenly realised who he reminded me of. It was an absurd connection to make. I thought of Joshua Braithwaite in his wedding photograph, standing upright and ready to smile. Someone had to be Braithwaite's champion. That task had fallen to me.

'Perhaps Mr Braithwaite was right, and there was ill-feeling on the part of the scoutmaster.'

Grainger sighed. 'Yes. Regretfully I did not probe further during that brief first talk with him. Braithwaite denied attempting suicide, but given the shame of the act and the seriousness of the penalties one would expect that.'

Is it Russians who throw their glasses in the fireplace and smash them? I felt such a mixture of emotions. Here was an attractive, intelligent man, easy in his manner and yet on this one topic of Mr Braithwaite he was so bloody complacent and ready to judge that I felt like flinging not just the sherry glass but the bottle.

'Was there anything else in your notes?'

'Only that his denial of suicide may have been delusional.'

'I see. Well, thank you.'

For reinforcing my prejudices against talking cures.

'More sherry?' he asked.

'Better not,' I said reluctantly. 'Don't want to mow down the local population on my way back. But tell me, who was on the staff when Mr Braithwaite was here? Are any of them still with you?'

He opened his desk drawer and took out a log book. As he flicked through its pages, he said, 'It was still early days for us. We had just two orderlies, and neither of them are still with us. One was . . .' He ran his finger down the page. 'Here we are . . . Stafford, M. Malcolm I think. He was here until last Christmas. Good chap. He'd lost an eye but he didn't miss much in spite of that. I gave preference to chaps who'd been wounded, with the thought that the officers would feel they were among their own. It seemed to work.'

'Where is Stafford now?'

'He and his wife went to Kent to take over a public house after the death of his brother-in-law. The other orderly . . . here we are – Kellett, P. He wasn't with us very long. Don't think the work suited him.'

I held my breath. No one had mentioned that Kellett worked here. But then, I hadn't asked. Surely there couldn't be two P Kelletts in the area? 'Do you remember if Mr Kellett had a particular war disability?'

'Yes. He was still coming to terms with it. Gave him a bit of gyp. Lost a hand. Apparently, according to some of my audience last night – stayed for a chat after my talk – poor man died only this week. Terrible accident.'

I struggled to stay composed and to collect my thoughts. Dr Grainger looked through his journal to find Kellett's leaving date, which was shortly after Braithwaite's disappearance.

Why had I spent the best part of a day creaming out non-existent facial wrinkles and trying on gowns in preparation for the Gawthorpes' party? And if only Kellett's

155

colleagues had gossiped to Sykes about his spell at Milton House, instead of telling tales about selling dyes and saving up for a cottage by the sea, we might have asked a crucial question of Kellett before it was too late.

Grainger looked suddenly concerned. For a moment I thought he was going leap across and take my pulse. 'What's wrong?' he asked. 'Did you know Kellett?'

'Not really. I met him briefly at the mill.'

'They're dangerous workplaces,' Grainger added, somewhat unnecessarily.

'Could Kellett have helped Mr Braithwaite – brought him clothes, a horse, or a bicycle, or escorted him to a safe place?'

'If he did, he didn't admit it to the police when the investigation was going on.'

'Thank you. You've been helpful. I won't take up any more of your time.'

He looked surprised. 'I don't hold Kellett responsible. Mr Braithwaite was in my care. I fell down on my duty. I shall regret that for the rest of my life.'

So you bloody well should, I thought.

He rose to walk me to the door. 'I want to show you something.'

Already the dismantling process was underway. Removal men carried boxes along the hall.

We flattened ourselves against a wall as two men carried a bedstead down the stairs.

In the lobby, Grainger stopped. 'Take a look at this painting.'

Light filtered in through the stained glass above the porch door. Then the door was opened by the removal men. We stood by an oil painting, full of light and shade – a stream, trees, an old stone bridge.

'Do you recognise the spot?' he asked.

It was a local scene, the beck and humpback bridge, and two children playing by the stepping stones. 'Is it where

156

. . . where Mr Braithwaite was found?'

'Yes. And it's his painting. Mrs Braithwaite donated it to the hospital. She didn't want it in the house, naturally enough, and couldn't destroy it.'

No one had told me that Braithwaite was such a talented artist. It gave an extra reason why he may have wanted to run away from the mill. If I had such a talent, I would want to pursue my art. He had caught the dappled light on the beck, the texture of the stepping stones, the movement of Edmund with his fishing rod, and Tabitha, clutching at her skirt with one hand and poking at the reeds with a stick, as if searching.

'What will happen to it now?'

'I'm not sure. I can't decide whether I should return it.' He rubbed his chin thoughtfully.

'They're his children, Tabitha and Edmund. I'm sure she'd want it, Tabitha I mean. Shall I take it with me?'

He looked suddenly relieved. 'I wish you would.'

'Let's put it in the boot of my car.'

I had risked driving up the dirt track.

He lifted the painting from the wall, along with the cobwebs that had accumulated behind it. When the removal men weren't looking, I snaffled one of their covers and draped it over the painting. I would not give it to Tabitha until after she married. It could be too unsettling.

Dr Grainger carried the painting outside. There was relief in his voice when he said, 'Thank you for taking this. I need no reminders of my time at Milton House, or of Mr Braithwaite.'

13

Sunday, 20 August 1916

GRAINGER

Talk about irony. Talk about bad timing. Yesterday, Grainger read a journal article about the decrease in suicides during wartime. Today, here he was lumbered with a potential suicide. Just his luck to fetch up in the one place in England in the week where a local worthy got himself dragged from a beck by boy scouts.

'Exceptional circumstances, Doctor Grainger,' the village constable had said.

At present, he could give his full attention to the few officers who formed the advance party of his patients in this new facility. The captain had developed a stammer, a twitch and a fearfulness that overwhelmed him. The lieutenant had been buried twice, once for twenty-four hours. His shuffling gait improved with the exercises prescribed by the physical training instructor. Grainger felt less sure of his own ability to help the man mend his mind.

It was a bloody nuisance, being asked to take in a civilian, a local bigwig at that. With a full complement of patients, he might have been able to refuse admission to Joshua Braithwaite. Not that Grainger lacked compassion, but suicidal mill owners were not part of his remit. Why does this get my ire up, he asked himself as he strolled the grounds, indulging in a little self-analysis. The insight he uncovered was not welcome. As long as he took care of officers back from the front, he could imagine himself to be still in the thick of things, pretend not to have been banished from London to the wilds of Yorkshire. For banishment it was. Grainger was a capital man, a London man from the roots of his hair to the tips of his neatly clipped toenails. He liked company, dinner parties, visits to the theatre and opera, to be in the throbbing centre of the country, the heart of the Empire, where events were decided and history made.

Having to probe the mind of a morose provincial held no charms. Grainger nodded to the gardener. The man tipped his cap as he approached a bed of cabbages, an ugly-looking knife in his hand.

Grainger tried to put a different interpretation on the task that lay ahead. Having to probe the despair of a manufacturing magnate might have possibilities. The man had lost a son after all. Such things mattered deeply in a culture where a business was handed down over the generations. With this in his thoughts, Grainger tried to quash his prejudices, telling himself that the mill owner may prove an interesting case. Presumably the man would need to be half-way intelligent to run a mill. Of course, possibly he would not be articulate, if his conversations ran to buying wool and turning it into cloth. This was not an occupation calling for introspection.

At nine o'clock on Sunday morning, Constable Mitchell escorted a protesting Braithwaite into the consulting room. Grainger was inclined to give the man the benefit of the doubt, and a reasonable amount of attention. After all, it could not be so cut and dried a case or the constable would have released him, or had him taken to prison.

The constable stepped outside and left Grainger alone with his uninvited guest.

Braithwaite made an unfavourable impression. Grainger's first thought was that the man had a gale force hangover. He was cut and bruised, his hair dishevelled, had slept in his suit.

Grainger hid his feelings and offered the man a seat.

Braithwaite seemed grateful, and ready to explain himself, but when he did the words did not make sense. Even in his confused state, Braithwaite had let it be known he was moneyed, influential, demanding to talk to his solicitor. He denied attempting suicide, denied drinking. He showed signs of paranoia. 'They' were out to get him. This life was over for him. He had to get out of here. In the next breath he claimed that he had not tried to drown himself. All that was stuff and nonsense born of spite.

It took all Grainger's skill to persuade the man to agree to have a rest, and sort out the matter tomorrow when he was more himself. It helped that Constable Mitchell came in at that moment, shaking his head sadly and saying, 'I'm afraid, Mr Braithwaite, the only alternative is the lock-up.'

'What about my wife?'

The constable shook his head.

Braithwaite cursed under his breath.

He was escorted to one of the second-floor rooms, with a view onto the moors. Perhaps that would calm him.

Short-term amnesia, Grainger might have said had he felt charitable. Or was it a case of a death wish the patient disguised from himself?

When the telephone call came, he felt unable to refuse to see Mrs Braithwaite, but did not look forward to the interview. He expected a matronly, tearful woman with high colour, no doubt wearing a print frock and summer hat. She would twist a hanky in her hand and plead her husband's case. There'd be some clumsy offer of a contribution to hospital funds in return for a favourable report on her husband's state of mind.

An orderly showed her in. She was tall, slender and

160

wore a riding outfit. In her left hand she held her hat and whip. He pushed back his chair and rose to meet her.

Coming towards him, she extended a cool right hand.

'So good of you to find time to see me, Doctor.'

'Do take a seat, Mrs Braithwaite.'

She took possession of the oak carver, crossing her long legs.

Now he recognised her from the public meeting that had been held in the Mechanics' Institute to announce the opening of the hospital. She was a woman who turned heads.

She looked round. 'This was the Nelsons' breakfast room. Mrs Nelson said it's lovely in the mornings, catches the sun.'

'Yes. This will be my consulting room.' At least she wasn't tearful and histrionic. She struck him as one of those people you could rely on to come to the point when she was ready. He refrained from asking the usual 'What can I do for you?' He hoped she would not ask him to do anything. Refusing her would be painful.

'I'm sorry that you have the trouble of taking custody of my husband. I'm sure it's not what you expected when you came to open up Milton House for the military.'

She so exactly guessed his thoughts. He murmured some non-committal reply, her sympathy taking him by surprise. Still, he felt sure she would make a damn good stab to influence him. She seemed to be assessing him, looking at him intently, her head tilted to one side. He recognised a pose of his own – a willingness to listen.

'Where were you before, Doctor?'

'I was in Harley Street, and St George's, then in France. I was asked to open this extra facility in the north.'

'I'm sure we're all very glad to have you here.'

'You must be anxious about your husband. I've spoken to him briefly. I plan to see him again when he has had the chance to recover somewhat.'

161

He would speak to Braithwaite when the man calmed down and found his manners.

'I understand you'll be making a report, on whether he truly did attempt suicide.'

'That's what I've been asked to do.'

'Then I am sure you will do it.'

He remembered that the policeman had mentioned that the Braithwaites had lost a son. He had expected her to give some mitigation for her husband's actions. She held the silence.

Something extraordinary seemed to be happening. She had the kind of magnetism that fills the room. He would never look at that chair again without imagining her sitting there, so calmly. In repose she was captivating, with wide cheekbones, glossy hair, bright, penetrating dark eyes, a chiselled nose and full lips, slightly parted. He remembered that at the public meeting she had a girl with her, her daughter perhaps. It may not be such a bad thing to be cast out into the wilds of Yorkshire after all.

He knew he would be able to ask her about her husband without having some emotional torrent pour onto his head. She was one of those rare women with great inner strength. He felt it.

'I suppose I must ask you, if it's not too painful . . . you must have an insight into your husband's state of mind. Has he behaved oddly lately?'

'I'm sorry. Please don't ask me. I don't wish to say anything that would influence you, or that might damage my husband.'

He waited for her to say more.

After a long time, she said, 'I expected Joshua to be strong when our son was killed. He wasn't.'

If she begins to cry, he thought, I may be able to touch her. If she stood and began to cry, I could take her by the shoulders and perhaps draw her to me. But she seemed to have such brittleness about her. She might splinter and break before she would cry.

She recrossed her legs and looked beyond him, out of the window.

'Have you had much opportunity to explore your surroundings, Dr Grainger?'

'No I'm afraid not.'

'Avoid the army target practice and the supposedly banned grouse shooters and you'll find some lovely rides across the moors. Do you ride?'

'I have no horse.'

She stood. 'I'm sorry to hear that. With your responsibilities, I'm sure you will be in need of recreation.'

'This is the lull before the storm. I'm expecting more patients any day now.'

'Then you must make the most of your time. Does Mrs Grainger ride?'

'I'm a widower.' He felt sure she would have known already. Women always did.

She nodded, expressing sympathy without words. 'May I show you something?' She walked to the window.

He followed and stood so close that he could feel the heat from her body, catch the scent of her hair.

They looked out at the glorious August day at a picture-book green land, a bevy of small white clouds casting shifting shadows on the distant hill.

'Over there. Across Reevock Moor, there's a lovely spot. You can see the whole valley. There's a clump of elms, and something of a tarn, very deep and dark. They say it covers an ancient settlement.'

'I shall make sure I visit there.'

She held out her hand. 'I would be much obliged if you would keep me informed of the progress of my husband's case.'

'Of course.'

'When you feel confident that it would not compro-

163

mise you, perhaps we could ride one day.'

An hour later, the orderly tapped on the door. 'There's a fine bay mare in the stable, doctor. Brought by a boy who said you'd know all about it.'

'Ah yes,' Grainger said, as if he were perfectly calm. 'Thank you.'

He knew that he would not easily be compromised. Had she meant to try to influence him, she could have done so earlier.

He folded the newspaper and handed it to the orderly. 'Does the horse look fresh?'

'Fresh as a daisy.'

'Then I shall take a ride.'

At first, he saw only her mare, tethered to a low branch. He dismounted, opened his mouth to call for her, thought better of it and looked about. Perhaps it was not her horse after all.

A mallard caught his eye as it swooped low and dived. There was a splash from further off, by a cluster of rocks. He saw someone swimming in the tarn, taking long strokes towards him. She emerged like Venus, only more lovely.

He averted his eyes, mouth dry. 'Thank you for sending the horse.'

'Will you come into the water, Gregory?'

'You have the advantage of me.'

'I hoped I would.'

'I don't know your Christian name.'

'Evelyn.'

'Isn't the tarn very cold, Evelyn?'

'Bitterly.'

Monday, 21 August 1916

Gregory Grainger couldn't sleep for thinking about

164

Evelyn Braithwaite, and their time together the day before. He was awake early enough to catch the first notes of the dawn chorus.

He had never known a woman like Evelyn, the way she glided from the water towards him, as if it were the most natural thing in the world, no rush or hurry about her. She had placed a picnic rug on the ground and stretched out on it to dry herself, drops of water from the tarn glistening on her pale body in the afternoon sunlight. She was slender. When she leaned forward, he noticed every sensational vertebra.

He'd said something clumsy and silly. 'Are you a naturist?' She seemed so at ease in her own skin.

She draped the towel around her shoulders and closed her eyes. 'Yes. I'm a naturist. I believe myself to be completely alone. I've no idea that someone is watching me, and wondering . . .' She hugged her knees.

Even then, fool that he was, he hesitated.

'Your husband . . .'

'This has nothing to do with him. I saw the way you looked at me in the Mechanics' Institute, when you came to talk about the work of the hospital. There was an instant connection between us, a kind of magnetism. Don't let it disappear in a smoke of words.'

He took a step towards her, and another.

She stretched out her hand and touched his thigh. 'There will be only one rule.'

'What's that?'

'Take off your bloody boots, man.'

He laughed then, and somehow knew it would be all right. Sitting down beside her, he tugged off his riding boots with difficulty, feeling awkward, like a boy. She moved her hand along his spine and, distractingly, hooked her thumb in the waist of his trousers. He placed his boots neatly, side by side, a little way off from the picnic blanket.

165

When he turned to look at her she lowered her eyes, just for a second, and the length of her lashes against her cheeks struck him as extraordinary.

She unbuttoned his shirt. 'You and I will have a lot to learn from each other.'

He kissed her, tasting her mouth, then loosed his braces and took off his shirt. Her head rested against his chest so that he only had to lower his head to feel her hair against his cheek.

Her fingers touched the flies of his trousers, with an almost innocent lightness, as if she were checking the number of buttons. Even then, he could not stop the thoughts. How could she? With a son dead, and a husband about to be charged with attempted suicide.

'Is this what's meant by magnetism?' she asked in a dreamy sort of voice.

'That involves an electric charge, attraction and repulsion.'

Her fingers touched him again. 'I think I can feel the electric charge.'

Moments later, they were naked, wrestling, struggling, in a hurry for their mouths to meet, for their bodies to be as close as it was possible to be.

She moaned as he penetrated her too quickly. And once was not enough. She made him lie beneath her, teasing him, coaxing him into submission until he could bear it no longer.

She kissed him gently, with a softness that did not seem meant for him.

When she broke free, she dressed quickly, with a shiver, telling him that he must give her a five-minute start so they would not be seen together.

He called after her as she galloped away, asking when he would see her again. The wind carried his words back to him. As he watched her ride to the horizon, he thought, she's keeping emptiness at bay, just for a short while.

*

When he returned to Milton House, Grainger learned that Joshua Braithwaite had partaken of a small meal of soup and bread. He braced himself to see the man and tapped on his door. When no answer came, Grainger tapped again and called, 'Mr Braithwaite! May I come in?'

Braithwaite was slumped in the chair, as if he had been dozing. He jerked into wakefulness.

'Are you ready to talk yet, Mr Braithwaite?' Grainger asked, feeling more kindly towards the man than he had earlier.

In the hospital uniform, Braithwaite appeared benign but when he spoke it was with controlled anger. 'Aye, I'm ready to talk. Where's my wife?'

At the very mention of Evelyn, a shudder ran through Grainger with such power that he half-expected Braithwaite to read his thoughts, to see the longing. 'She did visit earlier . . .'

'No she didn't. I've seen no one but that daft copper and your dim orderlies.'

'She called, but thought it best to leave you be.'

Braithwaite winced. 'Did she now?' His jaw tightened. 'I might have known.'

Grainger had come further into the room. He wanted to sit on the end of the bed but that was not the right thing to do. If he was to have a consultation with Braithwaite, it should be done properly, and notes made.

'I want to speak to my solicitor.'

'I'll speak to Constable Mitchell tomorrow. I'm sure contact can be arranged first thing in the morning.'

'I want to speak to him now.'

'It's Sunday.'

Braithwaite did not know what day it was, but hid his surprise, saying, 'Do you think I don't know what day it is? You must have me down for a barm pot.' He stood up. 'Let me get to a telephone. I pay Murgatroyd enough that he'll speak to me, Sunday or no Sunday.'

167

It seemed to Grainger to be a reasonable request. The man was first a suspected felon and only secondly a patient.

'There's a telephone in the hall.'

Without another word, Grainger led Braithwaite onto the landing and down the stairs. The telephone stood on a table, just near the consulting room door. Grainger went into his room, leaving the door ajar.

He listened as Braithwaite asked for a number, and waited, and waited. Braithwaite muttered a curse, clicked for a fresh line and asked for another number. This time, he was successful.

'Put Miss Braithwaite on,' he demanded. Then, 'What do you mean, she's not there? Where is she?' After a pause, he said, 'Yes. Yes. I forgot. If she comes, say her father needs to speak to her.'

He replaced the telephone.

Grainger came back into the hall, making it clear that he would escort Braithwaite upstairs.

'If my daughter telephones . . .'

There was something almost plaintive in Braithwaite's voice, and in the way he said 'If my daughter telephones', and not 'when', that Grainger simply nodded.

'I'll give instructions that you're to be brought to the telephone straight away.'

'I'd forgotten she's off with the VAD. She sometimes gets home on Sundays. Such a mess,' Braithwaite murmured to himself as he mounted the stairs, 'such a damn mess and muddle.'

Grainger called after him. 'Mr Braithwaite, you don't have to talk to me today, but perhaps I could give you a physical examination – just to check that everything is all right.'

'Everything's not all right is it? Far from it. And you prodding and poking me won't change that.'

*

That was Sunday. Now it was Monday morning. Grainger checked his clock. It was too early to call the servants. He went downstairs to the enormous kitchen. A scullery maid knelt by the range, setting chips of wood on rolled-up newspaper.

The orderly, Kellett, sat at the deal table drinking tea and smoking a cigarette. He stood up as Grainger entered.

'Anything wrong, sir?'

'I could murder a cup of tea.'

'I'll bring you one.'

'I'll have it here.' Grainger sat down.

Kellett fetched a cup and poured. Grainger remembered that he had been on duty during the night.

'Any disturbances?'

'Peaceful as babes, doctor. Except for Mr Johnson having one of his bad dreams.'

Kellett was a man who did not need encouragement to talk. Grainger only half-listened, and then not at all. He was wondering how soon he could see Evelyn again, and how they would manage it.

He rang the Braithwaite house. A housekeeper or whoever answered the telephone put her on.

'I wanted to thank you for yesterday, for sending the horse.'

It was important to be careful, he thought. You never knew what operator may be listening.

'It was my pleasure,' she said softly. 'Did you enjoy the ride?'

'Immensely.'

He should tell her that Braithwaite wanted to speak to her, but now he was conscious that the operator may be listening and if he started to speak about his charge in the same breath as a 'thanks for the horse', it could be misconstrued. As if she guessed his thoughts, she simply said, 'I'm glad, Doctor. Thank you for telling me.'

In one more second, he would be cut off from her. All

in a rush he said, 'Would it be possible for you to call at Milton House today?'

'Of course.'

'Say, three?'

'Three.'

Kellett came to him moments later, saying that Mr Braithwaite needed to use the telephone and was complaining about his door being locked.

'Escort him to the telephone,' Grainger said. 'And unlock his door.' He would telephone Constable Mitchell and tell him that Milton House was a hospital, not a prison. If Mitchell wanted Braithwaite locked up, let him do it. But before he had time to do that, Johnson tapped on his door, agitated and wanting to talk.

Captain Johnson had dreamed vividly from childhood. He had a memory of being made to stay alone in the nursery while the family prepared to set off on holiday.

'Get that child from underfoot,' he remembered his father saying.

Last night Captain Johnson dreamed himself back in the nursery. Filthy mud turned his nursery to a trench. As guns roared above him, Johnson heard his family leaving the house, shutting the front door, going on holiday without him, and he knew that he would be left – abandoned and suffocating – in a trench whose sides were collapsing in on him, filling his mouth and nose with mud, blood and death.

Grainger listened. He made notes. He wished he hadn't offered Johnson the chair that Evelyn had sat in. Was he being a fool? Johnson's dreams held no great mystery, but Grainger could not resolve the meaning of his own yesterday. What meaning should he, would he, place on yesterday? She had seduced him, but was that because of what she called the magnetism between them, or was that her way of punishing Braithwaite?

She had said, 'Don't ask me to talk.'

Talking was what he dealt in, but she was right. Talk

170

would muddy the waters between him and her. Grainger had read *The Rainbow*. He and his fellow medics talked of D H Lawrence and of free love – sitting in the pub by St George's. Women weren't like that, at least not in Grainger's experience. Now he had met Evelyn, he would never think that way again. She would colour the way he viewed the world, and womankind.

'What did your mother say when your father said "Get that child from underfoot"?' Grainger asked Johnson. It amazed him how it was possible to move in parallel along two quite discrete strands of thought.

Kellet was in the hall when Johnson went back to his room. Grainger saw him hovering by the door. He called him in.

'How is Mr Braithwaite this morning, Kellett?'

'Very quiet, Doctor.'

'Is he asking to use the telephone?'

'He has already.'

'And?'

'I believe he telephoned his solicitor but found him not available.'

'I see. And any communication with his family?'

'No, Doctor.'

'Thank you.'

Grainger felt a pang of pity for the man, and annoyance with Constable Mitchell for leaving the matter in such an unsatisfactory way. He called Kellett back. 'Ask Mr Braithwaite to come and see me in the consulting room.'

After a few moments Kellett returned.

'He's feeling distinctly down in the dumps, Doctor, and asks to be left alone. He'll speak to no one until he can contact his solicitor.'

'Very well.'

He had tried. No one could say he hadn't tried.

At five minutes to three, he looked out of the window.

171

The garden wall was already casting a shadow on the vegetable plot. Evelyn Braithwaite would come to the front door of course, not this way.

Three minutes to three; one minute to three; three o'clock; she would not come. All the same, he closed the blind, to keep the sun from the room and to shade against prying eyes.

At five minutes past three, an orderly came to announce Mrs Braithwaite.

'Please show her in.'

It seemed an age before the orderly returned, ushering her in, carrying something.

'Stand it just there if you would,' she said to the orderly, waving her hand towards the wall.

The picture was wrapped in brown paper. He saw through a small rip that it was a painting in a gilt frame.

'I believe the Nelsons took most of their pictures and you'll need something. This can be a start, perhaps for the landing?'

It seemed such a bizarre thing to do, and it could be construed as bribery. As usual, she seemed to read his thoughts.

'It has no financial worth. Just an amateur painting of a local scene that may cheer your patients.'

The orderly left, closing the door behind him.

'What are you thinking of? A painting?'

'I had to. Don't ask me why. Some things are hard to explain. Joshua did it and I just wanted it out of the house.'

Grainger felt a sudden dread. Perhaps she would be irrational, unpredictable, hysterical even.

'It's nothing,' she said. 'Believe me, Joshua would want you to have it, in appreciation of your taking care of him.'

The scene showed a bridge, with a fast-flowing brook, and a waterfall in the background. By the reeds a couple of children played, a girl and a boy.

It was good, an accomplished piece of work.

'I didn't know your husband was an artist.'

'He went to Art College, briefly. His older brother should have taken over the mill but he hightailed it to South Africa to search for gold. That sealed Joshua's future.'

'Did the older brother find gold?'

'I'll tell you another time. You wanted to see me?'

'Just a moment.' He locked the door. 'I don't think we'll be disturbed, but let's not take risks.'

'Indeed not.'

He was undoing her dress, which seemed to have so many buttons. 'This is very inconsiderate of you.'

'I thought you would like a challenge.'

'Shhh.'

He pressed his lips to hers, found her nipple, lifted her dress and let his hand caress her thigh.

'I'm going to be such a good friend to this hospital,' she murmured. 'Every week I shall come and read to a soldier.'

They made love with great urgency. She drew him away from the desk where he had wanted to take her, leading him to the chaise longue.

'Only every week?' he said, as she stroked his hair. 'If I don't have you every day I shall go mad.'

'You would grow tired of me.'

'Never.'

'I had better see Joshua, since I'm here, whether he will or no.'

She fastened her dress. It was a marvel to him that she could look so calm.

'I'll ask the orderly to bring him.'

It was Stafford who answered the bell.

'Would you please tell Mr Braithwaite that his wife is here to see him, and escort him here.'

This would be awkward. Grainger decided to take the seat on the chaise longue himself, leaving the two carver chairs for Evelyn and Braithwaite. No. That would be ridiculous. He would have to give them privacy, and wait outside.

173

Evelyn sat in that self-contained way she had, ankles crossed, palms upturned in her lap. They did not speak.

Grainger suddenly stood and went to the window. He drew up the blind and opened the window. Surely there must be the scent of sex in the room, and Braithwaite would know it at once.

Stafford returned. He was sweating and appeared agitated. 'Doctor.'

'What is it?'

When the tongue-tied man did not answer, Grainger went out with him into the hall.

In an urgent whisper, Stafford said, 'Mr Braithwaite's not in his room. He was there at three o'clock when I did the teas, but he's not there now.'

'Has anyone apart from Mrs Braithwaite been here asking about him?' Grainger had a sudden horror of someone having come to his door, or seen him with Evelyn through a crack in the blind. 'Might the constable have come to speak to him?'

Stafford shook his head.

'Think, man. Have you seen any of his workers or friends in the grounds?'

'Not a soul.'

'You're sure?'

'Not a one. And I was only saying to the cook, you'd have expected an enquiry after him from one of his fellow chapel-goers.'

14

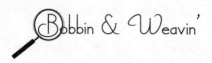

Bobbin & Weavin'

Sunday, 20 August 1916

ARTHUR WILSON

The chapel meeting room felt like a furnace by the time
Arthur Wilson brought the men's afternoon Bible class to
a close. He slid his notes on the Book of Job into the
battered brown briefcase that had served him well these
twenty-five years, and his father before him.

Wilson had needed no notes. *There was a man in the land
of Uz, whose name was Job; and that man was perfect and
upright, and one that feared God, and eschewed evil.* That man
of substance was hedged about with plenty, and everything was taken from him yet he sinned not. His oxen,
asses, seven sons and three daughters taken from him, yet
Job sinned not. He rent his mantle, shaved his head, fell
upon the ground and worshipped.

Not a man in the Bible class doubted that Wilson's
lesson was not about the upright Job but about the less
than upright Joshua Braithwaite, hedged about with plenty
through the generations yet who failed the simple test
when Satan gadded hither and thither in the world and
snapped up his son.

Wilson stood at the chapel meeting room window. He
relaxed a little, watching the men depart, still soberly
thoughtful from his instruction. But wait. One turned to
another, shedding the thoughtful expression. They

175

chatted. 'Braithwaite', he read on the man's lips. Another man turned back and looked at Wilson, staring boldly. They knew he was right to judge Braithwaite. They understood.

They were walking through the chapel yard gate in twos and threes. Suddenly it hit him. The men liked each other. That thought had never occurred to him before. The idea struck him as odd. But do they like me? That mattered not. He didn't want their liking, only their respect. As weaving manager that was his due. As a chapel leading light and instructor, that was his due. Wilson would have preferred a larger class, as it was before men took themselves off to war. But he made no attempts to make the lessons anything other than what they were: a serious study of the Good Book.

He watched the chapel caretaker open his house door and cross the scoured step into the yard. It had been a roasting day. The chapel and lecture hall windows were wide open to let in a little air. The caretaker entered the chapel. A window was closed from the inside, then another.

From along the corridor, a door slammed in the smaller meeting room. Light female footsteps trod the passage. Indistinct voices chirped like so many canaries. Arthur waited. After a moment, he picked up his briefcase and left the room slowly, giving time for the women to make their way through the yard.

Outside, he took a deep breath of the fine afternoon air, nodding to the taciturn caretaker, who touched his cap. As a prominent member of the chapel committee, Arthur Wilson expected no less.

Arthur feigned surprise when Neville Stoddard said into the back of his neck, 'Good afternoon, Wilson.'

'Good afternoon, Mr Stoddard.'

The two men fell into step. Unasked, Wilson informed Stoddard about the Bible-class topic. Stoddard grunted.

176

Wilson asked about the planned children's outing which Neville Stoddard was helping to organise. In previous years this task had been undertaken by Catherine Stoddard. Arthur guessed that Stoddard had stepped in so that he could report to his wife on the committee's progress. This would eliminate the excuse for female members of the Outing Committee to come to the mill house to see the ailing Catherine, shake their heads and go away saying to all and sundry, Oh, she did look real poorly.

'Bad business about Mr Braithwaite,' Wilson said, as they neared the post office. When Stoddard did not answer straight away, Wilson added, 'Of course I had no say in the matter. I wasn't on the scene. As assistant scout-master I was in another spot altogether. The younger lads needed to re-erect their tent.' Stoddard did not answer. 'Has there been news?'

'No,' Stoddard said curtly.

'Do you think I wouldn't have moved heaven and earth to have kept the law out of it?'

'No. I don't,' Stoddard said shortly.

Wilson snorted. 'You do me wrong, Mr Stoddard. As weaving manager, my loyalty is to the mill masters. If there's anything I can do in the matter, short of lying under oath, be sure I will do it.'

'You have done enough, Wilson.'

'Come, Mr Stoddard. There's nothing so bad that something good can't come of it.'

'I fail to see how, at present.'

Confound the man, Arthur felt his temper rising. Braithwaites had the upper hand now but it was only two generations since the better coat was worn by the Wilsons. Stoddard might be a stickler for profit and loss, keeping up output and the Lord knew he'd been smart enough to increase pay the minute men started joining up.

They were approaching the corner where Wilson

177

would turn off to his own street, where overlookers and managers lived, and his house right at the top – the best of its kind.

'I'll walk on if it's all the same, Mr Stoddard.'

'As you like.'

As manager, as a fellow chapel committee member, he was due more than this curt treatment. Now he began to worry. He could have stepped in yesterday. He could have gone to fetch Stoddard. There might be jobs at stake, his future at stake. True, there were other mills, but harsher places, and he didn't think at his age he could face starting all over again. Some might say he was past it.

And what did he have to show for it all? Nothing.

He glanced at Stoddard. The man looked grim. Without Braithwaite at the helm, Wilson wouldn't give the place six months. He happened to know contracts for khaki would be up for renewal. Stoddard would be too clumsy to shake the right hands and know who deserved a decent Christmas box.

Say that for Braithwaite, he could be sly and tricky while appearing hail fellow well met. Oh yes, Wilson knew that all right – to his own cost.

Braithwaite had run rings around Stoddard, too. Otherwise, why would Stoddard and his wife live in what was no more than a manager's house in the mill grounds when Braithwaite lorded it up the hill in his villa?

'Has there been any progress with my invention, sir?' Wilson asked.

Stoddard took a long step to avoid a wide crack in the flags. He looked at Wilson in surprise. 'Mr Braithwaite was dealing with that.'

'Only he said that on top of my outright payment for the loom picker, if it came to anything he would see me right.' This was not true. Wilson had accepted the twenty-five guineas offered and shook hands on it. But since then he had heard of a weaving overlooker in

178

Hebden Bridge who had gained immortality by having his name on a newly-designed lightweight shuttle. Wilson wanted immortality. This man from Hebden Bridge also, Wilson heard say, was to receive one penny for every dozen shuttles sold. Wilson wanted a penny a dozen for his pair of loom pickers. It would be a cushion in old age.

They were almost at the bridge. Stoddard stopped. He looked across at the Kelletts' house. 'I can never decide whether they have the best spot in the village or the worst. It's between the edge and the outskirts. What do you say?'

Wilson took out his pipe. 'I've no opinion in the matter.' Slowly, he filled the pipe, pressing in the Sweet Briar tobacco. He offered the tin.

Stoddard shook his head. 'Needs a new roof and won't have one this side of doomsday.' He brought out a small cigar. 'Some of the village children call Lizzie Kellett a witch.'

'She never sets foot in chapel.'

Who cared what she was called? Not Wilson. He kept his voice even. 'Kellett was once up to summat where there was black smoke outa the chimney. Kids'll reckon it's her spells.'

'And he's the devil?'

'He's devilish clever.' Wilson sucked at his pipe. This was getting somewhere near what he wanted to talk about. Kellett had prospered through selling the dyestuffs.

Wilson cleared his throat, plucked up courage and set out the new terms he had decided would be reasonable for the loom picker.

Stoddard looked at him in surprise. 'That was all settled on a handshake between you and Mr Braithwaite. Good day, Mr Wilson.' Without turning round, Stoddard called back to him. 'You should have come to me when you found Mr Braithwaite by the beck.'

Wilson fumed as he watched Stoddard walk on towards

the mill house. Stoddard was playing with him. Things were at a pretty pass all round. Done out of his rightful dues. His wife was the worst housekeeper in the world. She'd found where he kept his money and sent half his hard-earned savings to their widowed daughter. The nub of it was, he felt tired, and old, and unrewarded for all his hard work. Camping out in the woods last night with the boy scouts felt like a nail in his coffin. He couldn't sleep, couldn't lie right, could barely move his old legs this morning.

Wilson dabbed at his forehead. Damn this abominable heat.

Sometimes it seemed to Wilson that Marjorie provoked him deliberately. She made no effort to appear anything but drab, with her buttoned-up black clothes, like some widow, her greasy grey hair plaited and fastened up with big hairpins that fell out all over the show. One of them was popping out now. She pushed it back with a bony finger.

'What if it had been the other way round, and you'd been in the beck and he'd found you? It was a bad day's work.'

She timed her words so that he could not answer because Hettie lumbered in with their Sunday tea of lettuce, tomato and a slice of left-over mutton.

'Thank you, Hettie,' Marjorie said.

If he had told her once, he had told her a hundred times. She should not thank the skivvy. The girl should be doing the thanking, glad to have a place with a mistress who chose to turn a blind eye to her bushel of faults. But what other type of servant would Marjorie want around her? *Bad day's work* indeed. She had the cheek to reckon it could have been him. Did she really think that he, Arthur Wilson, could have been caught face down in the beck? He was true coin of the realm, Braithwaite the counterfeit. Everyone knew Braithwaite philandered his mucky socks

180

off. Upright all-on-the-shake-of-a-hand businessman filch a contract from a rival's back pocket. Take your invention for a mere pittance, an invention that could transform the weaving in a thousand mills.

Braithwaite might be the master and Wilson the man, but morally Braithwaite wasn't fit to piss in the same pot.

'What the blue blazes do you mean by that?' he demanded as Hettie's steps retreated down the tiled hall towards the kitchen.

'If we had been blessed with a son, and he had been killed, who knows how you would have felt?'

'But we weren't, and I wouldn't have been so weak-minded.'

He chewed with his mouth open in the way he knew irked her. When they were first wed, she asked him — actually asked him — not to slurp his soup. He never did anything but slurp now. Let her put up with it. Let her put up with everything. One useful part of being married so long was that he knew every little habit that grated on her.

She did not have the sense to leave it alone.

'People will think ...' She stopped. A look of alarm crossed her face, as well it might.

'What? What will people think? Go on, go on.'

'That you took the scoutmaster's side against your own master because you're still smouldering over that dratted loom picker. They'll say it was spite.'

'You'll say it was spite you mean. No right-minded person would blame me.'

How dare she say it was spite? It was a matter for the law. Anyone with an ounce of sense would know that. Constable Mitchell would stand on his head for a quiet life. He would have hush-hushed the whole episode. Joshua Braithwaite would have been home in his own bed, being doctored and danced attendance on if it had been up to Constable Mitchell.

'Some people will think it unchristian that you and Mr

Wardle dealt with Mr Braithwaite in that manner.'

'Unchristian! The man tried to commit suicide. How Christian is that? The man is a whited sepulchre, always has been.'

'He's only human. How would any man feel if their son was killed?'

'Thousands have lost sons. What kind of example is he setting? The whole scout troop – lads we're instilling duty and patriotism and high principles into – they have to know that cowardice of that kind must be punished severely.'

'I hope you won't say that if the mill goes under without him and we've to give up this house and find ourselves back where we started, which is nowhere.'

'How dare you woman?'

'How dare I? Because I may as well be hung for a sheep as a lamb.' Her eyes gave a spark of defiance that he had not seen for a long while. 'And if Joshua Braithwaite took it into his head to leave this world, I pity him and I understand. You make my life not worth living sometimes. God would forgive me if I shuffled off this mortal coil.'

His mouth fell open.

She glared at him. 'This war may have taught many that they must go on living regardless, when their hearts have been torn out. Perhaps it has also taught us that there is no need to go on to the bitter end.'

The door opened.

Silence held while Hettie brought slices of bread and butter that she had forgotten.

'Thank you, Hettie,' Marjorie said pointedly.

A thought struck Arthur Wilson like a bolt of lightning. Joshua Braithwaite had had his wife. Joshua Braithwaite had cuckolded him. That could be the only explanation for this worm turning on him, for her unexpected defiance, for her championing of a sinful suicide.

When they had finished eating, she got up and left the

182

table without a word. He knew what she was up to. She'd be out walking that damned dog of hers. He'd half a mind to do it in. He'd tried once, but Marjorie realised. She saw the empty dish and a couple of grains of bright-blue rat poison. Spooned soft soap into the beast's mouth till it spewed.

It wasn't a normal dog for a female to have, a great beastly Weimaraner with eyes like headlights. She'd stay out as long as she could, till dark, and beyond if there was a moon – keeping away from him.

They retired to bed. Marjorie sat on the stool before her dressing table, brushing her hair, as if it deserved brushing. The only reason they shared a room still was that he knew how dearly she did not want to and how much she would have preferred him to move across the landing and leave her alone.

He snatched the brush from her. She jumped.

He thwacked the brush flat on the crown of her greasy head. 'You think I don't know what all that was about earlier.'

She did that thing he hated, folding her arms about herself, refusing to look at him.

'I don't know what you're talking about, Arthur.'

'Sticking up for Braithwaite in that way.'

'I only said . . .'

'I should have guessed. He's done every other woman who's come within his little circle. It must have been when you were young and worth doing.'

Her mouth opened in surprise, she was about to protest. He brought his fist into her solar plexus with such force that she fell off the stool.

She lay there.

The dog started to bark, threatening him. He insisted it be kept outside, and now he was glad of that or the damn thing might decide to tear him to pieces. It occurred to him he could take it for a walk, throw its ball over a steep fell. Only it wouldn't walk out with him.

That was when the knocking came on the downstairs door. Hettie didn't trouble to stir herself. She'd be fast asleep.

Wilson opened the casement window and leaned out, expecting some news. Perhaps Braithwaite was dead after all. Perhaps Constable Mitchell had a good reason for sending him to the new hospital.

In the moonlight, he could not make out the figure.

'What is it?' he called.

'It's Paul Kellett.'

'What the blazes do thah want at this time of neeght?'

'I can't shout it. Come down. It'll be worth your while.'

That was Kellett all over. He didn't thee and thou any more. If the chamber pot had been full, Wilson might have tipped it on Kellett's head. But his second thought was that perhaps the man did have something to say that would be of interest. After all, he'd been thick as thieves with Braithwaite at one time. And now he worked at the new hospital.

Wilson did not beat his wife again that night. That was a job that required his full attention, and his full attention was now elsewhere.

Kellett had his collar turned up and his cap pulled down, like a man up to no good. Wilson didn't ask the fellow in but kept him in the porch.

'What's this about, Kellett?'

'Summat to your advantage, if you can toss a ball. Mr Braithwaite's in a spot of bother ...'

'Thah can say that again.'

'He wants to make it right, over the loom picker invention, whether he's around or not.'

'Conscience pricking him is it?'

'Pin yer lugs back and you won't be sorry. There's summat he rightfully wants out of his office. I said I'll fetch it for him. Only I don't have a key for't mill, and you

184

do. Give it to me and I'll go in under cover of dark and get what's lawfully his. Not a soul as will be any wiser. There's fifteen quid on account and fifty when he has his wallet by him.'

'And whose word have I got for that?'

'Mine.' Kellett put his hand in his pocket and brought out a five pound note.

'Bugger off. Him and thee made a fortune on them dyes.'

'Then you'll be daft to say no.'

'What is it he wants out of his office? Is he planning on legging it?'

'Less we know the better.' Kellett took another fiver from his pocket. 'It's a small thing I've to fetch.'

Wilson's hands itched to take the money.

'I'll be party to a crime if I let thee have key.'

'Not if I come in and help meself, and fetch it back and no one the wiser.'

'What's his new offer to me on the loom picker? He knows I was diddled.'

'What he give you was fair. I know cos it's what I got when I passed on me idea for a new drainage pipe in't dyehouse. If he comes through this trouble, you can have yer name on't picker and a cut of future sales.'

'And if he doesn't come through?'

Kellett offered his hand. 'He'll keep his word or you can cleave it from my flesh.'

Reluctantly, Wilson took Kellett's hand. 'I'd sooner deal with organ grinder than the monkey.' He nodded at a board on the porch wall. It had hooks and keys and a big old outdoor coat that smelled of dog.

Wilson moved the coat to reveal a key ring with two large keys.

Kellett reached for the key ring.

Wilson grabbed his wrist. 'Not so fast. What if safe's robbed and they chase me over it?'

185

Kellett gave a mirthless chuckle. 'I'm no safe cracker, daft bugger. Braithwaite wants a small thing, summat that's his.'

'Tell us what he's after, or there's no key leavin' this house.'

'He's after the key to his bank safe deposit box. Come with if you don't believe me.'

'I'm not coming with. On your head be it. But why should I give Braithwaite a way out?'

'Because ...' Kellett produced two more crackling fivers. 'Yer key'll be back on this hook before you can say poor old Job.'

'It better be.'

Above them, the casement window snapped shut.

15

Worstedopolis

Something rattled the window pane – a wind-blown twig, or a pebble signal from Sykes? I switched on my flashlight. Two thirty a.m.

My yawn was wide enough to catch a passing tram. If Neville Stoddard had let me look at the board meeting minutes, they would never have assumed this weighty importance for me. As it was, I felt sure there must be some clue to be gleaned about Joshua Braithwaite's state of mind, or of dirty dealings, prior to his disappearance. I drew on a bulky sweater and thick skirt over my silk pyjamas.

I tiptoed down the back stairs, using my flashlight, and left the house by the back door. For a moment I waited, to be sure no lights came on, but I had disturbed no one. Stepping out into the crisp, cold moonlit air shocked me into wakefulness. Almost Easter and the weather still arctic. In the distance, the mill loomed vast and forbidding, a massive dark shape on the skyline, its chimney pointing an accusing finger at the starry sky.

Sykes was in heavy shadow by the mill gates, his bicycle somewhere out of sight.

'You don't have to do this,' he whispered as I came closer. 'I'll go in and look at the minute books. From 1914 you said?'

I refused his offer. Having met the family, I felt sure I'd be able to pick up on any nuances that might provide hints – though of what I couldn't say.

Sykes produced a bunch of keys. He tried one in the lock of the wicket that was set within the larger gate. It did not work. He tried a second, a third, a fourth. The lock yielded.

We stepped through the wicket gate into the yard. The wind blew a strand of wool across my cheek. Sykes locked the gate behind us.

To our left stood a gatehouse, for the timekeeper who marked the cards of latecomers. To the right was the now devastated dyehouse. In the moonlight, the half-demolished wall, pile of bricks and slanted lintel took on a new horror. I stared at the ruins, the spot where I had photographed Kellett and his fellow workers and from where he must have run from the building moments before the roof caved in, screaming, running for his life, running to his death in the canal.

The door to the mill proved more difficult. None of Sykes' keys fitted the lock. He took something from his pocket that resembled a curved knitting needle and inserted it into the keyhole. After a few deft movements, the lock clicked open.

'Where will you be, Mr Sykes? You'll need to lock the door after me.'

'I'm coming with you.'

'No! Wait outside.'

He didn't budge. 'Kellett shouldn't have been in the dyehouse alone and you shouldn't be here on your own. Everyone needs back-up.'

He looked at his boots, not at me, and made no move to leave. It was no time to argue.

The place felt strange after my last visit when it practically rattled and hummed with a symphony of slams, whistles, crashes and roars. We wore soft shoes; thick walls kept out the wind. Only our own breathing disturbed the silence.

Once again, I passed the offices that had been such a hub

of activity during the day. Purchasing, Sales, Wages.

'I think it's this one – the secretary's office where I saw the minute books on the shelf.'

As we entered the airless office that reeked of cigarette smoke and tedious routine, I felt annoyed with Stoddard that his ridiculous secrecy had led to this middle of the night cloak and dagger stuff.

The feeling must have showed.

'It could be a daft waste of time, that's true, but you never can tell. Always best to follow your instincts.' Sykes reached to the shelf for the large bound volume, whose spine announced Company Minutes. He placed it on the desk. Then he pulled down an accounts book. I opened the minute book at August, 1916, intending to work backwards. Neatly typed pages have a way of looking entirely innocuous. If there was some skeleton in a cupboard, there would hardly be a diagram to tell me which cupboard. But I'd come this far.

Nothing seemed more certain than that reading these minutes would send me back to the land of nod. Intricate titbits of information gave me an insight into the difficult business of running a mill. But something significant did begin to emerge.

What seemed to me surprising was that prior to the spring of 1916 Braithwaite dominated every discussion. Yet months before his son's death, he had begun to abnegate responsibility.

On topics related to the renewal of fire insurance, the introduction of a new machine, replacing a loom, Braithwaite made no comments. Discussions, while Edmund was still able to attend, took place entirely between Stoddard, Evelyn, Tabitha and Edmund.

'Mr Braithwaite had no comment' became a frequent entry.

Why?

In previous meetings, 1914, 1915, he had led discus-

189

sions at every turn. No matter was too small for his personal attention. He had opinions about everything. Early in 1914, before Edmund and Tabitha were brought onto the board, he berated Stoddard for refusing to have electricity in the mill house when it had been installed in the mill. Stoddard, endearingly I thought, said he preferred gas light – it was gentler, and really that was not a matter for discussion in the board meetings as far as he was concerned.

One other topic caught my eye. In early 1916, it was proposed by Mr Stoddard to wind down activity at the dyehouse, due to shortage of labour. He proposed that piece dyeing should be contracted out.

I looked up from the minutes. 'Mr Sykes, you know you said about Kellett being out on the road, on his profiteering rounds with the German dyes?'

'Yes.'

'Take a look at this.'

Sykes read the paragraph I pointed out to him. 'Interesting.'

'Yes. I wonder at what point Kellett came back into the dyehouse. We know he went to work at the hospital for a short time. I wonder was it something of a comedown for him, to be back in the dyehouse doing dirty manual work, however skilled.'

'And well paid?' Sykes queried. 'Better than being an orderly I should think. Sounds as if his coming back got the mill out of a hole.'

'Anything interesting in the accounts?'

'Only by omission.' Sykes closed the accounts ledger. 'Whatever Braithwaite was earning from the sales of the von Hofmann dyes, it was going in his back pocket or under his mattress. It didn't come into the firm.'

'So why was he squirrelling away his ill-gotten gains? What was it for?'

Sykes replaced the accounts ledger on the shelf. 'People

who are used to raking in money don't need a why or a what for. They see the accumulation of wealth as part of God's plan.'

We both heard the sound at the same moment.

Footsteps echoing through the building. Footsteps on the stairs.

I recognised the step as it got nearer, a man walking steadily, as if he had a long way to go and must pace himself.

'Stoddard,' I whispered.

'What the blue blazes is he doing here at this time?'

Quickly I returned the minute book to the shelf.

Tabitha told me her Uncle Neville started work early. I checked my wristwatch. He started at four o'clock in the morning?

He had reached the corridor.

'Let me face him, Mr Sykes. I don't want him to know we're working together.'

Sykes thought for a moment, then nodded.

I stepped into the corridor. 'Good morning, Mr Stoddard. I thought if I got here early enough, you may agree to let me read those company minutes.'

He stopped. 'You! How did you get in?'

'I learned all sorts during my brief time volunteering with the Women's Police Service before I joined the VAD.'

Lie. I wished I did know how to pick a lock. Must get Sykes to teach me.

Stoddard paused. Don't go in there, I willed him. If he did, I felt sure Sykes would be behind the door and it would be up to me to keep Stoddard's attention while he flitted along the corridor.

Stoddard stood rooted to the spot, bursting with quiet fury. 'How long have you been in here?'

'Long enough.'

'Long enough to find what you wanted?'

191

'I could hardly do that when I didn't know what I was looking for.'

He flung open the door. The office, illuminated by the light from the corridor, looked undisturbed.

'Please don't worry about confidentiality, Mr Stoddard. I've abandoned my plans to set up a rival textile establishment a little further along the canal.'

His face was like thunder, but at least I had turned his attention from the office. For a moment Stoddard simply stared at me. I could sense Sykes, behind the door, holding his breath.

'What the blazes . . . What do you expect to find, woman? A minute saying, "Resolved by Neville Stoddard to oust and *disappear* Joshua Braithwaite so that he can take over the mill, step into Joshua's shoes . . ." and what?'

Marry his wife, I wondered.

'You said it, not I.'

'That's preposterous. Get out. Get out of my mill before I do something I regret.'

'Very well.' I turned and walked silently back along the corridor, holding myself erect and defiant but inwardly shaking. To my relief and consternation, Stoddard marched behind me, his boots drumming on the stone floor. At least Sykes would be able to find a hiding place.

I expected Stoddard to walk me to the door. He bounded beside me across the yard.

At the gate he looked round.

'Which way did you come?'

'The short cut across the fields.'

'On foot?'

'Yes.'

'Then we'll go back that way.'

'There's no need.'

'Oh I think there is.'

He tried to take my arm. I shook him off.

He fell into step with me as we turned to the path. His

192

breath made small clouds in the cold air.

Where the path narrowed, I led, he walked behind me.

The moon cast an eerie glow over the landscape, the dark shape of hedges and trees pinning us fast into time, time that seemed to stop. A white cloud floated across the moon.

The silence was unbearable, but neither of us would break it.

As we neared the house, I turned towards the back door.

'Servants' entrance?' he said mockingly. 'You must at least give me a demonstration of your lock-picking skills.'

'No need. I left the back door unlocked.'

'Then the front?'

'There's a bolt on the inside of the front door.'

I couldn't remember whether there was or not.

At the back door, he blocked my way.

'I'll wish you goodnight, Mrs Shackleton, or rather good morning.'

'Goodnight.'

'What? No apology for trespassing?'

'I was following my enquiries. I'm sorry for the way I did it but you left me no choice.'

'I'm disappointed. I thought you were intelligent, objective, principled. Really you're just silly, a silly girl.'

'A silly girl?' I heard my voice rise. Mistake. He was trying to bait me, and succeeded. 'Silly to want to find the truth for Tabitha? Silly because I'm logical, and follow my instincts?'

'Being logical is rather a male prerogative. And instincts are for animals, Mrs Shackleton. Instincts can get you into a lot of trouble. For instance, if I'd followed my instinct in the mill back there, I'd have knocked you flat for what you did. And if I followed my instincts now, you'd have a lot to raise your voice about. But I've made a fool of myself this week already. I'm not about to do it a second time.'

193

He stepped aside.

I pushed open the door.

'Go on!' he called. 'Let me see you safely inside.'

I had left my flashlight in the mill. When I closed the kitchen door behind me, and turned the key in the lock, it was utterly dark. The tears poured down my cheeks, tears of humiliation, tears of rage.

How dare he call me a silly girl, as if I hadn't a hope of success, as if there would be nothing else for me to do with my life than blunder about making a fool of myself.

Worse than that, I felt hurt and disappointed. I groped my way towards the back stairs, touching the wall as there was no banister. Something else struck me in the darkness with an unwelcome force. Stoddard and I had liked each other when we first met. He was kind, and intrigued by me, and I was impressed by him. Now, everything was shattered, and for what? I had found out that Joshua Braithwaite lost interest in his business. So what was new about that? I could have guessed as much. I flung myself onto the bed and stared through the drawn-back curtains at the moon.

Braithwaite had mentally moved away from involvement in the business, though he still attended the meetings. And he had certainly not lost his interest in making money. So what else was he thinking about during that period when he sent Kellett 'on the road' selling the illicit dyes? Kellett may have known, but he was dead. Mrs Kellett – might she hold a clue?

I thought back to how angry Evelyn was with her husband. What was it she had said, that she was sure there had been other women, but none that he cared enough about?

Perhaps that's where she was wrong, and Braithwaite had fallen in love. I preferred that idea to imagining him at the bottom of a mineshaft.

*

194

After just two and a half hours' sleep, I met with Sykes to consider our next move. We were both somewhat subdued as we sat in the Jowett on a side street in Bingley. This had been our agreed rendezvous point, in case anything went wrong at the mill, but it proved a bad choice. Children on their way to school made a whooping beeline for the car. Women suddenly found a reason to come into the street, a rug to beat, a dog to call.

Sykes was berating himself for not staying outside the mill, on look-out.

'What would you have done if you'd stayed outside?' Reluctantly, I set off driving to find a less exposed spot, slowing down beyond the railway station to avoid an argument with a muck cart. 'Those mill walls are too thick for warning whistles or owl hoots to penetrate. We were just unlucky that Stoddard turned up at four o'clock in the morning.'

'The man either has a guilty conscience or insomnia. But you carried it off like a trouper.'

'Trouper? I felt an almighty fool.'

'At least he escorted you home.' Sykes smiled. 'I think he's secretly taken a shine to you and your derring-do.'

I groaned. 'And was it worth it? All we did was confirm what we already know – that Braithwaite was detaching himself, from his business, from the family. But why? And for whom or what?'

The road wound us out of town. I pulled up by a stretch of land that could not decide between calling itself a meadow or a hill. A squirrel scampered up the tree beside us and leaped to a neighbouring branch.

'There was one other item in the accounts,' Sykes said. 'A payment of twenty-five guineas to Arthur Wilson for his drawings and sample of a loom picker.'

'Yes. That was mentioned in the minutes, too.'

'Didn't you say Wilson's wife brought up the loom picker as a reason why Wilson might be a killer?'

'She was far gone in her cups at the time.'

'From what I gathered at the Wool Exchange, Wilson might have had good cause to hold a grudge, thinking himself under-rewarded. And he was the assistant scoutmaster. That gives us two scoutmasters who might have had a reason for getting Braithwaite out of cold water into hot.'

'But Wilson works for Braithwaites. Would he risk his job, and Braithwaite's goodwill, by crying suicide?'

'He'd say "Wasn't me, guv. Was the other fellow".'

From overhead branches came the steady drip drip of rain onto the top of the car.

'Will you see what you can glean from Wilson? He doesn't like women.'

'I could try. Where does he drink?'

'He doesn't.'

Sykes made that little clucking sound out of the corner of his mouth, indicating extreme difficulty. 'It's never easy talking to teetotallers. You can't just drop in at the local.'

'He's a stalwart of the chapel. Perhaps it's time for your conversion.'

'Dunno about that. Is he likely to play the good Samaritan if I topple off my bike in front of him?'

I smiled at the image. Sykes would do it too, in the line of duty. 'If you come a cropper on your bike, he might put it down to the demon drink. All right. I'll have another go, perhaps I'll pay a social call on the Wilsons and see whether I can't draw him out. You might have another word with the dyeworkers, since you've chummed up with them.'

I didn't know how I would fit in my interviews in the short time available before I had to leave the Braithwaites, go home, and pack a trunk – ready to travel to London with my mother for Aunt Berta's party. Investigation or not, my life wouldn't be worth living if I absented myself from that most important of annual engagements.

*

Dr Alex Fraser was a short man with a kindly lived-in face. His wavy dark hair was parted in the centre and reached almost to the collar of his white coat. We discovered that he and Gerald once met at a medical conference, and he was sorry to hear that Gerald had not survived the war. However, this did not make him inclined to accede to my request for information.

The coroner had ordered a post mortem on Kellett. Dr Fraser, as the local pathologist, had completed that post mortem.

He tapped his pencil on the desk and said, 'I'm sorry, Mrs Shackleton. I pass on my findings to the coroner. What he does then is up to him.'

There was blunt Scottish stubbornness in his manner, a reluctance to break the rules. If I did not tread carefully, he would suddenly find an immediate pressing engagement and I would be out on my ear. I tried for fellow-feeling and sympathy.

'I'm acting for the widow. It was to me she confided her fears about poisoning after she described her husband's last moments. Having been married to a doctor, I know you have to follow procedures, but she hasn't slept since his death. If I could have some information . . .'

He shook his head. 'The widow can attend the inquest.'

'That won't be before Easter. In her state of health, I fear for her if I can't put her mind at rest.'

There was a slight relaxing around his eyes. 'You're not related to the Kelletts are you?'

That's what I should have claimed, but I did not look or sound like the daughter of a dyeworker.

Keep pushing.

I summoned my most tragic look. 'I have a letter of authorisation from Mrs Kellett, saying that I am acting on her behalf.'

'May I see it?'

'Of course.' I looked in my bag. I put my hands in my pockets, and tutted. 'It's in the car.'

He waited.

Damn him.

'I'll get it.'

I walked along the corridor and turned towards the way out, knowing I had no writing paper with me. A door opened and a nurse emerged. The room beyond her exhaled the whiff of stale tobacco and stewed tea. I went in. A young nurse sat turning the pages of a magazine.

Mustering my best hospital manner, I asked her for a pen and paper. 'I need to write a note for matron.'

The nurse obligingly found me pen and paper. In for a penny. Mrs Kellett, in her clear round hand, asked that Mrs Kate Shackleton be allowed to view the body, and to know the cause of death, was it poison?

I shivered as Dr Fraser and I entered the mortuary, passing tables where bodies lay covered with white sheets.

He shot me a quizzical look. 'You understand this is in confidence, and for the widow's information only?'

'Of course.'

'So was it you raised the alert over the stomach contents?'

'Mrs Kellett had suspicions. Mr Kellett was good at his job. She couldn't credit that lapse of attention. She also smelled something unfamiliar on his breath. His last breath, poor man.'

'And the widow told you, and you told the police.'

'Yes.'

We reached the farthest table. Fraser hesitated, his hand on the sheet.

'Dr Fraser, I was in the VAD for four years.'

'Yes. I guessed you were. Funny how one can always tell.'

He lifted the sheet as far as Kellett's stomach. A long scar marked where the scalpel had cut. Large, untidy stitches put him together again.

I looked at the body that had been Paul Kellett. His dark hair was matted, his eyes mercifully closed. It did not seem like him at all, this sculpted shape, the colour of dark moss. In my photograph, he had held pride of place among the dyeworkers, important and full of life.

'Was he taking anything for toothache do you know?' Fraser asked.

The question seemed ludicrous. This poor husk of a man was so far beyond a mere toothache.

'I don't know. Why do you ask?'

'With a body in this state, I may not have done an analysis of stomach contents, except to try and establish the time of death, digested food and so on.'

He drew the sheet to Kellett's chin, paused for a moment then covered his head, almost as if it would prevent the dead man hearing his pronouncement. 'He'd eaten a cheese and pickle sandwich and a pork pie, drunk beer – difficult to say how much. I also found a quantity of morphia, and of *Gelseminum sempervirens*.'

There was a neat darn in the sheet at the level of Kellett's chin. I had the absurd feeling that I ought to make some gesture, touch his arm, or say something. Sorry you never got to Bradford-on-Sea.

We walked back across the tiled floor. I waited until the mortuary doors swung closed behind us before asking, 'What is *Gelseminum sempervirens*? Why might he have taken that, and morphia?'

'Come back to my office and I'll explain.'

We returned to the windowless room. He pulled out a chair for me. 'Haven't written my report for the coroner yet, so when you speak to the widow, tell her that the smell on his breath may have been . . . Tell her that her suspicions will be taken note of. I expect she'll know what he was taking. Why I asked you if he'd had toothache – some people take *gel sem* as a pain relief for neuralgia or toothache.'

'What is it?'

199

'Tincture of *Gelseminum sempervirens* – it's the dried root and rhizome of yellow jasmine. The effects resemble those of nicotine, but with a stronger depression of the nervous system. Usually a patient would take the dose incrementally. I would prescribe forty minims. I'd say there was about two hundred minims in Mr Kellett's gut. He's not a giant of a man. People's tolerance to drugs is variable, but combining *gel sem* with morphia wasn't the smartest thing he ever did.'

'And what would be the effects – of the *gel sem*?'

'Giddiness, difficult eye accommodation, headaches, diarrhoea, and possibly severe depression. Now if you combine that with morphia . . .' He shook his head. 'He'd probably dropped off to sleep. The miracle is he came to at all.'

I took the photograph of him and his fellow dyeworkers from my brief case. 'There he is – just days ago. Full of life. Why would he have taken morphia?'

He picked up the photograph and looked at it closely. 'My guess is that he had a good deal of pain from the amputation.'

'Poor Kellett.'

'Foolish Kellett, if he overdosed himself.'

'Is that likely?'

He slid the photograph back to me. 'Some people can bear pain more easily than others. It can be intermittent too. That injury to his left arm, and his claw of a hand, there's no knowing how much gyp that gave him. It could be that he dosed himself on morphia, when it gave him trouble. A lot of old soldiers do. Now if on top of that he had jaw ache and someone said "try this", and gave him a twist of *gel sem*, he might well have taken it. But that will be for the coroner and an inquest to decide. Mine's the easy part of analysis and report. The drugs aren't the cause of death. That was the scalding from the exploding dye in the tank, the shock of cold water afterwards and heart failure.

It's a blessed relief for him he died. There wouldn't have been much anyone could have done for him in that state.'

My mouth felt dry. For a moment we were silent.

'Regarding the morphia, Dr Fraser. Do you believe he may have been an addict?'

'It's possible. I can't see it from his eyes in the photograph, but it's possible.'

'Would that be an expensive habit?'

He nodded. 'Could be.'

'So Mrs Kellett could be right. Someone may have laced his food or drink, knowing what effect it would have, and hoping the death would be passed off as a tragic accident.'

'That's not for me to say. I only report my findings. It's possible it was self-administered. Though if the wifey's right, she might have to answer awkward questions as to who made him the cheese and pickle sandwich and who drew the beer for him.'

I put the photograph back in my bag.

He gave me a curious glance. 'How do you come to know Mrs Kellett?'

'It's a long story.'

'I've time for a short break, if you'd like to tell it.'

I took a seat in the canteen while Dr Fraser went up to the counter.

He came back with a tray. 'This was the only cake they had I'm afraid.'

'It's fine. I like seedcake. Tell me, would a person know if he had been slipped a drug?'

'Taste. Though that could be disguised in food. Of course if he lies there unable to move and at the mercy of whoever administered it, he might begin to guess.'

'The symptoms you mentioned, headache, not focusing and so on, they could easily be mistaken for something else?'

Fraser nodded. 'Inebriation, concussion ... What do you have in mind?'

He broke off a piece of seedcake and popped it in his mouth.

'I'm not sure.'

'You're not just a friend of the family are you?'

'Not only that, no.'

'What?'

'I'm a private investigator.'

That was the first time I had said the words aloud. It felt good. But for how long would it feel good if I couldn't come up with more answers than questions?

16

Beating-up

Shedding, picking, beating-up. — three primary motions in weaving.

Saturday. Time for me to depart. I had to go home, pack my finery and be ready to travel with my mother to London. Sykes had tried to reassure me, saying I would see matters with a fresh eye on my return. I was not convinced.

Long before the Braithwaite household stirred, I drew the Indian shawl around my shoulders and sat in the window seat looking out over the fells. The more I found out, the less I knew about what might have happened to Joshua Braithwaite. The pieces of the jigsaw just did not fit. What was I missing?

Yesterday evening, I had intended to speak to Lizzie Kellett, but she had more visitors offering their condolences. This morning might be the best time to see her, before any more neighbours called to pay their respects. I would run the risk of waking her, but would take that chance.

Soon enough police officers from HQ would be calling on her with questions about the morphia and *Gelseminum sempervirens*. I preferred to get there first, before they frightened her out of her wits.

Lizzie's curtains were still drawn, but that didn't signify she slept. She would keep her curtains closed until after her husband's burial. I tapped on the door.

The cat came scurrying from further down the beck, carrying something in its mouth that wriggled. It waited for the door to open. After a moment, the cat gave up and stalked off in disgust. I tapped again, and then pushed the door gently. It opened just a little. Something was stopping it.

That 'something' was Lizzie Kellett.

She lay at the bottom of the steep stone stairs, her legs on the first step, as if she had tripped. She rested on her front, her head turned sideways, left cheek resting against the flagged floor. Because of her position, the right side of her face was pushed into a contorted leer. All colour had gone from her. Her face had the alabaster hue of a figure on a church tomb. Pale-blue veins mapped her hands and wrists. Her clenched left fist made a claw. The fingers of her right hand splayed flat. She looked more human than any of us could ever be, in that way that an unformed fledgling fallen from its nest is more a bird than some faraway eagle.

The long black skirt was rucked up above her knees, revealing wrinkled brown lisle stockings.

Slowly, I closed the door and retraced my steps along the path.

Constable Mitchell looked his age that morning. He was hastily buttoning himself into his jacket after hearing my news. 'Are you sure she's dead?'

'Quite sure, otherwise I would have pushed the door further open and gone in to see whether I could revive her. You'll see for yourself.'

'I'll be there straight away. There is something you could do for me, Mrs Shackleton.'

'Anything at all.'

'Could you bear to take her photograph?'

'Yes of course.'

'Then would you bring your camera to the cottage?'

'I'll go for it straight away and meet you there.'

'Better take a look for myself before I contact HQ. Then if I can tell them we have photographic evidence, they might let me move her. Course there won't be a difficulty if it's a straightforward trip down the stairs.'

I could sense he hoped it would be 'a straightforward trip down the stairs.' A suspicion stirring deep inside me said otherwise.

'Poor soul, eh?' Constable Mitchell sighed. 'She deserved a better death.' To give us more room, he propped open the inner door to the downstairs room with the spindly chair I had sat on to have my fortune told.

'*Did* she trip?' I asked. Her feet looked awkward, turning away in embarrassment, as if they wished to be somewhere else.

'Hard to say. Both shoes are cross-laced and tied in a double bow. That's a fair old bump on the back of her head.'

'These stone steps have a lethal edge to them.' I was putting the case for the accident, because I could hardly bear to think that here was another murder.

Constable Mitchell bent down and looked closely at the gash on Lizzie's head. 'CID were going to come over and question her regarding morphia and some other substance found in her husband's guts. She could have taken fright and flung herself down't stairs.'

So he had heard about the post mortem results on Kellett.

I could have acted surprised, but this seemed no time for games. 'Lizzie wouldn't have known they were coming.'

He looked up quickly. 'You knew though?'

'Yes, but I haven't breathed a word.'

It would be awkward to take a clear photograph of Lizzie's body, in such a confined space in a house with little light. 'If we pull back the curtains, there'll be a light source, and open this internal door as wide as possible.'

205

Perhaps the cat thought I could bring her back to life. It appeared on the window sill, minus its prey, looking on with interest.

'Could the cat have tripped her?' Constable Mitchell wanted it to be an accident as much as I did.

'The cat was outside when I arrived.'

The Reflex was already loaded with film. I would fix it on the tripod as I did not trust my hands to keep from shaking. As I set up to take the photograph, I remembered her standing by the doorway, just days ago, proudly holding the small sample of crêpe-de-chine.

'I have a magnesium flash in that bag. We can try that for one of the photographs but I'll see what I can do with the available light first.' I squeezed myself and the tripod into position.

'Can you get that?' he asked. 'The gash on the back of her head.'

I nodded.

He perched on his haunches and took a close look. 'The more I look at this injury, the less it appears accidental.'

I looked into the viewfinder.

'You mean that it may have been caused by a blunt instrument.'

I triggered the shutter, wound on the film, and shifted the tripod. 'Did you look round, Mr Mitchell? Has anything been tampered with or taken?'

'Not that I could see.'

I took two more photographs, then prepared the magnesium flash and gave it to him to hold.

The flash lit the scene. I prayed I had the correct exposure. 'I'll develop this right away.'

'Don't you need a darkroom?'

'I have everything I need with me. I'll use the cellar.'

'There's a couple of footprints I'd like you to photograph. If it rains, we'll lose them.'

I followed him outside.

'It's a size nine boot,' Mr Mitchell said.

The light was good and I felt confident that I would get a clear image.

'Can I do anything to help you with the developing of the photographs?'

'I just need some clean water. There's no tap in the house.'

'Back in a jiffy.'

With a shudder, I stepped over Mrs Kellett's body and back into her downstairs room. The hearth looked so cold and sad, grey ash that she would never shovel up and tip outside. Don't start to shake, I told myself. Take deep breaths. The black cat sat on the windowsill looking in.

I lit my way to her cellar with a candle, taking the camera and my canvas bag. Fortunately I have a foldable fabric lamp which can be used with a candle.

Constable Mitchell called to me from the top of the cellar steps. 'Can I come down?'

'Yes.'

We stood by the light of the candles. He watched as I prepared my dishes and set out the printing frame.

'Where would you like the jug of water?'

'Just here on the slab, please . . . and that bucket?'

'Here?'

'Yes. Thank you.'

Candlelight made an eerie glow and cast our tall shadows against the wall.

He spoke softly. 'I don't like to ask this, but do you feel brave enough to hold the fort for a short time? I need to go back to the house, to telephone headquarters.'

'I'll be all right. I have everything I need now.'

'I'm going to lock you in, Mrs Shackleton. There might be another multitude of weavers tapping to pay condolences. I'll also see who I can get to ward off nosy parkers until we've had time to examine the scene.'

Here was my opportunity to bring Sykes into the heart of the investigation. 'Don't take this amiss, Mr Mitchell, but I've someone working with me – recommended by my father, ex-force. His name's Jim Sykes. He's staying at the Ramshead Arms in Bingley. He'd be a great help until your chaps arrive.'

'Maybe,' he said thoughtfully. 'Saturday morning, and I don't know how quickly they'll get over here.'

The memory of my fortune telling visit tormented me. 'I came here to talk to Mrs Kellett about Joshua Braithwaite. Do you suppose there's any connection between my investigation and the deaths of Paul and Lizzie?'

He hesitated. 'I can't see it myself.'

I couldn't see it either, but that didn't mean there was no connection. Had Lizzie told someone about my questions? Someone who was afraid the Kelletts might be ready to spill some bloody beans? I felt a queasy lurch in my guts. It occurred to me that Lizzie had known much more than she was willing to say. Yet whatever secrets Paul and Lizzie kept had died with them.

'Don't imagine this had anything to do with Joshua Braithwaite, Mrs Shackleton. It may be that we're both wrong, and she tripped. It happens.'

The gash on Lizzie's skull did not somehow seem compatible with a fall down the stairs.

'When I've developed the photographs, do you mind if I look round, see whether I spot anything different between now and my previous visits?'

'As long as I look with you, then I know you're not disturbing evidence. We'll do it when I come back.'

I heard the key turn in the lock as Constable Mitchell left the house. For Lizzie's sake, I must make these prints perfect – then perhaps she could be moved. It was appalling that she lay dead, but at least we must try and give her some dignity.

For a long time I worked in silence. As I became absorbed in the work, my mind went into that peaceful blank state where there is no past, no future, no death, only this moment.

When Constable Mitchell returned, we went back upstairs with the fruits of my labour and spread the photographs on the table where Lizzie had set out her tarot cards. The prints were sharp and clear. Lizzie had what hairdressers call a double crown, and the gash had marred her lower crown.

'You've done a good job,' he said. 'It shows everything needed. And I've made a sketch of her position.'

I nodded. It was as if neither of us sufficiently believed in the power of a photograph to tell such a horrible truth, even when it was before our eyes.

'My sergeant's on the way from Keighley, and there'll be an inspector following on. Your man Sykes is coming too.'

'Thank you. Are you allowed to move her?'

'Not on my say so. It's being treated as a sudden unexplained death. We need the coroner's permission before the body can be moved, and the coroner will decide whether there's to be a post mortem. The inspector might regard it as an accident and if the coroner agrees, then I'll be able to take her upstairs to her bed and send for Mrs Broughton from the village to lay her out.'

'I hate to see her just lying there.'

'I know. They'll be as quick as they can. There's nothing more you can do now.'

'Except take a look around?'

'Yes.'

'Mrs Kellett told my fortune on the day I arrived. There was a postal order stub on the mantelpiece. She put it in the Rington's tea jar with the money I gave her.'

He lifted the lid carefully.

'No postal order stub. Was it completed with the name of a payee, or post office?'

'There was something written across, you know the way you do when it's just for yourself? I couldn't make out the name. It was for ten shillings.'

He raised his eyebrows. That was a lot of money for a weaver to be parting with.

Together we looked at the contents of a floral pattern biscuit tin from the cupboard. It contained her birth and marriage certificates and the birth certificate of her husband. Her maiden name was Dale. She paid several penny insurance policies. One book was marked for her burial. Other life policies named her husband, Paul Kellett, Arthur Dale who I guessed must be her brother, and Amy Dale. The 'Dale' on Amy's name was crossed out and 'Crosby' inserted. None were amounts that would be worth her life.

The sewing basket by the fender held a pair of men's grey wool socks, one with the darning mushroom tucked in, and a needle stuck through a partly finished darn. It crossed my mind to finish darning the grey sock in her work basket — just to do something — except that I never learned to darn.

Behind me, Constable Mitchell opened the kitchen drawer.

At the bottom of the sewing basket was a folded piece of paper, used as a holder for a needle, and a length of dark sewing thread. I took out the needle and unfolded the paper. This, too, was a postal order stub — again for ten shillings. On the line payee was the letter H.

I handed it to Constable Mitchell. 'She was sending money to someone.'

He took the stub and placed it on the table. 'Perhaps her sister or brother. She and Paul were fortunate, with two wages coming in.'

Constable Mitchell turned back to the drawer. 'Your business card's here.'

'Yes. I gave it to her. I thought she might think of something else to tell me about Joshua Braithwaite.'

210

The table drawer appeared undisturbed and yet the tiny book she had called her address book and into which she slipped my card was gone.

'There was an address book.'

'Are you sure?'

'A black cover, half the size of a postcard.'

Constable Mitchell made a note.

'Anything else?'

I shook my head.

'Let's take a look upstairs.'

'I didn't go upstairs.'

'No, but you seem to have a good eye. We won't touch anything.'

There was a tap on the door. 'That was quick!' Mitchell said, expecting his sergeant. But it was Sykes. Being nearer, he had arrived first.

We stepped outside onto the garden path to speak to him. I introduced Sykes to Mitchell.

'What can I do to help?' Sykes asked.

'Keep people away until my sergeant arrives.'

'Will do. Mind if I take a glance round? I have worked with CID, I know the rules.'

Mitchell nodded. 'But anything you spot, tell me and I found it, all right? I don't want to complicate my life with HQ.'

'Understood.'

Following Mitchell back into the cottage, I stepped over Lizzie's body and upstairs. Bedroom drawers contained her few items of clothing, neatly folded, smelling powerfully of mothballs. Her bed was made, corners tightly tucked, nightgown folded and placed under the pillow. A cupboard held a hoard of Sunlight soap bars, half a dozen candles, a new white sheet, snowy pressed nightgown and matching lacy cap.

If there had been anything in that room to incriminate a murderer, it was there no longer. A secret, if one she

211

kept, would go with her to the grave.

The grave – at the thought of that, I looked again at the contents of the hoard cupboard. She had placed her own laying-out stuff there, the sheet, the snowy white nightgown and pressed cap.

Looking at the smoothly ironed gown gave me a helpless feeling, and that strong sense that if I had not stirred up the past she may still be alive.

Mitchell was watching Sykes through the window.

I looked under the bed. The enamel guzzunder was mercifully empty. 'Look at this, Mr Mitchell.'

The floorboards sported a light covering of dust and fluff. I caught a sneeze just before it happened. One rectangular patch looked cleaner than the rest. Something had been dragged from under the bed, disturbing the fluff. Mitchell got down on all fours to look. When he stood up he scratched his head. 'Looks as if there was a box there.' He walked about the room again, looking for something that would answer the shape and size of the mark under the bed. 'Kellett had money. He was close about it, but everyone knew he raked in a packet during the war. Mystery was that he didn't throw it about, and kept on working all the hours God sent. Some said he was after buying a house by the sea.'

'Would he have kept his money under the bed?'

'Oh aye, he'd have done that all right. Cellar floods you see, or he might have stashed it down there somewhere.'

'If robbery was the motive, why not just break in while the two of them were at work?'

Mitchell thought for a moment, shaking his head as if the motion would set the pendulum of his brain swinging. 'You were on your way home today I believe?'

He wanted me and my smart observations off the premises before his sergeant arrived. 'Yes. I'm meant to be packing to go London but . . .'

'There won't be anything more for you to do here until

212

we've had the post mortem on Lizzie. You look to me as if a break wouldn't do you any harm.'

There was a tap on the downstairs door. Mitchell went down. It had been a gentle rap, not at all like a copper's. The voice was Sykes'.

'Something you should take a look at, Constable Mitchell.'

I perched on Lizzie's bed for a moment. She hadn't slept here last night. That's when she must have fallen – or been pushed. Sometime late yesterday after her neighbours had departed.

I watched from the bedroom window as Sykes led Mitchell down the bank, to the reeds by the humpback bridge. He was pointing something out. Some men carry cigarettes, matches and a penknife. Sykes produced an evidence bag from his inside pocket. Mitchell leaned down carefully to pick up a cricket bat. Sykes intercepted him and put the bag over the bat, lifting it carefully, handing it to Mitchell without looking at him. Tactfully, Sykes then walked away as a small crowd began to gather on the bridge. Time for me to leave.

I walked up the bank, carrying my camera bag, reaching the bridge as a car approached from the main street. The burly moustachioed sergeant sat at the wheel. His inspector climbed out of the car first. Spotting me with the camera bag, he gave me a grumpy acknowledgement for taking the photographs, and clearly wanted me off the scene as quickly as possible. The sergeant followed, looking so much the part that he could have been cast in a Keystone Cops film as the one who knots his brow and chases the villain. Behind us, Mitchell tramped about the bank – probably looking for a box of treasure in case it had been too heavy for the thief to carry.

From the small crowd on the bridge, Hector emerged.

'You must let me help you with your camera stuff!'

If I saw a photograph of Hector as a baby, I'm sure he

would have changed not a jot. He has a round, jowly face with sparse hair. His pale-blue eyes dart about as if looking for his mother.

He insisted on helping me onto his mount.

Being in the saddle allowed me to see the shiny patch on his crown when he adjusted his cap. 'You're losing your hair, Hector!'

'Yes. Terrible isn't it? I'll be bald by the time I'm thirty.'

'That should age you up a bit.'

He laughed, knowing immediately of Tabitha's worries about the difference between their ages. Straight away he said, 'It's abominable to laugh, after what's just happened. You must think we're a desperately unlucky village. First Kellett dying in that appalling way, and now Lizzie. What happened?'

'It looks like a fall down the stairs. But it's possible that both Paul and Lizzie's deaths weren't accidental. There may be a connection with Mr Braithwaite's disappearance.'

Hector stopped in the middle of the field and reached for the bridle. The horse came to a standstill. He produced a small stone bottle from his saddle bag, took out the cork, wiped the mouth on his sleeve and offered it to me. 'It's ginger beer.'

My first impressions of Hector had been of an affable, hearty young man. Now, watching him play for time, it occurred to me that he was not quite all he should be in the brains department. He was still a child who would not look out of place in his old boy scout uniform. I refused the ginger beer. He put the flagon to his lips and drank.

'Hector, I've had to look at two bodies this week. All I want from you is some information. You avoid talking to me about your time in the boy scouts . . .'

'Because . . .'

'Because you were one of the boys who found Mr Braithwaite, weren't you?'

214

I had struck home. His hand trembled slightly as he put the ginger beer bottle back in the saddle bag. 'Well, what if I was? It doesn't mean . . .'

'No more excuses, Hector. If you won't talk to me, then speak to the CID inspector. Let him decide whether there's a connection between then and now.' I yanked on the reins and turned to go back the way we had come.

It was a long moment before Hector called, 'I say, hold the horse, Kate! Don't go all official on me.' He hurried to my side.

'I'm right aren't I?' I said, sounding like a stern school-teacher, not turning back yet in case he thought I would relent.

'All right, all right. I'll tell you. Yes, I was one of the boys who found him. And I was the oldest.' He waited until I had turned the horse and we were once again cross-ing the field towards the Braithwaites' house. 'Soon as I sent young Ashworth to fetch the scoutmaster I knew I'd done the wrong thing.'

'Why do you say that?'

'Because Mr Braithwaite seemed dazed. He just said to me, "Bugger off. Leave me be." If I had buggered off and let him be, he might have come round, he would have got up, and got home eventually. Instead, it became this . . . It just got out of control. The minute I saw Mr Wardle's eyes — Scoutmaster Wardle, the way he looked, a kind of triumph. And Mr Braithwaite groaned, and he didn't have the strength, but he tried to kick out.'

'I don't see what else you could have done.'

'There was something not quite right, all us lads felt it. "You saw this," Mr Wardle said. "You may be called upon to give an account." I gave Mr Braithwaite my handker-chief to wipe his face and hands. He didn't have the strength so I did it for him. There was blood on his mouth, as if someone had punched him. I dipped the hanky in the beck and wiped his mouth. His front tooth was loose.'

215

'This was with Mr Wardle looking on?'

'I can't remember. Perhaps Mr Wardle hadn't reached us and I was just trying to help Mr Braithwaite. His knuckles were scraped, as though he'd been in a scrap. The face of his watch was cracked. There was a bit of check material caught in the watch chain.'

I tried not to sound incredulous or critical. 'Did you say anything about this at the time?'

'I put the scrap of material in my pocket, and forgot about it until later, until it was too late.' He spoke to the grass, to cover a lie or his puzzlement.

'What did you do with the watch, and the material?'

'I tucked the watch in his pocket. I kept the bit of check. Still have it, with my scouting bits and pieces, my axe and my whistle and so on. I was going to give it to you . . .' he tailed off miserably.

'You still can give it to me. As soon as possible. Hector, from what you say about Mr Braithwaite's loose tooth and scraped knuckles, perhaps you're right and he had been in a fight.'

'I suppose I thought he'd been duffed up.'

'Why did you think he'd been attacked?'

'Stands to sense. A man of Mr Braithwaite's standing wouldn't start a fight. I feared someone had taken him by surprise and got the better of him. From the scrapes on his knuckles he'd fought back but come off worse, and he'd be too proud to admit it. Someone must have given him a real pasting. He was like one of those punch-drunk boxers.'

'Do you have any idea who might have attacked him?'

He blushed and shook his head. 'No, I don't know.'

'Hector? Hector, please look at me.' Reluctantly he turned his troubled face and gazed at me. He gulped, then said, 'I knew Uncle Arthur was angry with Mr Braithwaite, but I didn't know why. I suppose I thought it may have been Uncle Arthur, attacking from behind. He

216

was supposed to have been with us, supervising the camp, but he was nowhere to be seen. Arthur Wilson is not a gentleman. I wondered if this snatch of stuff might have been from his shirt.'

'But it wasn't?'

'I asked Auntie Marjorie, what was Uncle Arthur's opinion of check shirts. He has a low opinion and doesn't own one. Says that check shirts are a disgrace to the human race.'

'Wouldn't he have been wearing a scouting uniform?'

'He and Mr Wardle wore what they pleased. I didn't know what Uncle Arthur had on under his coat.'

If it had been anyone else but Hector telling the story, I would have not have believed his confusions and assumptions.

'I'm still not sure why you didn't tell Constable Mitchell what you've told me.'

Hector looked as though he would burst into tears. 'He would have badgered me and I might have said too much.'

'I have a feeling you might not have told me this if Mr and Mrs Kellett had not been killed.' And if I hadn't threatened you with the CID.

'Perhaps not.'

'So, you think there's a connection and that's why you're telling me now.'

'It's nothing I know for sure, just a feeling. I can't tell Tabby that I was part of her father's downfall. Yet if I keep it to myself it'll eat away at me. I'm hoping you'll say . . .'

'What?'

'That the cracked watch face, the scrap of material, that what I've told you would make no difference. That it all would have happened anyway. I loved Tabby even then. She was magnificent and entirely out of my reach. I was just a gangly idiot.'

So what's changed, I asked myself. The horse tired of standing still and began to move again. Looking down on

217

Hector gave me a distinct advantage.

'Go on, Hector.'

'After what happened with her father, I wanted to tell her. It would have given me an excuse to speak to her, if I could have found my tongue. I hung about their house and grounds, waiting. Then someone told me she'd gone away, and that she had a chap who'd returned wounded, and she'd gone to see him. And of course she was in the VAD. She only ever came home for short visits, and by the time I'd hear "Tabby Braithwaite's home" she'd be gone.'

'You thought Mr Braithwaite had been attacked. Was there anything else unusual about him?'

Hector patted the horse's neck absent-mindedly. He looked at the ground as though searching for a four-leaf clover.

'That was the odd thing, Kate. He didn't seem to know me, know who I was. All right, so I was just another boy in scout uniform. But really, I'd expected him to remember me. We were supposed to be helpful to people in the scouts, good turns and all that sort of stuff. I was wandering about one Saturday, thinking about being helpful, and also looking for shelter from the rain. It'd started to rain stair rods. I went into the Braithwaites', hoping to see Tabitha to tell you the truth, but also thinking I might shelter in one of their out-buildings. Mr Braithwaite was there. He was obviously busy and I hoped he might be taking the motorbike to pieces or something. But he was packing stuff into the sidecar. When I offered to help he was a bit rude to me.'

'Can you remember what he was packing?'

'No. Not after all this time, except one thing, one odd thing.'

'What was that?'

'He was packing a bucket and spade. And I thought, no wonder he's being rude. He's gone mad. Losing Edmund has sent him mad with grief, that's what I thought. He let me clean the motorbike, and gave me a tanner. So he should have remembered me.'

'How did he seem in himself on that day he was packing the motorbike?'

'Sad of course. He'd lost Edmund you know, but cheerful as well. Isn't that odd? Sad and cheerful.'

'Hector, thank you for telling me. I'll keep your confidence. I'm sure what you did or didn't do that day wouldn't have made any difference.'

He opened the second gate. I held the horse steady until he closed it again, so slowly that the horse grew impatient, threw back its head and snorted a cloud of air from its nostrils.

'There's something else.'

'Go on.'

'I knew I'd made a pig's ear of everything, calling the scoutmaster and so on. So on the Monday, it was a school holiday, I took myself over to Milton House because I heard that Mr Braithwaite had been taken there. I saw him.'

'Where?'

'He was walking in the grounds. He spoke to me at the side gate. It wasn't locked, but we just spoke through the bars of the gate. He seemed a bit more himself, and he asked me to do something for him.'

'Kate! Hector!' It was Tabitha, hurrying across towards us from the house.

'Good Lord,' Hector said. 'She mustn't know.'

'You can tell me later. This could be important.'

He gulped, waving to Tabitha who had slowed down now that we walked towards her.

The four of us sat down to breakfast. I was not very hungry but knew I should have something before my journey home. Hopes of seeing Mrs Braithwaite's reaction to the news of Lizzie Kellett's death were dashed. She had

219

heard about it from her maid, and Tabitha had been told by Becky.

Tabitha sipped tea and nibbled at half a slice of toast. 'Horrible, horrible,' she said, over and over. 'To think of poor Kellett scalded, and blackened by dye, and then the shock of the freezing beck, and now this. Do you think Mrs Kellett hit the bottle? Marjorie Wilson had given her a flask of brandy. If she's unused to drink, she could have tripped down the stairs.'

Tabitha gave up on her half slice of toast. She looked as if she might be sick as she watched Hector tuck into eggs, bacon, well-done sausages, black pudding and fried bread. With a dramatic glance around the table and a tremor in her voice, she asked, 'Is there a curse on this place?'

Mrs Braithwaite attempted to look serene, but her eyelid twitched. She toyed with a kipper. 'Nothing is connected, Tabitha, and yet everything is. Perhaps we live in a time of shadows. But the shadows will pass. We will see a better tomorrow. What else can we do but keep on going? You and Hector have your wedding to think of. Now you must decide on the honeymoon. It's mad to have left it so late.'

Hector was caught with a mouthful and made a valiant attempt to chew it down in something of a hurry so as to help his future mother-in-law in her efforts to change the subject. 'There's some caverns opened up at Stump Cross.'

Tabitha turned a lighter shade of pale. 'Caverns?'

Hector grimaced as Evelyn's well-shod toes kicked his ankles.

'Paris would be grand, if you don't mind doing the talking, Tabby.'

'My mind won't work.' Tabitha moved crumbs from the edge of her plate so they made a small island in its centre. 'I can't think.'

'Nonsense, dear. It's tragic, and obviously they were

220

our employees and we'll have a responsibility to see things done properly, but we weren't close to the Kelletts.'

Hector crunched his fried bread.

'Eat something, Tabitha. Keep your strength up,' Mrs Braithwaite ordered. 'You too, Kate.'

We finished breakfast. Evelyn and Tabitha went upstairs. I managed to detain Hector with the excuse that I wanted him to draw me a map of the most direct route from Bridgestead back to Leeds. Pencil in hand, he drew a dot. 'This is Bridgestead. You are here . . .'

'Keep drawing, Hector. But tell me, what did Mr Braithwaite ask you to do for him that day?'

'I can't draw and talk.'

'Then just scribble. I know the way.'

'Do you? Then why . . .? Oh I see. Right.' He pressed so hard on the pencil the point broke.

'You saw Mr Braithwaite by the side gate of Milton House?'

'Yes. He looked different, in that hospital uniform they used to put men in.'

'Hospital blue,' I prompted.

'Yes, a bit like workmen's overalls. Quite the wrong outfit for Mr Braithwaite. I'll never forget his bruised face, and the cut on his lip. He knew who I was, and that I'd helped him with the motorbike. He asked would I do something for him, and there'd be a shilling in it when he had his wallet by him. I agreed straight away, just glad to help him in his troubles, and to do something for Tabitha Braithwaite's father.'

He came to a full stop, and gazed at the useless pencil. I made a powerful effort to quell my rising impatience as he drew a small pen knife from his pocket and started to sharpen the pencil point.

'He swore me to secrecy. Wanted me to find where his motorbike had got to. I said it was probably where he always kept it. He said it wasn't or he wouldn't be asking.

221

He said it was just the job for a boy scout – and to look in all the likely places till I found it, then come back and tell him, or tell Mr Kellett.'

'And did you?'

'Yes. It was in one of the outbuildings at the mill. He must have forgotten he'd left it there. I went back to tell him. He wasn't by the side gate, so I just walked in through the front gate, trying to look as if I had some business there.'

The pencil point was well and truly sharp. Hector turned it round and began to sharpen the other end.

I wanted to reach out and stop him whittling the pencil any further. There'd be none of it left.

'There weren't many people about. One soldier sitting on a bench said good morning to me. Another was trying to walk straight. I felt bad. The last thing they would want was some stupid boy gawping. I nearly went up to one of them and asked should I join the army. Some lads my age did get away with it. I wish I had now. I wish I'd taken part. I'd be more of an equal with Tabby.'

'I'm glad you're telling me all this, Hector. It could be really helpful. Go on.'

'Then I saw Mr Kellett. I knew him of course because he lived by the beck and I used to go there sometimes, fishing for tiddlers. I sauntered up to him and told him where the motorbike was. Poor chap. He was quite small, wasn't he?'

'And?'

'He said, "Thanks, young Gawthorpe. Mum's the word." So you see, he wanted me to say nothing. I did as he asked. I never mentioned wiping Mr Braithwaite's mouth, or the scrap of material, or looking for the motorbike. I was as good as my word. Until now.'

There is something about boys who are up to no good – a shiftiness, a lightness of step. These two were running along the Bingley road, carrying something. They turned, about to disappear into a hedge.

I drove alongside, pipped the horn and brought the car to a stop.

'What have you got there, boys?'

The elder held tightly to the top of a moving sack, his face set in a defiant glare. 'Nowt!'

The younger ran dirty fingers through his basin-cut brown hair.

'What is it?' I asked again. 'If you tell me, you can have a ride on the running board.'

They exchanged looks. The older flickered his eyes at the younger, unwilling to tell me himself but giving permission. Later he would be able to say, *You snitched, not me.*

'It's a black cat.'

'What do you intend to do with it?'

The older boy held the sack tightly, his knuckles turning white. 'It can kill people.'

I stepped from the car cautiously. They could run and I would never catch them.

'I can tell you for sure that cat was outside when the accident happened to Mrs Kellett.'

Bravely, the younger boy piped, 'It's a witch's cat.'

'Just a minute, please.' They looked on with interest as I reached into the car for my bag and took out my purse. 'I'll give it a new home, away from the village. And I'm not a witch.'

The older boy grew bold. He looked directly at me. 'You don't look like a witch, miss.'

'How much do you want for it?'

Being asked to name a price left them speechless, but only for a moment. The older boy held onto the bag with difficulty now as the cat struggled.

'It's evil,' he warned.

'No. Animals aren't evil. It's people who do bad things. Animals only want to live.'

We agreed on sixpence for the cat, and a further

sixpence if they would help me transfer it to a more comfortable place for its journey. I feared the cat would die of fright if it travelled in a sack. It might die of fright anyway.

I opened the larger of my canvas bags and took out my precious black box with its lid to keep it pristine. With only a few scratches to my hands and wrists, I managed to push the cat into the box, with the lid open a little so that it would not suffocate. The cat sat next to me in the front seat. The boys clambered onto the running board and held tight for the next half mile of my journey.

I toyed with the idea of treating the lads to a speech, pointing out the error of their ways, but it would have fallen on deaf ears. They were entirely absorbed in the novelty of a motor car ride as far as the crossroads.

Even after the boys jumped off, the mewling cat made it impossible for me to think. It miaowed persistently. I spoke soothingly. It stopped miaowing for a moment.

'Are you still alive, cat?'

It was.

The mind is a terrible and a marvellous thing. Even when you are totally distracted and believe all thoughts have fled, some picture will suddenly insert itself and demand attention.

The pictures came thick and fast. Mrs Kellett lying dead. A footprint, an abandoned cricket bat. Another picture wasn't mine at all but sprang directly from Hector's memory into my brain: Joshua Braithwaite talking to him through the bars of the gate.

I talked to the cat, asking its name and telling it everything would be all right.

Naturally, being a cat, it disbelieved me.

When I arrived home, Mrs Sugden met me with a message from Sykes. 'Mr Sykes says to tell you that the initials on the cricket bat were EB.'

EB. Edmund Braithwaite.

Mrs Sugden looked at the box in my arms that seemed to move of its own accord, and a screech came from it. She took a step back. 'What the blue blazes is that? That box is alive.'

'I thought we might like a cat.'

17

Scouring

Scouring: Washing the fabric to remove grease, dirt and any other impurities picked up during processing.

Sookie, my newly acquired loquacious marmalade-eyed cat, leaped from the box and ran under the kitchen dresser.

'I want you to keep her in for a few weeks, Mrs Sugden.' I poured milk onto a saucer and placed it by the edge of the dresser. 'Find her some scraps, eh?'

Mrs Sugden blew out her cheeks. 'She won't run off! A cat knows when it's fallen on its feet.'

'All the same, let's keep her in for now. She's had a bit of a shock.'

'It'll do its muckment under there. Be a right to-do having to shift that dresser to clean under it. I'll butter its paws, that'll make sure it won't stray. I don't suppose it's ever had butter.'

'Oh I should think it will have. It's a country cat.'

'Country folk are the worst. They've no sentiment over animals – it'll have had to catch mice for a living there.'

'She can do that here, once she's settled.'

I felt a powerful obligation to keep the cat safe but did not have the energy to debate about it. 'Just keep her in for a day or so.'

Being chum to Tabitha and playing house guest for Evelyn while poking in my beak, lying and tying loose ends, had proved a strain. My limbs ached, my head throbbed. Having kept up some semblance of energy for the drive home I now felt near to exhaustion. The words "Wreck of the Hesperus" sprang to mind, strapped to the ship's bow in the fearful storm.

Mrs Sugden turned her attention from the cat to me.

'You look dreadful. What's happened?'

'An awful lot.' How do you begin to recount two murders, the total failure of progress in searching for Braithwaite, and a series of events that made no sense? I shook my head. 'Not now.'

'You get yourself to bed. Rest. I'll bring you something up.'

For once, I did not argue. To be in my own bed sounded like heaven. In no time, Mrs Sugden brought bed warmers and beef tea. One of the best things about going away from home is coming back. Gerald and I had chosen this house together. Small and sunny, with big bay windows, it had come with its own ancient black cat that died and was buried by Gerald in the garden. Now by tragic twists the black cat had returned.

I love my little house. For all the Braithwaites' luxury, my tiredness was not only due to the emotional strain of the murders, and getting up in the middle of the night to break into the mill. I had stayed reasonably polite, on best behaviour with Evelyn, Tabitha and the evasive Hector for days.

I fell asleep, to the peering and disappearing faces of black cats, Lizzie Kellett, Paul Kellett and Joshua Braithwaite wearing his wedding-day smile. After that, I knew nothing until eleven o'clock the next morning.

I woke from a dream in which the gate clicked. In the dream I knew it was Gerald coming home.

I heard his voice. *I was only missing. I lost my memory. They didn't know who I was. I didn't know myself, but I'm back now.*

I opened my eyes but there was no one.

A few minutes later, Mrs Sugden tapped on the door. 'Are you awake?'

227

My answer was meant to be yes but came out as a great groaning yawn. I sat up in bed, perfecting my yawn, smoothing out my cheeks and running my fingers over what felt like bags, more like portmanteaus, under my eyes. *A wrinkle on the face is like a crinkle in a piece of tissue paper. You'll easily smooth it out.* I don't think so.

I reached out to grasp the cup of tea.

Mrs Sugden set down a slice of toast on the bedside table. 'That Mr Sykes called. I told him to come back later.'

'When?'

My drawing room looks out onto the garden. Through the bay window, I saw that in spite of the cool April, green buds had multiplied on my apple tree in the few days I had been away.

Between the door and the window stands a baby grand piano on which, when I have time, I like to thump out ragtime tunes. My old school friend, who is married to a New York banker, sends me sheet music. This interest in ragtime gives both of us the opportunity to be considered fashionably scandalous.

Though I am not a brilliant pianist, playing takes me into a different world. I placed the sheet music for *St Louis Blues* on the stand and began to pick out the tune. This delayed the moment when I had to try and make sense of the events of the past five days.

At four o'clock Sykes and I sat in wing chairs on opposite sides of the hearth. A small fire burned brightly in the grate.

He draped one leg over the other. Sitting opposite him like this, in the stillness of late afternoon, I noticed he was thinner than I thought. The bones of his knees made a sharp angle in the crease of his trousers. He took his notebook from an inside pocket.

He waited for me to begin.

I crossed the room to pick up my notebook from the oak bureau, more as a prop than a necessity. 'The main question is, are the deaths of Kellett and Mrs Kellett connected to our investigation? Has someone turned windy? And if so who, or why?'

Sykes does not make huge expressive movements when he speaks, but has a habit of moving his large hands just a little from the wrist when putting forward an idea, opening his palm as if to make an offer, or turning his hand the other way when something does not quite fit. He did that now. 'We have no evidence of a connection. I hear from my contact in Keighley that Scotland Yard have been notified.'

'Then while I'm away in London, perhaps you could find out what you can from your contact and keep me in touch?'

He nodded.

I gave Sykes an account of my visit to the mortuary and the conversation with Dr Fraser, about the morphia and *gel sem* found in Kellett's stomach. 'Dr Fraser thinks the morphia was to ease the pain of his amputation. Someone could have increased the drug dose unbeknownst to Kellett. That would have dulled his senses. Kellett himself told me, when I toured the mill, that just a moment's misjudgement and the vat of dye could be lethal.'

'Did Mrs Kellett say why anyone may have wanted to do Kellett harm?'

'She thought it could be envy. Because they had money put by to start a new life. She didn't name any particular person, only that everyone knew about their plans, all the dye workers.'

Sykes stroked his chin. 'Mitchell's inspector is treating the motive as theft.'

'The cash box from under the bed?'

'Yes.'

'It puzzles me, Mr Sykes. Why didn't the thief just

229

break into the house when the Kelletts were at work, and take what he wanted?'

Sykes shrugged and shook his head. 'Mrs Kellett had a lot of people tramping through her house paying condolences. Maybe the thief thought someone else would get to the money first, or that she'd pack her bags and go live with one of her relatives. Keighley CID believe they've got the weapon, and the time. Her last visitor left at nine o'clock on Friday, and you found her at eight o'clock on Saturday morning, so that gives just eleven hours in which the murder could have taken place.'

The thought of Lizzie so coldly arranged on the stone steps of the cottage made me shudder. I picked up the tongs and placed a cob of coal on the fire.

'It was in the earlier part of those eleven hours. She hadn't gone to bed on Friday night.'

I pictured the neatly made bed, the folded nightdress.

We had both almost imperceptibly turned towards the fire, as if for comfort. Sykes said, 'I'm not sure that whoever did her in went to the house with that intention.'

'Why do you say that?'

'He, or she, hadn't taken a weapon. It looks likely that the cricket bat was the weapon. The perpetrator fled the house with it in his hands, probably blood and hairs still on it, and dropped it in the beck, expecting it to float downstream. Only it was caught in the reeds. If we're fortunate there'll be prints on the handle. Whoever dropped it must have been in a hurry. It's thought to have been in the house. Apparently Miss Braithwaite took it to Mrs Kellett as something that had belonged to her brother Edmund. It was meant to entice him back from the spirit world. Miss Braithwaite says she left the bat at the cottage.' He smiled ruefully. 'I got that titbit from Mitchell, as my reward for letting him take the credit for finding it.'

I closed my eyes, feeling a cold fury with myself. The mental picture was clear from my first visit to Mrs Kellett.

The cricket bat was lying by the dresser. The cat had used it as a scratching post. 'I did see that cricket bat. Why didn't I notice it was missing when Lizzie was killed?'

'It might have come back to you. These things happen, when there's a lot to take in.'

I stared at the fire as a new lick of flame cut through the coals. This kind of detecting was a far cry from tracking down a missing soldier. But was there some comparison in the motives? The war had complicated life. A person could begin again, using someone else's identity card. A live man could take the identity of the dead. A soldier may have a good reason for abandoning his once nearest and dearest. Perhaps that was true of Braithwaite too, in spite of wealth and position. Yet in looking for Braithwaite, there was no clear trail. No stolen identity cards, only a jumble of odds and ends.

What else had I missed, and what else did I remember?

'Mrs Kellett's address book was gone from the table drawer, I spotted that. But the cricket bat was part of the general clutter of the house and didn't seem significant, until you found it.'

'Address book? Why would someone take that do you think?' Sykes opened his palms as if he expected me to drop a solution into his hands.

'I don't know. To delay her relatives being informed? Constable Mitchell said the Keighley chaps would make enquiries of her workmates, so they can track down her sister and brother.'

I passed Sykes my notebook. 'I saw three postal order stubs at Mrs Kellett's. One was blank but two had initials – one on the payee line and the other on both the payee and post office lines, written in black ink, probably at the post office. Constable Mitchell has kept the stubs, but I made a note.'

Sykes copied my note. 'I'll see what I can make of it.'

I stood up. 'I've one or two things to show you, in the

dining room. They may give us an extra insight into Braithwaite's state of mind.'

Sykes unfolded himself from the chair and followed me. 'And when we know the missing man well enough, he will speak. We hope.'

I had placed the painting of the children by the beck in the centre of the window seat. Now I turned it, placing it to the left so that it caught the light. 'Evelyn gave it to Dr Grainger to hang in Milton House. He was clearing out. Rather than leave it there, I took it. Eventually I'll give it to Tabitha.'

Sykes took a pair of steel-rimmed spectacles from his top pocket. He glanced at the painting, and then at the initials J.B. in the bottom right corner.

While he studied the painting, I put my other displays on the dining room table: the photographs, the map, the scrap of material that Hector had taken from Joshua Braithwaite's watch chain when he found him in the beck.

'This is a good painting,' Sykes said. 'Braithwaite was truly talented. That might give him a reason for wanting to break away from his life at home, and at the mill. Perhaps he thought of himself as an artist, a frustrated genius. He's caught the light on the water so perfectly, and the clouds practically float. The children are painted with such tenderness.'

'Yes. Tabitha, and Edmund.'

I suddenly realised that Dad had made an excellent choice in recommending Sykes to me. Not many police-man, not many people, would look at a painting and see so much.

In the light from the window, the water of the beck glinted as it would in real life when caught by the sun. Tabitha said he painted it quickly, but every stone on the humpback bridge seeped age and damp. Tabitha, her skirt tucked up, leaned forward, poking a stick into the water. Edmund crouched on his haunches, holding a child's fishing rod with net. By the

232

waterfall, there was a smudge, like a stain, and on the bridge a grey shape that marred the painting, almost as if it had been accidentally leaned against another painting. Sykes pointed out these imperfections.

'I know. I didn't notice them when Dr Grainger first gave it to me. You only see the smudges in a good light.'

'Could something have been painted over?' Sykes asked. 'Would this smudge on the bridge have been his wife?'

'And Joshua painted her out?'

'If he did, that would be a reason for her to give it away. She wouldn't destroy it, not when it's of her children, but she would have been angry with him.'

I swear Sykes almost added 'that's marriage', but changed his mind. I wondered about his marriage, and how his wife felt about him putting work first and coming to see me on a Sunday afternoon.

I took the painting out of the light and leaned it against the wall. 'There's a chap at the museum, something of a specialist in cleaning and restoring paintings. I'll ask Mrs Sugden to get in touch with him to come round and see what he makes of this.'

'Good idea,' Sykes said.

Like me I guessed he would feel relieved if we could solve one tiny mystery – even if only the secret of the painting.

I spread my photographs on the table.

'This is Tabitha's fiancé, Hector Gawthorpe, the ex-boy scout.'

'Ah yes, he escorted you from the bridge, carrying your camera bag.' Sykes smiled.

'And he finally decided to tell the truth and shame the devil. This is the scrap of material he's held onto all these years. It was caught on Joshua Braithwaite's watch chain when he was found in the beck.'

I told Sykes how Hector and two other boys had found Braithwaite.

233

Sykes examined the material, holding it between finger and thumb. 'It's a heavy weave.'

'I know. Poor Hector imagined it might have been from his uncle's shirt. Heaven help the mill when he gets in there.'

Sykes replaced the scrap of material onto the table. 'His uncle?'

'Arthur Wilson, the assistant scout master. He's weaving manager at the mill.'

'Ah, the inventor. Hector could be onto something. What else did he have to say?'

'A week or so before he went missing, Braithwaite packed some stuff into his motorcycle sidecar, including a bucket and spade.'

'Bit old for that wasn't he?'

'Well, yes. Hector thought he was losing his marbles through grief, that it was Edmund's bucket and spade.'

A sudden thought struck me like a thunderbolt. It was too mad to contemplate. I put a hand to my forehead to make the thought go away.

'What is it?' Sykes asked, his voice suddenly full of concern.

'Oh nothing, just one of those mad ideas. What if Edmund didn't die? What if he held a grudge, he deserted, and came back and murdered his father?'

Sykes gave a lot of concentration to the items on the table, and then looked through the window, as if for inspiration. Finally, in a low voice, he said, 'Edmund was killed, on the Somme. I took the liberty of checking with one of his surviving comrades – a lad in Bingley who drinks in the Ramshead.'

I felt suddenly foolish, and I also knew that Dad had told Sykes about how I could never let go, and how I always half-expected Gerald to come back.

With careful fingers, Sykes straightened the photographs on the table. 'So do we think Braithwaite may have been headed for the seaside?'

I made my voice sound very even, as if no mad idea ever struck my brain with the force of lightning. 'Possibly. But who was getting on beaches in 1916? They were full of barbed wire and look-out posts weren't they?'

'And which seaside?' Sykes said thoughtfully. 'Where would you go in his place?'

'Me? I'd try somewhere new. The family used to go to Grange-over-Sands. Locals there would recognise him. He'd choose the opposite coast, Scarborough, Whitby, Filey.'

Sykes gave an amused laugh. 'Some folks would choose the opposite end of the country. But if he made a preliminary trip in advance with bucket and spade then it couldn't have been so very far away.'

'And it sounds well planned, as if he knew exactly what he was doing.'

'Yet that doesn't tie up with his being in such a confused state when he was found at the beck.' I lifted the painting from the window seat and sat down, nodding to Sykes to join me. 'Hector said that Mr Braithwaite didn't recognise him by the beck, but that by Monday, when he saw him again through the hospital gates, he was more himself.'

Sykes stretched out his legs and contemplated his toe caps. 'How did Hector account for that confusion?'

'He said Braithwaite had been seriously duffed up, including a cut lip and a bruise. He was too dazed to remember Hector as the boy who'd cleaned **his** motorbike. But by Monday, when Hector went to Milton House, Braithwaite was sufficiently recovered to ask Hector to do him a good turn.'

'Which was?'

'Braithwaite wanted Hector to locate his motorbike and to tell him, or Kellett, where it was. Kellett was working at Milton House Hospital.'

'Was he now? That's interesting. And Braithwaite had forgotten where he left his motorbike?'

'Apparently. Hector located it in one of the outbuildings at the mill.'

'So Kellett could have brought the bike to Milton House – or somewhere nearby – and Braithwaite could have gone off to build sand castles, stopping only to empty his safe deposit box on the way.'

I tried to remember where I'd heard that before, the mention of a safe deposit box.

Sykes said, 'The sister of the landlady at the Gaping Goose works in the mill offices as a secretary. When Joshua Braithwaite went missing, so did the key to his safe deposit box at Thackreys' Bank.'

'How does she know?'

'Jane wasn't supposed to know that Braithwaite taped the key to the underside of his desk. But she'd spotted him scrabbling about there once or twice and worked it out. She's a sharp lass and doesn't miss much. Anyhow, it wasn't there after he went missing. She checked.'

'So did Braithwaite get his hands on the safe deposit box key, or did someone else?'

Sykes shook his head. 'Jane didn't tell anyone at the time, not even the police. She's someone who takes the "secret" in the word secretary a little too seriously. She finally confided in her sister last month, when they were talking about Tabitha's wedding.'

For the first time, I felt some hope on Tabitha's behalf. With a motorbike, with money from his safe deposit box, Braithwaite might well at this very moment be standing on a cliff, by his easel, looking out to the horizon, paintbrush in hand.

I tried to remember who else had mentioned a safe deposit box key, and then it came back. Tipsy Marjorie. I shut my eyes and tried to remember the disjointed conversation we'd had on the ride between the

Gawthorpes' and her stone terrace house on the cobbled street in Bridgestead. 'Marjorie Wilson said that it would help to know who got to the safe deposit box, and that if it was Joshua Braithwaite, then . . . what were her words? "If he got to that, then the bird could have flown."'

'But he didn't find his way to freedom on the Clyno motorbike. That's still in the outhouse at the mill, looking very sorry for itself. I took the opportunity to have a good look round.'

I had also been in that outhouse, and now that he mentioned it I remembered seeing a motorbike. I had tucked my camera bag away there on the day Tabitha and I walked across the moors.

'When did you look round?' I asked, amazed at how many places Sykes found his way to.

'On the ill-fated night we went to look at the books. Because a lot of threads lead back to that mill, and to Stoddard and his size nine boots.'

'Size nine? You mean like the boot prints on the bank outside Lizzie's house?'

'Yes.'

Moments ago, I had mentally congratulated Dad on finding Sykes for me. Now I decided he was utterly mad, and way off course.

'Half the men in the village probably wear size nines. You're wrong about Stoddard. He wouldn't hit a defence-less woman over the head with a cricket bat. And he doesn't need a box of guineas from under a widow's bed.'

Is this what policemen did, I wondered, picked on a name and found reasons for that person to be guilty? Stoddard was the one who had kept the business going, cared for his dying wife, thought of Joshua as a brother, behaved entirely admirably as far as I could see – apart from his lapse of judgement in proposing marriage to Evelyn Braithwaite. Of course I couldn't expect him to think kindly of me, not since he had caught me in the office in the middle of the night.

I had a brainwave. 'If there are fingerprints on that cricket bat, I can give you something that will eliminate Stoddard.'

I went to the room under the stairs that I use as a dark-room. The bobbin Stoddard had given me was still in the camera bag. I carried the bag into the dining room.

'This bobbin has Stoddard's fingerprints all over it. Take it. If you're right, and there are fingerprints on the cricket bat, he can be eliminated.'

Of course that gave me one other thing to do. As well as giving my statement to the chaps from Scotland Yard, I would now have to be fingerprinted to eliminate my own prints from the bobbin.

We had talked for over an hour, agreeing that Kellett probably knew more than was good for him. I began to gather up the photographs from the table.

'If Kellett did help Braithwaite to fly free, he may have known Braithwaite's whereabouts.'

Sykes nodded.

It followed that if Kellett knew, so did his wife. Once Kellett was silenced, the next step would be to put Mrs Kellett out of harm's way. One killing was made to look like a works accident, the second a burglary gone wrong. But what if that was just a cover story for both murders and the true motive was to silence the Kelletts? It seemed too preposterous that Braithwaite might come back, as it were from the dead, in order to keep his new life secret.

'What?' said Sykes, reading my face.

I told him the outlandish idea.

He smiled. 'Why not? We ought to keep an open mind. Anything is possible.'

I showed him the pencil dots on the Ordnance Survey map. 'These are the caves and potholes that have been explored since Braithwaite's disappearance. No one has found so much as a shoelace.'

238

Before putting away the photographs, I lingered over Evelyn's photograph. 'What do you think to her?'

'She's an attractive woman.'

'Yes. With two beaus.'

'Two?'

It pleased me that I was the one with the information. 'On the night of the party, Neville proposed to Evelyn. I didn't intentionally eavesdrop . . .'

'Pity.'

'I was on the terrace and heard him.'

'And?'

'She turned him down. She's having an affair with Dr Grainger. My guess is it's being going on for a long while.'

Sykes perked up. 'Before Braithwaite disappeared?'

'That I don't know. Evelyn knows that I know. I could tell by her manner after I came back from seeing Grainger.'

'Do you have a photograph of this Grainger chap?'

'No. This is going to sound silly. I usually don't mind asking people if I can take their photograph for my rogues' gallery, but I didn't like to ask him. Perhaps because I thought he might misconstrue the request.'

Sykes burst out laughing, which annoyed me.

'Sorry,' he stifled his laughter. 'Excuse the mirth, but I can imagine it. If this chap has made a conquest of Evelyn Braithwaite, he probably thinks he's God's gift, does he?'

'I suspect that conquesting was the other way round.'

'Going back to Stoddard, his proposal to the widow gives him an added reason to tidy loose ends. When he caught you in the offices, he told you it was his mill.'

'He's already a director. He has nothing to gain. When Kellett died, Stoddard was at the Gawthorpes' party. We'd all been together since early evening.'

'Passion,' Sykes said flatly, the word sounding foreign to his lips. 'What part does passion play?'

It was a good question. But it was not Evelyn's passions

that interested me, except on a personal level. Braithwaite was a ladies' man. Everyone knew it. 'I have an idea, Mr Sykes. First thing tomorrow, I'm going to try and see Braithwaite's solicitor. Professional men always confide in their solicitors, to make provision for a mistress or a wrong side of the blanket child.' I knew this from reading novels but liked the sound of my own voice saying it as if I had been born with the knowledge.

Sykes looked impressed.

'I got his name from Tabitha and made a telephone call to his secretary a couple of days ago. Come with me tomorrow on the train. I'll talk to him, and then you and I can meet afterwards and I'll give you chapter and verse.'

'Where does he have his office?' Sykes asked.

'Bradford.'

'Worstedopolis,' Sykes said. 'Where else?'

est mohair suit

On that blustery Monday morning, Mr Sykes and I met by the tram stop and rattled our way to town, heading for the railway station.

'Good luck,' he wished me as we stepped out among the throng at Forster Square station in Bradford.

He had an errand at the main post office, and we agreed to meet in half an hour at the nearby tea rooms.

Mentioning the Braithwaite name —Yorkshire's equivalent of Ali Baba's Open Sesame — had netted me an eleven a.m. appointment with the legal beagle to Bradford's mill-owning millionaire set.

A well-turned out chap whose mohair suit did nothing to improve his appearance, he had the look of a cherubic baker of pork pies, his plump-cheeked face topped with wispy white hair. Watery blue eyes, narrowing in an attempt to look canny, gave him a peevish air. Folds of flesh cascaded in layers onto the stiff shirt collar that cut into his neck. He enlivened the usual dark three-piece suit with a maroon tie and gold pin that matched his cuff links. His white podgy hands looked as if they'd knead dough with great patience. If he were descended from a baker, I reckoned it must have been the chap from Pudding Lane who in 1666 made London burn like rotten sticks. Once we were seated on either side of his document-piled desk he fingered a heavy gold fountain pen, big enough to count as an offensive weapon.

A small smile curved his plump lips as he looked at me

and saw money. 'My secretary tells me you wish to make a will. And that you're a friend of Miss Braithwaite's.'

'I should make my will, that's true, but not today.'

He laced his fingers together, resting them on a clean white blotter edged in a stiff green leather frame. 'A will is an important undertaking. We could discuss the generalities and make a future appointment at your convenience.'

'There's another matter, also, another reason for my being here.'

His listened without comment as I repeated the story of Tabitha Braithwaite's desire to find her father, and her hope that Joshua Braithwaite would walk her down the aisle.

On cue, the telephone rang. As I paused in my story, his secretary put her head around the communicating door.

He gave a cluck of annoyance, telling Miss Conway he did not wish to be disturbed.

'But it's Miss Braithwiate, Mr Murgatroyd, on a pertinent matter, she says.'

Guessing he would demur at passing on information, I had asked Tabitha to telephone.

He picked up the receiver. I could hear Tabitha's excited and eager explanation and request.

'This is most irregular, Miss Braithwaite and without Mrs Braithwaite's permission . . .'

A pause.

'Good morning, Mrs Braithwaite and how . . .'

Well done, Tabitha. She had persuaded her mother to back me up. Perhaps it was my thank you from Evelyn Braithwaite for keeping quiet about her liaison with Dr Grainger.

When he replaced the telephone in its cradle, Mr Murgatroyd called to his secretary to bring in the Braithwaite files.

Miss Conway came from poverty's doorstep. Her black

242

skirt shone brown with age, the neat blouse was frayed at the collar. Dark hair folded in old-fashioned pleats showed a touch of grey. Bringing with her a powerful waft of body odour, she placed an armful of files on his desk. He doesn't pay her enough. Mean sod. Or perhaps she looked after a sick mother, her wages swallowed by nourishing soups, leaving nothing for a bar of soap.

There were manila folders tied with red legal tape faded to pink, sturdy brown envelopes and dusty parchments. Like the disembodied head of a zephyr in the corner of a renaissance painting, Mr Murgatroyd puffed out his cheeks and blew a small cloud of dust in my direction.

'Despite Mrs Braithwaite's permission, I can only give you the broadest outline of the nature of the work we did, and do, for Mr Braithwaite and for the mill. Confidential commercial information, you understand.'

He frowned at Miss Conway as she emerged with a second armful of files. Was she on my side? Had she deliberately misunderstood his coded command to bring only what was of no consequence? The files fell from her arms.

Quickly, I came to the rescue, darting to the floor, pretending not to scan the front of every document I retrieved.

'Sorry,' Miss Conway murmured.

She slid away.

Mr Murgatroyd sifted through dusty files. 'As you see, there's far too much to enter into, and nothing here has any bearing on the events of August 1916.'

I pulled a handkerchief from my pocket and prevented a sneeze. 'Mr Murgatroyd, is there anything, among the papers or in your memory of Joshua Braithwaite, that would offer a clue to his state of mind, or to his disappearance?'

He sighed and fumbled with a loose knot of legal tape, as though it would tap some chord in his memory. 'Let me see now. My most recent instruction before that date . . .

243

Yes, here we are. I dealt with the purchase of two fields – land that adjoined the mill and the house. Mr Braithwaite had been eager to acquire it for some time. I also dealt with the transfer of money from the trust, when Miss Braithwaite came of age, and of course the change in his will shortly after his son died.'

'Wasn't it rather soon for him to be dealing with those matters? He was still in mourning.'

'It's never too soon for a person of property to put their affairs in order.'

He let a pause hang in the air, perhaps hoping I would forget all about my mission for Tabitha and suddenly see the good sense in entrusting him with my own last will and testament. I would appoint him my executor. The train to London would crash. I would die. Mr Murgatroyd would be up to his baker's elbows in all the dough that once belonged to me and Gerald. I would rather give the job to his unfortunate, impoverished secretary.

Among the documents retrieved from the floor, one bore the heading Application for a Patent. I wanted to know more. How much money had Wilson's invention earned for the Braithwaites?

'What about the patent that was applied for?' I asked.

Mr Murgatroyd shook his head so vigorously that the folds of fat on his throat wobbled.

'Patent?' The lines around his small eyes creased with suspicion. 'I made no reference to an application for a patent.'

'It's among the papers.'

'Oh that.' He gave a dismissive gesture, as if all in front of him counted for nothing and the only matters of importance were the dried fruit details lodged in his own currant bun brain. I wondered why he had asked for the papers to be brought since he had no intention of divulging the contents of any of them.

Some day I would write a textbook on how to be a

244

female detective in a man's world. Rule Number One: try not to let your animosity show. Your career as an investigator will be short lived if you cannot hide your feelings when you dislike, distrust or despise your interviewee.

'When Mr Braithwaite went missing, can you think of anyone from that time — friend, associate — he may have turned to?'

Mr Murgatroyd creased his forehead in pretence of thoughtfulness. He shook his head. 'He would not have wanted to lose face by going to a business associate. I cannot speak for any friends he may have had.'

The answer surprised me. Perhaps he really was trying to be helpful.

'Is there any lady outside the family that Mr Braithwaite made provision for in the event of his death? You would be the obvious choice for such a confidence.'

He actually blushed, as if I had added a teaspoonful of cochineal to the mix of his pastry face. At last, I had struck home.

'If there were any such document, and I am not at liberty to say whether there may or may not be, then it would be attached to the will, as a codicil, and Mrs Braithwaite would no doubt have seen it.'

'She would?'

'Yes. Mr Braithwaite kept a copy of his own will, naturally. Perhaps not a codicil if he lodged it with me and perhaps . . .'

A wave of thoughtfulness stopped his speech.

Here was the moment for my wooden spoon to stir his pudding. One of the letters in front of him told me the name of the Braithwaites' bank. 'Perhaps the copy of his will is in his safe deposit box at Thackreys' Bank?'

'Possibly,' he said cautiously.

'We know that Mr Braithwaite had possession of the safe deposit box key when he disappeared,' I asserted confidently. For all Murgatroyd knew, Mrs Braithwaite may have opened her cracked heart to me. 'It was his intention to visit the bank.'

I sighed, hoping this attitude signified my profound sympathy for Tabitha and Evelyn, rather than deep ignorance of whether Braithwaite ever did get his mitts on the key and if so, what then?

Murgatroyd scratched the back of his neck where the stiff collar rubbed. 'Yes. Banks are very cautious when it comes to their boxes. Mrs Braithwaite perhaps made the correct decision in choosing to wait. Seven years is a reasonable time for all sorts of dust to settle.'

The box could have been opened by the police during their search for Braithwaite, had they known of its existence. So Evelyn had not wanted the police to be at the bank and discover any dark secrets.

From the office next door came the steady tap tap and clank of the secretary's typewriter.

Murgatroyd shifted a little in his chair which was too small for his chubby frame.

I copied Sykes' trick of turning my hand at the wrist and finding the palm empty. 'I do hope I'm going to be able to help Tabitha and Mrs Braithwaite. Mrs Braithwaite has been so very patient.' I spoke as though she was my erstwhile friend whose stoic endurance I had witnessed at first hand for years. 'Many women would have sought to have a husband declared dead before the seven years.'

'Yes. Without a death certificate she would have had to show evidence of presumption of death. Family members do sometimes prefer to delay petitioning for a death decree. It might have been a different situation had there been financial hardship, say.'

Evelyn Braithwaite was the exemplary widow, playing the patient Penelope awaiting the return of her Odysseus.

'Mr Murgatroyd, are you aware of any particular friendship Mr Braithwaite may have had? Another woman, to be blunt. Miss Braithwaite believes her father is still alive and if he is, then having started a new life elsewhere would be one explanation for his continued absence.'

He drummed his fingers on the desk before giving his lawyer's answer. 'I am not in possession of information which would help you in your search to be of assistance to Mrs and Miss Braithwaite.'

'Do you believe Mr Braithwaite may have begun a new life, either with another woman, or perhaps to follow new pursuits? He was a painter after all. I believe he hadn't intended to go into the mill as a boy. There are precedents for businessmen to become tired of their life and seek a change.'

His lip curled in disapproval. 'Indeed, though not so many round here. We are a hard-headed lot in this part of the world.'

'Were his affairs left in order?'

The blue eyes held a look of startled reproach. 'Entirely in order.'

'Do you suppose he would have put his affairs so entirely in order after his son's death had he not expected some huge change in the pattern of his life?'

'That I cannot say. Suppositions are outside my realm, Mrs Shackleton.' There was a finality in his voice that said he had all but given up his hopes of writing a will for Kate Shackleton. 'Please do telephone us, Mrs Shackleton, if we can be of further help in the future. I'm afraid I'm due in chambers in a very short while. Miss Conway!'

The secretary wafted smokily into the room.

He waved her to take away the Braithwaite papers. 'Mustn't leave the office with the wrong set of documents.'

He stood as I rose to go. In the doorway, I turned.

'Mr Murgatroyd, why did you not go to Milton House when Mr Braithwaite asked you to, on the morning of 21 August?'

He hesitated for just too long. 'That was the week of our family holiday in the Lake District.'

247

Behind him, Miss Conway turned, surprise showing on her face. She took a breath as if about to speak, then thought better of it and returned to her own office.

I thanked Mr Murgatroyd for his time and found my own way out onto the bustling thoroughfare. What was it my father had said? If you ask the right questions you can get information even from a professional whose intention it is to withhold it. So much for my great technique! But one inspired guess had proved correct. Joshua Braithwaite tried to enlist his solicitor's help in his hour of need, and did not get it.

Sykes was waiting for me in the Forster Tea Rooms as arranged. Sitting at a table facing the window, he folded his newspaper, and motioned to the waitress to bring tea.

'Well?' he asked. 'What did you think to our Mr Murgatroyd? I've seen him in court once or twice.'

I pulled a face that was meant to show I found him devious, inefficient, crooked and boastful, but probably showed my defeat.

'Mr Braithwaite put in a call to him from Milton House, and he did not respond. On holiday, supposedly, but I don't believe him.'

'It could be that he didn't want to risk his reputation by being involved in a case of attempted suicide.'

I sat with my back to the window. 'Tell me if he leaves the building. He claims to be due in chambers shortly, but I think that was just to be rid of me. Braithwaites did take out at least one patent on an invention. If that's for the loom picker and it's been a financial success, Wilson has some cause to feel aggrieved. He'd be angry with Braithwaite. There'd be a motive.'

'Possibly, though a bit drastic to kill over an underpayment.'

'People can simmer with resentment at life's unfairness, Mr Sykes.'

He nodded. I could see that he knew that well enough.

We agreed that he would stay on top of the investigation, and keep me abreast of the progress of the police enquiries and the results of the post mortem on Mrs Kellett.

I gave him my address in London. 'Do write to me. I want to keep up with everything. I wish there was more to go on regarding the postal orders, and Mrs Kellett's relatives. Someone must know where her brother and sister are.'

He walked me back to the railway station, for the train to Leeds.

'I hope you enjoy your trip to London, Mrs Shackleton.'

I walked through the barrier towards the steam and noise of the platform. When I turned to wave, Sykes was still standing there. He smiled and raised his hand in a salute.

19

 Soft dress goods

My mother reached out a hand to steady herself as we walked back from the dining car to our carriage. 'There's something about eating on a train that cheers me up, I don't know why. The unexpectedness of it perhaps.'

Our fellow travellers had left the train at Grantham. We had the compartment to ourselves. Mother took out her compact, looked at herself critically and powder-puffed her perfect nose, smiling at her miniature self in the small round mirror.

I sat with my back to the engine, watching the landscape we left behind, aware of my mother's delight in the journey. She travels not simply from Wakefield to London, from a house rented by the West Riding Constabulary to a grand house in Chelsea. The journey gives her title an outing. Leaving behind her role as Mrs Hood, police superintendent's wife, she metamorphoses into the elegant Lady Virginia, daughter of the late Lord and Lady Rodpen. Her sister Ethelberta married a mere baronet and so the delicious irony for Mother is that in spite of marrying a commoner, she takes precedence over her sister. They make a joke of it, but I suspect mother finds it more amusing than does Aunt Berta.

Mother leaned across. She wore a striped velvet two-piece costume in royal blue with calf-length fringed-hem skirt. The long jacket, over a creamy silk blouse, reached just below her hips. The jacket was open to the waist, with three silver buttons at hip height. Her hat, in a slightly lighter shade, took the shape, of an elaborate upturned jelly on a plate. Her shoes were elegant buttoned-up black patents with Cuban heels and ornamental bows. Everything was new.

I was glad to be wearing my skirt and cardigan set, which at one year old is the newest item in my wardrobe, barring the borrowed gown from Tabitha.

'That's a very well-cut costume,' Mother said approvingly, 'but it's that "ghost of khaki" no-colour colour again.'

'I like these shades, Mother. And if it's good enough for Coco Chanel, it'll do for me.'

'You should have come over with your trunk yesterday. We could have made sure you don't need tucks in your clothes.'

'I haven't lost weight.'

'Looks like it to me.' She sat back, hands folded in her lap, gazing at me steadily as if she had to find out all over again who I am.

'I want to talk to you, Katie.'

'All right.'

Was this to be a mother-daughter chat about why I didn't come home more regularly, or move a little closer to her and Dad? I braced myself for questions.

Her mouth made a little smile, but her eyes looked sad. 'You were my lucky charm. When you came to us, I'd given up all hope of children. I thought I'd be one of those sad women for whom it just didn't happen. There is a certain amount of barrenness in the animal kingdom, you know, so why should we humans be different?'

'I'm glad you think I was your lucky charm.'

'I hope I didn't scoop all the luck from you. I hope there'll be some left.'

The conductor, strolling along the corridor, paused to look in at our compartment. He touched his cap. Mother inclined her head, and waited until he had passed.

251

'It only happened when I'd given up hoping, or even thinking about it. You were seven.'

'I know. I remember very well. It was when I saw the baby clothes in the drawer that I realised.'

'You were wonderful. Such a good little helper.'

'I'd never seen twins before. It felt like a fairy story.'

Mother reached over and this time did take my hand. 'It's like your own personal miracle when you have a child, Katie. I can hardly bear the thought that you're closing your mind to that possibility.'

I let her hold my hand just a moment longer, not to be unkind. 'There's nothing I can do about that.'

'You mustn't give up. It's how long since Gerald was killed . . . four years?'

'Since he went missing' — I could not bear that word killed, not in the same breath as Gerald's name — 'it's four years on Saturday.'

She spoke softly. 'He's not coming back, Katie.'

'I know that.'

Whistle blowing, our train sped through a local station. On the platform, a woman and a small child were seated on a bench. The child waved. A man on crutches in a demob suit stared dully at the train.

'Berta has invited someone who . . .'

'Mother, I'm not interested, not after last year.'

'Don't jump to conclusions.'

'Honestly, you've no idea what the men out there are like. They're the most total rejects, atrocious. Last year . . . that old lecher . . .'

'He was a mistake.'

'They're all a mistake.'

Mother was thoughtful for a moment and then decided to come to the lecher's defence. 'Perhaps he was just a little enthusiastic, bowled over by you.'

'He will be bowled over if I see him again.'

'Some men, they see a wedding ring, and they hear a

young woman's a widow ...'

'So I'm to take off my wedding ring? Or wear a sign, *Yes I'm available but no pawing until we've known each other ten minutes.*'

Mother sighed and gave up, for the moment.

I gazed out of the carriage window. Green fields sped by, hedges and ditches, wildflowers, lambs, birds in the trees. There is something so damned obvious and annoying about April. It gets under one's skin without asking. Something in us seems primed to drown in longings, to fall in love with a man seen from the top of a tram, or some mysterious person who might be just around the corner.

'Hasn't there been anyone you've found the least bit attractive?' Mother asked plaintively.

'No one suitable.'

'Oh blow suitable. Your father wasn't suitable.'

'No one I could see a future with, let's put it that way.'

Mother sighed. 'Don't become a mistress, dear. It wouldn't suit you. And you're still young.'

'I don't feel young.'

'I was your age when I had the twins. I wouldn't have liked to have left it very much longer.'

I shut my eyes, feeling suddenly weary. The April effect evaporated. Being witness to two horrible deaths left me feeling emotionally scooped out. I pretended to sleep, and very soon did, for a long stretch of the journey to London.

Aunt Berta has a way of making a person feel very special. When she heard Mother's worries that I had lost weight, she came to my room with her maid and insisted we look through every item in my trunk as it was unpacked.

'You see, Aunt Berta, Mother's worrying about nothing.'

Aunt Berta nodded. 'All the same, we'll go out shopping. There's some lovely material in Liberty's, and I have

253

the latest pattern books from Paris. You're invited to a wedding I hear?'

'Yes. Tabitha Braithwaite's. We were in the VAD together. She's marrying in May.'

'Goodness, we're almost in May. Easter next week, then May around the corner. Have you bought a hat?'

'No.'

'And have you selected a wedding outfit?'

'Not yet.'

She beamed with delight. 'Then that will be our task. You must have a picture hat. That should be chosen first, then the gown. People always get it the wrong way round. A wedding will make a pleasant change for you. Does Miss Braithwaite have brothers?'

'She had one brother, Edmund. He was killed on the Somme.'

'How sad. And the bridegroom, who are his people?'

'Oh . . . they have land and farms with tenants, that sort of thing.'

Aunt Berta put a hand on my arm. 'I'm glad you're getting out and about. Your mother worries about your investigations and your photography, but I think it's downright plucky.'

On the evening of the birthday dinner party, I stood with Aunt Berta and Uncle Albert in the hall, to greet arrivals. The Conan Doyles' carriage drew up.

Aunt Berta nudged me. 'Sir Arthur and Lady Jean are about to set off on a tour of America but wouldn't miss my party. They're very fond of you, you know, Katie. For two pins they'd ask you to accompany them.'

My aunt blissfully ignores inconvenient facts, such as the gulf between the Conan Doyles' beliefs and mine. They're skipping off to America to promote spiritism – knock-knocking on the door of the beyond.

'I should like to go to America, Aunt, but not just now.'

254

'We must look into that,' Mother said. 'An Atlantic voyage would do us good, but I don't suppose your father will spare the time.'

'Then you and I must go.'

'When?' Mother asked.

Why do I say these things?

Fortunately we were interrupted. When Sir Arthur and Lady Jean swept in, I went into the ballroom with them. Sir Arthur is so intense, but there is always some gem of wisdom to be got from him. Occasionally a person will say something that gives you another way of looking at the world, and he can do that better than anyone else I know. They have known me since I was a little girl. Lady Jean is always charming. All the same they do try to convert me to spiritism. I refuse to try and contact Gerald in the beyond.

Gerald was a great fan of Sir Arthur's historical novels and passed them to me. The last time I met Sir Arthur, I had a dream that we did contact Gerald and he wanted to talk about Sherlock Holmes.

I chatted to Sir Arthur and Lady Jean about their planned trip to America, and all the engagements arranged for them.

Lady Jean is a great one for getting other people to talk. I found myself telling them about the Braithwaite case.

When he heard that Joshua Braithwaite was found in the beck, Sir Arthur's interest sparked immediately. I led him into the library where I had my photographs tucked onto one of the lower bookcases. Truth to tell, I hoped he might have some astonishing insight into the case of the missing Joshua Braithwaite.

Lady Jean followed, as if she had decided never to let her husband out of her sight.

'How extraordinary!' He examined the photograph of Tabitha with the waterfall in the background. 'This is so like Cottingley where the fairies were spotted and photographed by those two young girls. You'll have seen my book on that?'

'Yes.' I tried to sound both interested and non-committal. No photographer worth their salt would imagine that those photographs were anything other than total fakes, but nevertheless Sir Arthur and his Spiritualist friends had chosen to believe there really were fairies.

Sir Arthur spoke with barely suppressed excitement. 'This gentleman who has disappeared, he may well have found his way through to the fairy world. I do firmly believe there are places on this earth — muddied as it is with our materialism, conflict and greed — where we can cross the line into that other world, that parallel universe of grace and joy. Behind the waterfall. There may be a clue.'

'Mr Braithwaite didn't find his way into a parallel universe. The scout leader called the local bobby. He was arrested and taken to hospital.'

'And perhaps found his way back to the waterfall? This is most fascinating. It would be astonishing to have evidence of a man breaking through the barrier between this world and the next, propelled by grief, drawn by the call of his dead son. Take a look, Jean.' He passed the photograph to Lady Doyle.

She creased her brow thoughtfully and said, 'Mmmm,' in a most intelligent and thoughtful tone of voice.

I needed to divert Sir Arthur from his other-world views if there was to be an earthly chance of his talking sense. 'When Mr Braithwaite was found in the beck, he claimed not to have intended suicide. He was in a poor way, confused, bruised, with cuts to his face. It's possible he'd fallen or been attacked. I don't believe he was trying to find his way to another world.'

Sir Arthur looked saddened by my scepticism but obliged me with his speculative glance. 'The clothes that he wore then — were they examined? Did they have marks

256

consistent with a fall? Say, if the lapels had been tugged, or some such thing, there might have been an assailant. It is best to look thoroughly, explore the most obvious details first.'

'There was no note in the policeman's account about his clothing being examined. He did have a scrap of material caught in his watch chain.'

'What sort of material?'

'It's something between textured cotton and webbing, in a check, beige and red. I haven't got the piece with me, but I did take a photograph.'

I produced the photograph from my briefcase. I had colour-washed it to reflect its faded beige, with red and black stripes, like a poor imitation of a tartan.

Sir Arthur examined it closely. 'Some kind of upholstery, or lining. A heavy cotton weave?'

'Yes.'

'Probably woven in Lancashire.'

He passed the photograph to his wife. If she was already bored with me, she hid it well, saying graciously, 'Mmmm. I do believe you're right, my dear.'

Sir Arthur narrowed his eyes thoughtfully. 'This confusion the gentleman experienced, had he been treated for any ailment or disease? Certain medicines induce symptoms such as those you describe, or it could be that he had glimpsed the other world and if so I should be most interested to know the effect that would have on a man's mind.'

'I don't know whether he was undergoing treatment. The regular village doctor was in the army. If Mr Braithwaite was ill the chances are he would have been relying on whatever home remedies he usually turned to.'

Could Braithwaite's confusion have been caused not by his being duffed up as everyone thought, but by the overdose of some drug?

'It would be wise to eliminate the obvious,' Sir Arthur

said sagely. 'I'll send over my *materia medica*. You might find it useful to take a look. If so, I shall treat you to one of your own as mine is full of youthful scribbles in the margins. Keep it until we return from America.'

'Thank you. I should very much like to see it.'

Sir Arthur beamed with pleasure at the prospect of doing me a good turn. This caused Lady Doyle to smile graciously.

They watched me pack the photographs back into my briefcase. 'The art of investigation is in asking the right questions,' I said.

'Knowing what questions to ask is the hardest thing in the world.' Lady Jean smiled – as if she would always know what questions to ask but would be too ladylike to voice them.

Sir Arthur leaned towards me. For a moment I expected an avuncular hand on my shoulder, but that is not his way. 'You might ask yourself, Why am I so afraid of the unknown? Believe me, I know. I've seen my mother, my brother, my son. I've spoken to them. If you want to contact your poor dead husband, then do try. He may be waiting on the other side to give you a blessing, and permission to go on living.'

I snapped the briefcase shut. 'But I am going on living.'

Lady Jean took Sir Arthur's arm. The two exchanged a look of such love and conspiracy that it made my heart hurt.

I took the briefcase upstairs to my room.

As I came downstairs, Aunt Berta pounced. 'There you are, my dear.' She grasped my elbow firmly and manoeuvred me across the ballroom.

'I believe you and this gentleman have met? This is Dr Grainger. Dr Grainger, my beloved niece, Mrs Shackleton.'

At that moment, the gong sounded for dinner. Aunt Berta disappeared to do the honours elsewhere.

'Lovely to see you again so soon, Mrs Shackleton.'

Dr Grainger gave a winning smile which did not win me. He had wasted no time in shutting up Milton House Hospital and leaving it, and Evelyn, behind.

'I'm intrigued, Dr Grainger. How did you wangle an invitation to my aunt's birthday bash?'

He reddened slightly with embarrassment. 'You mentioned that your father knew Professor Podmore . . .'

'He's a very old friend of my uncle's.'

'You know I'm working with the professor? He took pity on me and mentioned me to your aunt.'

'I see.'

And of course Aunt Berta would have jumped at the chance of inviting an up and coming eligible man with all his limbs and no glaring defects.

Dr Grainger offered me his arm. I didn't need an arm. He had obviously been out of society too long and had pre-war manners.

He said, 'I wangled an invitation because I wanted to see you again. Hope you don't mind.'

'Dr Grainger, last year I was seated between a lecher and a ninny. At least I can be sure you will not presume to stroke my thigh or recite bad verse.'

My father once asked Sir Arthur how it was he could have been so dispassionate in defending Sir Roger Casement, when everyone knew the man to be a traitor. Sir Arthur had answered that Roger Casement was not in his right mind when he committed the offence, and that it was necessary for men of judgement (it was always men) to make allowance for human weaknesses, inherent flaws and mental failings that could not be helped.

I bore this in mind as I took Dr Grainger's arm.

Aunt Berta's dinner party has shrunk over the years. Pre-war it had been a great social event, then for five years, she would not celebrate at all. Only Mother came to be with her during those times, and my mother never failed her. Aunt Berta had her first child on her twenty-

259

fourth birthday. Albert Tobias would have been the same age as me had he lived, thirty-one. Mother once told me that it was after she saw Albert, picked him up from his cot and sang a nursery rhyme to him, that she hurried back to Yorkshire determined to adopt a child. Me.

We were, by Lord and Lady Pocklington's standards, a modest gathering of fourteen. The Conan Doyles sat either side of Uncle Albert, with Professor Podmore to Jean Doyle's left and Mrs Podmore opposite her husband. Mrs Podmore is on the board of a children's charity and shamelessly canvases for funds at every opportunity. I sat beside Professor Podmore and talked to him, and to Dr Grainger opposite me, about their progress towards the opening of the Maudsley Hospital. Professor Podmore has visited the United States of America and so was able to chat to the Conan Doyles about the places they would visit. On my left sat the old world colonel who was at the siege of Ladysmith and whose conversation seems frozen in time. If one elicits his opinion on any event after 1900 he seems as puzzled as a child who missed the lesson on Rivers of England. Fortunately cousin James' wife Hope was seated opposite the colonel. Hope very agreeably prompts others to speak and reveals nothing. She has a slightly oriental air but I am not sure whether this is due to her high cheek bones or the enigmatic look in her mysterious grey-green eyes. Cousin James is Something-in-the-War Office, so perhaps Hope Knows Things and keeps quiet to avoid inadvertently spilling National Secrets into the soup.

My mother had her usual place on Uncle Albert's right, opposite cousin Malcolm, the middle son who scraped through the war with a limp and a nervous twitch. There is something touching about him that makes my heart ache. He is married to the fair Penelope who also gallantly listened to stories of Ladysmith.

Mercifully the dinner passed without the Conan Doyles

260

or Dr Grainger mentioning my investigations. I resolved to tell mother as soon as we returned to the drawing room, before anyone else got in before me.

'Professionally?' she said, her voice rising. She led me to an alcove in the far corner of the room. 'You have become a professional private detective? I don't understand.'

After this, I took refuge in talking to my cousins whom I do not see from one year to the next. Twice, Dr Grainger made moves towards me. Once Hope intervened to question him about the meaning of dreams. When Dr Grainger and I did speak, it was in the company of others. The colonel was most anxious to talk to Dr Grainger, about his dreams of Ladysmith.

There is something to be said for getting up at six o'clock in the morning, and it is this: If you get up at six o'clock, you avoid those mad, exhausting dreams that come between seven and eight. However, I rarely rise at six. On the morning after my aunt's dinner party, it was nearer nine.

I looked at myself in the bathroom mirror, slightly more presentable after several face-splashings. Someone tried the door. I would have to vacate soon. I drew on my robe and combed my hair so as not to give anyone a fright as I walked along the landing to my room.

Putting the pieces of the Braithwaite mystery together was like one of those spinning tops. If you looked at it in stillness, the images and the sections were all discretely painted in bright colours. When the top began to spin, those hues became a blur and a dazzling pattern that bore no relation to the neat pictures of the top when still.

I sat on the bed and tried to think through what I had learned. My brain refused to function. With a sigh, I dressed and gave up trying. Perhaps I should simply wait, go on investigating and see what other connections might be thrown up from my unconscious mind. A nagging voice told me this probably arose from laziness and was not an idea that would have found its way into the manuals of detection lodged at Scotland Yard.

I breakfasted alone since Mother and Aunt Berta were still in their rooms and Uncle Albert had left for the Foreign Office.

After breakfast I placed a telephone call to Mrs Sugden.

'Any news of any kind?' I asked after we had exchanged pleasantries about the weather in London and Leeds – showery but bright and cold for the time of year.

'Mr Duffield telephoned from the newspaper library. He says he has put some information in the post to you.'

'I see. Did he say what? Or has it arrived?'

'He posted it this morning. I expect it will be here by second post. Shall I send it on to you? Only I do believe you are having a respite from brain work and that is why I did not give him Lady Pocklington's address.'

'Yes, do send it on. And has the painting been cleaned yet?'

'The restorer will be here at 10.30 this morning.'

'I'll talk to you later then.'

'Enjoy yourself. Forget about it all, that's my opinion. Wherever he is or is not, Joshua Braithwaite won't be fretting over you.'

'Thank you, Mrs Sugden.'

I returned to my room. A neat brown paper parcel sat on the dressing table, my name and address written in Sir Arthur's clear hand. With my nail scissors I snipped the string at its sealing wax. It was, as promised, his copy of the *materia medica*, his name inscribed on the fly leaf. The book was much marked with his comments. He must have used it not only when he was a medical student, but in connection with his research for the Sherlock Holmes stories for there was a great deal of underlining of poisons and their effects.

His short note read, *To my dear Kate wishing you much success in your endeavours. Look to the waterfall. The fairy waterfall may provide the doorway to a new and richer life. A.C.D.'*

As I pulled on my outdoor shoes, I thought how simple it would be if we could really and truly slip through a waterfall into another life, like Charles Kingsley's poor Tom. Instead, I intended to explore the world of the patent office.

Is having a "no-stone-unturned" mentality a hindrance or a help? Without any great hopes of enlightenment, it seemed a good idea to look at the inventions that came from the world of the Bridgestead mill. When totally stumped, poke in corners. If Arthur Wilson had come up with an invention that had the potential to make a fortune and not been properly reimbursed, that could stoke bitterness, resentment and envy that might be a motive for murder.

As I opened Aunt Berta's front door onto a showery day, the butler called me back to the telephone. I half expected Mrs Sugden to have remembered some other message for me.

It was Dr Grainger. Might I possibly meet him for lunch? There was something he had wanted to say last night and hadn't found the moment. He named his club and asked whether he might meet me there.

'If it's all the same to you, let's meet at the Cavendish Club.' I preferred to be on home turf.

'As you wish.'

'Shall we say twelve?'

We did say twelve. I picked up my bag and notebook.

'Will you have the car, or shall I call you a taxi, madam?' the butler asked.

'I shall take the tube, but you might ring the Cavendish Club and book a table for two for Mrs Shackleton – 12.30 today.'

I wondered what Dr Grainger may want to say to me.

The Patent Office has the same hushed atmosphere as the British Museum Library, but with something else in the mix along with steeped thought. Perhaps the hope of all the inventors gives the place an edge of nerviness. A disapproving old head turned as my feet tapped across the tiled floor. The high domed ceiling and long windows flooded the room with light. At wooden bench-like tables that I imagine must be made in their hundreds for every fine library in the land, men pored over dusty tomes, making pencil scribbles into their books or onto scraps of paper. I had a sudden image of fiery rage seething under a bald pate as some intellectual labourer discovered Charles Blogg had pipped him to the post in the search for the unique filament that would create an everlasting light bulb or the close-coupled link that would allow the hitching of railway carriages at a greater rate of knots. Perhaps some of these gentlemen were out-and-out thieves, taking a bit of this invention and a smattering of that with the intention of coming up with a piston-fired bike or a self-driving motor car.

A young man of about twenty-one years of age sat on a high stool behind a desk, between pillars at the far end of the room. In hushed tones, I asked for the records of textile patents applied for since 1914. He disappeared into the inner sanctum beyond the pillars.

Finding a seat at a nearby table, I waited. What was I looking for? How could this search help me to find out what had happened to Joshua Braithwaite? The phrase clutching at straws came into that part of my mind that always takes the mocking, cynical view of my activities. Another voice in my head said, Go on looking for pieces of the jigsaw.

The clerk lowered two heavy volumes onto the table in front of me. 'Five more to come.'

'How is the material ordered?'

'Chronologically. You'll find a list of inventions by applicant, with a brief description, at the beginning of each volume. Textiles are contained within other industrial patents applied for.'

The world must be teeming with inventors. Notebook and pencil at the ready, I scanned the pages for familiar names, for words that might connect to the textile industry. I could not in every case tell from the brief descriptions whether these devices related to textiles or some other industry. Where an applicant's name was stated, I had no confidence, given the secrecy in the world of mill owners, whether this was some pseudonym. There was a comb dabbing brushmaker, a deburrer, a rotary dobby. All these patent applications bore the inventors' names: Burns, Twitchell, Hartley. So here was a way for clever men of technical ability to leave their mark on history. 'Oh my grandfather invented the Automatic Wool Sliver Comber that bears his name.'

But none were connected with the Braithwaites.

The volume for 1915 proved more fruitful. In May of that year, there was an application for the patent of The Bridgestead Picker. I looked up the details. A drawing and measurements outlined a picker of lightweight metal to be used with all looms and to reduce weft and warp breakages and eliminate the probability of oil stains on expensive cloth.

The application for the patent was signed by Joshua Braithwaite. According to Marjorie, Arthur Wilson was paid what he regarded as a pittance for his invention. And he did not have his name attached. That would annoy me. But enough to kill?

I looked up and caught the clerk's eye. He came across to me.

'Would you be able to tell me whether this patent was granted?'

265

He nodded, making a note of the number.

It did not take him long to return, carrying a ledger, a strip of paper marking the page. He stood beside me, opened the ledger and directed my gaze to a line. The patent was granted.

'Would much use be made of something like this? Has it been widely manufactured, do you know?'

'The only time I ever get to know such things is if I read it in the newspapers. With something like this, you'd need to ask a mill owner I dare say.'

I blinked my way out of the building, umbrella unfurled, and walked along Chancery Lane where I hailed a cab to 28 Cavendish Square.

During the war, we women of the Voluntary Aid Detachment had nowhere in London we could call our own. It was not unusual for me to turn up on Aunt Berta's doorstep with half a dozen VAD girls in tow who hadn't a place to lay their heads. At last, here was a place we could go, opened two years ago, a splendid Ladies' Club with moderate charges.

Our husbands, brothers and sons had their war memorials. VADs had this proud place where we could meet and look forward to an uncertain future.

Entering its portals, seeing the photograph of the Princess Royal on the wall, was like coming home.

20

Blending

Blending: Wools from different fleeces but of similar qualities are mixed together.

As I approached the Cavendish Club reception desk, I caught a glimpse of Dr Grainger in the lounge. He sat on a sofa, turning a page in *The Times*.

Alfred the porter has a prodigious memory for faces but this time excelled by remembering my name. 'Your guest is in the lounge, Mrs Shackleton. And we have a telephone message for you.' He handed me a note.

Ah, that was why he knew my name!

'Thank you.'

For Mrs Sugden to track me down to the Cavendish, she must have something important to tell me.

I handed the note back to Alfred. 'Would you please put a call in to this number?'

He nodded.

'I'll say hello to my guest while you're getting connected.'

Dr Grainger folded the newspaper and stood to greet me.

'Thank you for agreeing to lunch, Mrs Shackleton.'

I felt unaccountably suspicious of him. I perched on the edge of the settee and asked, 'Did you enjoy the evening?' The frost crackled in my voice.

'Yes. I felt honoured to be asked.'

'And I wonder what it is that you couldn't say yesterday evening.'

Note to myself, I thought. Do not sound so hostile. He probably can't help being a social-climbing philanderer.

'You're asking questions already. I hoped I might get one or two in today. Such as, will you have a drink before lunch?'

'Yes, a dry sherry would go down well. And I shall need to take one telephone call when it comes through.'

'Of course.'

Was there something just a touch sarcastic in his tone? Not that I cared.

What a joy to see the waitress in her VAD uniform! It took me back to the old days. She took his order for two dry sherries.

For a few moments we chatted about the party. Dr Grainger had gone with my cousins to a club and danced till dawn, he confided. He had the headache to prove it.

It disturbed me that he had wriggled his way into my family. I could not feel easy in his company. Nor could I quite say why. Surely I wasn't so prejudiced that I could dislike the man intensely for having had an affair with Evelyn Braithwaite – an affair that might be still going on for all I knew.

For all I knew. That might be it. It was to do with wanting to know. He was a prodder and poker into people's motives and actions, and so was I. Perhaps that was why this invisible line of tension ran between us when we met. Who knew what, and who knew most. A competition for omniscience. Well, I didn't feel I would come racing through the line first. Too many jigsaw puzzle pieces and not enough picture for that.

The waitress brought sherry.

Dr Grainger lit my cigarette. 'Shall we make an agreement?'

'Such as?'

'Question for question. But because you already interrogated me at Milton House, I must have two questions for every one that you ask.'

268

It made me smile to think he was as wary of me as I of him.

'There! You smiled. We don't have to interrogate. We could just sit and chat and see what comes out.'

'Very well. But can we get one thing out of the way first, Dr Grainger?'

'That's a question, so I'm due two. Answer: yes.'

'My aunt tries to matchmake for me. I don't encourage it and I don't wish it.'

He gave a short breathy whistle. 'That puts me in my place. And it does clear the air. Thank you.'

The look that crossed his face as he whistled was so fleeting that I could not tell whether he was genuinely disappointed or simply pretending to be disappointed out of politeness.

My telephone call came through. I apologised and walked to the hall.

Mrs Sugden put the picture restorer on the line to speak to me. I listened to what he had to say.

'I see. Yes. Would you describe the figure please, age, appearance? . . . I see. Thank you. Yes, do please continue the work.'

I asked to speak again to Mrs Sugden. 'Would you please get in touch with Mr Sykes, and tell him what the picture restorer has just told me?'

I returned to the lounge, feeling dazed.

'Are you all right?' Dr Grainger asked.

'Yes – just had a bit of a surprise about something that's all. Shall we go up to lunch?'

We both plumped for onion soup. He chose the pork chop, I decided on steak and kidney pudding.

I was glad he suggested a good wine. It was brought quickly and after one or two sips we both began to relax. He told me more about his work preparing for the opening of the Maudsley Hospital, how glad he was to be back in London.

'I'm glad it's working out well for you.'

Suddenly he looked guilty.

'I'm sorry. I didn't mean to harp on about myself so much. You were married to a doctor I believe?'

'Yes. A surgeon.'

He nodded.

For a moment we were silent. There is so little one can say when one contemplates the great waste we have all come through, that we stumble through still, gathering up the broken threads of our lives.

Over the soup, I talked about Gerald, how we met by chance in the summer of 1913. Gerald had a post at Leeds General Infirmary and would come over to Wakefield where I lived with my parents. We knew the train timetable by heart.

'And will you stay in Leeds, or perhaps come to London?' He cut into his pork chop, looking rather enviously at my steak and kidney pud.

I shrugged. 'I've no particular reason to come to London.'

A week ago I would have had no particular reason not to. Now I was a private detective with an employee in Leeds, and a case to solve.

The dining room was filling up. I recognised one or two women by sight from the grand opening of the club two years ago.

'You like it here, don't you?' Grainger asked.

'I do.'

'Good choice. There aren't many clubs in London where you'll get such a good value lunch.'

That's because so many former VADs are damned hard up, idiot.

We finished the main course. I wondered when he would find his way to saying what he had failed to tell me last night.

He dabbed at the corner of his mouth with the servi-

270

ette. 'Before the war, I got to know Josephine Tuffnell. Did you ever meet her?'

'Yes.' She was one of the 1912 debutantes, a great beauty, with a title in the family that went back almost as far as my mother's and aunt's. 'I heard her play and sing once. She's very good and seemed charming.'

They were all charming. Who knows what had happened to her since?

'We were close, but . . . I wasn't approved of by the family. Last night, or in the early hours, when I left the others, I walked along the Embankment, and I thought of her and wondered what she was doing now.'

'Why don't you find out?'

'Do you think I should?'

'Yes.'

'It's ridiculous, isn't it, that I'm asking you this. I hope you don't mind.'

'Not at all.' I didn't say that it was a great relief to me, nor that there was a touch of disappointment in that relief. 'Why didn't the Tuffnells approve of you?'

'Her family decided that a mere medical man of no fortune was quite unsuitable.'

'I don't think the family has a great fortune?'

'No – only the title and there's a tumbling family pile that will go to her brother. But I believe there's a great need for ready cash and I don't answer that need.'

'How sad.'

'I caught sight of her a few weeks ago, when I came to town for a Maudsley meeting . . .'

Liars should have good memories. He had told me only last week that he was still considering his options.

'. . . I was on an omnibus and she was walking along the pavement. I got off at the next stop, but she'd disappeared. I'd like to see her again, but I'm not sure whether it's a good idea, after everything that's happened. We've all changed . . . and I've had all that time in Yorkshire . . .'

271

Now we were at the crux of the matter. He might satisfy my curiosity about his affair with Evelyn. I wanted to know, but dreaded that he would be a man who kisses and tells.

'Will you be keeping up any of the Yorkshire connections?' I asked in what I hoped was a tactful tone.

'Don't think so. That's a closed chapter.' He shut his lips tightly and concentrated on spearing a potato. So he was not going to prattle about Evelyn, thank goodness.

'Everything's different now, Dr Grainger. For most girls, no prince is going to come along. Even the dimmest of parents realise that. If Yorkshire's a closed chapter, try and see Josephine again. Besides, she'll be of an age to make up her own mind now.'

He leaned forward, a puzzled frown on his face. 'But how? What should I do after all this time?'

I stifled a laugh. Here he was, a widower, having had an affair of who knew how long with Evelyn Braithwaite, a psychiatrist at the helm of the soon-to-be major psychiatric hospital, and he was asking me for advice on his love life. A bit bloody rich!

'You could write her a letter.'

'I'm not sure she would get it. My letters were intercepted before.'

'Then wait outside her house, preferably in the rain, a bouquet of flowers in your hand.'

'You're right! I shall.'

He raised his glass to clink mine.

'Is this why you wanted to meet for lunch? For advice on your love life?'

Because if so you should have offered to take me to the Ritz, Tightwad.

'No. No, sorry. I shouldn't have even brought that up.' He ran his hands through his hair. 'The truth is . . . well, it's this . . . the thing is, when we talked before, I wasn't entirely candid.'

'Really?' I exaggerated my surprise. Which of the notcandids did you have in mind, I wanted to ask. There were several. 'You did put me off by saying you had yet to finish preparing a talk about the dreams of the men you'd been treating. In fact, you must have given that speech at least half a dozen times.'

His jaw tensed. He tugged at his collar. Either he was very poor at covering his emotions or he was deliberately acting ill-at-ease. 'I'm sorry. It was an untruth. I didn't know what you wanted. I felt uneasy about Braithwaite's disappearance. Culpable you might say. I needed time before being able to address the matter.'

We waited until the waitress had taken our plates.

Although our puddings had not arrived, he toyed with his spoon. 'May I tell you something in absolute confidence?'

'Please do.'

'Evelyn Braithwaite wasn't my patient. She did now and then read for the patients, or write a letter, or sit and talk. But she came to Milton House primarily for reasons that I can't divulge.'

'You don't have to, but in saying that you already have! I had worked it out.'

'You know?'

'I saw you together.'

Our apple crumble arrived.

I waited, spoon poised for his next admission.

'Tell me, Mrs Shackleton, if I may ask, when you embark on these investigations of yours, it's clearly a great and diverting challenge.'

'That's your question?'

'Not quite. When you conclude the investigations, do you feel an immense satisfaction?'

'Not always. Arriving at the truth can be uncomfortable.'

'Then it's the chase you like, the search?'

I smiled. 'I'm very glad that the object of your desires

273

is Josephine Tuffnell and not Kate Shackleton.'

'And the answer?'

'I haven't stood back to think about that. It's just something I started to do almost accidentally.'

'When?'

He wanted me to say that I had begun after Gerald went missing. He expected that I did this work out of a great sense of loss, to find some meaning in the absence of the man I loved.

'Too many questions, Dr Grainger. Eat your apple crumble while it's still hot.'

He made a gesture of surrender and took a spoonful of apple crumble and custard. 'This reminds me of boarding school.'

'You must have gone to a good boarding school, Dr Grainger. Our custard had far more lumps.'

'If we're going to compare childhood custard, I think you should call me Gregory.'

'Agreed. It's Kate.'

'I know. It's a lovely name.'

It was one of those impossible to control teapots. However carefully you pour, something drips onto the table cloth. He watched me make a mess of pouring, and sighed.

'Take over yourself if you can do any better,' I offered.

'It's not that. There's something I'm going to have to tell you now, that I should have said before. This is very difficult. I don't know how to own up.'

'Is this why you rang me, what you couldn't say last night?'

'Yes.'

'Then just say it.'

'That Monday, the day Joshua Braithwaite went missing, I saw him.'

'In the hospital?'

He nodded, spooning sugar into his tea and stirring very

274

slowly. 'But also – outside of the hospital, on the hills. Evelyn was with me, in the consulting room. He'd tried to telephone his solicitor, on both days, and got nowhere. He'd asked about Tabitha, who was away, and asked about his wife. Well, Evelyn had said she didn't want to see him. The next morning, he was due before the magistrates. Anyway, after we'd ... talked, Evelyn thought perhaps she ought to see him.'

'This was before you spotted him on the hills?'

'That's right. I can't remember now whether it was her idea to see him, or my idea. Mr Braithwaite had asked for her. I called an orderly to fetch Mr Braithwaite to the consulting room. The orderly came back to tell me Mr Braithwaite was nowhere to be found. He'd gone.'

'What time would that have been?'

'About four o'clock.'

'Did Evelyn seem surprised?'

'Yes, very. I must admit it crossed my mind that she may have been manipulating me in order to give her husband time to vamoose, but later I realised that wasn't the situation. I went upstairs, to his room, and sure enough he was gone.'

'What would he have been wearing?'

'The hospital blues. His own clothing had been taken away, as a precaution. I told the orderly to search, search the building and the grounds. You know the size of that place.'

'The orderly, was it Kellett by any chance?'

'No. He was off duty, it was the other chap, Stafford. Anyway, I looked out of the window. From the upstairs windows you get an excellent view across the moors.'

'Yes, I know that area. Tabitha and I walked there one day and we saw Milton House. It seemed much nearer to the road from there. It's actually a fair way off.'

'That may be, but that's where he was. I'm sure it was he – running across the fells, a small figure in blue. I went to fetch binoculars to make sure.'

'What did you do then?'

'I went downstairs and told Evelyn. She said that sounded like him. He was a great runner as a younger chap, took part in fell races and so on.'

'And then?'

'I was all for ringing Constable Mitchell. He was the one who'd given me responsibility, though it was the last thing I'd wanted. Evelyn asked would I wait. She didn't want any more of a hoo-ha and scandal than there'd been already.'

'That's a bit rich, given that she could have probably put the hat on things much earlier.' I could have bit my tongue. Not only because of the indiscretion but because he may think me jealous of his affair with Evelyn.

He showed no sign of reacting to my remark, except to say, 'Be that as it may, I agreed. I said I'd get a search going round the grounds and roundabout, and only then call the constable.'

'So what was Evelyn's plan?'

'She was on horseback. She would intercept him. In the event, she couldn't find him.'

'She probably called Stoddard at the mill?'

'No. She didn't use the telephone.'

'Tell me, Gregory, in what direction was Joshua Braithwaite running?'

'A south-westerly direction.'

'Towards . . .?'

'I suppose generally in the direction of Bradford.'

Towards Worstedopolis. Where else would a mill master run?

'And Kate, it's embarrassing to admit this, but given that I delayed reporting it and so on, I didn't tell Constable Mitchell that I'd seen Braithwaite.'

We sat for a while in silence. I thought about what Sir Arthur had said last night when I had recounted Hector's

276

description of how Joshua Braithwaite did not recognise or remember him when dragged from the beck, and that he appeared disoriented and confused. Up to now we had all assumed it was because Braithwaite had been attacked. Now I wondered could there be another explanation.

'Was Mr Braithwaite on any medication – for some ailment or illness?'

Gregory took out his cigarette case and offered it to me.

He lit our cigarettes. 'I should be able to answer that question, but I can't. Why do you ask?'

'It might explain why he was not his usual self – and why he was found in such odd circumstances.'

'He wouldn't let me examine him. I did offer. I thought he may have had a hangover, but apparently he was teetotal. It could be that he had taken something. I assumed that he'd been roughed up, or overexerted himself in some way.'

'Yes, that's what I thought.'

'I'm sorry. I realise that's not much help.'

There was no ashtray on our table. Gregory reached across and took one from a nearby table.

'Gregory, I don't know when I'll see you again, and I really would like to get to the bottom of this mystery for Tabby's sake. Is there anything else, anything at all you can tell me?'

He concentrated hard on his cigarette. I was asking him what Evelyn Braithwaite may have divulged.

'I had heard he was not the most faithful of husbands. You have a theory don't you?'

'I have a straw I'm clutching.'

'If I knew what you were thinking I might be able to help.'

'I'm conjuring with the possibility that he never intended to commit suicide, just as he said. That he had a plan to go away with another woman, but that someone tried to stop him, perhaps the woman's husband.'

'So he could be alive somewhere, living a bigamous existence?'

'There is that possibility.'

He tapped the ash from his cigarette. So many emotions seemed to cloud his face that I could not make out his thoughts. Regret for ever being involved? A sense of guilt because of letting Braithwaite run off across the moors?

'I hope you find him, Kate, though I'll tell you this without breaking any confidences. Evelyn wouldn't have him back at any price.'

'It's not Evelyn who asked me to find him. If I find him, it will be for Tabby.'

The VAD waitress cleared our plates. She smiled at me, not that I had ever met her but we all knew each other.

Gregory put on his Homburg. We shook hands in the lobby.

'Promise me we'll have lunch again next time you're in London, Kate.'

'Yes, we shall. And by then I hope you'll reintroduce me to Josephine Tuffnell.'

He took out a card. 'You can contact me at Professor Podmore's rooms on Harley Street. I'm based there for the time being, until we're set up at the Maudsley.'

I watched from the window as he set off with a spring in his step, heading for the tube. He had offered to share a cab, and drop me off while he went on to resume work at the hospital. But Mother and Aunt Berta would be coming to meet me, with a shopping trip in mind.

Before they arrived, there might just be time for me to make a telephone call to Tabitha that would push my investigation forward.

The receptionist gave me permission to use the office telephone. I put through a call, keeping my fingers crossed that Evelyn or her maid would not pick up the receiver.

I could tell by the way Tabitha answered that she expected it to be Hector. When she realised it was me, she adjusted her voice by an octave, so that she sounded her age.

'Where are you calling from, Kate?'

'The Cavendish Club.'

'Oh how wonderful! I ache to be in London. I would love to be lunching at the Cavendish. Did you have the one and thrupenny lunch and are all the waitresses in our uniform?'

'Yes and yes. But Tabitha, I hope you can help me. There's something I want you to find out, and some information.'

'What is it?'

'The information first. Did your father have any complaints about his health immediately before he went missing? Dr Grainger couldn't help me on that. Does anything occur to you?'

'Nothing huge, like heart attacks or anything.'

'What about other ailments?'

'Well yes, I do remember now as it happens. Hector's father had a painful shoulder, couldn't raise his arm, and that reminded me that Dad once had that too.'

'Immediately before he went missing?'

'Oh no, just one year when we were on holiday at Grange and he was trying to finish a painting. But the shoulder made me remember. You see Hector's mother had neuralgia last week . . .'

I sighed, prepared to listen to a health report on Hector's entire family before Tabitha would get to the point and answer my question.

'And . . .?' I urged.

'Well, Dad had neuralgia as well. I remember thinking it might make my birthday dinner even worse than it would have been – what with not having Edmund there – if Dad's neuralgia played up. Do you think that might have had something to do with his going missing?'

'Not directly, no. Was he taking anything for it?'

'Oh yes.'

'Do you remember what?'

'No, but I could enquire. Mother might remember, or the housekeeper might. You see, we've had no doctor in the village for ages. I suppose he might have gone to Bingley or Keighley and seen someone there, a doctor or a chemist. Perhaps there'll be something in the bathroom cabinet still.'

'See what you can find out for me. But there's one other thing I'd like you to check, and to do this first please. Where did your father keep his art materials?'

There was a long pause. I could hear her brain ticking. 'I can't remember.'

'What I want to know, Tabitha, his paints, brushes, his easel, did he take them anywhere before he left for good, perhaps a week or so before? If you can find out for me, that might be one more clue.'

When I spoke to Tabitha, I felt like a girls' adventure storyteller. But it worked.

'I say! That's something we didn't think of. He didn't take any of his suits, only what he stood up in, but that would . . .'

'Don't get your hopes up, Tabitha. Just find out as soon as you can. Ring me back. I hope I'll still be here and not whisked away on the shopping trip.'

'Oh I do wish I could come with you.'

'Soon as you can, eh?' I gave her the number.

I heard Mother and Aunt Berta before I saw them. They sailed into the lobby in a swish of chiffon and linen, Mother in lilac and Aunt Berta in blue, each with a tiny veiled hat and the grand manner that increases by several octaves when they are together.

'It is so modern to be in a club that's for women,' Aunt Berta pronounced. 'Who would have thought it when we were Kate's age?'

'It's all very convenient for girls who need this sort of thing,' Mother said doubtfully. 'Girls who don't have a home and family behind them.'

I could see that they were ready to surge into Bond Street, Regent Street and Oxford Street, but attempted to delay them in the hope of hearing from Tabitha.

Fortunately my aunt and mother agreed that a pot of Darjeeling and a slice of Madeira cake would fortify us for the shopping ordeal that lay ahead. We made ourselves comfortable on the chintz chairs in the drawing room.

'The pace out there is so hectic,' Aunt Berta said. 'There's far too much rushing about.'

'Goodness me.' My mother glanced disapprovingly at my notebook. 'You've been at it again, haven't you? What a strain you put on yourself, my dear.'

For my mother, a strain consisted of arranging far too many anemones or interfering in housekeeping of which she understood nothing.

'I don't find it a strain. It interests me.' That sounded lame, even to me.

Fortunately, the tea arrived.

No sooner had I poured than the porter came to the drawing room to tell me I had a call.

I excused myself and took the call. 'Tabby?'

'Yes it's me. What a connection we have, almost as if you're in the next room.'

'Yes. All the better to hear what you have to tell me.'

'Well, I didn't know where Dad kept his painting stuff. Mother's out riding, so I asked our housekeeper. Well, she did know. Dad used the summerhouse, out beyond the veg plot. Mrs Kay and I trotted along there. She's the soul of discretion, and very reliable.'

'And?'

'This is the good part. There is nothing. Not a paint-brush, not a palette, not an easel – except for a broken one that he wouldn't have wanted. Oh, and some empty paint pots and a couple of brushes with their bristles chewed away. '

'Do you think his art materials may have been thrown out, or given to someone?'

'This is where it's encouraging. Mrs Kay has both keys. No one has been in there for an age. My mother never goes into the summerhouse – though she says now and again that she keeps meaning to have the place bottomed out.'

'Right. Well, that's interesting. Thanks, Tabby.'

'Do you think it's significant, Kate?'

'I'm not sure.'

'You must or you wouldn't be asking. If Dad took his art materials, then he intended going off to paint – like that what's-his-name Gauguin. He was the one who escaped to the South Sea Islands and left everyone behind wasn't he?'

'Kate!' The voice boomed from the drawing room. 'Your tea is getting cold, my dear.'

'And, Tabby, did you find out, was your father taking any medicines?'

'Oh, I forgot, hold on . . .'

'No, it's all right. Just let me know when you can. We'll talk again soon.'

When Mother, Aunt Berta and I stepped outside into the April afternoon, fortified with tea and heading for the stores, I felt pleased and optimistic. It was spring, after all, and two people were in love: Tabitha Braithwaite with Hector and Gregory Grainger with Josephine.

In spite of everything, the world would keep on turning.

21

Perching

Perching: When a cloth comes off the loom, it is thoroughly examined for faults. Defects which can be repaired in the next stage of manufacture are marked with chalk. Faults which cannot be mended are marked with a piece of string in the selvedge.

It was Good Friday. There would be no return home before Tuesday because we were engaged to stay with Aunt Berta and Uncle Albert over the Easter weekend, with Dad due today. He'd be pleased to know that Sykes was a great help.

After breakfast, I escaped to Uncle Albert's library to open the two letters that had come - Sykes' first. It made me smile to read his admission that he was wrong about Stoddard or, as Sykes cryptically referred to him, "the gentleman in question" – murdering Lizzie Kellett.

Dear Mrs Shackleton

You were right and I was wrong about the gentleman in question. Size nine boots he may have, but his are bespoke. The pattern of sole left on the bank by the cottage is that of a workman's boot – bought in the nearby town and repaired by a local shoe mender who has provided the police with a list of names of individuals who wear that boot which is popular.

As to the cricket bat, fingerprints were taken. These do not resemble those on the bobbin you provided – again clearing the gentleman in question.

Sykes' disappointment was evident. He had taken a strong dislike to Stoddard. I suspected this was because he felt bad about letting me into the mill and standing by while Stoddard discovered me there. It was a matter of pride. If he could have found Stoddard guilty of more than outwitting us, he would have been a happy man.

Sykes' letter continued.

> *Mrs Sugden sent word for me to come and see the cleaned oil painting. (The restorer had done his work and left when I arrived.) We were correct in surmising that the smudges constituted an act of concealment, even vandalism. The grey smear on the bridge being removed, there appears a petite, dark-haired woman aged about twenty-five, painted as something of a beauty in a flowered summer frock. At the foot of the waterfall, an infant floats in a Moses basket. Mr Winterton, the restorer, gave Mrs Sugden to understand that the woman and infant had been added to the scene at a later date. They were subsequently painted over inexpertly, not by the artist, but well enough for an unobservant person not to notice anything odd at first glance.*
>
> *Is this Braithwaite's "other family"? I shall pursue this line of enquiry.*
> *Yours respectfully*
> *J R Sykes*

Good question, Mr Sykes. No surprise that Evelyn wanted the painting out of her sight or that she could not bring herself to destroy a work that showed her own children at play. I may have to rethink my plan of giving the painting to Tabitha after her marriage. She may not appreciate her father's attachment to a woman as young, or younger, than herself and the existence of an unknown sibling set to inherit Edmund's bucket and spade.

The second letter came from Mr Duffield at the news-paper library, forwarded by Mrs Sugden.

Dear Mrs Shackleton

When you last made enquiries of me, you asked me to tell you if I could recall any further information regarding the matter you were investigating. The reporter I mentioned to you, the late Harold Buckley — and reporters these days do not come up to his calibre by a long chalk — would sometimes give me a carbon copy of stories of his that were spiked. 'For posterity, old chap. For posterity,' he would say. I searched through my system because bells rang after you left. However, I cannot find what I know I once had. It evades me. It kept me awake two nights running, wondering whether some blighter tampered with my files. The gist of it was something like this. Harold talked to two or three of the boy scouts. They all had chapter and verse over what to say regarding finding Mr J.B., which made Harold suspicious. People, old or young, do not come up with the same story over a set of events. You only need to think about what is coming out over the Great War now to know that, and it is also true of road traffic accidents.

One of the scouts said something that made old Harold prick up his ears, but blow me down if I can remember what it was. The boy's comments made him think that behind Braithwaite's disappearance was the old, old story of a man Running Away, as we always say in the papers, with a woman. Does that help?

So the reporter had picked up on the idea that Braithwaite was off with another woman. At last, perhaps we were on the right track. Find the dark-haired beauty painted by Joshua Braithwaite, and we may find the man himself. Mr Duffield's letter continued.

However, I did come across another matter from that time, one of Harold's pieces that I enclose, only because I know the poor old chap would smile in his grave to think someone still read his copy. At the time, due to wartime censorship, only officially sanctioned information found its way onto our pages.

The Cleckheaton *and* Spenborough Guardian *printed a piece in 1919, and I am only sorry we did not do it here, in honour of Harold. He wrote this piece with great caution, not mentioning that picric acid, utilised in the manufacture of dye stuffs, was being used to make explosives.*

Of course Harold knew his piece would be spiked — but that was a point of honour with him: write the truth and shame the devil. Someday the truth would out.

Yours sincerely
E Duffield

I unfolded the newspaper article written by Mr Duffield's favourite reporter. This would have been composed just after Braithwaite disappeared, the day of the explosion, the day I met Tabitha at St Mary's Hospital and gave her a lift to the station so that she could find the widow of the shell-shocked man whose death we witnessed.

The black of the carbon copy smudged my fingers as I lay the flimsy page of quarto on the table and smoothed out the creases.

LOW MOOR DISASTER

On Monday, 21 August, a series of violent and continuing explosions occurred at the Low Moor works, a subsidiary of the Bradford Dyers' Association. An initial tremendous blast rocked places as far away as Leeds, York and Huddersfield. Those people at a distance from the scene thought that Zeppelin bombs had been dropped.

Initial reports say that none of the women and girls employed in the factory was killed. Workers and residents from nearby properties fled to the safety of the woods and countryside. School teachers escorted their charges to safety.

Attempts to fight the ensuing violent conflagration were valiantly undertaken by the Low Moor Works Brigade. It is feared that these men, and members of the workforce who bravely attempted to halt or contain the continuing explosions, may have lost their lives. First to arrive on the scene were firemen from Odsal, soon to be reinforced by men from Central station. The force of the blasts was so great that within a short time, these heroic men were blown off their engine which was destroyed. The firemen who escaped death have been taken to the Infirmary. At present we have no death toll.

Scattered debris from the explosions damaged property within a radius of two miles. The shell of a gasometer was ruptured. Escaping gas ignited within seconds, converting the foul smell into an immense pillar of flame and thence into a plume of vile, choking black smoke whose heat quickly transformed the area to an unbearable furnace.

To see the people camped on the land four miles from their own homes is a piteous sight. Some do not know whether they have homes to return to. Others congregate at the Infirmary. With great dignity, they await news of the injured. On this fateful day, the war being fought on foreign shores by our brave men and boys has come home to challenge the courage of those they left behind.

Coincidence. It could be nothing more than coincidence that so much happened on that one day. So much happens every day, only we do not know about it. There could be no connection between Braithwaite and the explosion at Low Moor, unless it was that he may have supplied the picric acid that went into the explosives.

The first explosion was just after 2.30 p.m. Joshua Braithwaite was seen by Gregory Grainger running across the fells at four o'clock. For there to be a connection with his disappearance, he would have had to deliberately run ten or more miles to seek out death in a living hell.

Yet why, when he had an arrangement with Paul Kellett to bring his motorbike to him, did he set off running?

I hurried upstairs, changed into divided skirt and jacket, and borrowed a cross-bar bicycle that had belonged to my cousin. Cross bars are such an encumbrance and entirely unnecessary. They make manoeuvring round tradesmen's vans and taxi cabs terribly tricky. The London air was foul. I regretted not having a scarf to cover my mouth. Only when I came closer to Harley Street did it occur to me that Gregory Grainger may already have taken himself off to the country for the long weekend.

I rang the bell for Professor Podmore's rooms. A porter showed me into a waiting room but I felt too agitated to take a seat.

Five minutes later, Gregory appeared, a look of concern on his face. 'Is something wrong, Kate?'

'No, nothing's wrong. Just a question, following on from yesterday.'

'Won't you come upstairs?'

I declined, not wishing to make polite conversation with Professor Podmore or have the treat of a guided tour round the consulting rooms.

'Gregory, how soon on that day, 21 August, did people in Bridgestead and at Milton House hear about the explosion at Low Moor?'

He frowned. 'Let me think. The staff knew before I did. News travelled like wild fire.'

'So Mr Braithwaite would have heard?'

He looked thoughtful. 'It's possible. I can't really say.'

'How did people find out?'

He raised an eyebrow and looked out of the window at my bicycle propped by the railings.

'Seeing your bike brings it back. I believe the news reached the mill first. It was someone who'd delivered yarn, not on a bike of course. There was also this gangly boy scout used to turn up, offering to do good deeds for the officers – fetch tobacco, newspapers, that kind of thing. He could have brought the news, or one of the butcher's or baker's lads.'

'Thanks, Gregory. Sorry to have called you from your work.'

'Hang on a minute, Kate. Don't rush off.'

It was late the following Tuesday evening when Sykes and I met to share information. He came to the house and we sat by the fire, Mrs Kellett's cat on the hearth rug between us. If Sookie could have spoken, things might have been much easier. Not only did the cat not speak, she pretended not to listen as we tossed information and ideas to and fro.

We tried out explanations as to why Braithwaite had set off running. It could be that he saw an opportunity and took it. There may have been some arrangement with Kellett to meet with the motorbike at an agreed spot. But it made no sense that Braithwaite would have risked sparking off a search for himself without being able to get well away from the area.

Sometimes I wish I'd studied phrenology. Never too late. I could locate that part of my brain that thinks and tip-tap with my fingertips to spring it into action.

The nagging connection with Low Moor would not go away. 'Do you think it was something to do with the Low Moor explosion?'

Sykes sat back in his chair, one leg draped over the other, his pendulum foot swinging. 'Go on,' he said, as if I had some well-developed theory rather than a tickle of a half-thought.

We were both feeling grumpy at hitting brick walls. Here we were with eighteen days to go to Tabitha's wedding, and still no sign of the elusive Joshua Braithwaite.

I tried to turn what niggled me into something like a coherent idea. 'Well ... what have we got so far? We know Braithwaite supplied picric acid to Low Moor Chemical Works, being the good and patriotic war-profiteer. I don't know how these things work, whether there was a volatile batch, or dampness ... or, I don't know ... I'm not a chemist. Could there have been some reason for him to feel culpable?'

For a moment we sat in silence. Sykes had something in his notebook. I could tell by the way his fingers itched to open it and move on.

'Let's bear that in mind,' Sykes said. 'I'm no chemist either so we're plodding in the dark.'

He opened his notebook. I wasn't ready to let go of the possible Low Moor connection yet.

'Speak for yourself, Mr Plod. I intend to switch on a light.'

He bristled at the plod soubriquet. 'What light would that be then?'

'The newspaper librarian, Mr Duffield? He's the chap who sent me an account of the Low Moor explosion, written at the time.'

'Yes, historically interesting, a tragic disaster. But I don't see how it helps.'

Neither did I, but I persisted. 'Mr Duffield said that the *Spenborough Guardian* printed an article about the explosion, in 1919. An article written three years on from the explosion is bound to give us more information than was available at the time. I'd like you to go to Spenborough.'

He started to laugh, rocking back and forth, almost falling off the chair across his intertwined legs.

'What's so funny?'

'You think there's a place called Spenborough, like there's a Knaresborough?'

'And isn't there?'

'It's a municipal borough. Takes in Gomersal, Cleckheaton and Liversedge, on the River Spen.'

'It's not that funny. So Gomersal, or Cleckheaton, or Liversedge. Wherever the newspaper has its office.'

He calmed himself and made a note. 'I expect that'll be Cleckheaton, since its full moniker is the *Cleckheaton and Spenborough Guardian*. Does Mr Duffield give a date for the article?'

'No. Serves you right for laughing. I hope you have to read a year's newspapers to find it.'

'That's my thanks is it? For turning up information about the postal order.'

He had my attention, just as he intended.

He flicked open his notebook but did not refer to it. With the solemnity of a witness in the dock, he said, 'Mrs Kellett went to Bingley to buy a postal order each week. She'd go religiously after work on a Friday and though the post office was closed, the general store part of the shop was open and the owner, a Mr Ronald Dobson, would keep it for her under the counter. He always thought that she sent something to her sister or brother. Postmasters and mistresses come in two types in my book, the upright keepers of confidences and the nosy blighters. The post office was the Dobsons' business and so were the doings of everyone who came through its doors. Mrs Dobson, while dusting the counter, happened to notice that Mrs Kellett would fill out the order in the name Horrocks. She couldn't make out the post office name, but it began with the letter W.'

I nodded my appreciation.

Sykes consulted his notebook, as if he didn't quite believe what he had written. 'I thought Dobson was mistaken at first, about the ten shillings. That was a hefty whack, but he was adamant.'

'Where did Mrs Kellett get that much money to spare?' I asked.

He shook his head. 'Search me. Happen fortune telling pays better than we think. Maybe the spirits look after their own – or did up to a week last Friday in poor Mrs Kellett's case.'

I felt gloomy again. All this was fine and impressive, but a post office beginning with W could be anywhere from Wigan to Worcester. So where did we go from here?

'I'll take a photograph of the woman in the painting and see whether anyone in Bridgestead recognises her.'

Sykes nodded. 'And if you're right that there's a Low Moor connection, I can think of two post offices within easy reach that begin with W. Wibsey and Wyke. I'll take a look at the street directories and see if I can find a Horrocks.'

'Won't that take ages?'

'Probably. Shall I do that before or after I hike to Spenborough?'

Sookie swished her tail. She looked accusingly at Sykes. I wondered if she was thinking the same as I was, that if Sykes were a dog, he'd be a bloodhound.

Leaving Bradford for an outlying village is like travelling from the centre of a spider's web up one of its narrow threads, through fumes and smoke.

A massive mill on our left belched out steam. The roaring sounds through its vents made an awesome symphony of sound. Gerald used to say that if he were a composer, he would capture the throb and whine of industry and set the sound to percussion and strings.

All the lanes and roads had a similar look: mills with many windows, grimy cottages huddled next to each other, some with their windows converted to display goods and a shop sign above the door.

Sykes sat beside me in the passenger seat of the Jowett, bristling with so much unease he made my skin prickle. It occurred to me that having an ex-policeman in the car would come between me and my motoring reveries. Surely his constabulary sensibilities should not make him squirm at a mere two miles over the speed limit.

'What's eating you, Mr Sykes?'

'We're attracting attention, Mrs Shackleton, in case you hadn't noticed.'

'I often attract attention.'

'I'm sure you do. Only I am used to blending in, looking inconspicuous so as not to draw attention to myself.'

I glanced at his black boots.

It would take a while for me and Mr Sykes to become used to each other. However it did impress me that he knew the way to Chapel Fold, Wibsey, where we hoped to find our casher of postal orders.

'Turn left at the top of the hill.'

I gave an exaggerated hand signal and turned. A knot of out of work men tossing a coin on the street corner paused in their game to stare at us.

Mr Sykes sighed.

'Is there something about my driving that's upsetting you?'

'You know what they're all thinking?'

'I'm afraid my powers of detection don't extend to reading minds.'

'They're thinking, "Why isn't the chap driving?"'

'Then I'd better have two signs made, one for each side of the motor. "BECAUSE IT'S HER CAR".'

With that constabulary air of suspecting everyone in the

world of felonies, Sykes gazed at two men waiting to cross the road.

'And he can't drive,' he said glumly.

'Why on earth not?'

'It just never came my way to learn.'

'Anyone can learn to drive, Mr Sykes.'

'Call me Jim. I'm working for you and being given a moniker by a lady boss makes me uneasy.'

'What if it makes me uneasy to call a man of your standing and experience by his first name? And you're four years older than me.'

'Jim's easy to say.'

'All right. I'm Kate.'

'I can't call you Kate. It's Mrs Shackleton.'

'To say I'm "the boss" as you put it, you seem to be the one who's laying down the law.'

'It has to be proper.'

'I'm sure "it" will be. And why didn't you drive in the force?'

'Not one of the chosen.' He turned to look at me, staring at my hands on the wheel. In a gloomy voice, he said, 'You see, you can talk and drive. How many people can do that?'

'I don't know. Are you going to tell me?'

'It was a rhetorical question. You need to stop by that lamp post. Chapel Fold might be a bit tricky for the vehicle.'

We walked down a steep cobbled street past ramshackle workshops, a severe chapel and well-kept graveyard. Chapel Street gave way to Chapel Fold.

The door to number ten was propped open. A stout grandmotherly woman, with greying hair and pale skin deeply lined, was standing at a table, her hands in a large earthenware bowl, kneading bread dough.

I tapped on the door. 'Mrs Horrocks?'

'Who's askin?' Her pale watery eyes searched mine.

'I'm Mrs Shackleton, and this is Mr Sykes.'

'You're a policeman,' she said accusingly.

Sykes took off his hat and nodded. 'Ex-policeman. How did you know?'

'The boots. It's all right. I've nothing against you. My uncle was in the force.' She looked suddenly anxious. 'Has summat happened to one of my lassies?'

Sykes left it for me to answer. 'No. We've come from Bridgestead, where I believe you have a connection.'

The transformation was instant. The sudden wariness made her physically draw back. She looked as though she would like to slam the door shut, but thought better of it.

'You better come in.' She placed a white tea cloth over the earthenware bowl of dough and set it on the hearth.

A jug of water stood by the sink. 'Let me!' Sykes picked up the jug and poured it over her hands which she held over a basin. She peeled off a lump of dough that had attached to the back of her hand.

At the table we sat on three tall buffets, Mrs Horrocks lowering herself cautiously with stiff movements.

My first impulse was to jump in and begin to ask questions, but I waited, seeing what she would say.

Without the dough on her hands, she became bolder and stared at me. 'Bridgestead. It's out Keighley way.'

It was a good try at ignorance. When searching for missing soldiers, I had come across people who would say nothing until they knew what you were after.

I wanted to be absolutely sure we had the right person. 'Before I say anything more, would you please confirm to me who it is sends you the postal order and in what amount?'

She set her mouth in a stubborn line. 'I've nowt to say about that.'

'Mrs Horrocks, this is only to make quite sure that we are bringing this news to the ears that should receive it. Are you Nancy Horrocks?'

'Yes.'

'And do you receive a postal order every week?

When she didn't answer, Sykes said, 'We could ask the Wibsey post mistress.'

'All right, so it's for ten bob. And it's spent as soon as it's got. I've nowt to give back if that's what you're askin'.'

'Could you tell me why Mrs Kellett sends you a postal order?'

'That's between me and her.'

'Have you known her long?' I needed to know how close they were. For all I knew, Mrs Kellett could be a relation of Mrs Horrocks.

'I don't know her. Never met the woman. Now what's this about?'

Sykes was looking at the table, and I guessed he must be trying very hard not to join in, which I appreciated.

'Mrs Horrocks, I'm very sorry to tell you that Mrs Kellett has died.'

A great sigh came from her. 'Poor woman. There was never no note about being sick. I had no notion.'

'She wasn't sick. She met with an accident.'

'In the mill?' A look of horror crossed her face. She closed her eyes as if to shut out scenes of hair or hands caught in machinery, a flying bobbin acting as lethal shot.

Quickly, so as not to prolong her imaginings, I said, 'No. In her own home. She was found at the bottom of the stairs. Just a day after her husband was killed in an accident at work. The police are investigating.'

'Will they be coming here?'

'I couldn't say. I don't believe they know about you, not yet.'

She took a hanky from her pocket and blew her nose.

'I'm sorry to press you, but if I don't someone else will. Could you please tell me why she sent you the money. What was your connection?'

'She was a good friend to my daughter Agnes. That's all I can say.'

'May I speak to Agnes?'

She shook her head.

'We could come later. Is she at work?'

'My other daughters are at work, Beatrice and Julia, and Julia's husband. They'll all be back later. We're not short. We'll manage without the ten bob. There's an end of it.'

'And Agnes?'

'Mrs Kellett will have her reward in heaven, poor creature.'

'If Agnes is no longer living here, and she was the person Mrs Kellett knew . . .'

'They worked together at mill. Agnes lodged with her.'

It came back to me. Now who had said it, who had mentioned that Mrs Kellett had a lodger, 'the bonniest lass in the mill'. Ah yes. It was Marjorie on the night of the Gawthorpes' party.

'Mrs Horrocks, where is Agnes now?' I spoke as gently as I could. Her lower lip trembled and her voice seemed shaky.

'Agnes died. Mrs Kellett said she'd help me. And she's been good as her word. Right up to the beginning of this month.'

I looked across to Sykes. He didn't meet my gaze. There was a child's black rubber ball by the fender. A child's drawing was pinned on the wall.

Mrs Horrocks saw me look at them. She clenched her fist. 'No one is having the child. He's mine now.'

'The money was for the child?'

'Mrs Kellett was godmother. She said she'd help. Don't ask me why. Maybe she felt guilty that Agnes got herself in that way while she was under the Kelletts' roof.'

'Do you know who the child's father is?' Could it have been Kellett, I wondered. I pictured him as he was in the

297

photograph, cocky, full of himself, someone who might well have taken advantage of a young lodger.

Mrs Horrocks stood up, too angry to sit still, knocking over the buffet with the suddenness of her movement. 'I don't know and I don't care. And whoever he is, they're not having him back. When it all happened, I'd gone back to Manchester to nurse my sick mother. Agnes wrote to me that she'd married, was with child, and then again that she was a widow. All in the space of a twelve-month. Of course she wasn't wed.'

Sykes picked up the buffet and stayed on his feet until Mrs Horrocks sat down again, the gentleman, but also the policeman.

'How did Agnes die?' I asked.

'Of a broken heart, I say. The death certificate said brain haemorrhage.'

'When?'

'1917.'

Reluctantly, I retrieved the photograph I had taken of the figure in the painting, the young woman on the hump-back bridge.

'Is this Agnes?'

A small cry came from Mrs Horrocks. She reached out and took the photograph by the corner, lifting it towards her. The print fluttered as her hand shook. She closed her eyes tightly. An angry tear escaped onto her lined and wrinkled cheek. 'She doesn't look real.'

'It's from a painting. There was a Moses basket in the picture too, with an infant, Agnes' child I think.'

She slapped at her tears. Her mouth trembled. 'What do you want with us? You're not having Frederick.'

'What age is Frederick?'

'Coming up seven.'

'Mrs Horrocks, you didn't meet Mrs Kellett, but did you ever meet her husband?'

She shook her head. 'No. I never met neither of them.

298

That's what was so strange and kind that Mrs Kellett kept to her vow to help the child. I allus meant to get the train out there one day and say a thank you. Now it's too late.'

'What will you do now? Will it make a big difference to you, not having the postal order?'

She shrugged. 'Since we was better off, I been putting a few bob by for Frederick. He's a clever lad, might make summat of hisself if he's a mind.'

'Here's where you can get in touch with me.' I gave her my card, thanked her and we went outside.

She followed us to the door. 'When's Mrs Kellett's funeral? It would be right for us to pay respects.'

'We'll let you know the date,' I said.

We walked back to the High Street, where the Jowett had gathered a circle of admirers.

'Why don't you try your hand at driving, Mr Sykes?'

'Not round here. Too many horses and carts.'

He climbed into the car first and slid across to the passenger seat.

'We're making a guess that Braithwaite was the father, because he painted the lass.' As he spoke, Sykes watched me coax the car into motion. 'Kellett could've been the father. She stayed in their house.'

'That crossed my mind. It's possible. But he was off with the army for a year from 1914. If Frederick is coming up seven, he would have been born in . . . 1915. I think Mrs Horrocks knows very well who the father is. She said it was strange and kind that the Kelletts sent money. There'd be nothing strange about it if Kellett was the father.'

'Stop!' Sykes shouted suddenly.

I braked, so that he jerked forward and the map fell from his hands.

'What on earth's the matter?'

'It just occurs to me. If we turn round and drive in the other direction, we're heading for Cleckheaton and your

299

article in the Clecky and Spen *Guardian*. Office is on Northgate.'

I glared at him. 'You planned that all along. You're pretending it's only just struck you.'

He smiled that superior smile. 'Would I do that, Mrs Shackleton? Boss?'

As I did an about-turn, earning a rude yell from a van driver, he said smugly, 'In the force, the cars all had rudders.'

'And you still couldn't drive.'

Constable Mitchell looked as though he'd won a prize for his ship in a bottle. He beamed a friendly smile and asked me into the police house office.

Dad had told me that the Braithwaite case left a shadow over Mitchell's reputation. HQ thought he had not handled the situation well. It made no difference that he had obtained his sergeant's permission for taking Braithwaite to Milton House Hospital. It was Mitchell's initiative and had turned out badly.

This was not a bobby under a shadow. Something had changed. A new sense of importance filled the room. He sat upright like a man wearing a new corset.

'I solved the case,' he said simply. 'Arthur Wilson's under arrest, charged with murdering Mrs Kellett. We'll have him on Kellett's death too.' He nodded at the telephone as if it would back him up. 'Super's been on, congratulating me.'

'Well, congratulations from me too. How did this come about, Mr Mitchell?'

'Good solid police work, Mrs Shackleton. I was able to hand CID measurements and photo of the boot print, so there was something to look for. Being a manager, Wilson wasn't a man who repaired his own footwear. Cedric, the shoe mender, narrowed down the list, and Wilson was on it. The cricket bat was examined for fingerprints. I provided the measurements of the spot the box occupied, under the bed. Course, I was told off for interfering with a crime scene, but if a bobby can't look over his own patch, what use is he?'

He seemed to have forgotten that Sykes found the cricket bat and I checked under the bed, but he looked so happy. It would be cruel to remind him.

'Of course you helped,' he said, unable to stop smiling. He reached for his pipe, ready to give me chapter and verse.

'Oh?'

'Scotland Yard went to search Wilson's house while he was at work. At knocking off time I looked out for him passing, asked him in to get him chatting. That's where you came in.'

'And how did I help?'

'He holds a grudge against you for siding with his wife on the night of the Gawthorpes' party. You showed him up by escorting Marjorie home. He reckons you're one of these new women. You've deeply unsettled the female population by driving your car about and prying into other people's affairs.'

And here I was, chiding myself for being so entirely conventional. I rose in my own estimation. Constable Mitchell did not need encouragement to continue.

'Well, like I say, I waylaid Wilson on the way home. Kept the coast clear for CID to give his place the once-over. Wife made a cup of tea and brought in a plate of digestives. Wilson was that busy denigrating every female born the wrong side of 1880 that he let me keep him talking while the search went on. They found the box with the cash, and his fingerprints, not the boots cos he was wearing them.'

Something told me this all sounded a little too easy. 'And did Wilson confess?'

'Not at first. Blamed his poor wife. Said Marjorie was

301

mad and a drunk, which no one round here would have a great quarrel with. He said she was allus round at Lizzie Kellett's asking for her fortune telled. Happen she was round there paying her condolences, copped for a bad fortune and swung out over it, he said. When he was presented with the evidence, of the footprint and the fingerprints, well then he caved in. Said Kellett had owed him money and he'd gone to ask for it after Kellett died. Mrs Kellett wouldn't budge an inch. He knew the money was there somewhere. He thought he was entitled.'

'What made him believe he was entitled to money?'

The constable shook his head. 'Search me. Envy? Kellett had done better than him, in spite of both of them being clever fellers. He's owned up to murderin' Mrs Kellett, but he denies having owt to do with Kellett's death.'

'Do you believe him?'

Constable Mitchell's pleasure dimmed. He sighed and the smile had fled. 'Lads at Keighley have him secure. They'll get a confession out of him soon enough. He laced Kellett's food all right. Wilson got greedy. Simple as that.'

'Did the CID chaps find morphia and *gel sem* in Wilson's house?'

'No. They reckon he was clever there, got just as much of the drugs as he needed and no more. He doped Kellett's food first, then went off to the party at the Gawthorpes'. Fixed himself up with a perfect alibi, or so he thought. He wasn't so clever when it came to killing Mrs Kellett.'

It struck me that given Wilson could only hang once, it was odd that he would own up to one murder and deny the other, but I kept the thought to myself.

Mitchell crossed to the filing cabinet and opened a drawer. He took out a cash box, unlocked it and brought out two wage packets. 'Wilson missed this, and so did we. Mrs Kellett's pinafore was hanging behind the cellar door, pay packets in her pocket — hers and Kellett's.'

302

'What will happen to them?' I asked, feeling unbearably sad that the pair of them should leave behind untouched wage packets.

'They'll have relatives coming across for the funeral. Inspector says for me to hand it to the next of kin, as long as there's no squabbling as to who that should be. No use being official over a few bob. Kellett's treasure trove will probably go in the same direction but with more formality.'

'Had Mrs Kellett opened her wage packet?'

He unsealed the flap and tipped the contents onto the table. 'I reckon she had, and resealed it, so at least she'll have known of Mr Stoddard's little kindness.'

'What kindness was that?'

He fingered a coin and separated it from the rest. 'Look, see – there's an extra guinea. I went across to the mill to enquire of Mr Stoddard. He explained that he'd given her extra, on account of her having to bury her husband. Naturally she wasn't in work that Friday, but he sent the packet across and paid her for a full week's work. Paid both for a full week's work.'

It seemed to me such a pity that the one day Lizzie could take off work was because her husband had died. 'How is Marjorie taking the news of her husband's arrest?'

The constable paused for a moment. He returned the wage packets to the cash box, locked it, and replaced it in the filing cabinet. When he turned back to me, he looked solemn, and full of sympathy for the prisoner's wife. 'No one's seen Marjorie. She walks that dog of hers at ungodly hours of the night and early morning. The wife called, but she wouldn't answer the door to her. That young lass she had working for her, she's paid her off – sent her home to her mam.'

I called at the butcher's before knocking on Marjorie's door. As I'd hoped, the dog was inside and not out in his kennel. He barked. I opened the letter box. 'Charlie! I've got a bone for you.' Charlie stood behind the door, wagging his tail and jumping on his hind legs. 'Good boy, Charlie.' Inside the house, a curtain twitched. 'Marjorie! It's Kate. Let me in. I've brought a marrow bone for Charlie.'

Charlie stopped barking. I could hear her voice, hushing him, pulling him back from the door. 'Just leave it on the step,' she said.

'Let me in, Marjorie. I won't go away.' Charlie started barking again. The door opened. Before she had time to change her mind or snatch Charlie's bone from me, I pushed my way in.

Charlie leaped at me as though I were his long lost friend. I gave him the bone as quickly as I could so he wouldn't accidentally eat my hand at the same time. He bounded off down the hall, the bone gripped in the vice of his jaws as if we might ask to share it with him and he would hate to refuse.

Marjorie's hair was all undone, hanging in greasy strands below her shoulders. Her mouth turned down, her eyes looked blank with misery. I caught a strong whiff of unwashed body. She spotted dog hairs on the black sleeves of her cardigan and brushed at them with bony hands. She showed no sign of moving from the hall.

'Can we go sit down somewhere, Marjorie?'

She looked round as if the house was a strange place to her and she did not know what room we might be allowed to enter. 'He's everywhere, you see, that's the trouble. That's why Charlie and me go walking, but I can't go in the daylight. Not now. People staring.'

'The kitchen?' I asked. It struck me that Arthur Wilson would not often have been in the kitchen and we would be safe from the memory of his presence there.

She nodded and led the way down the hall, to where Charlie had escaped already. The dog looked up politely,

304

wagged his tail and continued to gnaw at the bone. This seemed to soothe her a little, and she sat on a Bentwood chair by the empty range, pushing strands of hair behind her ear. I put the kettle on the gas ring and lit a match. The teapot was cold and had not been emptied. When she thought I intended to go to the back door and throw the old tea leaves on the garden, she shuddered. Instead, I emptied the leaves into a newspaper. 'I've brought us a pork pie each, and one for Charlie.'

There was a shawl across the back of the chair. I put it around her thin shoulders. She looked so cold. 'It must have been a terrible shock for you, to have Mr Wilson arrested.'

When I put the cup of tea in her hand, the cup rattled in the saucer. She would have been better sitting at the table. I stood a buffet by her and put the saucer on it, so she only had the cup to deal with. Charlie went to the door with his bone. She did not object when I turned the key and shot back the bolts so that the dog could go into the yard.

'That'll leave us free to eat our pork pies,' I said.

For the first time she smiled. 'Oh aye. He'd have it out of your hand soon as look at you, thinking you meant it for him. Well, I'll have no one worrying at me to "get rid of the damn dog".' She made no attempt to pick up a piece of pork pie, though I had quartered it with a sharp knife to make it manageable. She stared at it for a long time, and then said, 'I'll have a dollop of brown sauce. It's in that cupboard.'

'Say when.' I tipped up the sauce bottle.

'When.'

'Were you here when the police came to search?'

'They asked me to leave. Take Charlie for a walk, and stay away from the direction of the mill. Do you think Arthur did it? It's hard to believe that he killed someone else. I allus thought it'd be me.'

305

'He's confessed, to killing Mrs Kellett, but not Paul.'

'Oh no, he wouldn't kill Paul.'

'The police think he did.'

She gave a snort. 'They would.'

'Why do you say he wouldn't kill Paul?'

'I can't put it into words. They stood by each other, in that way fellers do.' She picked up the second piece of pork pie. I guessed she hadn't eaten or drunk for a long time, nor slept by the look of her. A hot bath and a change of clothes wouldn't have gone amiss. She licked brown sauce from her fingers.

'Marjorie, I'd like to help you if I can. I don't expect you'll want to stay here.'

As if she hadn't heard me, she said, 'Oh I told the police he wouldn't have killed Paul. Not that they liked each other over much but they were two of a kind in wanting to get on. Only Paul had that bit more luck, and he was the one in Mr Braithwaite's confidence.'

'In what way was he in Joshua Braithwaite's confidence?'

'If Mr Braithwaite had waited till dark that day, it was Paul Kellett would have fetched him the motorbike to get away. It was Paul came asking Arthur to go back on the story about the suicide. Well, Arthur said he couldn't. It wasn't him that saw. It was that other chap, and all the boy scouts. Only by then, Arthur knew he'd done wrong in going along with it. It's a wonder it never cost him his job.'

'So Kellett was going to help Mr Braithwaite get away from the hospital before he was brought up in front of the magistrates the next day on a charge of attempted suicide?'

'I listened in. That night when Paul Kellett came braying on the door, I earwigged to see what it was all about.'

'And what was it about?'

306

She listened, putting her head to one side, brushing back the hair that fell over her face. 'Charlie wants to come in.'

I went to the door. Sure enough, Charlie stood there, wagging his tail, the bone in his mouth, pushing past me into the kitchen. I sat down again, and he came at me, pushing the bone towards me, growling.

'He wants marrow tekin out of bone.'

For a moment, I waited, thinking Marjorie would do this.

'He's asking you,' she said. 'He likes you.'

From what Constable Mitchell had said, I suspected that Charlie was the only male creature in the village who did like me.

'Right, Charlie.' I took a knife from the drawer and held out my hand for the bone. Marjorie and the dog watched me.

Charlie dropped the bone at my feet. In the short time he had spent outside, he appeared to have buried the bone and dug it up again. It was covered in slaver and soil. I held it gingerly, stabbing the knife into the bone, dislodging the soft pink marrow, dropping a piece to him. He wolfed this down.

'Why didn't Mr Braithwaite wait until nightfall, if Kellett was going to bring him a motorbike?'

The dog licked my hands, trying to hurry me up.

'Because news came through over't explosion. There was a delivery of yarn at mill, and news came with it. Soon as he heard, Mr Braithwaite waited for no one. He was off to Low Moor.'

Her words hit me like a blow. The knife slipped from my hand and clattered to the floor. Charlie backed off in alarm. Concentrate. I did not want to lose a finger during the course of my investigations. I picked up the knife and now carefully scraped the marrow to the top of the bone, within reach of a dog tongue.

'Here, Charlie.'

307

The water ran freezing cold as I rinsed my hands under the tap. 'Why?' I asked. 'Why did Mr Braithwaite go to Low Moor?'

'You might refresh Charlie's bowl while you're at it,' Marjorie suggested.

I tipped hairy, greasy water from an earthenware bowl down the sink and refilled it.

Tasks completed, I sat down again, and waited for an answer.

'That lass who'd had his bairn, she worked there. Don't ask me what a weaver was doing getting herself a job in munitions. Money I expect. She was a proud lass. Told Lizzie she wouldn't be a kept woman. We never thought, me and Lizzie, never thought he'd leave his wife and family and the mill, turn his back on it all for her.'

I rubbed my hands to get some warmth back into my fingers, and to give me time to think. So I was right about Low Moor, and right about the young woman on the bridge, and the baby.

Marjorie was looking at Charlie with admiration as he attacked his bone with new vigour.

I had one more print of the young woman on the bridge. I took it from my bag and passed it to Marjorie. 'Do you recognise her?'

'That's her,' Marjorie said. 'Daft 'aporth. Agnes. Bonny lass. Foolish, but then who am I to talk?'

'Who else knew about Braithwaite and Agnes, and the baby?'

'The only ones that knew for sure about Agnes and the bairn were the Kelletts. Lizzie told me. It got Arthur's goat, guessing we knew summat he didn't.'

'Yet Arthur was in on it somehow. You said Kellett came here that Sunday night. You heard them talking.'

'Oh aye, Paul came here. He wanted Arthur's keys for the mill, so he could fetch summat for Mr Braithwaite.'

'Do you know what it was?'

308

'Aye. The key to his safe deposit box. I wasn't supposed to know but I worked it out. Arthur got money for that bit of slyness, handing over the keys, though not as much as he felt hisself entitled to. And it rankled with him that Lizzie went on doing well.'

'In what way did Mrs Kellett go on doing well? And how did Arthur know?'

Marjorie picked pork pie crumbs from her apron and popped them into her mouth. She looked at me puzzled, and for a moment I thought she would reach for a bottle of her favourite tipple and that I would learn no more today.

'What did you ask me?'

I repeated my question. 'You said Mrs Kellett went on doing well. And that Arthur knew, and resented that.'

'Oh aye, that's it. Every Friday Mr Stoddard give out the wage packets to the managers. Arthur, being weaving manager, said that Lizzie Kellett's envelope was allus that bit heavier. He said that Stoddard paid her more than was written on't packet, week in, week out. It drove him wild to know why.'

'Why did *you* think the pay packet was heavier, Marjorie? Did Mrs Kellett ever say?'

'She sent money for the upkeep of Agnes' child. Braithwaite never contacted Agnes again, no more than he contacted his wife and daughter. He left Agnes and the little lad to fend for themselves.'

Charlie dropped his bone and came across, nuzzling at Marjorie, licking her hand.

'So you never put an end to your husband's curiosity and told him why Mrs Kellett got more money?'

'I did not. Nowt to do with me. Arthur said it was so she would keep her gob shut.'

'He thought that Mrs Kellett was blackmailing Stoddard?'

'Daft bat. Lizzie wouldn't have blackmailed no one.'

309

She stroked Charlie's head. 'Rich int it? Ten bob a week for the child of a millionaire.'

And eleven shillings for Mrs Kellett, I thought. The extra guinea in her last wage packet was not to cover the costs of Kellett's funeral, as Stoddard had told Constable Mitchell, but to pay for the upbringing of Frederick Horrocks, and to keep Mrs Kellett's silence about Frederick's paternity.

The upright Stoddard had lied to the police.

Did Stoddard truly believe the whole guinea went to Agnes Horrocks? Or had he, for years, paid Mrs Kellet in order to protect his cousin Joshua Braithwaite's reputation?

But all that took second place in my thoughts as I stood on the humpback bridge trying to make sense of what I knew. Agnes worked on munitions at Low Moor. Braithwaite had heard about the explosion and set off running to find her, not waiting for Kellett and the motorbike, and the key to the safe deposit box at Thackreys' Bank.

And according to the editor of the *Cleckheaton and Spenborough Guardian*, who had attended the inquest on the Low Moor explosion, the death toll was thirty-eight, including "a male person unknown".

But the explosion occurred at 2.30 p.m. and Joshua Braithwaite was seen running across the moors at 4 p.m. So it couldn't be him, could it?

22

The Warp

The coroner had allowed Paul and Lizzie Kellett's bodies to be released for burial.

The morning of the funeral broke blustery enough to frighten off rain. I crossed my fingers as I drew on my black coat. Nothing worse than a wet muddy funeral.

Sykes was watching out for me as I drew up outside his house. As he closed the door behind him, I noticed curious faces looking down from a bedroom window, a woman and two children. I waved as I got out of the car to let Sykes in.

'Do you want to try driving, Mr Sykes?'

'Oh no. Won't risk that so close to home, and on the day of a funeral.'

One excuse would have been enough.

'Just let me know when you are ready to screw your courage to the steering wheel.'

On a quiet stretch of road beyond Saltaire, he took a deep breath and said, 'Right. I'll have a go.'

At least an ex-policeman starts off with a little knowledge – hand signals. I gritted my teeth and praised him for the whole hundred yards that he was willing to drive.

When we arrived at Bridgestead, I dropped Sykes off on the main street, so that he could go to the police house to pester Constable Mitchell. I would scrounge breakfast at the Braithwaites'.

Tabitha looked up from buttering toast and ordered me to sit down.

'Have you had breakfast?'

Evelyn looked pale and drawn. Compared with the confident figure I had met on my first visit, she looked like a woman who was unravelling before my eyes. For a moment I felt a pang of pity. If my guess was correct, she and Gregory Grainger had been lovers for almost seven years. That was a longer time than Gerald and I had together. First Edmund killed in action, Joshua unfaithful, Gregory at the other end of the country. Now two of her workers killed and another accused of their murder.

I helped myself to a rasher of bacon and a sausage from the dishes set out on the sideboard.

Tabitha asked me about my visit to London. I told her the blue dress was a huge success.

She smiled. 'Comes to something when my dress gets out more than I do. Still, we've plumped on Paris for the honeymoon, and it's my resolution that Hector and I shall have a spectacular time.' As she rose from the table, the sleeves of her red satin dressing gown with its fiery dragons turned into wings. 'I'd better get changed. Mustn't be late for the funeral.'

She left the table.

'Close the door!' Evelyn called after her. 'You weren't born in a field.'

Evelyn was studying a pot of marmalade carefully, as if it presented a deep puzzle. She looked at me with barely disguised fury.

'It must have been lovely for you, to get away to London.'

The simplest and expected answer was to agree that it was.

'Did you see anyone we know?' she asked pointedly, her fury seeping away.

Should I tell her? No point in lying. 'Dr Grainger came to my aunt's birthday dinner. The professor he works with attended and so he brought him along.'

312

She lowered her head. Her hands clung to each other. 'I won't go to the chapel. I'll come to the cemetery.'

'Evelyn!' I wanted to offer some comfort, but did not know how. 'It was none of my doing that Dr Grainger came.'

With a sigh she pushed herself up from the table. 'It's all right. It's over between us. I thought we might go to London together, but that was nonsense on my part. It's better this way.'

Stoddard seemed to me a far more suitable person for Evelyn than Dr Grainger. Stupidly, I started to say that, and then hoped she did not realise that I had overheard him propose to her at the Gawthorpes' party.

'Neville?' She looked at me in astonishment. 'Some things are just not possible.'

Tabitha took my arm as we walked along the drive on our way to the chapel. 'About what you asked me, regarding Dad's neuralgia. He *was* taking something for that.'

'Do you know what he was taking?'

'Something from Aunt Catherine. She was our treasure trove of medicines, poor woman. Is it important?'

'It might explain his confused state of mind that day.'

'And have you found out anything else? I know you haven't had a lot of time.'

I took a deep breath. 'I'd better tell you this, in case it comes out some other way. Your father had been seeing a young woman.'

If it had not been for the existence of a half-brother, I might have kept that information to myself. To my surprise the news did not seem to worry Tabitha, but rather to raise her hopes.

'You think he went away with her?'

'It did strike me as possible, but I now know that didn't happen.'

We walked against the wind towards Bridgestead and

313

the chapel. Mill workers made their way in twos and threes towards the chapel. Older women wore shawls around their shoulders or on their heads. The younger women wore coats and hats or headscarves.

'On the day your father went missing, there was a series of explosions at Low Moor.'

For the briefest time, Tabitha's hand tightened on my arm.

'What does that have to do with Dad?'

'I think that's where this young woman worked, on munitions.'

The sky had turned white. Once the wind dropped, we could be in for snow.

Now I had to say it, just to prepare Tabitha, in case.

'Thirty-eight people died as a result of that explosion. Among the bodies . . .'

She stopped suddenly. 'Dad's fancy woman?'

'No. The women got out.' The article in the *Cleckheaton and Spenborough Guardian* had not included all the details of the tragedy, but the editor had attended the coroner's inquest into the deaths and had been willing to tell Sykes and me what he heard. 'There was one unidentified man.'

Tabitha's voice came out breathless, as though my words winded her. 'You're not suggesting . . . that just doesn't . . . just because she, this woman . . .' Tabitha rubbed at her forehead with her fist. With her other hand she steadied herself against a low wall.

'It's unlikely to be your father, but best to rule out the possibility.'

'Then don't say . . . I want something definite. When you asked me about his painting stuff and I told you it had gone you made me think . . .'

I felt furious with myself for not waiting, for my need to keep her in the picture. My blow-by-blow account had turned out to be just that – heavy blows. I reached out to her. 'I'm still working on that.'

I did not say that I was also waiting to hear whether

314

there was a pathologist's report on the unidentified man. For once, I had used my influence, getting Dad to ask for any such information to be sent to Keighley, Constable Mitchell's headquarters.

We were on the flat now, nearing the chapel. Tabitha had recovered a little from her shock at the directions my enquiries had taken. Hector stood by the chapel door, top hat in hand, waiting patiently for Tabitha. He had watched our progress and looked concerned as he took her arm. 'Uncle Neville's inside already.'

Hector greeted me briefly, expecting me to walk in with them, but I let them go first and found a seat near theback. The whole of Braithwaites' Mill must have been granted time off to attend. Women in shawls, headscarves and turbans were seated in the rows in front of me. Men occupied the other side of the chapel, caps lying on the kneeling board.

Sykes slid in beside me.

The minister read the service.

I wondered whether Mrs Kellett would have preferred a different kind of funeral where her spiritualist beliefs would have been acknowledged. What a small world this was, that Mrs Kellett had lived here all her life. She must have thought she would go on and on, living into old age as her own mother had. A few sobs came from her workmates, hankies pulled out, noses blown.

I heard Stoddard's deep bass voice before seeing him, near the front ahead of his workforce, leading the singing. He then took to the lectern. No one coughed or blew their nose as he spoke into the hushed chapel of the deep shock the village felt at the death of two such good neighbours and good workers in so untimely and violent a fashion. He begged for mercy for their souls, and prayed that justice would prevail.

'He's keeping it short so they can all bugger off back to work,' Sykes whispered. I hit him sharply him in the ribs with my elbow. He grunted in pain as the final hymn began.

Constable Mitchell and his wife had slipped in at the back of the church. As we came out, Mrs Mitchell and their small grandchildren split off and headed home.

'It does the young uns good to learn to be solemn at funerals,' Mitchell confided as we walked behind the coffins to the cemetery at the back of the chapel. He looked round quickly. 'Come and see me this afternoon, eh?'

White misshapen clouds scudded at speed across the bright blue sky. The wind moaned through an oak tree.

Evelyn had avoided the chapel service and simply waited by the newly dug grave. Tabitha and Hector joined her.

The crowd of mourners thronged the cemetery. I stayed with Sykes, on the edge, observing.

People formed themselves into groups. The chief mourners, Mrs Kellett's sister and brother and their families, stood close to the grave. I did not straight away notice the odd-woman-out. It was Evelyn's gaze that drew my attention. Evelyn glanced across the grave, stared for a moment, and then averted her eyes, but not quickly enough to hide the look of pure hatred. Stoddard noticed the change in Evelyn, and he looked in the same direction.

I glanced to my right, then whispered to Sykes, 'That's her. Mrs Horrocks said she was dead.'

'The woman in the painting?'

'Yes.'

She wore a smart black coat, black shoes and a small hat with a flimsy veil that stopped short at her eyebrows. The child, a boy of about seven years old, was also dressed in black, a cut-down suit with a jacket that imitated a man's, and dark trousers reaching just below his knees.

Mrs Kellett's sister began to cry. Her husband put his

arm around her. He couldn't find a handkerchief. The mystery woman in black handed her one.

'I'm very sorry for your loss.'

The sister blew her nose. 'Thank you. There's some sandwiches and a pot of tea in the chapel hall.'

The woman seemed undecided. The boy looked at her hopefully.

Stoddard stepped towards them. He said, in a kindly voice, 'You were a workmate of Lizzie's once, I believe? In the weaving shed?'

'No.' She grasped the child's hand. 'She once or twice attended the same church as me.'

'What church was that?' Stoddard asked.

She seemed as though she would not answer then tossed her head back and said, 'The Spiritualist church in Bradford.'

Stoddard all but snorted, but managed to keep his kindly tone. 'It was good of you to come. Is this your child?'

'Yes.'

'You'll be going back for refreshments?'

She hesitated.

The mill workers were already leaving, and not in the direction of the chapel hall but back to work.

I came between Stoddard and the woman and child. 'I'll show this lady the way.' I took her elbow and we walked to the gate.

'I'm not off back for refreshments. I've a train to catch.' She shook free of me.

I turned back. Evelyn was watching us. She spoke to Stoddard.

It gave me an unwelcome feeling of déjà vu to be back at the High Street café – the place where Tabitha and I had met to discuss her father's disappearance. It was unnerving to sit opposite someone who was the image of Agnes

317

in the painting. She had only agreed to talk because she was early for the train back to Bradford.

'Will it be all right if Mr Sykes takes Frederick to the park?'

She nodded warily, but a moment after changed her mind and leaped to her feet to run after them.

'It's all right, Miss Horrocks.'

She hurried onto the street, with me in pursuit. 'You want the child.'

'No. You have my word. Mr Sykes is taking the boy to the park, as I said. It will give us time to talk.'

'What do you want to talk about? You got me here offering a lift but we've legs. If you're trying to kidnap . . .'

'No one wants to harm your nephew. Your mother must have told you we called to see her.'

'So it was you, enquiring about the postal orders, and telling Mam about Mrs Kellett. Look, he may not be my child, but he's ours. He's Mam's grandson and he's going nowhere.'

'You must be Beatrice, or Julia?'

She hurried on, calling back, 'I'm Beatrice, and not gabbing to you while your accomplice makes off with our lad.' Rushing across the road between a horse and cart and a delivery boy on his bicycle, she caused the cyclist to swerve. Eyes only for the child, she stepped into horse muck without noticing, quickening her pace until there was a moment's distance between her and them.

When I caught her up, she had calmed down a little. 'I came today to pay respects to the Kelletts. I brought the child so he could do the same. There were times before Julia married and I got a job when we hadn't a crust. Mrs Kellett's ten bob kept us from clemming.'

'Earlier, when Mr Stoddard asked if you had worked in the weaving mill, I think he must have been mistaking you for your sister. You're very much alike.'

318

She paused mid-stride and turned to me. 'Did you know her?'

'Not personally. But the photograph I left with your mother, the one from the painting done by Joshua Braithwaite. Agnes is standing on the old bridge across the beck ...'

'Her stranded on a bridge. That's where he put her all right, with all his promises. And a Moses basket for the child! He might as well have put him in one and sent him floating down the river to be caught in reeds or to drown, for all the mind Joshua Braithwaite paid him.'

'I believe he did care about her, and Frederick.'

'Believe as you please. He dumped her and the child and went off.'

'Why would he have done that? He left a family, a business, a home.'

'Oh I heard about all that. If you ask me, our Agnes wasn't the only woman in his life. He probably tossed a coin and went with the one he liked the best.'

We had reached the park gates. Sykes let go of the boy's hand. Frederick bounded onto the grass like a horse hearing the starter's pistol. Then he turned and waved to Beatrice. She waved back.

'Will you tell me what happened to your sister?' I asked Beatrice.

'She died three months after Bigshot Braithwaite let her down. She'd found work in a chemist's shop. Whilst she was at work, she collapsed. The chemist tried to revive her. She was rushed to St Luke's, but it was too late.'

'I'm sorry.'

Frederick had spotted the children's play area with swings, roundabout and slides. He approached shyly. We were still in Easter week and other children played there. I remembered that feeling of being the stranger, on the edge of the group, wondering would you be accepted.

Sykes hung back, watching Frederick enter the playground.

'Beatrice, when you say Braithwaite let Agnes down, how did that come about?'

'He made promises to her. It was wrong. I knew no good would come of it. I told her that, but she wouldn't have it. They loved each other, she said, and loved the child. He said he'd come to her, on the Saturday. The house was rented in Robin Hood's Bay. He'd given her a key, and the address and everything. She waited, all packed and ready, and so excited. Of course he didn't come, or send word. She waited, all day, and all the next day. When Monday came, she gave up hoping and went back to work.'

'Were you there?'

'Yes. I was the one told her not to be so soft in the head. He'd no intention of coming. I told her if she didn't get back to work, she'd lose a good job.'

'So were you looking after Frederick while she went to work?'

'No. She left him with an old woman down the street. That's why we asked Mam to come in the end, to be sure Fred was properly taken care of, and it's a good thing we did, given that Agnes wasn't much longer for this world.'

Now that she had slowed down, Beatrice noticed her shoe and wiped it on the grass verge to try and get rid of the horse muck, turning her foot sideways to wipe it on the grass.

I plucked some leaves. 'If we go to the horse trough, you'll be able to get your shoe clean.'

After she had cleaned her shoe, we both sat on the bench. 'It was my fault. I was too hard on Agnes for being a fool. She listened to me, that he wasn't coming. She went to work.'

'Where did you work?'

'At Wibsey Mills.'

I tried to keep my voice calm. If Marjorie Wilson was wrong, and Agnes had not worked at Low Moor on munitions, there would have been no reason for Braithwaite to change his plans and to impulsively set off to find her.

'Were you both employed at Wibsey Mills?' I asked. 'You and Agnes?'

She shut her eyes for a moment. 'No. She was at the Low Moor Works, filling shells. On the one day she might have stayed at home, still hoping for a different life, I'd bullied her into going back to work. She got caught up in that damned explosion, ran miles to find Fred and the old woman. She was never the same again after that.'

'You weren't to know.'

'Never the same Agnes after that day, all that running, the stench of it. She started to get headaches. I'd say take an aspirin. I thought nowt of it, only that she got the headaches because she'd been let down so bad.'

We watched Frederick, who had managed to grab a swing. He waved for Sykes to come and push him, going higher and higher.

Beatrice's anger at Braithwaite and at herself had slid away. It's strange how we get so angry on behalf of someone we love, much more angry than they might be on their own account. Evelyn was angry with Joshua because of his infidelity, but she was angrier still because she blamed him for Edmund's death. Beatrice Horrocks, after all this time, was in a fury with Joshua Braithwaite because he had abandoned her sister. What would she do with all that anger if I told her what I thought to be the truth?

As if she knew something was coming, she went very still, folding her hands across her middle.

'I believe Mr Braithwaite tried to come for your sister on Saturday, and someone stopped him.'

'Whitewash!'

'I believe he was on his way to her on that Monday, that he would have come to the house, and that he went to search for Agnes because of the explosion.'

321

I had her attention now.

'And then what?'

'I'm not sure. There was one unidentified body found after the Low Moor explosion. It may have been his.'

She turned to me, white-faced, her mouth open. I immediately regretted telling her, but it was too late to stop. 'I can't know for sure, but I suspect he may have been caught up in the explosions.'

'The firemen wouldn't have let him through.'

'That's what I thought at first. The firemen were all killed. It must have been mayhem. The explosions went on for hours, explosion after explosion.'

Sykes and the boy were on their way back.

'The house in Robin Hood's Bay that Agnes mentioned to you, do you by any chance remember the address? You see I believe Joshua Braithwaite may have taken some of his belongings there. I'd like to check with the owner. That would at least give us some confirmation about his intentions.'

'I remember it all right. It was writ on an envelope, and on the mantelshelf for long enough.' She laughed bitterly. 'Did you see me drop summat in't grave?'

'No.'

'It was a key. Braithwaite give Agnes a great big iron key to that house, supposedly. I thought to chuck it in the mill stream. But I dropped it into the Kelletts' grave so Mrs Kellett can pass it on to poor Agnes and let her haunt the damn place.'

The missing address book popped into my head. Had someone thought to track down Agnes, in Bradford, or in Robin Hood's Bay? Could this child be as much at risk as Paul and Lizzie Kellett?

'What about if you and the child take a holiday, a sort of late Easter holiday?'

'I can't do that. He's back to school Monday. And I don't suppose Braithwaite rented the Robin Hood's Bay house for seven bloody years.'

'Someone killed the Kelletts. A man's been arrested for her murder . . .'

'I heard that feller confessed to both killings.'

'Frederick is Joshua Braithwaite's only son. You might be safer, just until this is cleared up, to take him somewhere else.'

'But the lad's a bastard, poor kid. He won't be coming into any property or whatever else from the Braithwaite fortune. And me mam's expecting us back.'

Nothing I said would make her change her mind.

Frederick came back with two ice creams and handed one to Beatrice. She patted the bench for him to sit beside her.

Sykes handed me a cornet. He licked one himself and gave a boyish grin. 'It's Easter holidays. Everyone should come to the park and have an ice cream.' He snapped the bottom off his cornet and scooped ice cream from the top. 'Did you ever do this, Frederick? Make a baby cornet?'

Frederick copied him.

At the park gates, I shook hands with Beatrice and wished her and Frederick good luck. Sykes said he would walk them to the station, and catch up with me later at the Bridgestead police house.

I arrived at the police house at the same time as Mr Mitchell. He leaned his bike against the railing, took off his bicycle clips and hooked them onto the handlebars.

Once inside, in spite of having asked me to come and see him, he seemed in no hurry to speak. A brown foolscap-size envelope lay on the table.

'I thought it'd be here. And being it's you that initiated the proceedings, you might as well sit in while I peruse it.' He drew a carbon copy of a typed report from the brown envelope. 'It's from the Bradford Coroner's office – a report on the unidentified man found at the scene of the Low Moor explosion. This was sent to Keighley, but they've biked it over to me, asking for my comments, being as how I knew Joshua Braithwaite.'

I waited while he read through the autopsy report on Mr X.

'Mr Braithwaite was five foot six, about ten stone. The height would be about right.'

He ran a finger down the page. If I didn't look, it may not be true. I closed my eyes.

After a long while, he said, 'This chap was dressed in overalls, what was left of the scraps on his body. Nothing under them, but then it was August and the hottest day of the year.'

My heart began to beat fast. Mitchell's finger paused partway down the page. He looked at me, and we shared the same thought. There is not a great deal of difference between hospital blues and overalls.

He was sparing me some of the grisly details. I would have to contrive to look at the report myself.

'How extensive were the burns?' I asked.

'Eighty-five per cent, poor blighter. But you see, it couldn't have been Mr Braithwaite. The explosion was around 2.30 p.m. and he was still in hospital at that time.'

'Mr Mitchell, the explosions continued into the next day. The gasometer went up. It must have been like a circle of hell.'

He shook his head as he read the report, picking on tiny details that convinced him he was right.

'There are points of similarity, true, but I don't reckon as how it's him.'

'Why not?'

'The man was Joshua Braithwaite's age and height. He had five gold fillings in his teeth. Now not many chemical workers have a gold filling, but some do – so you can't go on that. But I can assure you that Mr Braithwaite didn't have a missing front tooth. The unidentified man had a missing front tooth.'

I remembered what Hector had said. *I gave him my scarf*

to hold to his mouth. He was bleeding. His front tooth was loose.

I knew I'd been right, and yet to have it confirmed made me shudder. I didn't want to be right. I told Constable Mitchell what Hector had said.

He clamped his lips shut, clenched and unclenched his fists. 'It's always in the detail. I missed that. Now I wonder what else I missed.'

He picked up the telephone.

'You wouldn't have made a note of a loose tooth,' I said. 'Even if you had, it could have stayed loose for days.'

Mr Mitchell asked the operator to connect him to a certain dentist in Keighley.

While his attention was on the telephone call, I drew the report across the desk and began to read. The force of the explosion that killed Joshua Braithwaite must have been tremendous. He suffered broken ribs, a collapsed lung, and a fractured collar bone. His arm was broken in two places.

Mr Mitchell was speaking to someone at the dental practice. They held no records for Mr Braithwaite.

With mounting horror I read that Joshua Braithwaite had sustained bruises, a crushed elbow and a dislocated shoulder.

On the second call, to a Bingley dental practice, Mr Mitchell identified himself and asked the dentist whether Joshua Braithwaite had been a patient there. He put his hand over the mouthpiece. 'He's checking.'

We waited.

'Ah I see, yes. When was his last appointment?'

I could hear the hope for a miracle in his voice. He wanted the person on the other end to say that Mr Braithwaite popped in last week for an extraction.

'And what fillings were those?' He put his hand over the mouthpiece and nodded to me to pick up a pencil. I wrote as he repeated the information he was given. 'Right cuspidor or top eye tooth, gold filling; top right second molar or grinder, gold filling; bottom right second and third grinders, gold fillings; bottom left second grinder, gold filling. Thank you. Just a moment, please.' He pulled my note towards him and compared it against the information in the post mortem report. His mouth set in a grim line. 'I'll be coming to see you within the hour, sir, if you'll make yourself available please.'

He returned to his high stool with a sigh and picked up my notes. 'I'll read these back to you, Mrs Shackleton, so that you can double-check against the report. It would be terrible to make a mistake over this.'

Sometimes, you think if you look at print long enough, it will change its mind and say something else. It did not. We verified that the dental work matched that of Mr Braithwaite's.

Mr Mitchell stood up and paced the room. 'What was the man thinking of, running away from his family, his business, his own place, his people?'

'He was in love, and an artist. All those years, he'd been a round peg filling a very square hole.'

'In love!' The derisory edge to his voice spoke volumes.

I told him about Agnes Horrocks and Frederick, who must have been just a baby.

'Whatever possessed the man? He could have done what others do and provided for her. No one benefited. Everyone suffered.'

'Agnes lodged with Mrs Kellett while Kellett was away at war. That postal order stub I gave you – it seems that Mrs Kellett sent something each week to support the child.'

'Why would *she* send money?'

'I believe the money came out of the mill coffers – put in her wage packet each week. I expect that was a way of keeping the business of the child at arm's length, protecting Evelyn.'

Mr Mitchell shook his head and sighed. 'They don't

come much better than Mr Stoddard. Anyone else would have washed his hands of the trollop.'

He pulled on his helmet. 'I'm going to collect those dental records. Once I have them in front of me and I can see with my own eyes, I shall telephone my sergeant. I'll be obliged if you say nothing to Mrs Braithwaite before that.'

'Tabitha asked me to find him. She's the one I must tell.'

'His wife should know first. My sergeant will say how to proceed from here. In my opinion, we may want to ask Mr Stoddard to be present. He's been their sheet anchor all these years. He should be there for them when we break the news.'

Perhaps he should be there, for Evelyn. But it was Tabitha who had asked me to find her father, and it was Tabitha I must tell first.

Through the window, I watched Constable Mitchell put on his bicycle clips. He mounted the bike and pushed off, pedalling back down the hill towards the main road. He had asked me not to tell Mrs Braithwaite, but had not mentioned Tabitha.

The telephone operator connected me to the Braithwaites. I spoke to Tabitha, and asked her to meet me on the bridge. I believe if Mr Mitchell had not called Agnes Horrocks a trollop I may have done as he had asked and waited in the police house.

23

 On tenterhooks

Fastening the cloth on a framework to dry.

By afternoon, scudding white clouds chased any remaining streaks of blue from the sky. You could feel snow in the air.

I walked down the main street towards the humpback bridge. Once there, I stepped foot to foot trying to keep warm, hugging myself, watching the clouds of my breath. It was mad to ask Tabitha to meet me out here, yet somehow fitting to be close to the spot where Joshua Braithwaite had watched Tabitha and Edmund play and turned them into a work of art. I curled my toes and stamped my feet for warmth. Just here, Agnes Horrocks had preened in her summer dress, forever young, warm and full of life through Braithwaite's oil paints.

The thump against my back winded me and sent me reeling. I had to grab the stones on the top of the bridge wall to steady myself. It was Charlie. He nuzzled me, sniffing in my coat pocket as though he expected me to travel with marrow bones. 'Sorry, Charlie, it's not your lucky day.'

From a way off came a call – Marjorie, hiding, reluctant to show her face. I got the feeling that if I went towards the woods she would come and speak to me.

'Go on, Charlie. Back to your mistress.' He walked backwards for a few steps, and then turned and bounded towards the clump of trees.

How would I tell Tabitha? The simplest way would be best. *Your father is dead* ... As if she knew bad news awaited her, she took an age to appear. Then I caught sight of her, on horseback, riding towards the bridge. She waved. I waved back. I had expected her to be on foot, and that we would walk to the café and I would prepare her for bad news. Then we'd go to the police house.

No. That's not true. I could not imagine how or where to tell her.

She dismounted.

We walked down the bank to be out of the cold. Her horse trod gingerly, staying close beside her.

She looked happy. I guessed she had some news connected with her wedding. Perhaps they had booked the honeymoon hotel in Paris at last, or Hector had learned to say *bon jour*.

She glanced at my satchel. 'Are you out photographing again? You'll die of cold for your art!'

'No I'm not photographing, not just now.'

'Only Uncle Neville was asking. He thought you wanted to take a picture of the mill, for some competition. You'd said about photographing the looms when they were still – like some great crouching animal you'd said.'

I felt like crouching myself, disappearing under the bridge or finding my way to some new world through the waterfall. Only the sound of burbling water broke the late afternoon stillness.

'The photograph of the mill can wait.' Perhaps it would wait forever.

'Oh he insists. He said to say No hard feelings, whatever that means. Did you and he have words?'

So he had not mentioned my espionage incursion into the mill at the dead of night. 'I was perhaps a little too curious for his taste.'

She laughed. 'Told you. Told you what mill people are

329

like.' There was a false ring to her laugh, as though being deliberately light-hearted would arm her against me.

Her horse whinnied in protest at the steepness of the bank. She had to turn and lead him back.

'I've something to tell you, Tabitha, but perhaps this isn't the best time.'

Something in my voice made her catch the inside of her cheek with her teeth. Looking at her suddenly took me back to a road in France, where we stopped our ambulance that was already full, and hardly room for another casualty. For a moment, the air between us hung still and heavy.

'You've dragged me here, Kate. Better get on with it. Dad's gone to Tahiti?'

Suddenly my mouth felt dry. The first snowflake fell, landing on Tabitha's nose. I should not be telling her out here, but it was too late.

'Go on then,' she said. 'What is it that's so terrible that it needs to float away into the ether and not be confined by four walls?'

'Tabitha, I'm sorry to tell you that your father is dead. He was identified by his height and his dental records. His body was found at Low Moor. Mr Mitchell wanted to wait until his sergeant could be here, but I thought you should know now.'

Why did I think so? Because it was my case. Because Tabitha employed me. I must tell her, not some sergeant from Keighley who'd managed to do nothing at the time and less since.

She froze on the spot, like in a child's game of statues. Then suddenly she was shaking her head, clenching her fists. The horse stomped, its nostrils snorted small clouds of breath to her cheek as if in sympathy. She flung out her arm as if to strike me. 'You fool, Kate.'

I reached for her. She struggled as I grabbed and held her. Snowflakes landed on her eyelashes. She pushed me away and rubbed a fist on her eyelid. 'It can't be him. Why don't you just say you're sick of looking?'

I licked a snowflake from my lip, and tried to speak carefully. My words came out like some lawyer's voice that had nothing to do with Kate Shackleton or Tabitha Braithwaite. 'The previously unidentified man is the same height and build as your father. His dental records match. Constable Mitchell checked. No identification was made at the time, because there was no reason to suppose he would have been there. He was still at Milton House when the first explosion happened at Low Moor.'

'So it couldn't be him!' She pulled free and hurried away from me, leading the horse to the bridge. When I caught up, her face contorted with rage. 'I'm paying you to find him. You haven't found him.'

Say it quickly, I told myself, before she gouges out my eyes.

'I believe he went to Low Moor to find the young woman I told you about, Agnes Horrocks. She lived near there with her child, and she worked on munitions.'

She stood, glaring at me, her mouth open, shaking her head.

Too much to tell, I realised. It would have been better to have shown her the painting, explained the connection, let her take in one piece of information before the bombshell of his death. 'I'll come back to the house with you.'

She was trying to get her foot in the stirrup and could not. 'It can't be him. The Horrocks woman would have said something. All these years . . .'

'She didn't speak out because she thought he'd deserted her.'

It was a poor choice of word.

'Deserted her? Deserted her? What about us?'

She was crying now. A carter crossed the bridge, very deliberately not looking our way. I cast about for some-

331

thing, anything, to say that might help. 'At least you know he never intended to take his life.'

'I knew that already! And you're wrong. You can't go by somebody's teeth and know it's them. We've all got the same bloody gnashers.'

I took Gerald's silver hip flask from my satchel, unscrewed the top and handed it to her. 'It didn't mean he'd stopped caring for you. He would have been in touch, you know that.'

'How do I know it?'

'Because of the way you needed to find him. He would have needed to see you.'

The snow wasn't sticking. It fell on the bank and disappeared, as if it only came to play a trick, and remind us that there can be snow in April. Only in Yorkshire could you eat an ice cream in the park and an hour later turn into a snowman.

'He cared enough about you all to make sure the mill was in good hands, that you were all provided for. He was taking very little – his artist's materials and a few clothes.' I thought it best not to mention the bucket and spade that Hector had seen him packing. 'We don't even know for sure that the arrangement would have been permanent. Perhaps he just wanted to have a quiet holiday.'

'Mother would have known if there was another woman.' She took a sip from the brandy flask. 'Where was Dad supposed to be going?'

'Robin Hood's Bay.'

She looked at me blankly.

'It's a popular resort for artists. Near Whitby.'

'We didn't go over that way. We went to Morecambe and Grange.'

She turned away from me, and it may be that hearing he would go to the opposite coast struck some chord of truth. She looked at my silver flask, engraved with Gerald's initials.

'He might have been coming back in September or October,' I said.

'Or never.' Without looking at me, she asked, 'Who's going to tell this nonsense to Mother?'

'Mr Mitchell wants to take advice from his sergeant. He thinks your Uncle Neville should be there.'

'Then you tell Uncle Neville.'

This time her foot found the stirrup and she mounted, urging on the horse as if she couldn't wait to get away from me, and the harsh truth that she would not yet own up to believing. 'He'll look into it. Uncle Neville will find out there's been a mistake.' Turning back, she called over shoulder, 'You keep saying "I believe", so you're not sure. You've just got tired of looking and now you're guessing. It's all guesswork.'

The hooves on the cobbles hammered out her shock and disbelief, the sound thumping through my body. Tabitha flung out her arm. Something whizzed through the air. I turned to see the brandy flask hit the beck, clattering onto the stepping stones. I wanted to retrieve it but was shaking too hard.

How is it that the minute you do or say something, you know you've got it wrong? All that treading carefully and piecing together of scraps of information and then I had to blurt out the bad news when she's not even sitting down to hear. *You better sit down.* That's what people always say before the stake goes through your heart. Not I. *March up and down on this bridge. Struggle down the bank and up again. Let the snow settle on your eyelashes. Now here's the bullet.*

The least I could do was to alert her Uncle Neville, as she asked. Clambering down the bank to retrieve my flask I slipped, falling on my backside before getting my feet wet in the beck.

Mill workers were already heading home, joshing each other, lighting cigarettes. A few children had come from the village to meet parents.

333

Walking against the tide, I reached the mill gates. On one side of the yard, some clearing up of the dyehouse had begun, with bricks stacked on one side, stones on another and metal in a pile that could have been no use except as scrap.

On the other side of the yard, the door to the outhouse used as a garage stood slightly ajar. I caught sight of a motorbike and a neglected, detached sidecar. That was where I had hidden away my cameras on the day Tabitha and I wandered across the moor and I caught my first sight of Milton House. Something had struck me as odd at the time, and now I remembered.

I opened the door wider and went into the garage. As well as the motorbike, it held a pre-war Austin and a couple of push-bikes. As I approached the sidecar, the feeling that a tiny piece of the jigsaw would be found here made my fingers itch. I opened the top of the sidecar. You would expect it to be lined with that chequered material, one of those mock tartans that designers believe look jolly.

The lining had been stripped away. It was neatly done, as if someone had taken a sharp knife to it. Only at the very inner part of the sidecar where a person's feet would stretch had a scrap of material been missed. It was the texture as much as the faded pattern that told me this was as near as damn it to the scrap of material that had attached to Braithwaite's watch chain and been carefully preserved by Hector among his boy scout chattels.

Braithwaite's plan had been that Kellett would meet him with the motorbike and he would flee the hospital before his appearance at the magistrates' court. If Braithwaite *had* escaped on the bike, it would not be here now. Kellett would not have given himself away by bringing the bike back.

If only I'd had five minutes with Kellett, to ask the poor man the right questions, then everything may have been

334

solved. Of course that's presuming he would have answered me.

Leaving the garage behind, I walked to the mill house door, raised the knocker and let it fall.

Slow footsteps trudged along the tiled hall. An old woman in a long black dress and white apron gazed up at me through misty cataracts.

'Is Mr Stoddard at home?'

'He's still in't mill, madam.'

I hesitated, just a moment too long. She opened the door wider. 'Step inside won't you?'

Perhaps I could use the house telephone and just tell him what I had to say – that Evelyn and Tabitha needed him.

No. I should watch his face.

'Will he be back shortly?'

'Are you all right, madam? You look a little shaky. Will you have a glass of water?'

It amazes me that people whose vision should resemble life seen through a net curtain can be so observant.

'I will have a glass of water. Thank you.'

'Go in there. I'll fetch it.'

The parlour she showed me into doubled as a dining room. An elaborate candelabra gas lamp hung from the ceiling. With the shutters partially closed, the room breathed gloom. Its walls were papered in a deep maroon. A huge oak sideboard held two oval glass cases. One trapped a glass-eyed green parrot and a preening cockatoo who ignored each other and gazed reproachfully at me. In the other case, a sad-eyed owl seemed not to notice the crouching vole by its claws.

I guessed that some previous mill manager had used these creatures to give natural history lessons to his children.

The piano lid was firmly shut, with no music in sight. Eight chairs sat around a large oval dining table, designed for a big family. I pictured Neville Stoddard eating there alone each evening.

Listening for the housekeeper's return, I edged my way between the table and the sideboard.

On an impulse, I opened the sideboard drawers, then the cupboards, not knowing what I was looking for. There was nothing unusual: Sheffield cutlery, Derbyshire pottery, a cut-glass bowl.

The old woman came back, bringing a glass of water.

I took a drink.

'It's a lovely room,' I lied, playing for time, wondering what I might discover here. 'Do you keep anything I could take for a headache?'

She shook her head. 'The master doesn't get headaches.'

'I see.'

'There might be something in the mistress' cabinet. None of us go in there though.'

What was it Tabitha had told me when I asked was her father taking any medication? Yes, now I remembered. 'Ah yes, Miss Braithwaite told me that Aunt Catherine was the family treasure trove of medicines.'

The housekeeper opened her mouth to answer. The telephone began to ring. She shuffled into the hall.

If she would disappear into the kitchen, I might risk going up the stairs and looking at the medicine cabinet for myself.

No such luck. The housekeeper returned.

'That was Mr Stoddard on the telephone. He asks you to go over to the office. I told him you have a headache. He says I'm to get something for you.'

'Thank you.'

She hesitated. 'Will an aspirin satisfy?'

'Do you mind if I come up with you?' For a person with a headache, I was beside her at the door too quickly, too eagerly. 'Then I can look myself.'

She hesitated.

'I'm sure Mr Stoddard won't mind,' I said. 'I've never seen round a mill house.'

A massive portrait, far too big for the house, hung in the stairwell. A whiskered patriarch stared disapprovingly as we climbed the stairs, the housekeeper leading the way.

There were three bedrooms. The door to one was slightly ajar. On the opposite side of the landing, the housekeeper led the way into a light airy room, with faded pink wallpaper, white nets and brocade curtains. I looked for something that resembled a medicine chest but saw only a washstand.

'It's all in here, madam.' She opened the cupboard door, peered closely, then stood aside while I looked.

I wanted her to leave. She did not leave. The washstand cupboard was packed with medicines in plain, blue and brown bottles. I sniffed at one that had no label – a kind of liniment; the second, some sweet-smelling tincture; and the third, unmistakeably, morphia. There were liver powders, Epsoms salts, and a packet labelled *gel sem*. *Gelseminum sempervirens* – the substance found in Kellett's gut along with morphia.

'Medicines fascinate me,' I said, by way of explanation. 'Don't they you?'

'No, madam. The aspirins is there, in that little bottle.'

'Ah yes, thank you.'

I opened the bottle and swallowed an aspirin, hoping that it was indeed an aspirin.

Why had I never suspected Stoddard, not even for a moment? Who, on that Saturday when Braithwaite tried to go to Agnes, would have stopped him? His cousin Neville Stoddard. If Braithwaite had set off on his bike with the sidecar, the one person he would have had to explain to was Stoddard. *The mill's in your hands now, Neville.*

Evelyn had refused to listen to her husband. What was

337

it she had said? On the landing, he had asked her to talk to him. He had something to say. She refused to hear what he had to say. Stoddard would have listened. Fought with him even. Packed him into the sidecar and tried to take him home. Perhaps Braithwaite had escaped and gone running, running down the bank. Mrs Kellett could have seen him. Then Kellett promised to help. They both knew too much, Paul and Lizzie Kellett. Until I came, he could rely on their secrecy, buy their silence. But when I began to ask questions, he sensed danger and acted. Kellett's death was meant to look like an accident. I shuddered to think that if Arthur Wilson hadn't got to her first, Stoddard might have killed Lizzie.

But Wilson had simmered with resentment for far too long. The Kelletts prospered, first from the selling of the German dyewares in war time and then from Mrs Kellett's too-heavy pay packet. It wasn't fair. Wilson had received what he considered a paltry sum for his invention, and his name not even honoured when the picker was manufactured. He knew there was money to be had and he went to the Kelletts for his fair share of the booty. Mrs Kellett must have told him to sling his hook. He lost his temper and killed her.

But as far as Stoddard knew, I was ignorant of everything still – except of course I had just told Tabitha that the unknown male casualty at Low Moor was her father. And if Tabitha had told Evelyn already, then . . .

I held my head high, gripped my satchel too tightly, and strode towards the mill. Keep it simple, I told myself. Tabitha and Evelyn need him. When he hears that, Stoddard will go to them.

It reassured me to see that the caretaker, a skeletal man with a high boot resting on his sweeping brush, was waiting by the door for me, practically bouncing in his attempt to draw my attention.

'Mrs Shackleton?'

'Yes.'

'I'm to show you up. Mr Stoddard has a surprise for you, though I'm not supposed to say.'

'What is it?'

He puffed out his cheeks, shook his head and tapped the side of his nose.

I relaxed a little. If Stoddard had a surprise for me, then he could not be expecting me to have become suspicious of him. *Don't let it show*, I told myself. *Stay calm.*

'This way, madam.'

I followed the old man up two flights of stairs, a third, and a fourth to the top floor.

'It's lightest up here.'

And it was lightest. As well as the great windows that extended to the ceiling, there was light from glass panels in the roof, and from the open goods door in the wall. The snow had stopped, leaving dots of moisture on the high windows.

Stoddard beamed at me. He switched on the electric lights.

I turned to thank the caretaker, but he was gone.

'Here we are,' Stoddard called. 'An ideal opportunity. Told you I dabbled in photography myself at one time. What do you think to this?'

'You're taking photographs?'

'Not I, my dear. This arrangement is for you. I hope my camera will suit.'

'For me?'

'Didn't you say something last time you were here about the All British Photographic Competition, and that you didn't imagine many entries would feature a mill? Well, I'm sure you're right, and here's your chance. "Mill at rest" you can call it. What do you make of the camera?'

It was was a Noiram reflex quarter plate. 'Yes, I have used one of these.'

'Good. Then you'll be familiar with it.'

339

'Yes. But, Mr Stoddard, I'm here for another reason. I'm not sure that either of us will want to be taking photographs when you hear what I have to say.'

'You see we've a carton of yarn packages ready to hoist up. I told the men to leave it. Watch this – it'll make a good picture – from an unusual angle, too.'

'Mr Stoddard . . .'

His attention was on winching up the box from the ground. The chain clanked. The carton swayed for a moment. He nodded to me to capture the image. It would be simplest to do as he expected. I looked through the lens and caught the swaying great square parcel of yarns. He held it still, steadying the winch.

'So that was an extra image you didn't expect,' Stoddard announced. 'Now for the looms.' He turned round the camera plate. 'Oops! Shouldn't have done that. You'll need to enter it into the competition as all your own work and now you've had an assistant.'

Though the looms were silent, they still held the yarns and cloth that would be continued by the weavers in the morning. It gave them an odd look, still and peaceful. In spite of everything, I yearned to take that photograph. I moved the camera further up the room so as to see a line of looms. Doing so also put off the moment when I had to tell him why I had come. He was watching me take the photograph and had produced another camera, a fixed focus Brownie.

'Your Brownie won't give you a good indoor picture,' I said.

'Perhaps not. All the same, I would like a photograph of you. Stand by the door opening, where we brought the yarn through. Then you'll have the light of the open door behind you.'

'Very well.'

I walked slowly back up the room. 'Mr Stoddard, I appreciate that you've taken this trouble for me, but I've

340

really come to say that Evelyn and Tabitha would like you to go over there as soon as you can.'

There. I'd said it. Let's hope we could now stop this and I could go home for the weekend and leave the family to come to terms with the news of Joshua Braithwaite's death.

He looked at me blankly.

'Tabitha specially asked for you,' I said. 'I was talking to her by the bridge.'

'And did she ask you to search my garage and my house?'

'What do you mean?'

'I saw you go into the garage.'

'I was just looking at your car.'

'And Mrs Laycock tells me you went upstairs, into Catherine's room.'

'I thought there might be something for a headache.'

'Why?'

'Why what?'

'Why were you searching?'

'I wasn't searching. I'm curious.'

'Yes. I'd noticed.'

'Perhaps we should go to your office. We could talk there.'

Once we got out of here and onto the stairs, we would see the caretaker. I'd be able to leave without any further to-ing and fro-ing. He was beginning to make me feel uncomfortable.

'Yes,' he said, as if answering a question. 'I'd like a photograph of you – framed just there in the doorway.'

He took my arm, so gently I thought for a moment he wanted to kiss me. He held me by the shoulders and looked down at me.

'We liked each other I think.'

'Yes.'

'When you came here, trying to help Tabitha, you

impressed me. A beautiful woman, intelligent, honourable – out to seek the truth. But you went too far. All the same, I'd like your photograph. Will you stand in that doorway please?'

He encircled me with one arm so that I couldn't move. I thought it best to stay calm, keep talking, bide my time.

'I know it might not come out terribly well, not like yours. But there's always time to take a photograph, if that's your passion. That's what it's all about these days. Follow your passion. Never mind honour, duty, hard work, marriage vows. I know why you're here. It was you went to see that woman, brought her to the funeral with Joshua's bastard, breaking Evelyn's heart all over again.'

'Her heart was never broken. She threw herself at Dr Grainger the moment she saw him.'

His grip on me loosened. 'That's a monstrous lie. Evelyn is incapable of any deception or foulness.'

I backed away from him. 'It was you, wasn't it? You fought Joshua Braithwaite when he tried to leave that Saturday.'

'I tried to knock some sense into him.'

'And did trying to knock sense into him come easier after you'd doped him, like you did Kellett?'

'No one will ever connect me to Kellett's death. It's absurd. Wilson will be hung for the sheep and the lamb.'

I was walking slowly, talking to him, walking backwards towards the door, ready to turn and run.

'You pushed him in your sidecar after you'd beaten him up. You tried to take him home but he got out and ran for the beck. That's why he was confused, not making sense when he was found. Because he was drugged and over-powered, but he still managed to get away from you.'

He started to laugh. 'I wouldn't have doped Joshua. Didn't need to. The fool doped himself because of his toothache. He wouldn't fight back, wouldn't fight me. Just ran. Like a coward. Running away from his responsibilities.'

'Or running towards them, towards Agnes and the child.'

I turned to run for the door. A sudden furious crash and bang of machinery startled me. He had flicked the looms into life. For a moment, I didn't know where the noise came from. He was behind me, dragging me back towards the loading door in the wall, with its four-floor drop to the ground below.

In the noise I could barely hear what he said. This time he held me securely. I screamed, but no sound could be heard above the din of the machinery. Then his hand was over my mouth and with his other hand he quickly switched off the looms, but without my being able to break free.

I dug in my heels but he had me in an iron grasp, like a clamp around my arms and chest. I tried kicking and caught his shin. His grip tightened.

'Your sympathies are in the wrong place, Mrs Shackleton. Kellett was the worst kind of blackmailer. Got his wife to do it for him. It's cost me a guinea a week for years.'

I bit his hand.

He twisted my arm. 'I hate hurting a woman, especially a good-looking one, but you're going to die as you step back to get a perfect photograph of mill machinery. I will be so distraught, and your fingerprint will be on the camera trigger.'

I tried to fix myself to the ground, and to kick out, but one movement outdid the other. He was too strong. We edged back towards the loading door. 'Trace all this evil back to Braithwaite. He corrupted. He called himself a teetotaller, but he supped with the devil.'

Teetering on the edge, swaying back and forth in a monstrous embrace, I could feel the icy cold on my back. For an absurd moment, I wondered would there be more snow.

'It could have been different, Kate, so different. Of course there never could have been anything between you and me. We're from different worlds. But even this death, you could have stood in the doorway and I could have said, *Step back, step back,* and taken your picture and one step back and you would have known nothing, except the fall. And I would have had a photograph to cherish forever.'

In a rush of air I was falling. I had expected him to go on talking and for my life not to end. In the seconds before I was pushed, a dog barked, and the sound of footsteps echoed in my imagination.

I grabbed the beam that jutted from the wall. Next to me the chain pulley swung back and forth in a thump thump rhythm, hitting me on the side of my body as I hung there, feeling my tendons would break, not able to get a proper purchase on the rough wooden beam that tore at my hands each time I tried to take a stronger hold.

Stoddard was leaning down, cursing me now, prising my fingers, trying to make me lose my grip. I didn't look up or down, just hung on for dear life, not knowing whether a scream or a cry found its way from my dry throat. My fingers ached to be free of the beam, and then they stopped hurting.

That pain changed shape. Stoddard had stopped prising my fingers.

Charlie leaned out where Stoddard had been. He barked, just once, then backed away. I heard a cry – the cry of a man being mauled by a dog.

Sykes leaned down towards me. 'If I stretch out my arm, can you take hold?'

'I don't know.'

'Hold on!' The second voice was Constable Mitchell's.

My arms stopped aching as I willed myself not to think of them, only hang on. Hang on.

Sykes reached down. I grabbed his hand.

'Come on, Katie lass, you can do it.'

As he pulled me up, I was able to push myself with the other hand by the beam. Then my head was level with the floor and somehow I was dragged inside. Sykes was saying something, his arm round my shoulder.

Stoddard, handcuffed, lay by the silent looms, the dog standing over him, looking at his throat with great interest.

'Hey up, lad.' Mitchell spoke to the dog with an uncertain tone that set Charlie growling.

'Charlie!' I called him and he came to me, a great long stream of saliva dripping from the side of his mouth. 'Good dog, Charlie.' He had probably saved my life.

When the dog left Stoddard's side, Mitchell pulled Stoddard to his feet.

'Let's be having you, sir.'

I averted my eyes as Mitchell escorted Stoddard from the end loom towards the door. Suddenly, he pulled from Mitchell's grasp, propelling himself towards me with a snarl. 'Stupid girl! I was trying to save her, Mitchell!'

As he lunged at me, trying once again to push me to my death, I stepped aside and stuck out my foot. It was a reflex action, like some child in a playground who seizes the moment when her bullying enemy comes skipping by. Charlie made a grab for the seat of Stoddard's pants, and in that moment he fell, through the loading door that he had meant to be my last exit from the world.

With a strangled cry, he dropped. I heard him crunch on the ground below.

24

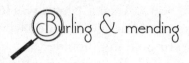

Burling & mending

*Broken ends are removed. Knots are pulled through to the back
of the fabric and any missing threads sewn in.*

Why? That question woke me in the night. The thought of
Stoddard's almost jovial attempt to murder me felt like
something from a nightmare. Tiny details loomed into
view – a smile, a gesture, the sound of his drawn breath.

Stoddard did not die. He lay on the ground, writhing in
agony. With that awful clarity that comes when you think
your mind must have stopped working, I remembered.
'There's morphia in the washstand in his wife's room.' I
turned to Constable Mitchell. 'It's what he used to drug
Kellett's snack. For pity's sake, give Stoddard some now.'

It was a long way for the ambulance and police car to come
from Keighley to collect Stoddard and take him into custody.

Sykes insisted on driving me home, steadily keeping to
ten miles an hour, watching the road ahead with a fixed
stare as if he thought it would make some sudden and
unexpected demand.

Once home, he asked for tweezers and painstakingly
removed splinters from my hands. Each splinter he placed
carefully onto a white linen serviette and tied with a
ribbon, as evidence.

After the desplintering, Mrs Sugden drew a bath for
me. I lay there as the water grew tepid.

Why? Stoddard had said himself that no one would link
him to Kellett's death. I could have proved nothing.

It was over. With Joshua Braithwaite now known to have died in the Low Moor explosion, my task was complete. So why did Stoddard try to kill me? My eyes pricked with tears at the injustice. What had I ever done but try to find the truth? Self-pity sent me to sleep. I woke knowing there was something I'd missed, but what?

During the night I woke every hour from confused dreams, falling dreams, murderous dreams. Gregory Grainger would say write them down, analyse them. It did not take a razor sharp analysis to make something – or nothing – of dreams that replayed fear. Braithwaite appeared, scraps of ragged hospital blue uniform stuck to charred flesh. A bruised and battered spectre, Braithwaite shook his head. His skull grinned, blood dripping from his gums in place of the missing tooth.

Mrs Sugden stood over me with a tray of tea, a boiled egg and bread soldiers.

'Best not stir today.' She set down the tray.

'I need to be up. I've to give a statement to the police.'

Plumping up my pillows, she said, 'Let them wait. And I'm sending for the doctor.'

'That's quite unnecessary.'

'Mr Sykes agrees with me on that. He says that a medical report might be required by the court.'

Then she told me I had a visitor. Only royalty and prime ministers give audiences from their beds. And when Mrs Sugden named my visitor, I felt like crawling under the sheets, but thought it best to get the interview over with.

Evelyn came in, carrying bright tulips from her garden. She placed them on the washstand and said that Mrs Sugden was bringing a vase.

'How are you?' she asked, with a sad, solicitous smile, as if I were recovering from a cold.

Mrs Sugden brought the vase, her face like thunder. 'Shall I get rid of her?' she mouthed from behind Evelyn's back.

347

With my eyes, I said no to that. I would hear what Evelyn had to say.

Evelyn took over and arranged the flowers. She took a penny from her purse and dropped it into the vase. 'The copper, you know. Tulips like it. It extends their life.'

She drew up a chair and sat by the bed. 'Have you given a statement yet?'

'Not yet.'

Mrs Sugden breathed heavy disapproval then left. I did not hear her footsteps retreat across the landing.

Evelyn leaned towards me. 'They're not sure that Neville will pull through.'

I was meant to be concerned?

'Evelyn, he tried to kill me.'

'You're mistaken, my dear. I spoke to a lawyer last night. It was a tussle between you. You were going to fall. Neville caught you.'

I closed my eyes, not bothering to reply.

'I'm sorry you had to step into this mess, Kate. I wish Tabitha hadn't asked you. I wish . . . all sorts of things.'

She spoke as though I had been invited into an untidy drawing room and really it should have been swept and the ornaments dusted.

'Evelyn, Neville Stoddard killed Kellett, and he tried to kill me.'

'The lawyer said they wouldn't be able to touch him for Kellett's death – especially since they have Wilson and he's confessed to it.'

'Stoddard is a killer.'

'No! It wasn't meant to be like that. Neville was just trying to give Kellett a fright. He didn't intend Kellett to die. The man had enough money to retire and live in style. Yet he wanted more, more and more. Neville thought that if he experienced a minor accident, that would give him a jolt. He'd realise it was time to give up blackmailing Neville about the bastard child. Neville was trying to protect me.' She spoke brightly, without an ounce of guilt.

'When did you know, Evelyn, that he killed Kellett?'

'Does it matter?'

'Yes, if you were an accessory.' I was glad to have the support of the pillows, and shut my eyes. Go away. Go away. She did not.

'Don't go all legal on me, Kate. Accessories to me are gloves and a handbag.'

She leaned forward, the perfect visitor, her eyes brimming with concern. 'You tripped. That mill can be a dangerous place.'

'Go away, Evelyn. He tried to kill me.'

I expected her to leave. She stayed put, sitting like a demure schoolgirl, ankles crossed, hands resting on her thighs.

Perhaps I dropped off, hoping she would have vanished by the time I woke. It may have been for a few seconds, or half an hour, but when I woke, it all fell into place. I jerked forward, suddenly alert, knowing. My dream of Braithwaite with the scraps of ragged hospital blue uniform stuck to charred and bruised flesh came back to me. His skull was not grinning, but trying to speak.

'It was you.'

Her mouth hardened. 'What are you talking about? What was me?'

I reached for my glass of water. She handed it to me. I took a sip, and immediately wished I hadn't, expecting she may have poisoned me.

I should have been speaking in a drawing room, surrounded by suspects, CID officers listening behind a velvet curtain, constables in an anteroom, ready to pounce. Instead, it was just the two of us, she so self-possessed, me with only the strength that comes from anger.

I propelled myself from the bed and stood over her.

'You knew your husband planned to leave you, leave the mill. You wouldn't speak to him, so he went to his cousin. Stoddard gave him something, for his neuralgia? For courage? He beat him up, told him not to be so stupid. He put him in the sidecar to fetch him home. Joshua escaped. That's when the boy scouts found him.'

She gave a light mirthless laugh and looked beyond me towards the drawn curtains. 'You have a vivid imagination.'

I held the back of her chair, and closed my eyes, seeing it all so clearly. That was why she was so concerned that Dr Grainger had come to my aunt's party. She feared for what he might say. 'You were at Milton House when your husband went missing from there. You saw him running across the fell and asked Dr Grainger to give you time to search. You went after him on horseback.'

'And what if I did? What of it?'

The description of Joshua Braithwaite's injuries had burned into my brain when I read the pathologist's report. I moved away from the chair, better to see her face as I recited the litany: broken ribs, collapsed lung, fractured collar bone, broken arm, gash on the head.

'Injuries inflicted by you, Evelyn. You trampled him.'

She gasped and a shudder went through her. 'It wasn't like that.'

'What was it like?'

'He'd turned mad. He drove his son away, poor Edmund, cornered into enlisting in the army. Then Joshua could be the young suitor, starting his life all over.'

'It's an old old tale, Evelyn. In most families adultery and loss of love doesn't lead to murder.'

She clutched her arms around herself for a moment and hung her head. I thought she had finished. To make her start again, I said, 'If I could interpret the injuries from the post mortem report, then a coroner could do the same. The evidence will be reviewed.'

350

I paced the length of the room, refusing to give in to the exhaustion that threatened to overwhelm me. 'His right arm was broken. He'd raised his arm to stop you.' The image came unbidden. Joshua Braithwaite, exhausted, turning to Evelyn, his arm raised in a supplicating gesture.

She looked up at me. 'If I confide in you, you'll understand. But you must say that what happened at the mill was an accident. Neville didn't push you. You fell.'

'Just tell me. I deserve to know.'

Evelyn spoke so quietly, I had to strain to hear.

'When I caught up with Joshua on the fells, in that moment, it was just me and him, as if everything bad had slipped away. He was tired out from running, beads of sweat on his face, and great wet patches of sweat under his arms and on his chest. He gave his smile, his special smile. We looked at each other and I wanted to help him, I truly did. And then he said, "There's been an explosion. I have to get to Agnes. I have to get to Low Moor, love." I don't know what did it. It might even have been that he still called me love when I wasn't his love. It might have been the way he said her name. I struck out with the whip. He fell. The horse reared. There was no avoiding what happened next. I tried to rein back, but Rowan almost threw me. Some rocks scattered under his hooves and after he reared, he came down, trampling Joshua. I tried to control him. Joshua managed to move. The horse kicked him. When I dismounted, Joshua was lying there, in great pain. I told him I'd come back with help.'

I felt sick. After everything, I did not want to vomit and have her fussing over me. It would be too humiliating. 'Don't tell me any more, Evelyn. Talk to your lawyer.'

She raised her hands, palms towards me, as if she were an opera singer who wanted to stop the applause in order to make an announcement. 'If I tell you, you'll understand. You wouldn't want to destroy Tabby, not after all the poor girl's been through. Everything I did, I did for

351

the best. By the time I got back with Neville, and with Kellett, Joshua was dead.'

'How long did you wait before going back?'

'No time at all. I swear it was as fast as I could.'

'And then?'

'It was me who told Neville what to do with the body. Joshua had wanted to go to Low Moor. "Take him to Low Moor," I said. I think I was hysterical by then. Kellett said nothing, waiting for Neville to make the decision. I just kept on and on – take him away, get rid of him. I don't want to know any more.'

I sat on the bed. We faced each other, Evelyn white and tense. After a moment, she began again.

'Kellett wouldn't have anything to do with it, except for fetching the motorbike and sidecar, which he said he'd agreed to do for Joshua. Neville and I carried Josh down to the lane and put him in the sidecar. We did it together. Joshua got his last wish – to be taken to Low Moor, only not in the way he'd wanted. And it made a clean end, an unidentified body in the burning rubble of the explosion.'

I felt sick with revulsion. She wouldn't look at me.

'That doesn't explain why Stoddard tried to kill me yesterday.'

'He thought you'd work it out.'

'You mean about your husband's injuries?'

'Yes.'

'That I would think over the injuries in the post mortem report and know that they were caused by him being trampled to death. Stoddard thought I would ask why all the lining – bloodied from Joshua – had been cut from the motorbike sidecar.'

'He only ever wanted to help me, and for the mill to prosper. If you give evidence against Neville, and he's convicted – or even if he's charged – the mill will collapse. Oh we say the looms are down because we're waiting for yarn, or there's a fault with the power, but the workers

352

know. They know that we prefer not to call it short time. We don't want word to get around that we're suffering hard times, like everyone else in textiles. You've come into a world you don't understand, Kate. Neville is the mill. The mill is Neville. If he goes down, two hundred workers go with him — lose their livelihoods. Between them they have five, six, seven hundred children. Who will feed those children, Kate? Will you?'

She stood up and walked to the door, turning back to face me.

This was the moment when eavesdroppers should have sprung into action and arrested her.

'I appeal to you, Kate. Say you were taking a photograph and stepped back too far. That you fell.'

The door opened. Sykes stood there, Mrs Sugden beside him.

Mrs Sugden hurried across to me and said, 'Your mother's just arriving. Please, get back into bed.'

'The doctor's here,' Sykes said.

I waited until Mrs Sugden had taken Evelyn downstairs.

Sykes sat in the chair vacated by Evelyn.

'What are you doing here, Mr Sykes?'

'I stayed last night. Slept downstairs, just in case someone came calling.'

'I hope you were listening at the door just now?'

He shook his head.

Evil sometimes wears a smiling face. Most people, me included, prefer to look only at the smile. The smile of evil would forever be that look of Stoddard's as he tried to kill me. With a heavy heart, feeling like an agent of destruction, I told the truth in my statement to the police. Before Stoddard could be charged with attempted murder, he died in hospital from his injuries, escaping justice.

Before he died, he confessed to killing his cousin Joshua Braithwaite. He had acted alone, he said, and dumped the body at the site of the Low Moor explosion.

I told the police the truth, but not the whole truth. What was it that kept me silent about Evelyn Braithwaite's admission? Perhaps it was for Tabitha's sake, or because of the lengths to which Stoddard had gone to protect Evelyn. Maybe it was because I wondered, if I'd been sitting in that saddle on that day, how I would have acted when the man I loved told me he wanted to be elsewhere. I believed her when she said it was an accident. Later, I wondered.

Did I do the right thing? Dad and Sykes and I talked it over. There would have been no evidence to link Evelyn to her husband's murder. She had told me in the belief that I would not betray her, and in an attempt to make me exonerate Stoddard.

Along with the horror of what she'd done, a grudging part of me admired her for her sheer bare-faced fury.

In the second week of June I received a cheque for my services in searching for the whereabouts of Joshua Braithwaite, Esquire. The cheque came not directly from Tabitha but through her solicitor. She could not bring herself to speak to me, or write to me, and I didn't blame her. The solicitor wrote that the cheque was from Mrs Hector Gawthorpe. So that answered one question. The wedding had taken place. The solicitor enclosed a hand-written note, which made me think that Mr Murgatroyd had not entirely given up on the idea of enticing me to be his client and writing my will. He said that the previously unmarked grave in Scholemoor Cemetery now bore a headstone commemorating Joshua Braithwaite.

He also said that Mr and Mrs Gawthorpe had sold the mill as a going concern. It was from Sykes that I learned Hector Gawthorpe had opened a car salesroom, and that Evelyn, her husband finally declared dead, was on an extended visit to the West Indies.

*

354

I stood by Joshua Braithwaite's grave one Sunday in August, with Gregory Grainger who had come north to give a fund-raising talk about the planned opening of the Maudsley. Along with Sykes, we had called for Beatrice and Frederick Horrocks.

On the way over, Beatrice thanked me for finding out that the cottage in Robin Hood's Bay had been in Agnes' name and would come to Frederick, along with a small legacy – a codicil to Braithwaite's will.

Gregory and I went to pay our respects at the memorial to the firemen who lost their lives in the explosion.

As we walked back through the cemetery, Gregory said, 'I know you'll probably say no, but I hope you'll say yes.'

'You're not still wanting me to intercede with Josephine Tuffnell?'

'That didn't work out. And to be honest, it was never really on the cards. If you'd given me even one nod of encouragement I wouldn't have mentioned Josephine Tuffnell.' His hand brushed mine.

'To what will I say no?'

'I've leave due. Would you like to motor up to the Lake District with me?'

I wanted to say yes. My body said yes, and that took me by surprise because it was the first time in a long while I had thought I might truly come back to life.

Gregory took both my hands in his and we smiled. 'Well then, what do you say, Kate?'

'I can't.'

He sighed his disappointment. 'May I ask why not?'

'It's too complicated.'

'If it's because . . .'

I put my finger to his lips. 'Don't. Best not.' On such moments, lives turn.

There would be too much between us when I looked at him. If only he had managed to hold onto Joshua

355

Braithwaite at Milton House, the man might have lived and so might Paul and Lizzie Kellett.

On the morning of the Kelletts' funeral, when I had inexpertly tried to console Evelyn for her loss of Gregory and had tried to suggest Neville was much more the man for her, she had said that it just was not possible. Now, of course, I knew why. They would look at each other and see blood.

If I looked at Gregory, I would see Tabitha's misery, Kellett's scalded body, Mrs Kellett's bird-like hands and wrinkled stockings. I would see an exhausted, undefeated Joshua Braithwaite running across the skyline of the fells. Attractive as Gregory could be, there was too much deceit between us, too many ghosts.

One piece of news did cheer me at the end of that summer. I came second in the All British Photographic Competition, with a stunningly sharp photograph of Mrs Sugden by her dung heap, alongside a gnome-like old chap who had come to shovel the manure into a rusty wheelbarrow for his allotment. I called my photograph "Muck Shovelling".

Acknowledgements

My research began with a visit to Armley Mills Museum, Leeds. Staff there and at Bradford Industrial Museum were most helpful. Eugene Nicholson, Curator of the Industrial Museum, guided me through archive material and publications. Former overlookers Mark Astley, once of Salts Mill, and Greg Kotovs, patiently answered questions about processes and machinery.

Mark Keighley, author of *Wool City*, shed light on wool production and manufacture.

Through the Society of Dyers and Colourists, in whose offices my sister Pat once worked, I was advised by Mr J M Crabtree, creator of the fastest black dye in England, and Andrew Filarowski, Technical Director. Dr Ian Holme, textile chemist and colourist, kindly supplied copies of his relevant publications.

Retired police officer Ralph Lindley, and Mary Lindley, helped bring to life the workings of law and order in a Yorkshire village. Sylvia Gill, whose family worked in the mills, offered sterling support.

The Low Moor explosion of Monday 21 August 1916 took place just a few miles from where I once lived. This tragic event has been documented by Ronald Blackwell and The Bradford Antiquary.

Thanks to my steadfast agent Judith Murdoch for her encouragement, and to Emma Beswetherick and Donna Condon of Piatkus who made the editing process a great pleasure.